MORE
THAN A
MISTRESS

MARY
BALOGH

A DELL BOOK
NEW YORK

More than a Mistress is a work of fiction. Names, characters, places, and incidents are the products of the author's imagination or are used fictitiously. Any resemblance to actual events, locales, or persons, living or dead, is entirely coincidental.

2010 Dell Books Mass Market Edition

Copyright © 2000 by Mary Balogh
Excerpt from *A Secret Affair* copyright © 2010 by Mary Balogh

Published in the United States by Dell Books, an imprint of The Random House Publishing Group, a division of Random House, Inc., New York.

DELL is a registered trademark of Random House, Inc., and the colophon is a trademark of Random House, Inc.

Originally published in hardcover in the United States by Delacorte Press, an imprint of The Random House Publishing Group, a division of Random House, Inc., in 2000.

This book contains an excerpt from the forthcoming novel *A Secret Affair* by Mary Balogh. This excerpt has been set for this edition only and may not reflect final content of the forthcoming edition.

ISBN 978-0-440-22601-7

Cover art by Franco Accornero

Printed in the United States of America

www.bantamdell.com

15 14 13 12 11

PRAISE FOR MARY BALOGH
AND
MORE THAN A MISTRESS

"A luscious Regency-era delight . . . Balogh will delight fans and new readers alike with her memorable characters and fast-paced, well-constructed plot." —*Booklist*

"Mary Balogh continues to reaffirm her place as an extraordinary star of the Regency genre. Her intelligent characters, who manage to cleverly find their way out of danger, gain our respect. Then she adds intrigue, romance and a fast pace to give us a book we won't be able to put down." —*Romantic Times*

"An intriguing mix of suspense and passion. This romantic story is hilarious in spots with characters who are well-rounded and lovable. . . . A sure-fire winner from one of this genre's finest authors." —*Rendezvous*

"Mary Balogh is an exceptional talent. . . . I encourage other readers to discover what Regency fans already know— Regencies can be as sensual and heartbreaking as any contemporary or historical romance in the hands of a master craftswoman like Ms. Balogh." —*Old Book Barn Gazette*

"Wise, witty and compassionate, Mary Balogh is an incomparable talent. I never miss a book." —JILL BARNETT, bestselling author of *The Days of Summer*

"An authentic London high society setting and smart, sexy dialogue." —*Publishers Weekly*

MORE
THAN A
MISTRESS

1

The two gentlemen who were in their shirt sleeves despite the brisk chill of a spring morning were about to blow each other's brains out. Or attempt to do so, at least. They were standing on a secluded stretch of dew-wet lawn in London's Hyde Park, facing in different directions, each ignoring the other's existence until the moment should come to take aim at each other and shoot to kill.

They were not alone, however, this being a duel of honor in which due process had been followed. A gauntlet had been thrown down, even if not literally, and challenger and challenged had progressed toward this morning's meeting through the medium of their seconds. Both seconds were now present, as were a surgeon and a gathering of interested spectators, all male, who had risen early from their beds—or had not yet gone to them after the revels of the night before—for the sheer exhilaration of watching two of their peers attempt to put a period to each other's existence.

One of the duelists, the challenger, the shorter and stockier of the two, was stamping his booted feet, flexing his fingers, and licking his dry lips with a drier tongue. He was almost as pale as his shirt.

"Yes, you may ask him," he told his second through teeth that he tried in vain to keep from chattering. "Not that he will do it, mind, but one must be decent about such matters."

His second strode off smartly to confer with his counterpart, who in his turn approached the other duelist. That tall, elegant gentleman showed to advantage without his coat. His white shirt did nothing to hide the powerful muscles of his arms, shoulders, and chest, as his breeches and top boots only accentuated those of his long legs. He was nonchalantly engaged in smoothing the lace of his cuffs over the backs of his long-fingered, well-manicured hands and holding a desultory conversation with his friends.

"Oliver is shaking like a leaf in a strong breeze," Baron Pottier observed, his quizzing glass to his eye. "He could not hit the broad side of a cathedral from thirty paces, Tresham."

"His teeth are clacking like trotting hooves too," Viscount Kimble added.

"Are you intending to kill him, Tresham?" young Mr. Maddox asked, drawing to himself a cool, arrogant stare from the duelist.

"It is the nature of duels, is it not?" he answered.

"Breakfast at White's afterward, Tresh?" Viscount Kimble suggested. "And Tattersall's after that? I have my eye on a new matched pair of grays for my curricle."

"As soon as this little matter has been taken care of." But the duelist was distracted both from straightening his cuffs and from his conversation by the approach of his second. "Well, Conan?" he asked, a touch of impatience in his voice. "Is there good reason for this delay? I must confess myself eager for my breakfast."

Sir Conan Brougham was accustomed to the man's cool

nerve. He had served as his second during three previous duels, after all of which his friend had consumed a hearty breakfast, unharmed and perfectly composed, as if he had been engaged for the morning in nothing more lethal than a brisk ride in the park.

"Lord Oliver is prepared to accept a properly worded apology," he said.

There were jeering noises from their acquaintances.

Eyes of such a dark brown that many people mistook their color for black looked back into Sir Conan's without blinking. The narrow, arrogant, handsome face to which they belonged was expressionless except for one slightly elevated eyebrow.

"He has challenged me for cuckolding him but is willing to settle for a simple apology?" he said. "Do I need to spell out my answer, Conan? Did you need to consult me?"

"It might be worth considering," his friend advised. "I would not be doing my job conscientiously if I did not thus advise you, Tresham. Oliver is a pretty decent shot."

"Then let him prove it by killing me," the duelist said carelessly. "And let that be within minutes rather than hours, my dear fellow. The spectators are displaying distinct signs of boredom."

Sir Conan shook his head, shrugged, and strode away to inform Viscount Russell, Lord Oliver's second, that his grace, the Duke of Tresham, did not acknowledge the necessity of any apology to Lord Oliver.

There was nothing for it then but to proceed to business. Viscount Russell in particular was anxious to have the meeting over with. Hyde Park, even this secluded corner of it, was a rashly public place in which to hold a duel, illegal as such meetings were. Wimbledon Common, the more usual venue for affairs of honor, would have been safer. But his friend had insisted on the park.

The pistols had been loaded and carefully inspected by both seconds. While an expectant hush fell over the spectators, the protagonists each picked up a weapon without looking at the other. They took up their positions back to back and at the agreed-upon signal paced out the regulation number of steps before turning. They took careful aim, each standing sideways in order to offer as narrow a target as possible to the other. They waited for Viscount Russell to drop the white handkerchief he held aloft, the signal to fire.

The hush became an almost tangible thing.

And then two things happened simultaneously.

The handkerchief was released.

And someone shrieked.

"Stop!" the voice cried. *"Stop!"*

It was a female voice, and it came from the direction of a grove of trees some distance away. An indignant buzz arose from the spectators, who had held themselves properly silent and motionless so that the protagonists would have no distraction.

The Duke of Tresham, startled and furious, lowered his right arm and turned in order to glare in the direction of the person who had dared interrupt such a meeting at such a moment.

Lord Oliver, who had also wavered for a moment, recovered fast, corrected his aim, and fired his pistol.

The female screamed.

His grace did not go down. Indeed at first it did not appear that he had even been hit. But a bright red spot appeared on his calf, an inch or two above the top of one perfectly polished leather boot, just as if suddenly painted there by an invisible hand with a long-handled brush.

"Shame!" Baron Pottier called from the sidelines. "For shame, Oliver!"

His voice was joined by others, all censuring the man who had taken unfair advantage of his opponent's distraction.

Sir Conan began to stride toward the duke while the crimson spot increased in diameter and the surgeon bent over his bag. But his grace held up his left hand in a firm staying gesture before raising his right arm again and taking aim with his pistol. It did not waver. Neither did his face show any expression except intense, narrow-eyed concentration on his target, who had no choice now but to stand and await his death.

Lord Oliver, to his credit, stood very still, though the hand that held his pistol to his side was trembling noticeably.

The spectators were silent again. So was the unidentified woman. There was an air of almost unbearable tension.

And then the Duke of Tresham, as he had done at every previous duel in which he had been engaged, bent his arm at the elbow and shot into the air.

The red spot on his breeches spread outward in rapidly expanding concentric circles.

It had taken iron willpower to remain standing when it felt as if a thousand needles had exploded in his leg. But even though incensed with Lord Oliver for firing his pistol when any true gentleman would have waited for the duel to be reorganized, Jocelyn Dudley, Duke of Tresham, had never had any intention of killing or even wounding him. Only of making him sweat awhile, of giving him time to watch his life flash before his eyes and wonder if this would be the one occasion when the duke, famed as a deadly shot but also known as a man who contemptuously wasted his bullet on the air during duels, would act untrue to form.

The needle points had taken over his whole person by the time he had finished and tossed the pistol onto the wet grass. He felt like agony personified and remained upright only because he would be damned before giving Oliver the satisfaction of being able to claim that he had been felled.

He was also still angry. An understatement. He was in a white-hot fury that might have been directed against Oliver had there not been a more obvious target.

He turned his head and looked with narrowed gaze to the spot at the edge of the trees where she had been standing a few moments ago, shrieking like a banshee. A serving girl, running an early-morning errand, no doubt, and forgetting one of the primary rules of service—that one minded one's own business and left one's betters to mind theirs. A girl who needed to be taught a lesson she would never forget.

She was still there, staring as if transfixed, both hands pressed to her mouth, though she had stopped her caterwauling. It was a pity she was a woman. It would have given him intense satisfaction to set a horsewhip whistling about her hide before being carted away to have his leg attended to. Deuce take it, but he was engulfed in pain.

Only a few moments had passed since he had fired his pistol and tossed it down. Both Brougham and the surgeon were hurrying toward him. The spectators were buzzing with excitement. He heard one voice distinctly.

"Well done, by Jove, Tresh," Viscount Kimble called. "You would have contaminated your bullet by shooting it into the bastard."

Jocelyn held up his left hand again without looking away from the woman by the trees. With his right hand he beckoned imperiously to her.

If she had been wise, she would have turned and run. He was hardly in a position to go chasing after her, and he doubted that anyone else present would be interested in running to earth on his behalf an unappealing, gray-clad slip of a servant girl.

She was not wise. She took a few tentative steps toward him and then hurried the rest of the way until she was standing almost toe to toe with him.

"You fool!" she cried with angry disregard for her place on the social scale and the consequences of talking thus to a peer of the realm. "What an utterly idiotic thing to do. Have you no more respect for your life than to become embroiled in a stupid *duel*? And now you have been hurt. I would have to say it serves you right."

His eyes narrowed further as he determinedly ignored the pulsing pain in his leg and the near impossibility of standing any longer on it.

"Silence, wench!" he commanded coldly. "If I had died here this morning, you would as like as not have hanged for murder. Have you no more respect for *your* life than to interfere in what is no concern of yours?"

Her cheeks had been flushed with anger. They paled at his words, and she stared at him wide-eyed, her lips compressed in a hard line.

"Tresham," Sir Conan said from close by, "we had better get that leg attended to, old chap. You are losing blood. Let me carry you with Kimble here over to the blanket the surgeon has spread out."

"*Carry?*" Jocelyn laughed derisively. He had not taken his eyes off the serving girl. "You, girl. Give me your shoulder."

"Tresham—" Sir Conan sounded exasperated.

"I am on my way to work," the girl said. "I will be late if I do not hurry."

But Jocelyn had already availed himself of her shoulder. He leaned heavily on it, more heavily than he had intended. Moving at last, shifting the weight off his injured leg, he found that the wave of agony made a mockery of the pain hitherto.

"You are the cause of this, my girl," he said grimly, taking one tentative step toward the surgeon, who suddenly seemed an impossible distance away. "You will, by God, lend me your assistance and keep your impertinent tongue safely housed behind your teeth."

Lord Oliver was pulling his waistcoat and coat back on while Viscount Russell packed away his pistol and came striding past Jocelyn to retrieve the other one.

"You would do better," the girl said, "to swallow your pride and allow your friends to carry you."

Her shoulder did not bow beneath his weight. She was rather tall and slender, but she was no weakling. She was doubtless accustomed to hard manual labor. She was probably equally accustomed to cuffings and beatings for impudence. He had never heard the like from a servant girl.

He was well-nigh swooning by the time he reached the blanket the surgeon had spread on the grass beneath an oak tree.

"Lie down, your grace," he instructed, "and I will see what damage has been done. I do not like the look of the positioning of that wound, I must confess. Or all the blood. I daresay the leg will need to come off."

He spoke as if he were a barber who had discovered a tuft of hair that did not blend well with the rest of the head. He was a retired army sawbones, supplied by Lord Oliver. Bloodletting and amputation were probably his answer to every physical ailment.

Jocelyn swore eloquently.

"You cannot possibly know that from a single glance," the serving girl had the temerity to observe, addressing the surgeon, "or make such a dire prediction."

"Conan," Jocelyn said, his teeth clamping tightly now in a vain attempt to control the pain, "fetch my horse." It was tethered not far away.

There was a chorus of protests from his friends who had gathered around him.

"Fetch his horse? He is as mad as ever."

"I have my carriage here, Tresham. Ride in that. I'll go and have it brought up."

"Stay where you are, Brougham. He is out of his mind."

"That's the fellow, Tresham. You show them what you are made of, old sport."

"*Fetch my damned horse!*" Jocelyn spoke from between his teeth. He had a death grip on the girl's shoulder.

"I am going to be very late," she scolded. "I will lose my employment for sure."

"And serve you right too," Jocelyn said, throwing her own words back at her, his voice devoid of all sympathy as his friend strode away to bring his horse and the surgeon launched into a protest.

"Silence, sir!" Jocelyn instructed him. "I will have my own physician summoned to Dudley House. He will have more regard for his future than to suggest sawing off my leg. Help me to my horse, girl."

But Lord Oliver appeared in front of him before he could turn away.

"I am not satisfied, I would have you know, Tresham," he said, his voice breathless and trembling as if he were the one who had suffered injury. "You will doubtless use the distraction with the girl to throw dishonor on my name. And everyone will laugh *at me* when it is known that you contemptuously shot into the air."

"You would rather be dead, then?" Death was seeming to be a rather desirable state to Jocelyn at that particular moment. He was going to black out if he did not concentrate hard.

"You will stay away from my wife in the future if you know what is good for you," Lord Oliver said. "Next time I may not accord you the dignity of a challenge. I may shoot you down like the dog you are."

He strode away without waiting for an answer, while another chorus of "Shame!" came from the gallery, some of whose members were doubtless disappointed that they were not about to witness the sawbones plying his trade on the grass of Hyde Park.

"My horse, girl." Jocelyn tightened his hold on her shoulder again and moved the few steps to Cavalier, whose head Conan was holding.

Mounting was a daunting task, and would have been quite impossible if his pride had not been at stake—and if he had not had the assistance of his silent but disapproving friend. It amazed Jocelyn that one small wound could cause such agony. And there was worse to look forward to. The bullet was lodged in his calf. And despite his words to the surgeon, he was not quite confident that the leg could be saved. He gritted his teeth and took the horse's reins from Conan's hands.

"I'll ride with you, Tresham," his friend said curtly. "You bloody idiot!"

"I'll ride on your other side," Viscount Kimble offered cheerfully. "And then you will have someone to catch you whichever side you choose to slide off. Well done, Tresh, old chap. You gave that old sawbones a right setdown."

The serving girl stood looking up at Jocelyn.

"I must be at least half an hour late by now," she said. "All because of you and your foolish quarreling and more than foolish dueling."

Jocelyn reached for one of the pockets of his coat, only to be reminded that he was still wearing just his shirt and breeches and top boots.

"Conan," he said testily, "oblige me by finding a sovereign in my coat pocket and tossing it to this wench, will you? It will more than compensate her for the loss of half an hour's wages."

But she had turned on her heel and was striding away over the grass, her back bristling with indignation.

"It is a good thing," Baron Pottier said, looking after her, his quizzing glass to his eye, "that shopgirls do not challenge dukes to duels, Tresham. You would be out here tomorrow morning again for sure." He chuckled. "And I would not wager against her."

Jocelyn did not spare her another thought. Every thought, every sense, every instinct became focused inward on himself—on his pain and on the necessity of riding home to Grosvenor Square and Dudley House before he disgraced himself and fell off his horse in a dead faint.

*　　*　　*

For two weeks Jane Ingleby had searched for employment. As soon as she had accepted the fact that there was no one in London to whom to turn for help and no going back where she had come from, and as soon as she had realized that the little money she had brought to town with her would not keep her for longer than one month even if she were very careful, she had started searching, going from one shop to another, one agency to another.

Finally, when depleted resources had been adding anxiety to the almost paralyzing fear she had already been feeling for other reasons, she had found employment as a milliner's assistant. It involved long hours of dreary work for a fussy, bad-tempered employer who did business as Madame de Laurent complete with French accent and expressive hands, but whose accent became pure cockney when she was in the workroom at the back of her shop with her girls. The pay was abysmal.

But at least it was a job. At least there would be wages enough each week to hold body and soul together and pay the rent of the small room Jane had found in a shabby neighborhood.

She had had the job for two days. This was her third. And she was late. She dreaded to think what that would mean even though she had a good enough excuse. She was not sure Madame de Laurent would be sympathetic to excuses.

She was not. Five minutes after arriving at the shop, Jane was hurrying away from it again.

"Two gents fighting a duel," Madame had said, hands planted on hips, after Jane had told her story. "I was not born yesterday, dearie. Gents don't fight duels in Hyde Park no longer. They go to Wimbledon Common."

Jane had been unable to supply the full names of the two gentlemen. All she knew was that the one who had been wounded—the dark, arrogant, bad-tempered one—had been called Tresham. And that he lived at Dudley House.

"On Grosvenor Square? Oh, *Tresham!*" Madame had exclaimed, throwing her hands in the air. "Well, that explains everything. A more reckless, more dangerous gent than Tresham it would be impossible to find. He is the very devil himself."

For one moment Jane had breathed a sigh of relief. She was going to be believed after all. But Madame had tipped back her head suddenly and laughed scornfully. And then she had looked around the workshop at the other girls, and *they*, sycophants that they were, had all laughed scornfully too.

"And you would have me believe that the Duke of Tresham needed the help of a milliner's assistant after taking a bullet through the leg?" Madame had asked. The question was clearly rhetorical. She had not paused for a reply. "You cannot take me for a fool, dearie. You saw some excitement and stayed around to have a gawk, did you? Did they take his breeches down to tend to his leg? I can hardly blame you for stopping to gawk at that sight. There is no padding in *them* breeches, I would have you know."

The other girls had tittered again while Jane had felt herself blush—partly with embarrassment, partly with anger.

"Are you calling me a liar, then?" she had asked incautiously.

Madame de Laurent had looked at her, transfixed. "Yes, Miss Hoity Toity," she had said at last. "That I am. And I have no further need of your services. Not unless—" She had paused to look about at the girls again, smirking. "Not unless you can bring me a note signed by the Duke of Tresham himself to bear out your story."

The girls had dissolved in convulsions of giggles as Jane had turned and left the workshop. As she strode away, she remembered she had not even asked for the two days' wages she had earned.

And what now? Return to the agency that had found her this job? After working for only two days? Part of the problem before had been that she had no references, no previous experience at anything. Surely worse than no references and no experience would be two days of work ended with dismissal for tardiness and lying.

She had spent the last of her money three days ago on enough food to last her until payday and on the cheap, serviceable dress she was wearing.

Jane stopped on the pavement suddenly, her legs weak with panic. What could she do? Where could she go? She had no money left even if she did decide belatedly that she wanted to go in search of Charles. She had no money even with which to send a letter. And perhaps even now she was being hunted. She had been in London for longer than two weeks, after all, and she had done nothing to mask her trail here. Someone might well have followed her, especially if . . .

But she blanched as her mind shied away from that particular possibility.

At any moment she might see a familiar face and see the truth in that face—that she was indeed being pursued. Yet she was now being denied the chance to disappear into the relatively anonymous world of the working class.

Should she find another agency and neglect to mention the experience of the past few days? Were there any agencies she had not already visited at least half a dozen times?

And then a portly, hurrying gentleman collided painfully with her and cursed her before moving on. Jane rubbed one sore shoulder and felt anger rising again—a familiar feeling today. She had been angry with the bad-tempered duelist—apparently the Duke of Tresham. He had treated her like a thing, whose only function in life was to serve him. And then she had been angry with Madame, who had called her a liar and made her an object of sport.

Were women of the lower classes so utterly powerless, so totally without any right to respect?

That man needed to be told that he had been the means of her losing her employment. He needed to know what a job meant to her—survival! And Madame needed to know that she could not call her a liar without any proof whatsoever. What had she said just a few minutes ago? That Jane could keep her job if she brought a note signed by the duke attesting to the truth of her story?

Well then, she would have her note.

And he would sign it.

Jane knew where he lived. On Grosvenor Square. She knew where that was too. During her first days in London, before she had understood how frighteningly alone she was, before fear had caught her in its grip and sent her scurrying for cover like the fugitive she now was, she had walked all over Mayfair. He lived at Dudley House on Grosvenor Square.

Jane went striding off along the pavement.

2

The Earl of Durbury had taken rooms at the Pulteney Hotel. He rarely came to London and owned no town house. He would have preferred a far less expensive hotel, but there were certain appearances to be kept up. He hoped he would not have to stay long but could soon be on his way back to Candleford in Cornwall.

The man standing in his private sitting room, hat in hand, his manner deferential but not subservient, would have something to do with the duration of the earl's stay. He was a small, dapper individual with oiled hair. He was not at all his lordship's idea of what a Bow Street Runner should look like, but that was what he was.

"I expect every man on the force to be out searching for her," the earl said. "She should not be difficult to find. She is just a green country girl, after all, and has no acquaintances here apart from Lady Webb, who is out of town."

"Begging your pardon, sir," the Runner replied, "but there

are other cases we are working on. I will have the assistance of one or two other men. Perfectly able men, I assure you."

"I would think so too," the earl grumbled, "considering what I am paying you."

The Runner merely inclined his head politely. "Now, if you could give me a description of the young lady," he suggested.

"Tall and thin," his lordship said. "Blond. Too pretty for her own good."

"Her age, sir?"

"Twenty."

"She is simply a runaway, then?" The Runner planted his feet more firmly on the carpet. "I was under the impression that there was more to it than that, sir."

"There certainly is." The earl frowned. "The woman is a criminal of the most dangerous kind. She is a murderess. She has killed my son—or as good as killed him. He is in a coma and not expected to live. And she is a thief. She ran off with a fortune in money and jewels. She must be found."

"And brought to justice," the Runner agreed. "Now, sir, if I may, I will question you more closely about the young woman—any peculiarities of appearance, mannerisms, preferences, favorite places and activities. Things like that. Anything that might help us to a hasty conclusion of our search."

"I suppose," his lordship said grudgingly, "you had better sit down. What is your name?"

"Boden, sir," the Runner replied. "Mick Boden."

Jocelyn was feeling quite satisfyingly foxed. Satisfying except that he was horizontal on his bed when he preferred the upright position while inebriated—the room had less of a tendency to swing and dip and weave around him.

"'Nuff!" He held up a hand—or at least he thought he did—when Sir Conan offered him another glass of brandy.

"'f I drink more, th'old sawbones will have m'leg off b'fore I can protest." His lips and tongue felt as if they did not quite belong to him. So did his brain.

"I have already given you my word that I will not amputate without your concurrence, your grace," Dr. Timothy Raikes said stiffly, no doubt aggrieved at being referred to as a sawbones. "But it looks as if the bullet is deep. If it is lodged in the bone . . ."

"Gerr irr—" Jocelyn concentrated harder. He despised drunks who slurred their words. "Get it out of there, then." The pain had been pleasantly numbed, but even his befuddled mind comprehended the fact that the alcohol he had consumed would not mask the pain of what was about to happen. There was no point in further delay. "Ged on—get on with the job, man."

"If my daughter would just come," the doctor said uneasily. "She is a good, steady-handed assistant in such cases. I sent for her as soon as I was summoned here, but she must have left Hookham's Library before the messenger arrived."

"Blast your daughter!" Jocelyn said rudely. "Get—"

But Conan interrupted.

"Here she is." There was marked relief in his voice.

"No, sir," Dr. Raikes replied. "This is merely a housemaid. But she will have to do. Come here, girl. Are you squeamish? Do you faint at the sight of blood as his grace's valet does?"

"No to both questions," the housemaid said. "But there must have been some mis—"

"Come here," the doctor said more impatiently. "I have to dig a bullet out of his grace's leg. You must hand me the instruments I ask for and swab the blood so that I can see what I am doing. Come closer. Stand here."

Jocelyn braced himself by grasping the outer edges of the mattress with both hands. He caught a brief glimpse of the housemaid before she disappeared beyond Raikes. Coherent thought vanished a moment later as everything in his body, his mind, his world exploded into searing agony. There was nowhere, no corner of his being, in which to hide as the physician cut and probed and dug deeper and deeper in search of the bullet. Conan was pressing down with both hands on his thigh to hold his leg immobile. Jocelyn held the rest of himself still by dint of sheer willpower and a death grip on the mattress and tightly clenched eyes and teeth. With dogged determination he concentrated on keeping himself from screaming.

Time lost all meaning. It seemed forever before he heard the physician announce with damnable calm that the bullet was out.

"It's out, Tresham," Conan repeated, sounding as if he had just run ten miles uphill. "The worst is over."

"Damn it to hell!" Jocelyn commented after using a few other more blistering epithets. "Can't you perform the simple task of removing a bullet, Raikes, without taking all morning over it?"

"I worked as fast as I could, your grace," his physician replied. "It was embedded in muscles and tendons. It is difficult to assess the damage that has been done. But haste on my part would almost certainly have crippled you and rendered amputation unavoidable."

Jocelyn swore again. And then felt the indescribable comfort of a cool, damp cloth being pressed first to his forehead and then to each of his cheeks. He had not realized how hot he was. He opened his eyes.

He recognized her instantly. Her golden hair was dressed with ruthless severity. Her mouth was in a thin line as it had been the last time he saw her—in Hyde Park. She had shed the gray cloak and bonnet she had been wearing then, but what was beneath them was no improvement. She wore a cheap, tasteless gray dress, primly high at the neckline. Despite his inebriation, which his pain had largely put to flight, Jocelyn seemed to recall that he was lying on his own bed in his own bedchamber in his own London home. She had been in Hyde Park on her way to work.

"What the devil are *you* doing here?" he demanded.

"Helping to mop up blood and now sponging away sweat," she replied, turning to dip her cloth in a bowl and squeeze it out before pressing it to his forehead again. Saucy wench.

"Oh, I say!" Conan had obviously just recognized her too.

"Who let you in?" Jocelyn winced and swore as Dr. Raikes spread something over his wound.

"Your butler, I suppose," she said. "I told him I had come to speak with you, and he whisked me up here. He said I was expected. You may wish to advise him to greater caution about the people he admits. I might have been anyone."

"You *are* anyone!" Jocelyn barked, tightening his grip on the mattress as his leg was moved and a universe of pain crashed through him. The doctor was beginning to bandage his wound. "What the devil do you want?"

"Whoever you are," the doctor began, sounding nervous, "you are upsetting my patient. Perhaps you—"

"What I *demand*," she said firmly, ignoring him, "is a signed note to the effect that you detained me against my will this morning and thus caused me to be late for work."

He must be drunker than he had realized, Jocelyn thought.

"Go to the devil," he told the impertinent serving girl.

"I might well have to," she said, "if I lose my employment." She was dabbing at his chin and neck with her cool cloth.

"Perhaps—" Dr. Raikes began again.

"Why should I care," Jocelyn asked her, "if you lose your job and are tossed out onto the street to starve? If it were not for you, I would not be lying here as helpless as a beached whale."

"I was not the one aiming a pistol at you," she pointed out. "I was not the one who pulled the trigger. I called to both of you to stop, if you will remember."

Was he actually, Jocelyn wondered suddenly, scrapping

with a mere laboring girl? In his own home? In his own bed-chamber? He pushed her arm away.

"Conan," he said curtly, "give this girl the sovereign she ran away from earlier, if you will be so good, and throw her out if she refuses to go on her own feet."

But his friend had time for only one step forward.

"She certainly *does* refuse to go," the girl said, straightening up and glaring down at him, two spots of color reddening her cheeks. She was having the unmitigated gall to be angry and to show it to his face. "She will not budge until she has her signed note."

"Tresham," Conan said, sounding almost amused, "it would take you only a moment, old chap. I can send down for paper, pen, and ink. I can even write the note myself, and all you will need do is sign it. It is her livelihood."

"The devil!" Jocelyn exclaimed. "I will not even dignify that suggestion with a reply. She may grow roots where she stands until a burly footman comes to toss her out on her ear. Are you finished, Raikes?"

The doctor had straightened from his task and turned to his bag.

"I am, your grace," Dr. Raikes said. "There is much damage, I feel it my duty to warn you. It is my hope that it will not be permanent. But it most certainly will be if you do not stay off the leg and keep it elevated for at least the next three weeks."

Jocelyn stared at him, appalled. Three weeks of total inaction? He could not think of a worse fate.

"If you will not write the note," the girl said, "then *you* must offer me employment to replace my lost job. I simply refuse to starve."

Jocelyn turned his head to look at her—the cause of all his woes. This was his fourth duel. Before today he had not suffered as much as a scratch. Oliver would have missed by a yard if this girl's screeching had not given him a broader target at which to aim and the luxury of aiming at an opponent who was not also aiming at him.

"You have it," he snapped. "You have employment, girl. For three weeks. As my nurse. Believe me, before the time is up you will be wondering if starvation would not have been a better fate."

She looked steadily at him. "What are my wages to be?" she asked.

Jane awoke disoriented early the following morning. There were none of the noises of drunken men bellowing and women shrieking and children crying and quarreling, none of the smells of stale cabbage and gin and worse to which she had grown almost accustomed. Only silence and warm blankets and the sweet smell of cleanliness.

She was at Dudley House on Grosvenor Square, she remembered almost immediately, and threw back the bedcovers to step out onto the luxury of a carpeted floor. After she had gone yesterday to give notice to her landlord and fetch her meager belongings, she had reported to the servants' entrance of Dudley House, expecting to be put into an attic room with the housemaids. But the housekeeper had informed her that the house had its full complement of servants and there was not a bed available. His grace's nurse would have to be placed in a guest room.

It was a small room, it was true, at the back of the house overlooking the garden, but it seemed luxurious to Jane after her recent experiences. At least it offered her some privacy. And comfort too.

She had not seen her new employer since yesterday morning, when she had so boldly—and so despairingly—demanded that he provide her with employment if he would not help her keep the job she already had. He had apparently taken a dose of laudanum after she and the physician had left, which the housekeeper had sneaked into a hot drink without his knowledge, and it had reacted with the enormous amount of alcohol in his system to make him violently sick before it plunged him into a deep sleep.

Jane guessed that the size of his headache this morning would be astronomical. Not to mention the pain in his leg. It was only through the skill of a superior physician, she knew, that he still had two legs today.

She washed in cold water, dressed quickly, and brushed out her hair before plaiting it with expert fingers and coiling it tightly at the back of her head. She pulled on one of the two white caps she had bought yesterday out of the wages she had earned at the milliner's. She had gone back there officially to give her notice and explain that she would be working for the Duke of Tresham. Madame de Laurent had paid up, too surprised to do otherwise, Jane guessed.

She left her room and made her way down to the kitchen, where she hoped to have some breakfast before she was summoned to begin her work as nurse.

He would make her prefer starvation to her current employment, he had predicted yesterday. She had no doubt he would try his best to make her life uncomfortable. A more arrogant, bad-tempered, ill-mannered man it would be difficult to find. Of course, there had been extenuating circumstances yesterday. He had been in considerable pain, all of which he had borne stoically enough, except with his tongue. *That* had been allowed to run roughshod over everyone within earshot of it.

She wondered what her duties would be. Well, at least, she thought, entering the kitchen and discovering to her chagrin that she must be the last servant up, her working life was unlikely to be as monotonous as it had been at Madame Laurent's. And she was earning twice the wages with board and room in addition.

Of course, it was to last for only three weeks.

*   *   *

His leg was throbbing like a mammoth toothache, Jocelyn discovered when he woke up. From the quality of the light in the room, he judged that it was either early morning or late dusk; he guessed the former. He had slept the evening and night away and yet had lived a lifetime of bizarre dreams in the process. He did not feel in any way refreshed. Quite the contrary.

It behooved him to concentrate on the mammoth toothache in his leg. He did not want even to think about the condition of his head, which felt at least a dozen times its usual size, every square inch of it throbbing as if some unseen hand were using it as a drum—from the inside. His stomach was best ignored altogether. His mouth felt as if it might be stuffed with foul-tasting cotton wool.

Perhaps the only positive note in an overwhelmingly negative situation was that if first impressions were anything to judge by, at least he was not feverish. It was the fever that killed after surgery more often than the effects of the wound itself.

Jocelyn jerked impatiently on the bell rope beside his bed and then vented his irritability on his valet, who had not brought his shaving water up.

"I thought you would wish to rest this morning, your grace," he said.

"You thought! Do I pay you to think, Barnard?"

"No, your grace," his man replied with long-suffering meekness.

"Then fetch my damned shaving water," Jocelyn said. "I have bristles enough on my face to grate cheese."

"Yes, your grace," Barnard said. "Mr. Quincy wishes to know when he may wait upon you."

"Quincy?" Jocelyn frowned. His secretary wished to wait upon him? "Here? In my bedchamber, do you mean? Why the devil would he expect me to receive him here?"

Barnard looked at his master with considerable unease.

"You *were* advised to stay off your leg for three weeks, your grace," he said.

Jocelyn was speechless. His household actually expected him to remain in bed for three weeks? Had they taken collective leave of their senses? He informed his hapless valet with colorful eloquence what he thought of the advice and interference of physicians, valets, secretaries, and servants in general. He threw back the bedcovers and swung his legs over the side of the bed—and grimaced.

Then he remembered something else.

"Where is that damned woman?" he asked. "That interfering baggage whom I seem to remember employing as my nurse. Sleeping in the lap of luxury, I suppose? Expecting breakfast in bed, I suppose?"

"She is in the kitchen, your grace," Barnard told him, "awaiting your orders."

"To attend me here?" Jocelyn gave a short bark of laughter. "She thinks to be admitted here to ply my brow with her cool cloths and titillate my nerves with her sharp tongue, does she?"

His valet was wise enough to hold his tongue.

"Send her to the library," Jocelyn said, "after I have retired there from the breakfast room. Now fetch my shaving water and wipe that disapproving frown from your face."

Over the next half hour he washed and shaved, donned a shirt, and sat while Barnard arranged his neckcloth the way he liked it, neat and crisp without any of the silly artistry affected by the dandy set. But he was forced to concede that the wearing of breeches or pantaloons was going to be out of the question. If current fashion had not dictated that both those garments be worn skintight, perhaps matters might have been different. But one could not fight fashion altogether. He did not possess breeches that did not mold his legs like a second skin. He donned an ankle-length dressing gown of wine-colored brocaded silk instead, and slippers.

He submitted to being half carried downstairs by a hefty

young footman, who did his best to look so impassive that he might almost have been inanimate. But Jocelyn felt all the humiliation of his helplessness. After he had sat through breakfast and read the papers, he had to be half carried again into the library, where he sat in a winged leather chair beside the fire rather than at his desk, as he usually did for an hour or so in the mornings.

"One thing," he said curtly to his secretary when that young man presented himself. "Not one word, Michael, about where I should be and what I should be doing there. Not even half a word if you value your position."

He liked Michael Quincy, a gentleman two years his junior who had been in his employ for four years. Quiet, respectful, and efficient, the man was nevertheless not obsequious. He actually dared to smile now.

"The morning post is on your desk, your grace," he said. "I'll hand it to you."

Jocelyn narrowed his gaze on him. "That woman," he said. "Barnard was supposed to have sent her in by now. It is time she began to earn her keep. Have her come in, Michael. I am feeling just irritated enough to enjoy her company."

His secretary was actually grinning as he left the room.

His head now felt about fifteen times larger than normal, Jocelyn thought.

When she came into the room, it was clear that she had decided to be the meek lamb of an employee this morning. Doubtless word had spread belowstairs that he was in one of his more prickly moods. She stood inside the library door, her hands folded in front of her, awaiting instructions. Jocelyn immediately felt even more irritated than he had already been feeling. He ignored her for a couple of minutes while he tried to decipher a lengthy, crossed letter written in his sister's atrocious handwriting. She lived scarcely a ten-minute walk away, but she had written in the greatest agitation on hearing about the duel. It seemed she had suffered palpitations and vapors and other indecipherable maladies so serious that Heyward, her husband, had had to be fetched from the House of Lords.

Heyward would not have been amused.

Jocelyn looked up. She looked hideous. She wore yesterday's gray dress, which covered her from neck to wrists to ankles. There was no ornament to make the cheap garment prettier. Today she wore a white bonnet cap. She stood straight and tall. It was altogether possible, he thought, mentally stripping her with experienced eyes, that she looked quite womanly beneath the garments, but one had to be dedicated to observe the signs. He seemed to recall through yesterday's nightmare of pain that her hair was golden. It was invisible now.

Her stance was meek. But her eyes were not directed decently at the floor. She was gazing steadily at him.

"Come!" He beckoned impatiently.

She came with firm strides until she was three feet from his chair. She was still looking directly at him with eyes that were startlingly blue. Indeed, he realized in some surprise, she had a face that was classical in its beauty. There was not a fault to find there, except that he remembered yesterday's thinned lips. In repose today they looked soft and exquisitely shaped.

"Well?" he said sharply. "What do you have to say for yourself? Are you ready to apologize to me?"

She took her time about answering.

"No," she said at last. "Are you ready to apologize to me?"

He sat back in his chair and tried to ignore the rampaging pain in his leg. "Let us get one thing straight," he said in the quiet, almost pleasant voice that he knew had every last member of his staff instantly quaking in his or her boots. "There is not even the smallest semblance of equality between us—" He paused and frowned. "What the devil is your name?"

"Jane Ingleby."

"There is not the smallest semblance of equality between us, Jane," he continued. "I am the master and you are the servant. The very *lowly* servant. You are not required to cap everything I say with some witty impertinence. You will address me with the proper respect. You will tack 'your grace' onto everything you do say. Do I make myself clear?"

"Yes," she said. "And I believe, your grace, you should watch your language in my hearing. I do not approve of having the devil's name and the Lord's name bandied about as if they were in everyone's nursery vocabulary."

Good Lord! Jocelyn's hands curved about the arms of the chair.

"Indeed?" He used his iciest voice. "And do you have any other instructions for me, Jane?"

"Yes, two things," she said. "I would prefer to be called Miss Ingleby."

His right hand found the handle of his quizzing glass. He half raised it to his eye. "And the other thing?"

"Why are you not in bed?"

3

Jane watched the Duke of Tresham raise his glass all the way to his eye, grotesquely magnifying it, while his other hand came to rest on top of the pile of letters in his lap. He was being enormously toplofty, of course, trying to frighten her. And half succeeding. But it would be certain suicide to show it.

His servants, she had gathered at breakfast, were all terrified of him, especially when he was in one of his black moods, as he was this morning, according to his valet. And he looked rather formidable, even clad as he was now in dressing gown and slippers over a crisp white shirt and expertly tied neckcloth.

He was a powerful-looking, dark-haired man with black eyes, prominent nose, and thin lips in a narrow face, whose habitual expression appeared to be both harsh and cynical. And arrogant.

Of course, Jane conceded, this must not be one of his better days.

She had approached the room with Mr. Quincy, the duke's pleasant, gentle-mannered secretary, and had decided to be what she was supposed to be—a quiet, meek nurse who was fortunate to have this position even if only for three weeks.

But it was difficult not to be herself—as she had discovered at great cost almost a month ago. Her stomach lurched and she withdrew her mind firmly from those particular memories.

"I beg your pardon?" he said now, lowering his glass to his chest again.

A rhetorical question. He did not, she guessed, suffer from defective hearing.

"You were told to stay in bed for at least three weeks and keep your leg elevated," she reminded him. "Yet here you sit with your foot on the floor and obviously in pain. I can tell from the tension in your face."

"The tension in my face," he told her with an ominous narrowing of his eyes, "is the result of a giant headache and of your colossal impudence."

Jane ignored him. "Is it not foolish to take risks," she asked, "merely because it would be tedious to lie abed?"

Men really were foolish. She had known several just like him in her twenty years—men whose determination to be men made them reckless of their health and safety.

He leaned back in his chair and regarded her in silence while despite herself she felt prickles of apprehension crawl up her spine. She would probably find herself out on the pavement with her pathetic bundle of belongings in ten minutes' time, she thought. Perhaps without her bundle.

"*Miss Ingleby.*" He made her name sound like the foulest curse. "I am six and twenty years old. I have held my title and all the duties and responsibilities that go with it for nine years, since the death of my father. It is a long time since anyone spoke to me as if I were a naughty schoolboy in need of a scolding. It will be a long time before I will tolerate being spoken to thus again."

There was no answer to that. Jane ventured none. She folded her hands before her and looked steadily at him. He was not handsome, she decided. Not at all. But there was a raw masculinity about him that must make him impossibly attractive to any woman who liked to be bullied, dominated, or verbally abused. And there were many such women, she believed.

She had had quite enough of such men. Her stomach churned uncomfortably again.

"But you are quite right in one thing, you will be pleased to know," he admitted. "I am in pain, and not just from this infernal headache. Keeping my foot on the floor is clearly not the best thing to be doing. But I'll be damned before I will lie prone on my bed for three weeks merely because my attention was distracted long enough during a duel for someone to put a hole in my leg. And I will be double damned before I will allow myself to be drugged into incoherence again merely so that the pain might be dulled. In the music room next door you will find a footstool beside the hearth. Fetch it."

She wondered again as she turned to leave the room what exactly her duties would be for the coming three weeks. He did not appear to be feverish. And he clearly had no intention of playing the part of languishing invalid. Nursing him and running and fetching for him would not be nearly a full-time job. Probably the housekeeper would be instructed to find other tasks for her. She would not mind as long as her work never brought her in sight of any visitors to the house. It had been incautious to come into Mayfair again, to knock on the door of a grand mansion on Grosvenor Square, to demand work here. To put herself on display.

But it was such a pleasure, she had to admit to herself as she opened the door next to the library and discovered the

music room, to be in clean, elegant, spacious, civilized surroundings again.

There was no sign of a footstool anywhere near the
hearth.

Jocelyn watched her go and noticed that she held herself very
straight and moved gracefully. He must have been quite befuddled yesterday, he thought, to have assumed that she was a
serving girl, even though as it had turned out she really was
just a milliner's assistant. She dressed the part, of course. Her
dress was cheap and shoddily made. It was also at least one
size too large.

But she was no serving girl, for all that. Nor brought up to
spend her days in a milliner's workshop, if he was any judge.
She spoke with the cultured accents of a lady.

A lady who had fallen upon hard times?

She took her time about returning. When she did so, she
was carrying the footstool in one hand and a large cushion in
the other.

"Did you have to go to the other side of London for the
stool?" he asked sharply. "And then have to wait while it was
being made?"

"No," she replied quite calmly. "But it was not where you
said it would be. Indeed, it was not anywhere in plain sight. I
brought a cushion too as the stool looks rather low."

She set it down, placed the cushion on top of it, and went
down on one knee in order to lift his leg. He dreaded having it
touched. But her hands were both gentle and strong. He felt
scarcely any additional pain. Perhaps, he thought, he should
have her cradle his head in those hands. He pursed his lips to
stop himself from chuckling.

His dressing gown had fallen open to reveal the bandage
cutting into the reddened flesh of his calf. He frowned.

"You see?" Jane Ingleby said. "Your leg has swollen and

must be twice as painful as it need be. You really must keep it up as you were told, however fretful and inconvenient it may be to do so. I suppose you consider it unmanly to give in to an indisposition. Men can be so silly that way."

"Indeed?" he said frostily, viewing the top of her hideous and very new cap with extreme distaste. Why he had not dismissed her with a figurative boot in the rear end ten minutes ago he did not know. Why he had hired her in the first place he could not fathom since he blamed her entirely for his misfortune. She was a shrew and would worry him to death like a cat with a mouse long before the three weeks were over.

But the alternative was to have Barnard fussing over him and blanching as pale as any sheet every time he so much as caught sight of his master's bandage.

Besides, he was going to need something to stimulate his mind while he was incarcerated inside his town house, Jocelyn decided. He could not expect his friends and family to camp out in his drawing room and give him their constant company.

"Yes, indeed." She stood up and looked down at him. Not only were her eyes clear blue, he noticed, but they were rimmed by thick long lashes several shades darker than her almost invisible hair. They were the sort of eyes in which a man might well drown himself if the rest of her person and character were only a match for them. But there was that mouth not far below them, and it was still talking.

"This bandage needs changing," she said. "It is the one Dr. Raikes put on yesterday morning. He is not returning until tomorrow, I believe he said. That is too long a time for one bandage even apart from the swelling. I will dress the wound afresh."

He did not want anyone within one yard of the bandage or the wound beneath it. But that was a craven attitude, he knew. Besides, the bandage really did feel too tight. And besides again, he had employed her as a nurse. Let her earn her keep, then.

"What are you waiting for?" he asked irritably.

"Permission? Is it possible that you deem it necessary to have my *permission* to supersede one of London's most eminent physicians and to maul my person, Miss Ingleby?" It annoyed him that he had not insisted upon calling her Jane. A nice meek name. A total misnomer for the blue-eyed dragon who looked calmly back at him.

"I do not intend to maul you, your grace," she said, "but to make you more comfortable. I will not hurt you. I promise."

He set his head back against the headrest of his chair and closed his eyes. And opened them hastily again. Headaches, of course—at least the caliber of headache that he had been carrying around with him since he regained consciousness a couple of hours before—were not eased when experienced from behind lowered eyelids.

She closed the door quietly behind her, he noticed, as she had done when she had gone in search of the footstool. Thank God for small mercies. Now if only she would keep her mouth shut. . . .

For the first time in a long while Jane felt as if she were in familiar territory. She unwound the bandage with slow care and eased it free of the wound, which had bled a little and caused the bandage to stick. She looked up as she freed it.

He had not winced even though he must have felt pain. He was reclined in his chair, one elbow resting on the arm, his head propped on his hand while he regarded her with half-closed eyes.

"I am sorry," she said. "The blood had dried."

He half nodded and she set about the task of cleansing the wound with warm water before applying the balsam powder she had found among the housekeeper's supplies.

She had nursed her father through a lingering illness until the moment of his death a year and a half ago. Poor Papa. Never a robust man, he had lost all his will to live after

Mama's passing, as if he had allowed disease to ravage him without a fight. By the end she had been doing everything for him. He had grown so very thin. This man's leg was strong and well muscled.

"You are new to London?" he asked suddenly.

She glanced up. She hoped he was not going to start amusing himself by prying into her past. It was a hope that was immediately dashed.

"Where did you come from?" he asked.

What should she say? She hated lying, but the truth was out of the question. "From a long way away."

He winced as she applied the powder. But it was necessary to prevent the infection that might yet cost him his leg. The swelling worried her.

"You are a lady," he said—a statement, not a question.

She had tried a cockney accent, with ludicrous results. She had tried something a little vaguer, something that would make her sound like a woman of the lower classes. But though she could hear accents quite clearly, she found it impossible to reproduce them. She had given up trying.

"Not really," she said. "Just well brought up."

"Where?"

It was a lie she had already told. She would stick with it since it immediately killed most other questions.

"In an orphanage," she said. "A good one. I suppose I must have been fathered by someone who could not acknowledge me but who could afford to have me decently raised."

Oh, Papa, she thought. And Mama too. Who had lavished all their love and attention on her, their only child, and given her a wondrously happy family life for sixteen years. Who would have done their utmost to see her settled in a life as happily domesticated as their own if death had not claimed them first.

"Hmm" was all the Duke of Tresham said.

She hoped it was all he would ever say on the subject. She

wrapped the clean bandage securely but loosely enough to allow for the swelling.

"This stool is not high enough even with the cushion." She frowned and looked around, then spied a chaise longue adorning one corner of the library. "I suppose you would rain down fire and brimstone on my head if I were to suggest that you recline on that," she said, pointing. "You could retain all your masculine pride by remaining in your library, but you could stretch your leg out along it and elevate it on the cushion."

"You would banish me to the corner, Miss Ingleby?" he asked. "With my back to the room perhaps?"

"I suppose," she said, "the chaise longue is not bolted to the floor. I suppose it could be moved to a place more satisfactory to you. Close to the fire, perhaps?"

"The fire be damned," he said. "Have it moved close to the window. By someone considerably more hefty than you. I will not be responsible for your suffering a dislocated spine even if there would be some poetic justice in it. There is a bell rope beside the mantel. Pull on it."

A footman moved the chaise longue into the light of the window. But it was on Jane's shoulder that the duke leaned as he hopped from his chair to take up his new position. He had flatly refused, of course, to allow himself to be carried.

"Be damned to you," he had told her when she had suggested it. "I shall be carried to my grave, Miss Ingleby. Until then, I shall convey myself from place to place even if I must avail myself of some assistance."

"Have you always been so stubborn?" Jane asked while the footman gawked at her with dropped jaw as if he expected her to be felled by a thunderbolt in the very next moment.

"I am a Dudley," the Duke of Tresham said by way of explanation. "We are a stubborn lot from the moment of conception. Dudley babes are reputed to kick their mothers with unusual ferocity in the womb and to give them considerable grief while proceeding into the world. And that is just the beginning."

He was trying to shock her, Jane realized. He was looking at her intently with his black eyes, which she had discovered from close up were really just a very dark brown. Foolish man. She had assisted in the birthing of numerous babies from the time she was fourteen. Her mother had raised her to believe that service was an integral part of a life of privilege.

He looked more comfortable once he was settled and had his foot resting on the cushion. Jane stood back, expecting to be dismissed or at least to be directed to present herself to the housekeeper for further orders. The footman had already been sent on his way. But the duke looked at her consideringly.

"Well, Miss Ingleby," he said, "how are you planning to amuse me for the next three weeks?"

Jane felt a lurching of alarm. The man was incapacitated, and besides, there had been no suggestive note in his voice. But she had good reason to be distrustful of gentlemen in their boredom.

She was saved from answering by the opening of the library door. It did not open quietly, as one might have expected, to admit either the butler or Mr. Quincy. Indeed, its opening was not even preceded by a respectful knock. The door was thrown back so that it cracked against the bookcase behind it. A lady strode inside.

Jane felt considerable alarm. She was a young and remarkably fashionable lady even if she would never earn full marks for good taste in dress. Jane did not recognize her, but even so in that moment she realized clearly the folly of being here. If the visitor had been announced, she herself could have slipped away unseen. As it was, she could only stand where she was or at best take a couple of steps back and sideways and hope to melt into the shadows to the left of the window curtains.

The young lady swept into the room rather like a tidal wave.

"I believe my instructions were that I was not to be disturbed this morning," the duke murmured.

But his visitor came on, undaunted.

"Tresham!" she exclaimed. "You are alive. I would not believe it until I had seen it with my own eyes. If you just knew what I have suffered in the past day, you would never have done it. Heyward has gone off to the House this morning, which is bothersome of him when my nerves are shattered. I declare I did not get one wink of sleep last night. It was most unsporting of Lord Oliver actually to shoot at you, I must say. If Lady Oliver was indiscreet enough to let him discover that she is your latest amour, and if he is foolish enough to proclaim his goat's horns to all the world with such a public challenge—and in Hyde Park of all places—then *he* is the one who should get shot at. But they say that you shot gallantly into the air, which shows you for the polished gentleman that you are. It would have been no more than he deserved if you had killed him. But of course then they would have hanged you, or would have if you had not been a duke. You would have had to flee to France, and Heyward was provoking enough to tell me that he would not have taken me to Paris to visit you there. Even though all the world knows it is the most fashionable place to be. Sometimes I wonder why I married him."

The Duke of Tresham was holding his head with one hand. He held up his free hand while the young lady paused to draw breath.

"You married him, Angeline," he said, "because you fancied him and he was an earl and almost as wealthy as I am. Mostly because you fancied him."

"Yes." She smiled and revealed herself to be an extremely pretty young lady despite her resemblance to the duke. "I did, did I not? How *are* you, Tresham?"

"Apart from a throbbing leg and a head ten sizes or so too large for my neck," he said, "remarkably well, I thank you, Angeline. Do have a seat."

The last words were spoken with considerable irony. She had already sat down on a chair close to the chaise longue.

"I will leave instructions on my way out," she said, "that

no one but family is to be allowed in to see you. You certainly do not need any visitor who might be inclined to talk your head off, poor thing."

"Hmm," he said, and Jane watched as he raised his quizzing glass to his eye and looked suddenly even more pained than before. "That is a repulsive bonnet," he said. "Mustard yellow? With that particular shade of pink? If you were intending to wear it to Lady Lovatt's Venetian breakfast next week, I am vastly relieved to inform you that I will be unable to escort you."

"Heyward said," the young lady continued, leaning forward and ignoring his opinion of her taste in bonnets, "that Lord Oliver is telling everyone he is not satisfied because you did not try to kill him. Can you imagine anything so idiotic? Lady Oliver's brothers are not satisfied either, and you know what *they* are like. They are saying, though not one of them was present, I understand, that you moved like a coward and prevented Lord Oliver from killing you. But if they challenge you, you simply must not accept. Consider my nerves."

"At the precise moment, Angeline," he assured her, "I am preoccupied by my own."

"Well, you may have the satisfaction of knowing that you are the talk of the town anyway," she said. "How splendid of you to *ride* home, Tresham, when you had been shot through the leg. I wish I had been there to observe it. At least you have diverted talk from that tiresome Hailsham affair and that business in Cornwall. Is it true that a beggar girl screamed and distracted your attention?"

"Not a beggar exactly," he said. "She is standing there by the curtain. Meet Miss Jane Ingleby."

Lady Heyward swiveled on her chair and looked at Jane in considerable astonishment. It was quite clear that she had not noticed there was anyone else in the room except her and her brother. Not that the curtain offered any great degree of shelter, but Jane was dressed as a servant. It was a somewhat reassuring realization that that fact made her virtually invisible.

"You, girl?" Lady Heyward said with an hauteur that gave her an even more marked resemblance to the duke. She could be no more than a year or two older than herself, Jane estimated. "Why are you standing there? Have you had her thrashed, Tresham?"

"She is my nurse," he said. "And she prefers to be called Miss Ingleby rather than *girl*." There was a deceptive meekness in his voice.

"Indeed?" The astonishment in the young lady's face increased. "How peculiar. But I have to run along. I was to meet Martha Griddles at the library twenty minutes ago. But I had to come here first to offer what comfort I could."

"What are sisters for?" his grace murmured.

"Precisely." She bent over him and aimed a kiss at the air in the vicinity of his left cheek. "Ferdie will probably be calling on you later. He was incensed by the dishonor Lady Oliver's brothers were trying to throw upon you yesterday. He was all for calling them out himself—every one of them. But Heyward said he was merely making an ass of himself—his very words, I swear, Tresham. He does not understand about the Dudley temper." She sighed and left the room as abruptly as she had entered it, leaving the door wide open behind her.

Jane stood where she was. She felt cold and alone and frightened.

What was the drawing-room gossip to which the Duke of Tresham's sister had so fleetingly referred? *At least you have diverted talk from . . . that business in Cornwall.*

What business in Cornwall?

"I believe," the duke said, "the brandy decanter is called for, Miss Ingleby. And inform me at your peril that imbibing more alcohol will merely intensify my headache. Go and fetch it."

"Yes, your grace." Jane was quite uninclined to argue.

4

*L*ord Ferdinand Dudley came less than an hour after Lady Heyward had left. He crashed the door back against the bookcase just as she had done and strode into the library unannounced.

Jocelyn winced and wished he had not sent the brandy decanter away as soon as he had set eyes upon it. He had just finished drinking a cup of chocolate, which Jane Ingleby had told him might settle his stomach and soothe his head. It had not achieved either desirable effect yet.

She melted back against the curtains again, he noticed.

"Devil take it!" his younger brother said by way of greeting. "Old Gruff-and-Grim tried to stop me from coming in here, Tresham. Can you imagine? Where do servants get such cork-brained notions?"

"Usually from their employers," Jocelyn said.

"Good Lord!" His brother stopped in his tracks. "You really are playing the invalid. Mama used to languish on that chaise longue whenever she had been dancing and gaming for three nights or so in a row and fancied herself at death's door. There's no truth to the rumor, is there?"

"There usually is not," Jocelyn replied languidly. "To which particular rumor do you refer?"

"That you will never walk again," his brother said, throwing himself down onto the chair on which Angeline had sat. "That you had to wrestle old Raikes down onto the floor to prevent his hacking off the leg. Honestly, Tresham, physicians these days would just as soon pull a saw out of their bags as take the time to dig around for a bullet."

"You may rest assured," Jocelyn told him, "that I was in no mood for wrestling anyone to the ground yesterday except perhaps that nincompoop of a surgeon Oliver took out to Hyde Park. Raikes did his job admirably well and I will certainly walk again."

"Just what I said," Ferdinand said, beaming at him. "It is in the betting book at White's. I have fifty pounds on it that you will be waltzing at Almack's within a month."

"You will lose." Jocelyn raised his quizzing glass to his eye. "I never waltz. And I never show my face at Almack's. All the mamas would instantly assume I was in the marriage mart. When are you going to dismiss that sad apology for a valet of yours, Ferdinand, and employ someone who can refrain from cutting your throat every time he shaves you?"

His brother fingered a small nick under his chin. "Oh, that," he said. "My fault, Tresham. I turned my head without warning him. The Forbes brothers are after your blood. There are three of them in town."

Yes, they would be. Lady Oliver's brothers had almost as bad a reputation as hell-raisers as he and his siblings did, Jocelyn thought. And since the lady was the only sister among five brothers, they were more than usually protective of her even now, three years after her marriage to Lord Oliver.

"They will have to come and take it, then," Jocelyn said.

"It should not be at all difficult since it seems my butler will admit anyone to my house who deigns to step up and rap on the knocker."

"Oh, I say!" Ferdinand sounded aggrieved. "I am not just anyone, Tresham. And I must protest your not asking me to be your second or even informing me that there was to be a duel. Is it true, by the way, that it was a servant girl who caused all the fracas? Brougham says she came storming into the house after you and got all the way to your bedchamber and gave you a tongue-lashing because she had lost her job." He chuckled. "I daresay that it is a very tall story, but it is a damned good one nevertheless."

"She is standing over there by the curtain," Jocelyn said, nodding in the direction of his nurse, who had stood like a statue ever since his brother's arrival.

"Oh, I say!" Ferdinand leaped to his feet and gazed at her with the keenest curiosity. "What the devil is she doing here? It is really not the thing, you know, girl, to interfere in a matter of honor. That is gentlemen's business. You might have caused Tresham's death, and then you would have swung for sure."

She was looking at Ferdinand the way she usually looked at him, Jocelyn saw. He recognized the signs—the further straightening of already straight shoulders, the thinning of the lips, the very direct stare. He waited with a certain relish for her to speak.

"If he had been killed," she said, "it would have been by the bullet of the man with whom he was dueling. And how foolish to call such a meeting a matter of *honor*. You are right to call it men's business, though. Women have a deal more sense."

Lord Ferdinand Dudley looked almost comically non-plussed as he took a scolding from a hideously clad servant.

"She comes equipped with a mind, you see, Ferdinand,"

Jocelyn explained with studied boredom, "with a double-edged tongue attached."

"I say!" His brother turned his head and looked at him, aghast. "What in thunder is she doing here?"

"Conan did not complete the story?" Jocelyn asked. "I have employed her as my nurse. I do not see why the rest of my servants should be at the receiving end of my temper for the coming three weeks while I am incarcerated in my own home."

"Devil take it," his brother said. "I thought he was funning!"

"No, no." Jocelyn waved one careless hand. "Meet Jane Ingleby, Ferdinand. But do have a care if it ever becomes necessary to address her again. She insists upon being called *Miss Ingleby* rather than *Jane* or *girl*. Which point I have conceded since she has stopped calling me nothing at all and has begun occasionally addressing me as *your grace*. My younger brother, Lord Ferdinand Dudley, Miss Ingleby."

He half expected her to curtsy. He half expected his brother to explode. This must surely be the first time he had been presented to a servant.

Jane Ingleby inclined her head graciously, and Ferdinand flushed and made her an awkward little bow and looked downright embarrassed.

"I say, Tresham," he said, "has the injury turned you daft in the head?"

"I believe," Jocelyn said, setting one hand to the aforementioned head, "you were about to take your leave, Ferdinand? Some advice, my dear fellow, though why I waste my breath giving it I do not know since Dudleys are not renowned for taking advice. Leave the Forbeses to me. Their quarrel is with me, not with you."

"Damned rogues and gangsters!" His brother bristled. "They would be better employed giving their sister a good smacking. How you could have got involved with plowing that particular piece of skirt, I do not know. I—"

"Enough!" Jocelyn said coldly. "There is—" He was about to say there was a lady present, but he caught himself in time. "I am not answerable to you for my affairs. Take yourself off now, there's a good fellow, and send Hawkins in to me. I intend to attempt to make clear to him that his future employment in this house depends upon his letting no one else beyond the doorstep for the rest of the day. If my head does not explode before nightfall and cause my brains to rain down on the books, I shall be very surprised."

Lord Ferdinand left and the butler stepped into the library a minute or two later, looking apprehensive.

"I do apologize, your grace—" he began, but Jocelyn held up one hand.

"I will concede," he said, "that it would probably take a whole regiment of seasoned soldiers and a battery of artillery to keep Lord Ferdinand and Lady Heyward out when they are determined to come in. But no one else today, Hawkins. Not even the Prince Regent himself should he deign to come calling. I trust I have made myself clear?"

"Yes, your grace." His butler bowed deferentially and withdrew, closing the door behind him with merciful quietness.

Jocelyn sighed aloud. "Now, Miss Ingleby," he said, "come and sit here and tell me how you plan to amuse me for the next three weeks. You have had plenty of time to think of an answer."

"Yes, I play all the most common card games," Jane said in answer to a question, "but I will not play for money." It had been one of her parents' rules—no gambling in their home for higher stakes than pennies. And no playing at all after half a crown—two shillings and sixpence—had been lost. "Besides," she added, "I have no money with which to play. I daresay you would derive no pleasure from a game in which the stakes were not high."

"I am delighted you presume to know me so well," he said. "Do you play chess?"

"No." She shook her head. Her father had used to play, but he had had strange notions about women. Chess was a man's game, he had always said with fond indulgence whenever she had asked him to teach her. His refusal had always made her want even more to be able to play it. "I have never learned."

He looked at her broodingly. "I do not suppose you read," he said.

"Of course I *read*." Did he think her a total ignoramus? She remembered too late who she was supposed to be.

"Ah, of course," he repeated softly, his gaze narrowing. "And write a neat hand too, I daresay. What sort of an orphanage was it, Miss Ingleby?"

"I told you," she said. "A superior one."

He looked hard at her but did not pursue the matter.

"And what other accomplishments do you have," he asked, "with which to entertain me?"

"Is entertaining you a nurse's job, then?" she asked.

"My nurse's job is exactly what I say it is." His eyes were looking her over as if he could see beneath all her garments. She found that gaze more than a little disconcerting. "It is not going to take you twenty-four hours of every day to change my bandage and lift my foot on and off cushions after all, is it?"

"No, your grace," she admitted.

"Yet you are eating and living at my expense," he said. "And I believe I am paying you a rather handsome salary. Do you begrudge me a little entertainment?"

"I believe," she told him, "you will soon be heartily bored with what I have to offer."

He half smiled, but rather than softening his face, the

expression succeeded only in making him look rather wolfish. He had his quizzing glass in his hand, she noticed, though he did not raise it to his eye.

"We will see," he said. "Remove that cap, Miss Ingleby. It offends me. It is remarkably hideous and ages you by at least a decade. How old are you?"

"I do not believe, your grace," she said, "that my age is any of your business. And I would prefer to wear a cap when on duty."

"Would you?" He looked suddenly haughty and not a little frightening with his eyebrows raised. His voice was softer when he spoke again. "Take it off."

Defiance seemed futile. After all, she had never worn a cap before yesterday. It had just seemed like a good sort of disguise, like something beneath which she could at least half hide. She was not unaware of the fact that her hair was her most distinctive feature. She reluctantly untied the bow beneath her chin and pulled off the cap. She held it with both hands in her lap while his eyes were directed at her hair.

"One might say," he said, "that it is your crowning glory, Miss Ingleby. Especially, I daresay, when it is not so ruthlessly braided and twisted. Which poses the question of why you were so determined to hide it. Are you afraid of me and my reputation?"

"I do not know your reputation," she said. Though it would not tax the imagination overmuch to guess.

"I was challenged to a duel yesterday," he said, "for having, ah, *relations* with a married lady. It was not the first duel I have engaged in. I am known as an unprincipled, dangerous man."

"Spoken with pride?" She raised her eyebrows.

His lips twitched, but whether with amusement or anger it was impossible to tell.

"I do have some principles," he said. "I have never ravished a servant. Or assaulted any woman beneath my own roof. Or bedded any who were unwilling. Does that reassure you?"

"Absolutely," she said. "Since I believe I qualify for sanctuary on all three counts."

"But I would give a monkey," he said softly, sounding as dangerous as he had just described himself, "to see you with your hair down."

The Lilliputians were swarming all over the Man Mountain, securing him with the greatest ingenuity—even his long hair—to the ground.

She was reading *Gulliver's Travels* to him, a book to which he could hardly object since he had left the choice of reading material up to her. She had wandered about the library shelves for a half hour, looking and fingering and occasionally drawing out a book and opening it. She handled books with reverence, as if she loved them. She had turned to him finally and held up the volume from which she was now reading.

"This one?" she had asked. "*Gulliver's Travels*? It is one of those books I have always promised myself I would read."

"As you wish." He had shrugged. He was perfectly capable of reading silently to himself, but he did not want to be alone. He had never particularly enjoyed his own company for any length of time—no, that was not true. But for the past ten years or so it had been.

He had been feeling considerable irritation as the true nature of his plight had become clearer to him during the course of the day. He was a restless, energetic man, who engaged in a dozen or more activities every day, most of them involving physical exercise like riding and boxing and fencing and—yes—even dancing, though never the waltz and never at that most insipid of all institutions, Almack's. Making love was a favorite activity too, of course, and that could be the most energetic exercise of all.

Now for three weeks, if he could bear the torture that long, he was to be inactive, with only visiting friends and relatives for company. And the prim, shrewish Jane Ingleby, of course. And pain.

He had distracted himself by dismissing his nurse and spending the afternoon with Michael Quincy. The monthly reports from Acton Park, his country estate, had arrived that morning. He had always been conscientious about them, but he had never before pored over them with quite such determined attention to detail.

But the evening threatened to be endless. The nights were the time when he did most of his living and socializing, first at the theater or opera or whatever fashionable ball or soiree was likely to draw the greatest crowd, and then at one of his clubs or in bed if the sport offered there seemed worth the sacrifice of a night with his male friends.

"Do you wish me to continue?" Jane Ingleby had paused and looked up from the book.

"Yes, yes." He waved one hand in her direction, and she looked down and resumed her reading.

Her spine, he noticed, did not touch the back of her chair. And yet she looked both comfortable and graceful. She read well, neither too fast nor too slowly, neither in a monotone nor with theatrically exaggerated expression. She had a lovely soft, cultured speaking voice. Her long lashes fanned her cheeks as she looked down at the book she held with both hands close to her lap. Her neck was long and swanlike in its elegance.

Her hair was pure spun gold. She had done an admirable job of making it look severe and insignificant, but the only way she could hope for success in that endeavor was to shave her head. He had noticed the beauty of her face and the loveliness of her eyes during the morning. It was only when she had removed her cap that he had discovered how far reality surpassed his growing suspicion that she was an extraordinarily handsome woman.

He watched her read as he rubbed the heel of his right hand hard over his thigh as if to ease the pain in his calf. She was a servant, a dependent beneath his roof, and without any doubt a virtuous woman. As she had observed in her usual pert manner during the morning, she was thrice protected from him. But he would dearly like to see that hair with all the pins and coils and braids removed.

He would not be totally averse, either, to seeing her person without the dreary, cheap, ill-fitting dress and anything else she might be wearing beneath it.

He sighed, and she stopped reading again and looked up.

"Would you like to go to bed now?" she asked him.

She could always be relied upon to return her own particular brand of sanity to a situation, he thought. Her expression was without the slightest hint of suggestiveness despite her choice of words.

He glanced at the clock on the mantel. Good Lord, it was not even ten o'clock. The evening had scarcely begun.

"Since neither you nor Gulliver is a particularly scintillating companion, Miss Ingleby," he said brutally, "I suppose that is my best option. I wonder if you appreciate how low I have been brought."

A night of sleep without either liquor or laudanum to induce slumber had not improved the Duke of Tresham's temper, Jane discovered early the next morning. The physician had arrived and she was summoned from her breakfast in the kitchen to the duke's bedchamber.

"You have taken your time," he said by way of greeting when she entered the room after tapping on his door less than a minute after the summons. "I suppose you were busy eating me out of house and home."

"I had finished my breakfast, thank you, your grace," she said. "Good morning, Dr. Raikes."

"Good morning, ma'am." The physician inclined his head politely to her.

"*Take that monstrosity off!*" the duke commanded, pointing at Jane's cap. "If I set eyes on it again, I shall personally carve it into very thin ribbons."

Jane removed her cap, folded it neatly, and put it into the pocket of her dress.

Her employer had turned his attention to the doctor.

"It was Miss Ingleby who changed the bandage," he said, apparently in answer to a question that had been asked before her arrival, "and cleansed the wound."

"You did an admirable job, ma'am," the doctor said. "There is no sign of infection or putrefaction. You have had some experience in tending the ailing, have you?"

"Yes, a little, sir," Jane admitted.

"She spooned purges into all the damned orphans when they overate, I daresay," the duke muttered irritably. "And I am not *ailing*. I have a hole in my leg. I believe exercise would do it more good than coddling. I intend to exercise it."

Dr. Raikes looked horrified. "With all due respect, your grace," he said, "I must advise strongly against it. There are damaged muscles and tendons to heal before they are put to even the gentlest use."

The duke swore at him.

"I believe you owe Dr. Raikes an apology," Jane told him. "He is merely giving you his professional opinion, for which you summoned him and are paying him. There was no call for such rudeness."

Both men looked at her in sheer astonishment as she folded her hands at her waist. And then she jumped in alarm as his grace threw his head back on the pillow and roared with laughter.

"I do believe, Raikes," he said, "that a splinter from the bullet in my leg must have flown up and lodged in my brain. Can you believe that I have suffered this for a whole day without putting an end to it?"

Dr. Raikes clearly did not. "I am sure, ma'am," he said

hastily, "that his grace owes me no apology. One understands that his injury has severely frustrated him."

She could not for the life of her leave it alone. "That is no excuse for speaking abusively," she said. "Especially to subordinates."

"Raikes," the duke said testily, "if I could go down on bended knee in humble sorrow at my words, I would perhaps do so. But I may not so exert myself, may I?"

"No indeed, your grace." The doctor, who had finished rebandaging the duke's leg, looked considerably flustered.

It was all her fault, of course, Jane thought. It came of having grown up in an enlightened home, in which servants had invariably been treated as if they were people and in which courtesy to others had been an ingrained virtue. She really must learn to curb her tongue if she was to have this chance of earning three weeks' salary to take with her into the unknown beyond it.

The Duke of Tresham submitted to being carried downstairs, though not before he had dismissed Jane and instructed her to stay out of his sight until he summoned her. The summons came half an hour later. He was in the drawing room on the first floor today, reclining on a sofa.

"My head appears to have returned to its normal size this morning," he told her. "You will be pleased to learn that you will not be much called upon to use any of your considerable resources in entertaining me. I have given Hawkins leave to admit any visitors who may call, within reason, of course. He has express instructions to exclude any milliners' assistants and their ilk who rap on the door."

Jane's stomach lurched at the very thought of visitors.

"I will excuse myself, your grace," she said, "whenever someone calls."

"Will you indeed?" His eyes narrowed. "Why?"

"I assume," she said, "it will be mostly gentlemen who will call. My presence can only inhibit the conversation."

He startled her by grinning at her suddenly, completely transforming himself into a gentleman who looked both mischievous and far younger than usual. And almost handsome.

"Miss Ingleby," he said, "I do believe you are a prude."

"Yes, your grace," she admitted. "I am."

"Go and fetch that cushion from the library," he instructed her. "And set it under my leg."

"You might say please once in a while, you know," she told him as she turned toward the door.

"I might," he retorted. "But then again, I might not. I am in the position to give the commands. Why should I pretend that they are merely requests?"

"Perhaps for the sake of your self-respect," she said, looking back at him. "Perhaps out of deference to the feelings of others. Most people respond more readily to a request than to a command."

"And yet," he said softly, "it appears that you are in the process of obeying my command, Miss Ingleby."

"But with a mutinous heart," she said, leaving the room before he could have the last word.

She returned with the cushion a couple of minutes later, crossed the room without a word, and, without looking at him, positioned it carefully beneath his leg. She had noticed in his bedchamber earlier that yesterday's swelling had gone down. But she had noticed too his habit of rubbing his thigh and baring his teeth occasionally, sure signs that he was in considerable pain. Being a proud man, of course, he could not be expected to admit to feeling any at all.

"Apart from the thin line of your lips," the duke said, "I would not know you were severely out of charity with me, Miss Ingleby. I expected at the very least that you would jerk up my leg and slam it down onto the cushion. I was all ready to deal with such a show of temper. Now you have deprived me of the opportunity to deliver my carefully rehearsed setdown."

"You are employing me as a nurse, your grace," she reminded him. "I am to comfort you, not harm you for my own amusement. Besides, if I feel indignation on any subject, I have the vocabulary with which to express it. I do not need to resort to violence."

Which was as massive a lie as any she had ever told, she thought even as the words were issuing from her lips. For a moment she felt cold and nauseated, her stomach muscles clenching in the now-familiar feeling of panic.

"Miss Ingleby," the Duke of Tresham said meekly, "thank you for fetching the cushion."

Well. That silenced her.

"I do believe," he said, "that almost elicited a smile from you. Do you ever smile?"

"When I am amused or happy, your grace," she told him.

"And you have been neither yet in my company," he said. "I must be losing my touch. I am reputed to be rather superior, you know, in my ability to amuse and delight women."

Her awareness of his masculinity had been a largely academic thing until he spoke those words and looked at her with the characteristic narrowing of his dark eyes. But suddenly it was no longer academic. She felt a totally unfamiliar rush of pure physical desire that did alarming things to her breasts and her lower abdomen and inner thighs.

"I do not doubt it," she said tartly. "But I daresay you have already used up this month's supply of seductive arts on Lady Oliver."

"Jane, Jane," he said gently. "That sounded remarkably like spite. Go and find Quincy and fetch the morning's post. *Please,*" he added as she moved toward the door.

She turned her head to smile at him.

"Ah," he said.

5

*A*ngeline came again in the late morning, escorted this time by Heyward, who had accompanied her in order to inquire civilly after his brother-in-law's health. Ferdinand came before they left, but more with the purpose of talking about himself than out of any great concern for his brother's recovery. He had become embroiled in a challenge to race his curricle to Brighton against Lord Berriwether, whose skill with the ribbons was rivaled by no one except Jocelyn himself.

"You will lose, Ferdinand," Heyward said bluntly.

"You will break your neck, Ferdie," Angeline said, "and my nerves will never recover so soon after this business with Tresham. But how dashing you will look tearing along the road as fast as the wind. Are you going to order a new coat for the occasion?"

"The secret is to give your horses their heads whenever you have a straight stretch of road," Jocelyn said, "but not to get too excited in a pinch and not to take unnecessary risks on sharp bends as if you were some circus performer. For both of which vices you are famous, Ferdinand. You had better win, though, now you are committed. Never make a boast or a challenge you are incapable of backing up with action. Not especially if you are a Dudley. I daresay you *were* boasting."

"I thought perhaps I might borrow your new curricle, Tresham," his brother said carelessly.

"No," Jocelyn said. "Absolutely not. I am surprised you would waste breath even asking unless you think a hole in my leg has made me soft in the brain."

"You are my brother," Ferdinand pointed out.

"A brother with a working brain and a fair share of common sense," Jocelyn told him. "The wheels on your own curricle were round enough when last I saw them. It is the driver rather than the vehicle that wins or loses a race, Ferdinand. When is it to be?"

"Two weeks," his brother said.

Damn! He would not be able to watch any part of it, then, Jocelyn thought. Not if he was obedient to the commands of that damned quack, Raikes, anyway. But in two weeks' time, if he was still confined to a sofa, his sanity might well be at stake.

Jane Ingleby, standing quietly some distance away, had read his mind, Jocelyn would swear. A single glance at her showed her with her lips compressed in a thin line. What did she plan to do? Tie him down until every last day of the three weeks had passed?

He had refused her request to be excused when his family members arrived. He refused it again later when more visitors were announced while she was taking his letters one at a time from his hand as he perused them and dividing them into three piles according to his instructions—invitations to be refused, invitations to be accepted, and letters whose replies would necessitate some dictation to his secretary. Most of the invitations, except for those to events some time in the future, of course, had to be refused.

"I will leave you, your grace," she said, getting to her feet after Hawkins, who seemed far more in control of his own domain in the front hall today, had come to announce the arrival of several of his friends.

"You will not," he said, raising his eyebrows. "You will remain here."

"Please, your grace," she said. "I can serve no function here while you have company."

She looked, he thought, almost frightened. Did she expect that he and his friends were going to indulge in a collective orgy with her? He would probably have dismissed her himself, he supposed, if she had not announced that she would leave. Now, out of sheer stubbornness, he could not let her go.

"Perhaps," he said, "all the excitement will bring on a fit of the vapors and I will need the ministrations of my nurse, Miss Ingleby."

She would doubtless have argued further if the door had not opened to admit his visitors. As it was, she scurried for the farthest corner of the room, where she was still standing when it occurred to him to look a few minutes later. She was doing an admirable job of blending into the furniture. Her cap was adorning her head again and covering every last strand of her hair.

They had come in a collective body, all his closest friends—Conan Brougham, Pottier, Kimble, Thomas Garrick, Boris Tuttleford—bringing hearty good cheer with them. There was a great deal of noise as they greeted him, asked rhetorically after his health, jeered over his dressing gown and slippers, admired his bandage, and found themselves seats.

"Where is your claret, Tresham?" Garrick asked, looking about him.

"Miss Ingleby will fetch it," Jocelyn said. That was when he looked and noticed her in the far corner. "My nurse, gentlemen, who runs and fetches for me since I am unable to reach the bell rope from where I recline. And who scolds and worries me into and out of the dismals. Miss Ingleby, ask Hawkins for the claret and the brandy, and have a footman bring a tray of glasses. Please."

"*Please*, Tresh?" Kimble chuckled. "A new word in your vocabulary?"

"She makes me say it," Jocelyn said meekly, watching Jane walk out of the room, her face averted. "She scolds me when I forget."

There was a raucous guffaw from his gathered friends.

"Oh, I say," Tuttleford said when his mirth had subsided a little, "isn't she the one who squawked out, Tresham, just when you were unnerving Oliver with your pistol trained at the bridge of his nose?"

"He has employed her as his nurse," Conan replied, grinning. "And has threatened to make her sorry she was born or something like that. *Is* she sorry, Tresham? Or are you?"

Jocelyn played with the handle of his quizzing glass and pursed his lips. "You see," he said, "she has a damnably annoying habit of answering back, and I have a damnable need for mental stimulation, penned and cribbed and incarcerated as I am and as I am likely to be for a couple of weeks or so longer."

"Mental stimulation, ho!" Pottier slapped his thigh and roared with merriment, and everyone else followed his example. "Since when have you needed a female for mental stimulation, Tresham?"

"By Jove!" Kimble swung his quizzing glass on its ribbon. "One cannot quite picture it, can one? How else does she stimulate you, Tresh? That is the question. Come, come, it is confession time."

"He has one immobilized leg." Tuttleford laughed again. "But I'll wager that does not slow you down one whit, does it,

Tresham? Not in the *stimulation* business. Does she come astride? And do all the bucking so that you can lie still?"

The laughter this time was decidedly bawdy. They were all in fine fettle—and getting finer by the minute. Jocelyn raised his quizzing glass all the way to his eye.

"One might casually mention," he said quietly, "that the female in question is in my employ and beneath my own roof, Tuttleford. Even I have some standards."

"My guess is, fellows," Conan Brougham said, more perceptive than the others, "that the notorious duke is not amused."

Which was a mistake on his part, Jocelyn thought a moment later as the door opened and Jane came back into the room, carrying two decanters on a tray. A footman came behind her with the glasses. She was, of course, the instant focus of everyone's curious attention, a fact that should have amused him as it would surely disconcert her. But he felt only annoyance that any of his friends would for one moment think him capable of the execrable taste of dallying with his own servant.

She might have tried to escape with the footman, but she did not do so. She retired to her corner with lowered eyes. Her cap was pulled lower than ever over her brow.

Viscount Kimble whistled softly. "A beauty in hiding, Tresh?" he murmured, too low for her to overhear.

Trust Kimble's eyes to penetrate her disguise. Kimble, with his blond god's good looks, was very much a ladies' man, of course. A connoisseur to equal Jocelyn himself.

"But a servant," Jocelyn replied, "under the protection of my own roof, Kimble."

His friend understood him. He grinned and winked. But he would not make any improper advances to Jane Ingleby. Jocelyn did wonder fleetingly why he cared.

The conversation quickly moved off into other topics since they could hardly discuss Jane in her presence. But no one seemed to consider it improper to discuss in her hearing Lady

Oliver's apparent enjoyment of her notoriety as she had played court to a host of admirers at the theater last evening; the presence of three of her brothers with her and Oliver in their box; the avowed determination of the brothers to call the Duke of Tresham to account for debauching their sister as soon as he was on his feet again; the ridiculous lengths to which Hailsham was going to prove that his eldest son, now nine years old and reputed to be mentally deficient, was a bastard so that he could promote the claims of his second and favorite son; the latest sensational details of the Cornish scandal.

"It is being said now that Jardine is dead," Brougham said on that last topic. "That he never did recover consciousness after the attack."

"It must have been one devil of a bash on the head," Kimble added. "The more sensational accounts insist that his brains were fully visible through hair and blood. London drawing rooms are filled with swooning females these days. Which makes life interesting for those of us who can be close enough to some of them when it happens. Too bad you are incapacitated, Tresh." He chuckled.

"As I remember it," Pottier said, "Jardine did not *have* a great deal of hair. Not too many brains either."

"He never regained consciousness." Jocelyn, attempting to shift his position to rid himself of a few cramps, inadvertently knocked the cushion to the floor. "Come and replace this, Miss Ingleby, will you? He never regained consciousness and yet— according to some accounts—he was able to give a perfectly lucid account of the attack and his own spirited and heroic defense. He was able to identify his attacker and explain her motive for breaking his skull. A strange sort of unconsciousness."

Jane bent over him and placed the cushion in just the right spot, lifted his leg onto it as gently as she always did, and adjusted the top of the bandage, which had curled under. But she was, he noticed when he glanced at her, white to the very lips.

He was almost sorry then that he had insisted upon her remaining in the room. Clearly she was uncomfortable in the company of all men. And no doubt with their talk. As stoic as she had been over his injury, perhaps the talk of hair and blood and brains had been too much for her.

"News of his death may be just as exaggerated," Garrick said cynically, getting to his feet and helping himself to another drink. "It could well be that he is simply ashamed to show his face after admitting to having been overpowered by a mere slip of a girl engaged in a robbery."

"Was she not clutching a pistol in both hands?" Jocelyn asked. "According, that is, to the man who never regained consciousness from the time she struck him with one of them until the moment of his demise? But enough of that nonsense. What sort of a cork-brained scheme is this that Ferdinand has got himself into? A curricle race against Berriwether of all people! Who made the challenge?"

"Your brother," Conan said, "when Berriwether was boasting that you will be eating humble pie at all your old sports now that you will have one lame leg to drag about. He was claiming that the Dudley name would never again be one to be uttered with awe and admiration."

"In Ferdinand's hearing?" Jocelyn shook his head. "Definitely not wise."

"No, not exactly in his hearing," his friend explained. "But Ferdinand got wind of it, of course, and came striding into White's with flames roaring from his nostrils. I thought for one moment he was going to slap a glove in Berriwether's face, but all he did was ask as polite as you please what Berriwether thought your finest accomplishment was apart from your skill with weapons. It was your skill with the ribbons, of course. Then came the challenge."

"And how much has Ferdinand wagered on the outcome?" Jocelyn asked.

Garrick provided the answer. "One thousand guineas," he said.

"Hmm." Jocelyn nodded slowly. "The family honor worth one thousand guineas. Well, well."

Jane Ingleby was no longer standing in her corner, he saw idly. She was sitting there very straight-backed on a low stool, her back to the room.

She did not move until his friends took their leave more than an hour later.

"Give me the damned thing!" The Duke of Tresham was holding out one imperious hand.

Jane, standing beside the sofa, where he had summoned her the moment after the drawing room door had closed behind his visitors, unfastened the ribbons beneath her chin and removed the offending cap. But she held it in her own hands.

"What are you intending to do with it?" she asked.

"What I am intending to do," he said irritably, "is send you to fetch the sharpest pair of scissors my housekeeper can provide you with. And then I am going to have you watch while I cut that atrocity into shreds. No, correct that. I am going to have *you* cut it into shreds."

"It is mine," she told him. "I paid for it. You have no right whatsoever to destroy my property."

"Poppycock!" he retorted.

And then to her horror Jane knew why he had suddenly blurred before her eyes. An inelegant sob escaped her at the same moment as she realized that her eyes had filled with tears.

"Good God!" he exclaimed, sounding appalled. "Does the wretched thing mean that much to you?"

"It is mine!" she said vehemently but with a lamentably unsteady voice. "I bought it and one other just two days ago.

They cost everything I had. I *will* not allow you to cut them up for your own amusement. You are an unfeeling bully."

Despite the anger and bravado of her words, she was crying and sobbing and hiccuping quite despicably. She swiped at her wet cheeks with the cap and glared at him.

He regarded her in silence for a few moments. "This is not about the cap at all, is it?" he said at last. "It is because I forced you to remain in the room with a horde of male visitors. I have hurt your sensibilities, Jane. I daresay in the orphanage the sexes were segregated, were they?"

"Yes," she said.

"I am weary," he said abruptly. "I believe I shall try to sleep. I do not require your presence here to listen to me snore. Go to your room and remain there until dinnertime. Come to me again this evening."

"Yes, your grace," she said, turning from him. She could not say thank you even though she knew that in his way he was showing her a kindness. She did not believe he wished to sleep. He had merely recognized her need to be alone.

"Miss Ingleby," he said when she reached the door. She did not look back. "Do not provoke me again. In my service you will wear no cap."

She let herself out quietly and then raced upstairs to her room, where she shut the door gratefully on the world and cast herself across the bed. She was still clutching the cap tightly in one hand.

He was dead.

Sidney Jardine had died and there was no way anyone on this earth was going to believe that she had not murdered him.

She clutched a fistful of the bedspread in her free hand and pressed her face into the mattress.

He was dead.

He had been despicable and she had hated him more than she had thought it possible to hate anyone. But she had not wanted him dead. Or even hurt. It had been a pure reflex action to grab that heavy book and the pure, mindless instinct of self-defense to whack him over the head with it. Except that she had swung the tome rather than lifting it and bringing it down flat, because it had been so heavy. The sharp corner had caught him on the temple.

He had not fallen but had touched the wound, looked down at his bloodied fingers, laughed, called her a vixen, and advanced on her. But she had sidestepped. He had lost his balance as he lunged and had fallen forward onto the marble hearth, cracking his forehead loudly as he went down. Then he had lain still.

There had been several witnesses to the whole sordid scene, none of whom could be expected to tell the truth about what had happened. All of whom doubtless would be eager to perjure themselves by testifying that she had been apprehended while stealing. The gold, jewel-studded bracelet that would seem to prove them right was still at the bottom of her bag. All those people had been Sidney's friends. None of them had been hers. Charles—Sir Charles Fortescue, her neighbor, friend, and beau—had been away from home. Not that he would have been invited to that particular party anyway.

Sidney had not been dead after the fall even though everyone else in the room had thought he was. She had been the one to approach him on unsteady legs, sick to her stomach. His pulse had been beating steadily. She had even summoned a few servants and had him carried up to his room, where she had tended him herself and bathed his wounds until the doctor arrived, summoned at her command.

But he had been unconscious the whole while. And looking so pale that a number of times she had checked his pulse again with cold, shaking fingers.

"Murderers hang, you know," someone had said from the doorway of the bedchamber, sounding faintly amused.

"By the neck until they are dead," another voice had added with ghoulish relish.

She had fled during the night, taking with her only enough possessions to get her to London on the stagecoach—and the bracelet, of course, and the money she had taken from the earl's desk. She had fled not because she believed that Sidney would die and she would be accused of his murder. She had fled because—oh, there were a number of reasons.

She had felt so very alone. The earl, her father's cousin and successor, and the countess had been away at a weekend house party. They had little love for her anyway. There was no one at Candleford to whom to turn in her distress. And Charles was not home. He had gone on an extended visit to his elder sister in Somersetshire.

Jane had fled to London. At first there had been no thought of concealment, only of reaching someone who would be sympathetic toward her. She had been going to Lady Webb's home on Portland Place. Lady Webb had been her mother's dearest friend since they made their come-out together as girls. She had often come to visit at Candleford. She was Jane's godmother. Jane called her Aunt Harriet. But Lady Webb had been away from home and was not expected back any time soon.

For more than three weeks now Jane had been well-nigh paralyzed with terror, afraid that Sidney had died, afraid that she would be accused of his murder, afraid that she would be called a thief, afraid that the law would come looking for her. They would know, of course, that she had come to London. She had done nothing to hide her tracks.

Worst of all during the past weeks had been knowing nothing. It was almost a relief to know at last.

That Sidney was dead.

That the story was that she had killed him as he had been apprehending her in the process of robbing the house.

That she was considered a murderess.

No, of course it was not a relief.

Jane sat up sharply on the bed and rubbed her hands over

her face. Her worst nightmares had come true. Her best hope had been to disappear among the anonymous masses of ordinary Londoners. But that plan had been dashed when she had so foolishly interfered in that duel in Hyde Park. What had it mattered to her that two gentlemen who had no better use for their lives were about to blow each other's brains out?

Here she was in Mayfair, in one of the grand mansions on Grosvenor Square, as a sort of nurse/companion to a man who derived some kind of satisfaction out of displaying her to all his friends. None of them knew her, of course. She had lived a secluded life in Cornwall. The chances were that no visitors to Dudley House over the coming weeks would know her. But she was not quite convinced.

Surely it was only a matter of time. . . .

She got to her feet and crossed the room on shaking legs to the washstand. Mercifully there was water in the pitcher. She poured a little into the bowl and scooped some up in her cupped palms, into which she lowered her face.

What she ought to do—what she ought to have done at the start—was simply turn herself over to the authorities and trust to truth and justice. But who were the authorities? Where would she go to do it? Besides, she had made herself look guilty by running away and by staying out of sight for longer than three weeks.

He would know what she ought to do and where she should go with her story. The Duke of Tresham, that was. She could tell him everything and let him take the next step. But the thought of his hard, ruthless face and his disregard for her feelings made her shudder.

Would she hang? *Could* she hang for murder? Or even for theft? She really had no idea. But she had to grip the edge of the washstand suddenly to stop herself from swaying.

How could she trust in the truth when all the evidence and all the witnesses would be against her?

One of the gentlemen downstairs had said that perhaps

Sidney was not dead after all. Jane knew very well how gossip could twist and change the truth. It was being said, for example, that she had been holding a pistol in each hand! Perhaps word of Sidney's death had spread simply because such an outcome titillated the senses of those who always liked to believe the worst.

Perhaps he was still only unconscious.

Perhaps he was recovering quite nicely.

Perhaps he was fully recovered.

And perhaps he was dead.

Jane dried her still-hot cheeks with a towel and sat down on the hard chair beside the washstand. She would wait, she decided, looking down at her hands in her lap—they were still shaking—until she had discovered the truth more definitely. Then she would decide what was best to do.

Was there a search on for her? she wondered. She pressed her fingers against her mouth and closed her eyes. She must stay out of sight of future visitors just in case. She must remain indoors as much as possible.

If only she could continue to wear her caps. . . .

She had never been a coward. She had never been one to hide from her problems or cower in a corner. Quite the contrary. But she had suddenly turned craven.

Of course, she had never been accused of murder before.

6

Mick Boden of the Bow Street Runners was standing in the Earl of Durbury's private sitting room at the Pulteney Hotel again, one week after his first appearance there. He had no real news to impart except that he had discovered no recent trace of Lady Sara Illingsworth.

His failure did not please him. He hated assignments like this one. Had he been summoned to Cornwall to investigate the murder attempt on Sidney Jardine, he could have used all his skills of detection to discover the identity of the would-be murderer and to apprehend the villain. But there was no mystery about this crime. The lady had been in the process of robbing the absent earl when Jardine had come upon her. She had hit him over the head with some hard object, doubtless taking him by surprise because he knew her and did not fully realize what she was up to, and then she had made off with the spoils of the robbery. Jardine's valet had witnessed the whole scene—a singularly cowardly individual in Mick's estimation since the thief had been a mere girl with nothing more lethal than a hard object to swing at him.

"If she is in London, we will find her, sir," he said now.

"If she is in London? *If?*" The earl fumed. "Of course she is in London, man. Where else would she be?"

Mick could have listed a score of places without even taxing his brain, but he merely pulled on his earlobe. "Probably nowhere," he admitted. "And if she did not leave here a week or more ago, she will find it harder now, sir. We have questioned every coaching innkeeper and coachman in town. None remember a woman of her description except the one who brought her here. And now we are keeping a careful watch."

"All of which is laudable," his lordship said with heavy irony. "But what are you doing to find her within London? A week should have been time enough and to spare even if you put your feet up and slept for the first five or six days."

"She has not returned to Lady Webb's, sir," Mick told the earl. "We have checked. We have found the hotel where she stayed for two nights after her arrival, but no one knows where she went from there. According to your account, sir, she knows no one else in town. If she has a fortune on her, though, I would have expected her to take another hotel room or lodgings in a respectable district. We have found no trace of either yet."

"It has not occurred to you, I suppose," the earl said, going to stand in front of the window and drumming his fingernails on the sill, "that she may not wish to draw attention to herself by spending lavishly?"

It would strike Mick Boden as decidedly odd to steal a fortune and then neglect to spend any of it. Why would the young lady even have stolen it, if she was living at Candleford in the lap of luxury as the daughter of the former earl and relative to this present one? And if she was twenty years old and as lovely as the earl had described her, would she not be looking forward to making an advantageous match with a wealthy young nob?

There was more to this whole business than met the eye, Mick thought, not for the first time.

"Do you mean she might have taken employment?" he asked.

"It has crossed my mind." His lordship continued the finger-drumming while he frowned out through the window.

How much money had been taken? Mick wondered. Surely it must have been a great deal if the girl had been willing to kill for it. But of course there had been jewels too, and it was time he explored that possible means of tracing the girl.

"I and my assistants will start asking at the employment agencies, then," he said. "That will be a start. And at all the pawnbrokers and jewelers who might have bought the jewelry from her. I will need a description of each piece, sir."

"Do not waste your time," the earl said coldly. "She would not pawn any of it. Try the agencies. Try all likely employers. *Find* her."

"We certainly would not want a dangerous criminal let loose on any unsuspecting employer, sir," Mick agreed. "What name might she be using?"

The earl turned to face the Bow Street Runner. "What name?"

"She used her real name at Lady Webb's," Mick explained, "and at the hotel those first two nights. After that she disappeared. It has struck me, sir, that she has realized the wisdom of concealing her identity. What name might she use apart from her own? Does she have any middle names? Do you know her mother's maiden name? Her maid's name? Her old nurse's? Any that I might try at the agencies, sir, if there is no record of a Sara Illingsworth."

"Her parents always called her Jane." The earl scratched his head and frowned. "Let me think. Her mother was a Donningsford. Her maid . . ."

Mick jotted down the names he was given.

"We will find her, sir," he assured the Earl of Durbury again as he took his leave a few minutes later.

Though it was a strange business. A man's only son was in a coma, one foot in the grave, the other on an icy patch. He might even be dead at this very moment. And yet his father had left him in order to search for the woman who had tried to kill him. But the man never left his hotel suite, as far as Mick knew. The would-be murderess had stolen a fortune, yet the earl suspected she might be seeking employment. She had stolen jewels, but his lordship was unwilling to describe them or to have them hunted for in the pawnshops.

A very strange business indeed.

After one week of moving between his bed upstairs, the sofa in the drawing room, and the chaise longue in the library, Jocelyn was colossally bored. Which was probably the understatement of the decade. His friends called frequently—every day, in fact—and brought him all the latest news and gossip. His brother called and talked about little else except the curricle race that Jocelyn would have given a fortune to be running himself. His sister called and talked incessantly on such scintillating topics as bonnets and her nerves. His brother-in-law made a few courtesy calls and discussed politics.

The days were long, the evenings longer, the nights endless.

Jane Ingleby became his almost constant companion. The realization could both amuse and irritate him. He began to feel like an old lady with a paid companion to run and fetch and hold the emptiness at bay.

She changed his bandage once a day. He had her massage his thigh once, an experiment he did not repeat despite the fact that her touch was magically soothing. It was also alarmingly arousing, and so he rebuked her for being so prudish as to blush and told her to sit down. She ran errands for him. She sorted his mail as he read it and returned it to Quincy with his instructions. She read to him and played cards with him.

He had Quincy in to play chess with him one evening and instructed her to sit and watch. Playing chess with Michael was about as exciting as playing cricket with a three-year-old. Though his secretary was a competent player, it never took great ingenuity to defeat him. Winning, of course, was always gratifying, but it was not particularly exhilarating when one could see the victory coming at least ten moves in advance.

After that Jocelyn played chess with Jane. She was so abysmally awful the first time that it was a measure of his boredom that he made her try it again the next day. She was almost ready that time to have given Michael a marginally competitive game, though certainly not him. The fifth time they played, she won.

She laughed and clapped her hands. "That is what comes, you see," she told him, "of being bored and toplofty and looking down your nose at me as if I were a speck on your boot and yawning behind your hand. You were not concentrating."

All of which was true. "You will concede, then," he asked, "that I would have won if I had been concentrating, Jane?"

"Oh, assuredly," she admitted. "But you were not and so you lost. Quite ignominiously, I might add."

He concentrated after that.

Sometimes they merely talked. It was strange to him to *talk* to a woman. He was adept at chitchatting socially with ladies. He was skilled at wordplay with courtesans. But he could not recall simply talking with any woman.

One evening she was reading to him and he was amusing himself with the observation that with her hair ruthlessly scraped back from her face, her eyes were slanted upward at the corners. It was her little rebellion, of course, to make her head as unattractive as possible even without the aid of the cap, and he hoped uncharitably that it gave her a headache.

"Miss Ingleby," he said with a sigh, interrupting her in the middle of a sentence, "I can listen no longer." Not that he had been doing much listening anyway. "In my opinion, with which you may feel free to disagree, Gulliver is an ass."

As he had expected, her lips tightened into a thin line. One of his few amusements during the past week had been provoking her. She closed the book.

"I suppose," she said, "you believe he should have trodden those little people into the ground because he was bigger and stronger than they."

"You are such a restful companion, Miss Ingleby," he said. "You put words into my mouth and thereby release me from the necessity of having to think and speak for myself."

"Shall I choose another book?" she asked.

"You would probably select a collection of sermons," he retorted. "No, we will talk instead."

"What about?" she asked after a short silence.

"Tell me about the orphanage," he said. "What sort of life did you have there?"

She shrugged. "There is not a great deal to tell."

It must certainly have been a superior sort of orphanage. But even so, an orphanage was an orphanage.

"Were you lonely there?" he asked. "*Are* you lonely?"

"No." She was not going to be very forthcoming with her personal history, he could see. She was not like many women—and men too, to be fair—who needed only the smallest encouragement to talk with great enthusiasm and at greater length about themselves.

"Why not?" he asked, narrowing his gaze on her. "You grew up without mother or father, brother or sister. You have come to London at the age of twenty or so, if my guess is correct, doubtless with the dream of making your fortune, but knowing no one. How can you not be lonely?"

She set the book down on the small table beside her and clasped her hands in her lap. "Aloneness is not always the same thing as loneliness," she said. "Not if one learns to like oneself and one's own company. It is possible, I suppose, to feel lonely even with mother and father and brothers and sisters if one basically does not like oneself. If one has been given the impression that one is not worthy of love."

"How right you are!" he snapped, instantly irritated.

He was being regarded from very steady, very blue eyes, he noticed suddenly.

"Is that what happened to you?" she asked.

When he realized just what it was she was asking, the intimately personal nature of the question, he felt such fury that it was on the tip of his tongue to dismiss her for the night. Her impertinence knew no bounds. But a conversation, of course, was a two-way thing, and he was the one who had tried to get a conversation going.

He never had conversations, even with his male friends. Not on personal matters. He never talked about himself.

Was that what had happened to him?

"I was always rather fond of Angeline and Ferdinand," he said with a shrug. "We fought constantly, as I suppose most brothers and sisters do, though the fact that we were Dudleys doubtless made us a little more boisterous and quarrelsome than most. We also played and got into mischief together. Ferdinand and I were even gallant enough on occasion to take the thrashing for what Angeline had done, though I suppose we punished her for it in our own way."

"Why does being a Dudley mean that you must be more unruly, more vicious, more dangerous than anyone else?" she asked.

He thought about it, about his family, about the vision of themselves and their place in the scheme of things that had been bred into them from birth onward, and even perhaps before then.

"If you had known my father and my grandfather," he replied, "you would not even ask the question."

"And you feel you must live up to their reputations?" she asked. "Is it from personal choice that you do so? Or did you become trapped in your role as eldest son and heir and eventually the Duke of Tresham yourself?"

He chuckled softly. "If you knew my full reputation, Miss Ingleby," he said, "you would not need to ask that question either. I have not rested on the laurels of my forebears, I assure you. I have sufficient of my own."

"I know," she said, "that you are considered more proficient than any other gentleman with a wide range of weapons. I know that you have fought more than one duel. I suppose they were all over women?"

He inclined his head.

"I know," she said, "that you consort with married ladies without any regard to the sanctity of marriage or the feelings of the spouse you wrong."

"You presume to know a great deal about me," he said mockingly.

"I would have to be both blind and deaf not to," she said. "I know that you look upon everyone who is beneath you socially—and that is almost everyone—as scions to run and fetch for you and to obey your every command without question."

"And without even a please or thank you," he added.

"You engage in the most foolhardy wagers, I daresay," she said. "You have shown no concern this week over Lord Ferdinand's impending curricle race to Brighton. He could break his neck."

"Not Ferdinand," he said. "Like me, he has a neck made of steel."

"All that matters to you," she said, "is that he win the race. Indeed, I do believe that you wish you could take his place so that you could break yours instead."

"There is little point in entering a race," he explained, "unless one means to win it, Miss Ingleby, though one also must know how to behave like a gentleman when one loses, of course. Are you scolding me, by any chance? Is this a gentle tirade against my manners and morals?"

"They are not my concern, your grace," she said. "I am merely commenting upon what I have observed."

"You have a low opinion of me," he said.

"But I daresay," she retorted, "my opinion means no more to you than the snap of your fingers."

He chuckled softly. "I was different once upon a time, you know," he said. "My father rescued me. He made sure I took the final step in my education to become a gentleman after his own heart. Perhaps you are fortunate, Miss Ingleby, never to have known your father or mother."

"They must have loved you," she said.

"Love." He laughed. "I suppose you have an idealized conception of the emotion because you have never known a great deal of it yourself, or of what sometimes passes for it. If love is a disinterested devotion to the beloved, Jane, then indeed there is no such thing. There is only selfishness, a dedication to one's own comfort, which the beloved is used to enhance. Dependency is not love. Domination is not love. Lust is certainly not it, though it can be a happy enough substitute on occasion."

"You poor man," she said.

He found the handle of his quizzing glass and lifted it to his eye. She sat looking back at him, seemingly quite composed. Most women in his experience either preened or squirmed under the scrutiny of his glass. On this occasion its use was an affectation anyway. His eyesight was not so poor that he could not see her perfectly well without it. He let the glass fall to his chest.

"My mother and father were a perfectly happy couple," he said. "I never heard them exchange a cross word or saw them frown at each other. They produced three children, a sure sign of their devotion to each other."

"Well, then," Jane said, "you have just disproved your own theory."

"Perhaps," he said, "it was because they saw each other for only a few minutes three or four times a year. As my father came home to Acton Park, my mother would be leaving for London. As she came home, he would be leaving. A civil and amicable arrangement, you see." One he had thought quite normal at the time. It was strange how children who had known no different could adapt to almost any situation.

Jane said nothing. She sat very still.

"They were wonderfully discreet too," he said, "as any perfect couple must be if the harmony of the marriage is to be maintained. No word of my mother's legion of lovers ever came to Acton. I knew nothing of them until I came to London myself at the age of sixteen. Fortunately I resemble my father in physical features. So do Angeline and Ferdinand. It would be lowering to suspect that one might be a bastard, would it not?"

He had not spoken those words to hurt. He remembered too late that Jane Ingleby did not know her own parents. He wondered who had given her her last name. Why not Smith or Jones? Perhaps it was a policy of a superior orphanage to distinguish its orphans from the common run by giving them more idiosyncratic surnames.

"Yes," she said. "I am sorry. No child should have to feel so betrayed even when he is old enough, according to the world's beliefs, to cope with the knowledge. It must have been a heavy blow to you. But I daresay she loved you."

"If the number and splendor of the gifts she brought with her from London are any indication," he said, "she doted on us. My father did not depend upon his months in London for pleasure. There is a picturesque cottage in a remote corner of Acton Park, Jane. A river flows at the foot of its back garden, wooded hills grow up around it. It is an idyllic setting indeed. It was home during several of my growing years to an indigent relative, a woman of considerable charm and beauty. I was sixteen years old before I understood just who she was."

He had always intended to give the order to have that cottage pulled down. He still had not done so. But it was uninhabited now, and he had given his steward specific orders to spend not a single farthing on its upkeep. In time it would fall down from sheer neglect.

"I am sorry," she said again as if she were personally responsible for his father's lack of taste in housing his mistress—or one of them anyway—on his own estate with his children in residence there. But Jane did not know the half of it, and he was not about to enlighten her.

"I have much to live up to, you see," he said. "But I believe I am doing my part in perpetuating the family reputation."

"You are not bound by the past," she told him. "No one is. Influenced by it, yes, perhaps almost overwhelmingly drawn to live up to it. But not compelled. Everyone has free will, you more than most. You have the rank, the wealth, the influence to live your own life your own way."

"Which, my little moralist," he said softly, narrowing his eyes on her, "is exactly what I am doing. Except now, of course. Such inaction as this is anathema to me. But perhaps it is a fitting punishment, would you not agree, for having taken my pleasure in the bed of a married woman?"

She flushed and looked down.

"Does it reach your waist?" he asked her. "Or even below?"

"My hair?" She looked back up at him, startled. "It is only hair. Below my waist."

"Only hair," he murmured. "Only spun gold. Only the

sort of magic web in which any man would gladly become hopelessly caught and enmeshed, Jane."

"I have not given you permission for such familiarity, your grace," she said primly.

He chuckled. "Why do I put up with your impudence?" he asked her. "You are my servant."

"But not your indentured slave," she said. "I can get up and walk out through that door any time I please and not come back. The few pounds you are paying me for three weeks of service do not give you ownership of me. Or excuse your impertinence in speaking with lascivious intent about my hair. And you may not deny that there was suggestiveness in what you said about it and the way you looked at it."

"Certainly I will not deny it," he agreed. "I try always to speak the truth, Miss Ingleby. Go and fetch the chess board from the library. We will see if you can give me a decent game tonight. And have Hawkins fetch the brandy while you are about it. I am as dry as a damned desert. And as prickly as a cactus plant."

"Yes, your grace." She got to her feet readily enough.

"And I would advise you," he said, "not to call me impertinent again, Miss Ingleby. I can be pushed only so far without retaliating."

"But you are confined to the sofa," she said, "and I can walk out through the door at any time. I believe that gives me a certain advantage."

One of these times, he thought as she vanished through the door—at least *one* time during the remaining two weeks of her employment—he was going to have the last word with Miss Jane Ingleby. He could not remember *not* having the last word with anyone, male or female, any time during the past ten years.

But he was relieved that their conversation had returned to its normal level before she left. He did not know quite how she had turned the tables on him before that. He had tried to worm out of her something about herself and had ended up telling her things about his childhood and boyhood that he did not care even to think about, let alone share with another person.

He had come very close to baring his heart.

He preferred to believe that he had none.

7

"Come here," the Duke of Tresham said to Jane after a game of chess a few days later, in which he had prevailed but only after he had been forced to ponder his moves and accuse her of trying to distract him with her chatter. She had spoken scarcely a word during the whole game. Jane had moved away to return the chess board to its cupboard.

She did not trust the tone of his voice. She did not trust *him* when she thought about the matter. There had been a tension between them during the past few days that even in her inexperience she had had no difficulty in identifying. He saw her as a woman, and she, God help her, was very much aware of him as a man. She breathed a prayer of gratitude as she approached the sofa for the fact that he was still confined to it, though she would no longer be employed if he were not, of course.

The thought of leaving her employment—and Dudley

House—in another week and a half was becoming more and more oppressive to her. In their careless conversation, his friends had several times referred to the fact that her father's cousin, the Earl of Durbury, was in London and that he had the dreaded Bow Street Runners looking for her. The friends and the duke himself appeared to be on her side. They jeered over the fact that she had overpowered Sidney, a man who was apparently not universally liked. But their attitude would change in a moment if they discovered that Lady Sara Illingsworth and Jane Ingleby were one and the same person.

"Show me your hands," the duke said now. It was, of course, a command, not a request.

"Why?" she asked, but he merely raised his eyebrows in that arrogant way he had and stared back at her.

She held them out toward him hesitantly, palms down. But he took them in his own and turned them over.

It was one of the most uncomfortable moments of Jane's life. His hands dwarfed her own, cupping hers loosely. She could easily have pulled away, and every instinct urged her to do so. But then she would reveal her discomfort and its only possible source. She felt the pull of his masculinity like a physical force. She found it difficult to breathe.

"No calluses," he said. "You have not done much menial work, then, Jane?"

She wished he would not sometimes lapse into calling her by the name only her parents had ever used. "Not a great deal, your grace," she said.

"They are beautiful hands," he said, "as one might expect. They match the rest of your person. They change bandages gently without causing undue pain. One wonders what other magic they could create with their touch. Jane, you could be the most sought-after courtesan in all of England if you so chose."

She pulled her hands back then, but his own tightened about them a little faster than she moved.

82 MaryMary Balogh

"I did add 'if you chose,' " he pointed out, a wicked gleam in his eyes. "What other magic can they create? I wonder. Are they musical hands? Do you play an instrument? The piano-forte?"

"A little," she admitted. Unlike her mother, she had never been any more than a proficient pianist.

His hands were still tight on hers. His dark eyes burned upward into her own. Her claim to be able to escape him at any time by simply walking out through the door was ridiculous now. By just a slight jerking on her hands he could have her down across him in a moment.

She glared at him, determined not to show fear or any other discomfort.

"Show me." He released her hands and indicated the piano-forte on the far side of the drawing room. It was a lovely instrument, she had noticed before, though not as magnificent as the one in the music room.

"I am out of practice," she said.

"For God's sake, Miss Ingleby," he retorted, "do not be coy. I always withdraw in haste to the card room whenever the young misses of the *ton* are about to demonstrate their party pieces at any fashionable entertainment. But I have degenerated to the point at which I am almost eager to listen to someone who openly admits that she plays only a little and is out of practice. Now go and play before my mind turns to other sport while you are still within grabbing distance."

She went.

She played one of the pieces she had committed to memory long ago, a Bach fugue. By happy chance she made only two errors, both in the first few bars and neither glaring.

"Come here," the duke said again when she had finished.

She crossed the room, sat in the chair she usually occupied, and looked directly at him. She had discovered that doing so protected her from being bullied. It appeared to suggest to him that she was capable of giving as good as she got.

"You were right," he said abruptly. "You play a little. A very little. You play without flair. You play each note as if it were a separate entity that had no connection with what came before or after. You depress each key as if it were simply an inanimate strip of ivory, as if you believed it impossible to coax *music* out of it. You must have had an inferior teacher."

The criticism of herself she could take quite philosophically. She had never had any illusions about her skills. But she bristled when he cast such aspersions on her mother.

"I did not!" she retorted. "How dare you presume to judge my teacher by my performance. She had more talent in her little finger than I have in my whole body. She could make it seem as if the music came from *her* rather than from a mere instrument. Or as if it came *through* her from some—oh, from some heavenly source." She glared indignantly at him, aware of the inadequacy of words.

He gazed at her in silence for a moment, a strange, unfamiliar glow in his eyes.

"Ah," he said at last, "you do understand, then, do you? It is not that you are unmusical, just that you are without superior talent of your own. But why would such a paragon come to an orphanage to teach?"

"Because she was an angel," Jane said, and swiped at the tears that threatened to spill onto her cheeks. What was the matter with her? She had never been a watering pot until recently.

"Poor Jane," he said softly. "Did she become a mother figure to you?"

She almost told him to go to hell, language that had never passed her lips before. She had almost sunk to his level.

"Never mind," she said weakly. "You do not own my memories, your grace. Or me either."

"Prickly," he said. "Have I touched a nerve? Go away now and do whatever it is you do during your hour off in the afternoons. Send Quincy to me. I have letters to dictate to him."

She walked in the garden as she did most afternoons except when it rained. Spring flowers were in glorious bloom, and the air smelled sweet. She was missing the air and exercise that had been so much part of her life in Cornwall. But fear was something that was closing about her more and more. She was afraid to go beyond the front doors of Dudley House.

She was afraid of being caught. Of not being believed. Of being punished as a murderess.

Sometimes she found herself on the verge of blurting the whole truth to the Duke of Tresham. Part of her believed he would stand as her friend. But it would be foolishness itself to trust a man renowned for ruthlessness.

After two weeks Jocelyn decided that if he had to spend another week as he had spent the last two he would surely go mad. Raikes had been quite correct, of course, damn his eyes. The leg was not yet ready to bear his weight. But there was a middle ground between striding about on both legs and lying with one elevated.

He was going to acquire crutches.

His determination to delay no longer strengthened after two particular afternoon visits. Ferdinand came first, bursting with the latest details of the curricle race, set for three days hence. It seemed that betting at White's was brisk, almost all of it against Ferdinand and for Lord Berriwether. But his brother was undaunted. And he did introduce one other topic.

"The Forbes brothers are becoming increasingly offensive," he said. "They are hinting that you are hiding out here, Tresham, pretending to be wounded because the thought of them waiting for you has you shaking in your boots. If they ever so much as whisper as much in my hearing, they will all have gloves slapped in their faces hard enough to raise welts."

"Keep out of my concerns," Jocelyn told him curtly. "If

they have anything to say about me, they may say it to my face. They will not have long to wait."

"Your concerns *are* mine, Tresham," his brother complained. "An insult to one of us is an insult to all. I just hope Lady Oliver was worth it. Though I daresay she was. I have never known a woman with such a slender waist and such large—" But he broke off suddenly and glanced uneasily over his shoulder at Jane Ingleby, who was sitting quietly some distance away, as usual.

Ferdinand, like Angeline and Jocelyn's friends, seemed uncertain how to treat the Duke of Tresham's nurse.

Trouble was brewing, Jocelyn thought restlessly after his brother had left. Just as it usually was over something or other. Except that normally he was out there to confront it. He had always reveled in it. He could not remember thinking, as he sometimes caught himself doing these days, that there was something remarkably silly and meaningless in his whole style of life.

The sooner he got out and back about his usual activities, the better it would be for his sanity. Tomorrow he would want to know the reason why if Barnard had not acquired the crutches he had asked for.

And then came the second visitor. Hawkins, come to announce the caller, looked disapproving. Jane Ingleby gathered up the book from which she had been reading and retreated to the corner where she always hid out while he entertained.

"Lady Oliver, your grace," Hawkins said, "wishing for a private word with you. I informed her ladyship that I was not sure you were well enough to receive visitors."

"Bloody hell!" Jocelyn roared. "You know better than to allow her over the doorstep, Hawkins. Get the woman out of here."

It was not the first time she had come to Dudley House. The woman knew no better, it seemed, than to call upon a gentleman in his bachelor home. And she had come at a time when half the fashionable world was out and about and might happen by and see her or evidence of her presence.

"I suppose," he asked rhetorically, "she came in Lord Oliver's town coach and that it is waiting for her outside?"

"Yes, your grace." Hawkins bowed.

But before Jocelyn could renew his command that the woman be removed from the premises immediately if not sooner, the lady herself appeared in the doorway. Hawkins, Jocelyn thought grimly, would be fortunate indeed if he did not find himself demoted to the position of assistant boot boy before the day was over.

"Tresham," she said in her sweet, breathy voice. She raised a lace-edged handkerchief to her lips as visual evidence of the distress of a woman of sentiment.

She was, of course, a vision of delicate loveliness in varying shades of coordinating greens to complement her red hair. She was small and slender and dainty, though she did also, of course, have the bosom that Ferdinand had referred to earlier.

He scowled at her as she wafted into the room, her hazel eyes clouded with concern for him. "You ought not to be here."

"But how could I stay away?" She continued wafting until she reached the chaise longue. She sank to her knees beside him and possessed herself of one of his hands with both her own. She raised it to her lips.

Hawkins, the arrant knave, had withdrawn and closed the door behind him.

"Tresham," she said again. "Oh, my poor, poor dear. You shot gallantly into the air, it is said, when you might easily have killed Edward. Everyone knows your prowess with a pistol. And then you bravely allowed him to shoot you in the leg."

"It was the other way around," he told her curtly. "And there was nothing brave about it. I was not paying attention at the time."

"A woman screamed," she said, kissing his hand again and holding it against one cool, powdered cheek. "I am sure I do not blame her, though I would have swooned quite away if I had been there. My poor, brave darling. Did he nearly kill you?"

"The leg is far from the heart," he said, firmly repossessing himself of his hand. "Do stand up. I will not offer you a seat or refreshments. You are leaving. Now. Miss Ingleby will show you out."

"Miss Ingleby?" Two spots of color appeared in her cheeks suddenly, and her eyes flashed.

He indicated Jane with one hand. "Miss Ingleby, meet Lady Oliver. Who is leaving—*now!*"

But Lady Oliver's look of jealous annoyance turned to indifference mingled with disdain when her eyes lit on Jane. What she saw, obviously, was a maidservant.

"You are cruel, Tresham," she said. "I have been worried half to death about you. I have been languishing for a sight of you."

"Which you have now had," he said briskly. "Good day to you."

"Tell me you have been pining for me too," she said. "Ah, cruel that you make me beg for one kind word."

He looked at her with something like loathing. "Frankly," he said, "I have scarce spared you a thought since I last saw you—at the Georges', was it? Or on Bond Street? I do not remember. And I daresay I will not spare you another thought once you have gone."

She was holding her handkerchief to her mouth again and looking at him reproachfully over the top of it.

"You are angry with me," she told him.

"My feelings, I assure you, ma'am," he said, "do not go beyond irritation."

"If you would let me explain——" she began.

"I beg you will spare me."

"I came here to warn you," she said. "They are going to kill you, you know. My brothers, that is, Anthony and Wesley and Joseph. In defense of my honor, which they do not believe Edward did convincingly enough. Or if they do not kill you, they will find another way to hurt you. They are like that."

Behaving with a ruthless disregard to honor must be a family trait, then, Jocelyn thought.

"Miss Ingleby," he said, "would you please conduct Lady Oliver to the door and see her on her way? And instruct Hawkins that I will have a word with him."

Lady Oliver was weeping in earnest. "You are hard-hearted, Tresham, as everyone warned me," she said through her sobs. "I thought I knew better. I thought you loved me. And I do not need a maid to show me out. I can see myself out, thank you."

Which she proceeded to do in a tragic performance that surely would have brought whistles from the pit of any theater had she been on stage, and a demand for an encore.

"Well, Miss Ingleby," Jocelyn said after an unseen hand had closed the library door, "what do you think of my paramour? Can you blame me for climbing into the lady's bed, married or not?"

"She is very lovely," she admitted.

"And your answer to my second question?" He glared at her as if she were somehow to blame for Lady Oliver's continued indiscretions. He would have expected the woman to avoid him above all others for the next lifetime or two.

"I am not your judge, your grace," Jane Ingleby said gravely.

"You condone adultery, then?" he asked, looking at her with narrowed gaze.

"No, of course not," she said. "It must always be wrong. Nevertheless, you were cruel to her just now. You spoke to her as if you loathed her."

"I do," he said. "Why pretend that I do not?"

"And yet," she said, "you lay with her and made her love you. But now you have spurned her when she braved propriety in order to come and see you and warn you."

He smiled. "Is it possible," he asked, "to be so incredibly naive? I made Lady Oliver love me, Jane? The only person Lady Oliver loves is Lady Oliver. And she has braved propriety so that the *beau monde* will believe that she and I are flouting convention and danger by continuing our liaison. The woman is an exhibitionist. It pleases her to be notorious, especially with someone like me. It delights her to have it said that she has tamed the heart of a Dudley—of the Duke of Tresham himself. She would love nothing better than for me to be compelled to shoot into the air three more times while her brothers use me for target practice. Five times if the other two brothers should descend upon town."

"You trivialize the lady's sensibilities," Jane said.

"I thought," he said softly, "you were not my judge."

"You would tempt a saint," she told him tartly.

"I hope so." He grinned. "But tell me, what has you so convinced that I have lain with Lady Oliver?"

She stared at him blankly for a few moments. "Everyone knows it," she said at last. "It is why the duel was fought. *You* told me."

"Did I?" he asked. "Or did I just allow you to make the assumption?"

"I suppose," she said, sounding indignant, "you are going to deny it now."

He pursed his lips and took his time about answering. "No, I think not," he said. "To deny it would be to give the impression that your good opinion matters to me, you see, Jane. I could not have you believing that, could I?"

She came closer and sat down on her chair again. She arranged the book open on her lap without any apparent care that she turned to the right page. She set her hands flat on the pages. She was frowning.

"If it is untrue," she asked, "why did you not deny it? Why did you fight a duel and risk death?"

"Jane, Jane," he said, "is a gentleman publicly to contradict a lady?"

"But you loathe her."

"I am still a gentleman," he said, "and she is still a lady."

"That is ridiculous!" Her brows snapped together. "You would allow her husband to believe the worst of you and her without telling him the truth? You would allow all of fashionable society to believe the worst of you?"

"Ah," he said, "but they love me for it, Jane. I am the bad, dangerous Duke of Tresham. How I would disappoint the *ton* if I were to insist that on this occasion I am as innocent as a newborn lamb. Not quite, of course. I did flirt with the lady on a few occasions. I often flirt with married ladies. It is expected of me."

"What nonsense you speak!" she said crossly. "And I do not believe you. You are telling me all this only so that you may laugh at me later and tell me what a simpleton I am to believe in your innocence."

"Ah, but, Miss Ingleby," he said, "I have already told you that your opinion matters not one whit to me."

"You are despicable," she said. "I do not know why I remain in your employ."

"Perhaps, Jane," he said, "because you need a roof over your head and food in your stomach. Or perhaps because you enjoy scolding me and chastising me with your barbed tongue. Perhaps because you are growing just a little fond of me?" He deliberately made his voice into a caress.

Her lips were set in a thin line. She stared grimly at him.

"Just remember one thing," he said. "I do not tell lies, Jane. I may acquiesce in other people's lies, but I do not tell lies of my own. You may believe me or not as you wish. Now put down that book and go and fetch me some coffee. And my mail from Michael Quincy. And the chess board."

"You will *not* call me Jane," she said, getting to her feet. "One day I will beat you at chess again even when you are concentrating. And wipe the complacency from your face."

He grinned at her. "Go and do what you have been told to do," he said. "*Please*, Miss Ingleby?"

"Yes, your grace," she said vindictively.

Why, Jocelyn wondered as she left the room, had it seemed so important to him, despite his denial, that she know the truth about Lady Oliver? He did not care tuppence what anyone thought. Indeed, he had always reveled in his rakish reputation even on the rare occasion like this when it was unearned.

Lady Oliver had boasted to her husband, probably during a quarrel, that the Duke of Tresham was her lover. And said husband, in high dudgeon, had issued his challenge. Who was Jocelyn to contradict the lady?

Why had he wanted Jane Ingleby to know that he had never bedded Lady Oliver? Or any other married lady, for that matter?

If Barnard did not have those crutches by tomorrow, Jocelyn thought suddenly, he would beat the man about the head with them as soon as they were in his possession.

8

W hat do you think you are doing?" Jane asked,
startled, when she walked into the library the
following morning to discover the Duke of
Tresham standing facing the window, propped on crutches.

"I *think* I am standing at the window of the library," he
said, looking back over his shoulder at her, his eyebrows raised
haughtily. "In my own home. Deigning to answer an impertinent question from an impertinent servant. Fetch your cloak
and bonnet. You may accompany me outside into the garden."

"You were told to keep your leg still and elevated," she
said, hurrying toward him. She had not remembered that he
was quite so tall.

"Miss Ingleby," he said, without changing his expression,
"go and fetch your cloak and bonnet."

He was a little awkward with the crutches at first, she noticed later, but that fact did not deter him from strolling outside with her for half an hour before they sat side by side on

a wrought-iron seat beneath a cherry tree. Her shoulder was almost touching his arm. She sat very still while he breathed in slowly and audibly.

"One takes many things for granted," he said, more to himself than to her, it seemed. "Fresh air and the perfumes of nature, for example. One's health. One's ability to move about freely."

"Deprivation and suffering can certainly act like wake-up calls," she agreed. "They can remind us to stop squandering our lives in unawareness and in attention to mere trivialities." If she were ever free again . . .

Her mother had died after a shockingly brief illness when Jane was barely seventeen, and her father had taken to his bed and died a little over a year later. She had been left with memories of happiness and security, which she had been young and innocent enough to expect to last forever. She had been left with Papa's cousin inheriting his title and taking over Candleford. And resenting her and courting her favor all at the same time and devising plans for her future that suited his vision but not her own. If she could have back just one of those days of her innocence . . .

"I suppose," the duke said, turning his head to look down at her, "I should turn over a new leaf now, shouldn't I, Miss Ingleby? Become that rarest of all social phenomena, a reformed rake? Defy my heritage? Marry a saint and retire to my country estate to become a model landlord? Sire a brood of model children and raise them to be model citizens? Live happily ever after in a monogamous relationship?"

He had made himself sound so abjectly meek that she laughed.

"It would be a fine thing to behold, I am sure," she said. "Have you proved your point for this morning? Your leg is hurting, is it not? You are rubbing your thigh again. Come indoors and I shall make you comfortable."

"Why is it," he asked her, "that when you say such things,

Jane, I forget any idea of turning over a new leaf and feel very unsaintly indeed?"

He had leaned slightly sideways. His arm was against her shoulder and there was no space on her other side to shuffle across to. She stood up.

That feeling of almost unbearable tension was happening altogether too often. With him, of course, it was deliberate. She believed he delighted in making suggestive remarks to her and looking at her with his eyes half closed. He was amusing himself by teasing her, knowing very well that she was affected. And she *was* affected. She could not deny that the sight of him—even the very *thought* of him—could quicken her blood. That the careless touch of his hand could make her ache for more.

"Take me back inside, then," he said, getting up and onto his crutches without her assistance, "and perform whatever nursing duties you deem necessary. I will come meekly, you see, since you are not in the mood for dalliance."

"And never will be, your grace," she assured him firmly.

But it was a statement and a resolve that were to be tested later that very night.

Jocelyn could not sleep. He had been suffering from insomnia for a week or more. It was understandable, of course, when there was nothing to do after eleven o'clock at night—sometimes even ten—but go to bed and picture in his mind all the balls and routs then in progress and to imagine his friends moving on afterward to one of the clubs until dawn sent them homeward.

Tonight his sleeplessness was combined with a terrible restlessness. He could feel temptation grab almost irresistibly at him—the sort of temptation that had often got him into trouble when he was a boy until he had learned to curb his urges, especially when his father was at Acton. Finally he had suppressed them completely—except when occasionally they burst through all his defenses and would not leave him alone.

On such occasions he usually went to a woman and stayed with her until there was no energy left for anything but sleep and a return to his normal way of life.

He thought with brief wistfulness of Jane Ingleby, but he turned his mind quickly away from her. He enjoyed teasing her, flirting with her, annoying her. And of course she was powerfully beautiful and attractive. But she was off-limits. She was a servant beneath his own roof.

Finally, at something past midnight, he could resist no longer. He threw back the bedcovers, hoisted himself upward with his crutches, and hobbled through to his dressing room, where he donned shirt and pantaloons and slippers but did not bother with either waistcoat or coat. He did not light a candle as he did not have a third hand with which to carry it. He would light some downstairs.

He made his way slowly and awkwardly down to the ground floor.

Jane could not sleep.

The Duke of Tresham no longer needed a bandage. The wound had healed. He was getting about with crutches. He was restless and bad-tempered and would soon be going out. He would not need her.

He never had really needed her.

She would probably be dismissed even before the three weeks were at an end. But even if not, there was only one week left.

The world beyond the doors of Dudley House had become a frightening place that she dreaded having to step into. Every day one visitor or other referred to what was known as the Cornish incident. Today the duke and his friends had chatted merrily on the subject.

"I wonder," the blond and very handsome Viscount Kimble had said, "why Durbury stays shut up in the Pulteney almost all the time instead of enlisting the aid of the *ton* in apprehending his niece or cousin or whatever the devil relationship the woman has to him. Why come to town to search for her and then hide away and let the Runners do all the work?"

"Perhaps he is grieving," the brown-haired, pleasant-faced Sir Conan Brougham had suggested. "Though he does not wear mourning. Could it be that Jardine is not dead after all but is merely skulking in Cornwall with a broken head?"

"That would be in character," the duke had said dryly.

"If you were to ask me," Viscount Kimble had observed, "the woman should be awarded a medal rather than a noose if he *is* dead. The world will be a better place without the presence of Jardine in it."

"But you had better watch your back with the rest of us once you leave the sanctuary of this house, Tresham," Sir Conan had added with a chuckle. "Look out for a fierce wench wielding a pair of pistols or a hefty ax. Accounts vary on which she used to do the dastardly deed."

"What does she look like, pray?" the duke had asked. "So that I may duck out of sight when I see her coming."

"A black-eyed, black-haired witch as ugly as sin," Sir Conan had said. "Or a blond Siren as beautiful as an angel. Take your pick. I have heard both descriptions and several others between the two extremes. No one has ever seen her, it seems, except Durbury, who is keeping mum. Have you heard about Ferdinand's new team? I daresay you have, though, and from the horse's mouth itself, so to speak. Will they decide to travel north when he gives them the signal to proceed south, do you suppose?"

"Not if he is a true brother of mine," the duke had said. "I suppose he bought a frisky pair that will take a year to tame?"

The conversation had proceeded on that topic.

Now Jane could not sleep. Or even lie still. She kept seeing

Sidney's parchment-pale face and the blood on his temple. She kept thinking of the earl's coming to London to search for her. And of the Bow Street Runners combing its streets and questioning its inhabitants to discover her whereabouts. She kept imagining herself taking her fate in her own hands and leaving Dudley House to confront the earl at the Pulteney Hotel.

It would be such a relief to come out of hiding, to have everything out in the open.

To be thrown into jail. To be publicly tried. To be hanged. *Could* an earl's daughter be sentenced to hang? An earl could not. But could his daughter? She did not know.

Why was her father's cousin not wearing mourning? Was it possible that Sidney was not dead after all? But it would be foolish to hope.

She threw back the bedcovers eventually and stopped even pretending to be settled for the night. She lit her candle, threw her cloak about her shoulders, and left her room, not even bothering to dress or to put on shoes. Perhaps she could find a book in the library into which to escape until her brain quieted down.

But she became gradually aware of something as she descended the stairs. Some sound. By the time she reached the bottom it was quite obvious what it was.

Music. Pianoforte music.

Coming from the music room.

But who could be producing it? It was far too late for visitors. It must be well past midnight. Besides, there was no light in the hall. The servants had all retired to bed. There was a thin thread of light beneath the music room door.

Jane approached it gingerly and rested her hand on the knob for several moments before turning it and opening the door.

It was the Duke of Tresham.

He was seated on the pianoforte bench, his crutches on the

floor beside him. He was hunched over the keys, playing without sheet music, his eyes closed, a look almost of pain on his face. He was playing something hauntingly beautiful, something Jane had never heard before.

She stood transfixed, listening. And experiencing again, with a constriction of the heart, the feeling that the music came not from the instrument or even from the man but through them from some divine source. She had not believed there could be another musician with a talent to match her mother's.

But now she was in his presence.

Five minutes or more must have passed before the music ended. He sat, his hands lifted an inch above the keyboard, his head bowed, his eyes still closed. It was only in that moment that Jane realized she was a trespasser.

But it was too late. Even as she thought of withdrawing and closing the door quietly behind her, he turned his head and opened his eyes. For a moment they looked blankly into hers. And then they blazed.

"What the devil are you doing here?" he thundered.

For the first time she was truly afraid of him. His anger appeared somehow different from any she had seen in him before. She half expected him to get up and come stalking toward her.

"I am so sorry," she said. "I came down for a book and I heard the music. Where did you learn to play like that?"

"Like what?" he asked, his eyes narrowing. He was recovering from his shock, she could see, and was looking more himself. "I dabble, Miss Ingleby. I was amusing myself, unaware that I had an audience."

He had retreated, she realized suddenly, behind a familiar mask. She had never thought of him before as a man who needed defenses. It had never occurred to her that perhaps there were depths to his character that he had never shown her, or any of his visitors either.

"Oh, no," she said, aware even as she spoke that perhaps it would be wiser to remain silent. She stepped right into the room and closed the door. "You are no dabbler, your grace. You have been gifted with a wondrous and rare talent. And you were not amusing yourself. You were embracing your talent with your whole soul."

"Poppycock!" he said curtly after a brief silence, "I have never even had a lesson, Jane, and I do not read music. There goes your theory."

But she was staring at him with wide eyes. "You have never had a lesson? What were you playing, then? How did you learn it?"

She realized the truth even as she asked the questions. He did not answer her but merely pursed his lips.

"You do not wear it loose even to bed?" he said.

Her hair. He was talking about her hair, which was in a thick braid down her back. But she was not to be distracted.

"It was your own composition," she said. "It *was*, was it not?"

He shrugged. "As I said," he told her, "I dabble."

"Why does your talent embarrass you?" she asked. "Why are you eager to belittle and even deny it?"

He smiled then, slowly. "You really do not know my family," he told her.

"I suppose," she said, "that playing the pianoforte, composing music, loving it, is something quite unworthy of a Dudley male."

"Bordering on the effeminate," he agreed.

"Bach was a man," she said, walking toward him and setting her candle down on the pianoforte beside the candelabrum that had been giving him light. "Were all the famous composers effeminate?"

"They would have been if they had been Dudleys." He grinned rather wolfishly at her. "Bare feet, Jane? Such shocking dishabille!"

"According to whom?" She would not allow him to change the subject. "You? Or your father and grandfather?"

"We are all one," he said. "Like the trinity, Jane."

"That is blasphemous," she told him firmly. "Your father must have been aware of your talent. Something like that cannot be hidden indefinitely. It will burst forth, as it has tonight. He did not encourage you to develop it?"

"I soon learned never to play when he was at home," he said. "Not after he caught me at it twice. I never did particularly enjoy having to sleep on my front all night because my rear was too sore."

Jane was too angry to say anything. She merely stared at him with compressed lips—at the hard, cynical, dangerous rake who had had all traces of his more sensitive, artistic nature thrashed out of him by a father who had been ignorant enough and weak enough to fear all things feminine. Why was it that men of that type did not realize that the mature, balanced person, regardless of gender, was a fine mix of masculine and feminine qualities? And here was this foolish man trying to live up to the ideal set him by ignorant men—and doing rather a good job of it most of the time.

He turned his attention back to the keyboard and began to play softly. This time it was a familiar tune.

"Do you know it?" he asked without looking up.

"Yes," she said. "It is 'Barbara Allen.'" One of the lovelier and sadder folk songs.

"Do you sing?" he asked her.

"Yes," she admitted softly.

"And do you know the words?"

"Yes."

"Sing them, then." He stopped playing and looked at her. "Sit on the bench here beside me and sing. Since you have come, you might as well make yourself useful. I shall try to play as if my fingers were not all thumbs."

She did as she was bidden and watched his hands as he

played some introductory bars. She had noticed before that he had long fingers. Because he was the Duke of Tresham, it had not occurred to her then that they were artistic hands. It was obvious now. They caressed the keys as if he made love to the music rather than merely produced it.

She sang the song through from beginning to end, long as it was. After an initial self-consciousness, she forgot everything but the music and the sad story of Barbara Allen. Singing had always been one of her greatest joys.

There was silence when the song came to an end. Jane sat straight-backed on the pianoforte bench, her hands clasped in her lap. The duke sat with his hands poised over the keys. It was, Jane thought, without quite understanding the meaning of the thought, one of life's most blessed moments.

"My God!" he murmured into the silence. It did not sound like one of his all-too-common blasphemies. "Contralto. I expected you to have a soprano voice."

The moment passed and Jane was very aware that she was sitting beside the Duke of Tresham in the music room, clad only in her nightgown and outdoor cloak, her braid loose down her back. With bare feet. He was wearing very tight pantaloons and a white shirt open at the neck.

She could think of no way to stand up and remove herself from the room without making a grand production out of it.

"I have never in my life," he said, "heard such a lovely voice. Or one that adapted itself so perfectly to the music and the sentiment of the song."

She was pleased despite her discomfort.

"Why did you not tell me," he asked her, "when I had you play for me and gave you an honest assessment of your talent? Why did you not tell me that you sing?"

"You did not ask," she told him.

"Damn you, Jane," he said. "How dare you keep yourself so much to yourself? A talent like yours is to be shared, not hidden away from the world."

"Touché," she said quietly.

They sat side by side in silence for a while. And then he took her hand in his and held it on the bench between them. Suddenly half the air seemed to have been sucked from the room.

"You ought not to have come down," he said. "Or you ought to have crept into the library and chosen your book and ignored your curiosity. You have caught me at a bad time."

She understood his meaning. It was a bad time for her too. They were firmly caught in a situation that was unfamiliar to them. In a mellow, somewhat melancholy mood. Alone together—as they often were, of course. But entirely alone this time, with no servants moving about beyond the door. Late at night.

"Yes" was all she could think of to say. She stood up then, drawing her hand free of his. Yet everything except her common sense yearned to stay.

"Don't go," he said, his voice unusually husky, and he swiveled around on the bench until he sat with his back to the pianoforte. "Don't leave me yet."

It was a moment—and only a moment—of decision. She could listen to common sense, say a firm good night, and walk from the room. He could not—and would not—stop her. Or she could stay in a situation that was charged with tension and against which her defenses had been lowered. There was no time to debate the matter with herself. She took the couple of steps that brought her directly in front of him.

She lifted both hands and set them on his head as if in benediction. His hair was silky and warm beneath her fingers. His hands came to rest on either side of her waist and drew her toward him. He sighed and leaned forward to bury his face between her breasts.

Fool, she told herself as she closed her eyes and reveled in the physical sensations of his touch and his body heat and the smell of his cologne. *Fool!* But the thought was without conviction.

When he finally lifted his head and looked up at her, his dark eyes fathomless, she went down onto her knees on the floor between his spread thighs. She did not know why she did so, whether at the guidance of his hands or from some instinct that did not require thought. She set her arms along the tight fabric over his thighs, feeling their firm, muscled strength, and lifted her head.

He was leaning over her, and his fingers touching her face were feather-light and tipped with a heat that scorched its way into the depths of her femininity. He cupped her face with his hands before kissing her.

She had been kissed before. Charles had been her beau for four years as well as her dearest friend forever. On a few occasions she had been alone with him and had permitted him to kiss her. She had liked his kiss.

Now she realized she had never been kissed before. Not really. Not like this.

Ah, never like this.

He scarcely touched his lips to hers. His eyes were open, as were hers. It was impossible to lose herself in sheer physical sensation even though every part of her body sizzled with awareness and ached with desire. It was impossible not to know fully what was happening and with whom. It would be impossible afterward to tell herself that she had been swept away by mindless passion.

This was not mindless.

He feathered kisses over her cheeks, her eyes, her temples, her nose, her chin. And returned to her mouth, which he touched softly, teasingly, with his lips, coaxing her to kiss him back in the same way.

A kiss was not necessarily just lips pressed to lips, she discovered in growing wonder. There was the warm, moist flesh behind her lips, which he touched and stroked with his tongue. There was her own tongue moving lightly across his top lip and back over the bottom one. He touched its tip, sliding over the top of it deep into the cavity of her mouth. There were sucking and stroking and soft, wordless moans in her voice, in his.

And then his arms closed about her as he leaned farther over her, half lifting her against the taut strength of his chest, and they shared a deep, hard, openmouthed embrace that had her clinging and pressing and yearning for more.

At last she was down on her knees again, his hands spread over her own on his thighs, his dark, heavy-lidded eyes gazing down into hers.

"We will have to punish each other for this in the morning, Jane," he said. "It will be amazing how different it will all seem then. Forbidden. Impossible. Even sordid."

She shook her head.

"Oh, yes," he insisted. "I am just a rake, my dear, with nothing on my mind except covering you on the floor here and taking my wicked pleasure deep inside your virgin body. And you are the wide-eyed, innocent dove. My servant. My dependent. It is quite impossible. And definitely sordid. You think that what has happened is beautiful. I can see it in your eyes. It is not, Jane. That is merely what an experienced rake can make a woman think. In reality it is the simple lustful, raw desire for sex. For the quick, vigorous mating of bodies. Go to bed now. Alone."

Both his face and his voice were harsh. She got to her feet and stood away from him. But she did not immediately turn to leave. She searched his eyes with her own, looking into the mask that he had settled firmly in place. The impenetrable mask. He was gazing back at her with a mocking half smile on his lips.

He was right. What had happened had been entirely physical. And very raw.

But he was wrong too. Her mind could not yet grapple with what exactly was wrong with what he had said. It just was. He was wrong.

But yes, it was quite impossible. And without a doubt this would all appear very different in the morning. She would not be able to look calmly at him tomorrow as she was doing now.

"Good night, your grace," she said.

"Good night, Jane."

He had turned back to the pianoforte by the time she had picked up her candle, left the room, and closed the door behind her. He was playing something quiet and melancholy.

She was halfway up the stairs before she remembered that she had come down for a book. She did not turn back.

9

Yes, a stool will do nicely," Jocelyn said with a careless wave of his hand to the servant who had asked.

It would do more than nicely. He had come to White's Club in his town carriage rather than riding, but he really ought to have used his crutches after descending instead of just a stout cane. His boot was pressing uncomfortably against his still-tender right calf. If he was not careful he was going to be compelled to have the boot cut off again when he returned home. He had already lost his favorite pair that way the day of the duel.

"And fetch me the morning papers too," he instructed the servant, lifting his leg onto the stool without any outer appearance of effort but with a grateful inward sigh.

He had left the house early so that he would not have to encounter *her* before leaving, and she was herself an early riser. He picked up the *Morning Post* and scanned the front page, scowling as he did so. What the devil was he about, escaping early from his own home so that he could postpone coming face to face with a servant?

He was not sure which of two facts he was most ashamed of—if shame was the right word. Embarrassment might be more accurate. But neither was an emotion with which he had much recent acquaintance.

She had caught him playing the pianoforte. Playing one of his own compositions. And he had kissed her. Damnation, but he had been alone and inactive for too long and had broken one of his cardinal rules and had sunk to a new low in his own esteem. If his leg had not been aching enough to distract him, he probably would have laid her on the floor and availed himself of the treasure that had lain beneath the flimsy barrier of her nightgown. She would not have stopped him, the silly innocent.

"Tresham? By God, it is! How are you, old chap?"

Jocelyn was happy to lower his newspaper, which he had not been reading anyway, in order to greet acquaintances, who were beginning to arrive for their morning gossip and perusal of the papers.

"Hale, hearty, and hopping along at roughly my usual speed," he replied.

The next several minutes were taken up with cheerful greetings and jocular witticisms about the Duke of Tresham's leg and the elegant stool on which it reclined and the stout cane propped beside his chair.

"We were beginning to think you were enjoying playing court at Dudley House, Tresh," Viscount Kimble said, "and were going to settle to it for life."

"With the delectable Miss Ingleby to minister to your needs," Baron Pottier added. "You are wearing your boots again, Tresham?"

"Would I come to White's in my dancing slippers?" Jocelyn raised his eyebrows.

But Sir Isaac Wallman had picked up on an interesting detail. "The delectable Miss Ingleby?" he said. "The nurse? The one who screamed during the duel? Ho, Tresham, you rogue. Now how exactly has she been ministering to your needs?"

Jocelyn raised his quizzing glass and regarded the little dandy through it, looking him over slowly from head to toe.

"Tell me, Wallman," he said in his most bored accents, "at what ungodly hour of the night did you have to rise to give your valet time to create that artistry with your neckcloth?" It would have been overelaborate even for the grandest of grand balls. Though maybe not for a soiree with the Regent, that prince of dandies.

"It took him a full hour," Sir Isaac replied with some pride, instantly distracted. "And he ruined eight neckcloths before he got it right with this one."

Jocelyn lowered his glass while Viscount Kimble snorted derisively.

The pleasantries over with, the conversation moved to the London-to-Brighton curricle race set for two days hence and to the somewhat reclusive presence in London of the Earl of Durbury, who had come to search for his son's murderess. It was a major disappointment to several of the gentlemen present that the earl was not appearing everywhere in order to regale a bored *ton* with the macabre details.

Sidney Jardine, who had been elevated to the position of heir to an earldom on the accession of his father to the title a year or so before, had never been popular with his peers. Jocelyn's only dealings with him had come during a *ton* ball a couple of years before when Jardine, in his grace's hearing, had made a coarse remark fully intended for the ears of a young lady and her mama, who had both declined his invitation to the former to dance. Jocelyn had invited the man to stroll with him on the terrace beyond the ballroom.

There he had instructed Jardine pleasantly enough to take himself off home without further ado or to hell if he preferred unless he chose to stay and have his mouth washed with soap. And when a furiously bristling Jardine had tried to issue a challenge, Jocelyn had raised his quizzing glass to his eye and informed his would-be adversary that it was an immutable rule with him to duel only with gentlemen.

"I am of the school of thought," he said now, "that Lady Sara Illingsworth should be congratulated rather than censured. If she is wise, though, she will have removed herself far from London by now."

"She did not go by stage, though, Tresh," Viscount Kimble said. "I have heard that the Runners have done a thorough investigation. No one of her description has been traveling on any one of them."

"She has learned wisdom since her arrival here, then," Jocelyn said. "Good for her. I daresay she was provoked. Why else would any young lady bash a gentleman over the head?"

"You should know, Tresham," Sir Isaac said with a titter, and won for himself another steady perusal through the ducal quizzing glass.

"Where is Ferdinand stabling his new horses?" Jocelyn asked of the group at large, though he was still looking at an enlarged and visibly uncomfortable Sir Isaac. "And where does he exercise them? I daresay he is busy preparing them for the race. I had better get over there and see if he is like to murder himself on Friday. He was never the world's most skilled judge of horseflesh."

"I'll come with you, Tresh," Viscount Kimble offered as Jocelyn lowered his foot from the stool and turned to grasp his cane. "Do you need any assistance?"

"Come within three feet of me at your peril!" Jocelyn growled while he hoisted himself upright as gracefully as he was able and gritted his teeth at the needle-sharp pain that shot up his right leg. "And I don't need your escort, Kimble. I came in the carriage."

It was an admission that aroused a fresh burst of amusement and witticisms from his acquaintances, of course.

Jane would give him a royal scolding for this when he got

home, Jocelyn thought, and was instantly annoyed at himself for even thinking of home.

He found his brother exactly where he expected to find him, exercising and training his new horses. At least Ferdinand had a good eye for his matched pair, Jocelyn discovered with some relief. They were not just a pretty pair, but superb goers too. The trouble was, of course, that Ferdinand had not had the handling of them for nearly long enough to race them, besides which point he was a restless and impulsive and reckless young man—a typical Dudley, in fact—with impatient hands and a tendency to make colorful use of all the most profane words in his vocabulary when he was frustrated.

"You have to let your hands talk firmly yet seductively," Jocelyn said with a sigh after one particularly hair-raising tirade occasioned by the horses' refusal to act as a team. "And you have to give your voice a rest, Ferdinand, or by the time you reach Brighton there will be none of it left with which to cheer your own victory."

"Damned cattle," his brother grumbled. "I have bought a couple of prima donnas."

"What you have bought," Jocelyn told him, "is an excellent pair that was cheap at the price. What you have to do, preferably before Friday, is teach them who is master."

He was not entirely without hope of winning his substantial bet at White's. Ferdinand was a notable whip though a somewhat erratic one, who appeared to believe that superiority consisted in taking unnecessary risks.

"Now, with *your* curricle, Tresham," Ferdinand said with studied nonchalance, "I would leave Berriwether five miles behind my dust. It is lighter and better sprung than my own."

"You will have to be content to leave him only two miles behind your dust, then," Jocelyn said dryly.

"I'll be giving Wesley Forbes a thrashing one of these days," Ferdinand said later when the brothers were relaxing in his bachelor rooms, Jocelyn with his right foot up on a low table. "He was making offensive remarks at Wattier's last night about people who stagger about on crutches to convince the world of their weakness but forget which leg they are supposed to have injured. Sometimes they lurch along with the right leg raised, he said, and sometimes with the left. He thinks he is the world's sharpest wit."

Jocelyn sipped on his glass of claret. "He could not have been referring to me, then, could he?" he remarked. "Don't be drawn, Ferdinand. You do not need a brawl this side of the race. And never on my behalf. The very idea!"

"I would have planted him a facer right there in the card room," Ferdinand said, "if Max Ritterbaum had not grabbed my arm and dragged me off to Brookes's. The thing is, Tresh, that not a one of them will have the bottom to say anything like it to your face. And you can be damned sure that none of them will be decent enough to slap a glove across your cheek. They are too craven."

"Leave them to me," Jocelyn said. "Concentrate on the race."

"Let me refill your glass," Ferdinand said. "Have you seen Angeline's latest monstrosity?"

"A bonnet?" Jocelyn asked. "The mustard one? Atrocious."

"Blue," his brother said, "with violet stripes. She wanted me to take her walking in the park with it perched on her head. I told her that either it or I would go strolling with her, but not both together. I would be the laughingstock, Tresham. Our sister was born with a ghastly affliction: no taste. Why Heyward encourages her by paying the bills is beyond me."

"Besotted with her," Jocelyn said. "As she is with him. No one would ever guess it to see them together, or *not* together, which is more often the case. They are as discreet about it as if they were clandestine lovers."

Ferdinand barked with laughter. "Lord," he said, "imagine anyone besotted with Angie!"

"Or with Heyward," his brother agreed, idly swinging his quizzing glass from its ribbon.

It was an enormous relief, he reflected some time later as he made his way home, to be getting his life back to normal.

If Jane had thought for one moment that what had happened the night before had meant something to the Duke of Tresham, it did not take her long to learn the truth. Not that she *had* thought it, but sometimes one's emotions defied reason.

He did not return home until late in the afternoon. And even then he did not summon Jane, but closeted himself in the library with Mr. Quincy. It was almost dinnertime before he sent for her.

He was still in the library. He was seated on the chaise longue, his right leg elevated on the cushion. He was fully dressed minus his right boot. He was also scowling.

"Not one word," he said before she had even thought of opening her mouth. "Not a single word, Miss Ingleby. Of course it is sore and of course Barnard had the devil of a time pulling off my boot. But it is time it was exercised, and it is time I took myself off out of here during the daytime. Else I will descend to rape and debauchery."

She had not expected him to refer to last night after being absent all day. Last night seemed rather like a dream. Not perhaps their embrace, which was something so far beyond her experience or expectations that she could not possibly have imagined it, but the sight and sound of the Duke of Tresham playing the pianoforte and coaxing magic from its keys.

"I suppose," he said, turning his black eyes and his blacker scowl on her for the first time, "you thought it was love, Jane? Or affection? Or some fine emotion at least?"

"No, your grace," she said. "I am not as naive as you seem to think me. I recognized it as physical desire on both our parts. Why should I believe that a self-acknowledged rake would have any fine feelings for his servant? And why would you fear that a woman like me would fall for your dangerous and legendary charm when I have been subjected to your ill temper and profane tongue for more than two weeks?"

"Why would I *fear*?" His eyes narrowed. "I might have guessed that you would have the last word on the subject, Jane. How foolish of me to imagine that I seriously discomposed you last night."

"Yes," she agreed. "I daresay your leg is somewhat swollen. You will need to bathe it in cold water. Keep it submerged for a while."

"And freeze my toes?"

"I imagine," she told him, "that that discomfort is better than watching them turn black over the coming weeks."

He pursed his lips and there seemed for a moment to be a smile lurking in his eyes. But he did not give in to it.

"If you are planning to go out again tomorrow," she said, "I beg leave to be given the morning free, your grace."

"Why?" His frown returned.

Her clasped hands turned cold and clammy at the very thought of her reason, but she could no longer give in to the paralysis of terror. She must sooner or later venture beyond the sheltering doors of Dudley House.

"It is time I looked for other employment," she said. "I have less than one week left here. Indeed, I am not really needed now. I never have been. You never needed a nurse."

He stared at her. "You would leave me, would you then, Jane?"

She had been firmly repressing the pain she felt at the thought of doing just that. The pain just did not have either a rational or worthy cause. Though, of course, she had seen a startlingly different side to him in the music room last night.

"My employment here will soon be at an end, your grace," she reminded him.

"Who says so?" He was staring at her broodingly. "What poppycock you speak when you have nothing else to which to go."

Hope stirred. She had half thought of asking him—or of asking the housekeeper, who hired the servants—if she could stay on as a housemaid or scullery maid. But she did not believe she would do so. She would not be able to bear living on at Dudley House in a more menial capacity than the one she had held so far. Not that she could allow pride to dictate her actions, of course.

"It was agreed," she said, "that I remain to nurse you while your injury forced you to remain inactive. For three weeks."

"There is still almost a week left, then," he said. "I will not hear of your searching for something else, Jane, until your time here has been served. I do not pay you to spend your mornings flitting all over London looking for an employer who will pay you more than I do. How much *do* I pay you?"

"More than I earn," she said. "Money is not the issue, your grace."

But he was being stubborn. "I will hear no more about it for at least another week, then," he said. "But I have a job for you on Thursday evening, Jane. Tomorrow. And I will pay you well for it too. I will pay you what you deserve."

She looked warily at him.

"Don't stand by the damned door as if poised for flight," he said irritably. "If I wished to pounce on you, I would do so no matter what the distance. Come closer. Sit down here."

He pointed to the chair where she usually sat.

There was no point in arguing that at least. She did as she was told even though doing so brought her uncomfortably within the aura of his masculinity. She could smell his cologne and remembered how it had been very much a part of last night's sensual experience.

"I am hosting a grand entertainment here tomorrow evening," he said. "Quincy is just now writing out the invitations and having them delivered. There will be only a day's notice for the invited guests, of course, but they will almost all come. Invitations to Dudley House are rare enough to be coveted, you see, despite my reputation. Perhaps because of it."

She would remain for every moment of the evening behind the closed door of her room, Jane thought, clasping her hands very tightly in her lap.

"Tell me," the duke said, "do you possess any garment more becoming than that atrocity you are wearing and the other one you alternate with it, Miss Ingleby?"

No. Oh, no. Definitely not. Absolutely, without question not.

"I will not need it," she said firmly. "I am not going to be one of your guests. It would be unfitting."

His eyebrows arched arrogantly upward.

"For once, Miss Ingleby," he said, "we are in perfect accord. But you have not answered my question. Do take that mulish look off your face. It makes you look like a petulant child."

"I have one muslin frock," she admitted. "But I will not wear it, your grace. It is unsuited to my employment."

"You will wear it tomorrow evening," he informed her. "And you will do something prettier with your hair. I will find out from Barnard which of the maids is most adept at dressing hair. If there is none, I will hire one for the occasion."

Jane was feeling somewhat sick to her stomach.

"But you have said," she reminded him, "that I cannot be one of your guests. I will not need a muslin dress and an elaborate coiffure to sit in my room."

"Do not be dense, Jane," he said. "There will be dinner and cards and conversation and music—provided by a number of the ladies I am inviting. All ladies are accomplished, you know. It is a common fallacy among mothers, it seems, that the ability to tinkle away at a pianoforte keyboard while looking suitably decorative is the surest way to a man's heart and fortune."

"I wonder," she said, "what has made you so cynical."

"Do you?" He smiled in that wolfish way of his. "It comes of growing up with an earl's title and the rank of a marquess, Jane. And of becoming a duke at the tender age of seventeen. Time and again I have proved myself to be the blackest-hearted villain in all England. But every mama with a marriageable daughter still fawns over me as if I were the Angel Gabriel, and every papa courts my acquaintance. Not to mention the simpering young maidens themselves."

"One of these days," she said tartly, "you are going to fall in love with one of those maidens only to discover that she will laugh your courtship to scorn. You have little respect for female intelligence, your grace. You believe yourself to be the greatest matrimonial prize in Christendom and therefore despise all those whom you believe to be angling after you. There are *some* sensible ladies in this world, I would have you know."

He pursed his lips again, a gleam of definite amusement in his eyes now. "For my pride's sake, Jane," he said, "might we extend that to include the Islamic world as well as just Christendom?"

He was quickly learning, Jane thought, how to burst her bubble.

"But we digress." He looked at her more soberly, and Jane felt fingers of apprehension creep up her spine. "You, Miss Ingleby, are going to be the main attraction of the evening. You are going to sing for my guests."

"No!" She stood up abruptly.

"Ah yes," he said softly. "I will even accompany you. I believe I must have admitted to the *ton* from time to time that I dabble. I do not fear that my manhood will be in jeopardy if I merely accompany a vocalist. Do you believe I should?"

"No," she said. "No to the whole thing, I mean. I will not do it. I am not a public performer and have no wish to be. You cannot make me and do not think you can. I will not be bullied."

"I will pay you five hundred pounds, Jane," he said softly.

She drew breath to continue and snapped her mouth shut again. She frowned.

"Five hundred pounds?" she said incredulously. "How ridiculously absurd."

"Not to me," he said. "I want you to sing in public, Jane. I want the *beau monde* to discover what I discovered last night. You have a rare talent."

"Do not think to flatter me into agreeing," she said. But her mind had already whirled into motion. Five hundred pounds. She would not need to work for a long time. She could disappear into a more secure hiding place than this house. She could even move away to somewhere the earl and the Bow Street Runners would not think of looking.

"Five hundred pounds would free you from the necessity of searching out instant employment, would it not?" he said, obviously reading her thoughts, or at least some of them.

But first she would have to face a houseful of guests. Was there anyone in London, she wondered, apart from the Earl of Durbury, who knew her real identity, who had ever set eyes on her as Lady Sara Illingsworth? She did not believe so. But what if there *were* someone?

"I will even say please, Jane," the Duke of Tresham said, his voice falsely humble.

She looked reproachfully at him. Was there even the remotest chance that the earl would be among the guests? There was one way of finding out, of course. She could ask Mr. Quincy if she could look at the guest list.

"I will think about it," she told him while her stomach performed an uncomfortable flip-flop.

"I suppose," he said, "that is the best I can expect from you for now, is it, Jane? You cannot capitulate too soon or it will seem that you have allowed yourself to be overpowered. Very well. But your answer must be yes. My mind is set upon it. We will do some rehearsing tomorrow afternoon."

"You are rubbing your leg again," she said. "I suppose you will not admit that you were foolish to go out today and more foolish to stay out so long. Let me call someone to help you up to your room, and let me have some cold water sent up to you."

"I have been attempting to teach my brother to distinguish the front end of a horse from the rear," he said. "I have wagered a hefty amount on him at White's, Miss Ingleby, and am quite determined that he will win the race."

"How terribly foolish men are," she said. "Their minds are totally bent on trivialities, their energies spent on matters of insignificance. If Lord Ferdinand is hurt on Friday, you will perhaps realize that he is of far more importance to you than the mere winning of a bet."

"If you have finished your scolding," he told her, "you may do what you yourself suggested, Miss Ingleby, and summon the heftiest footman you can find."

She left the room without another word.

What if her description was circulating London? she thought suddenly. What if she stepped into the music room on Thursday evening and the assembled guests arose en masse to point accusing fingers at her?

She could not help the foolish feeling that in some way it would be a relief.

10

*J*ocelyn did not often entertain, but when he did, he did it in lavish style. His chef grumbled belowstairs at having been given no notice at all of the monumental task of preparing a grand dinner to begin the evening and a tasty supper to sustain it at midnight. But he set about the task with a flurry of creative energy instead of resigning on the spot as he threatened to do whenever he stopped work long enough to draw breath.

The housekeeper did not complain, but marshaled her troops with grim determination to banish every speck of dust from the rooms that would be used for the entertainment and to have every surface polished and gleaming. She arranged the lavish mounds of flowers that Michael Quincy had ordered.

As Jocelyn had predicted, almost everyone accepted his invitation even though doing so doubtless involved the breaking of other commitments at the last moment. The chance to attend a dinner and soiree at Dudley House did not come often.

Jocelyn instructed his housekeeper to select or to hire a maid accomplished at dressing a lady's hair. He did toy with the idea of also taking Jane Ingleby to a fashionable modiste and commanding that an evening gown be made up with all haste—he had considerable influence with two or three of London's most exclusive dressmakers—but he did not do so. She would without doubt make a fuss and end up refusing to sing. Besides, he must not make her look too much the lady, he decided, or his guests would be wondering about the propriety of her having spent almost three weeks beneath his roof as his nurse.

He spent some time during the afternoon in the music room with her, rehearsing two contrasting songs to show off her voice as well as an encore, the possibility of which she protested was nonsense, but which he insisted was not.

He found, as he dressed for the evening, that he was feeling nervous. A fact that thoroughly alarmed him and made him despise himself heartily.

When she had been younger, when her parents had both been alive and healthy, there had been frequent picnics, dinners, and dances at Candleford Abbey. They had loved entertaining. But Jane did not believe they had ever invited anywhere near fifty guests at one time. And even those parties she remembered had been a long time ago. She had been just a girl.

She sat in her room for several hours before getting ready to go downstairs, listening to the distant sounds of voices and laughter, imagining what was happening, what was yet to happen before she was summoned to sing. But it was impossible to predict the exact time of the summons. *Ton* parties, Jane was aware, were quite unlike their counterparts in the country, which almost never continued past eleven o'clock or midnight at the very latest. Here in town no one seemed to consider it strange to be up all night—and then, of course, to sleep all the following day.

She might not be called down before midnight. She would collapse in a heap of the jitters if she had to wait that long.

But finally she could see from the clock on the mantel that Adele, the French maid who had been hired for the evening just to dress her hair, would be knocking on her door in ten minutes' time. It was time to get dressed.

It was far too late to regret agreeing to this madness. There was no one among the guests—she had perused the guest list with great care—who might know her identity. But the Earl of Durbury was in town. What if everyone at tonight's gathering had been furnished with her description? Her stomach lurched. But it was too late.

She determinedly pulled off her maid's frock and drew over her head the carefully ironed sprigged muslin dress she had set out on her bed earlier. It was a dress perfectly suited to afternoon tea in the country. It was not at all appropriate for an evening party even there, of course, but that did not matter. She was not a guest at tonight's entertainment, after all.

She shivered with mingled cold, excitement, and fear.

She had never meant to hide when she fled to London. What she should have done after making the ghastly discovery that Lady Webb was not at home, Jane thought belatedly, was to stay at the hotel where she had taken a room and apply to the earl's man of business in town for funds. She should have boldly proclaimed to all the world that she had been abused and assaulted by a drunken rogue during the earl and countess's absence from Candleford and had quite justifiably defended herself by hitting him with a book and removing herself far from proximity to him.

But she had not done it, and it was too late now.

She was in hiding. And about to show herself to fifty members of the crème de la crème of British society.

What *utter* madness.

A female voice laughed shrilly in the distance.

Someone tapped on Jane's door, making her jump foolishly. Adele had arrived to dress her hair.

At eleven o'clock Lady Heyward, Jocelyn's hostess for the evening, announced the end of the card games that were in progress, while Jocelyn himself directed a few footmen in the moving of the drawing room pianoforte to the center of the room and the arrangement of chairs about the room's perimeter. The musical part of the evening was about to begin.

Several of the younger ladies volunteered or were persuaded to play the pianoforte or to sing. One gentleman— Lord Riding—was brave enough to sing a duet with his betrothed. All the recitals were competent. The guests listened more or less attentively and applauded politely. This was, after all, a familiar form of evening entertainment to them all. Only a few of the acknowledged patrons of the arts ever hired professional artists, but on those occasions the evening was heralded as a private concert.

Finally Jocelyn got to his feet with the aid of his cane.

"Do feel free to stand up and move about for a few minutes," he said when he had everyone's attention. "I have engaged a special guest for your entertainment before supper. I shall go and bring her down."

His sister looked at him in surprise. "Whoever can she be, Tresham?" she asked. "Is she waiting in the kitchen? Where on earth did you find her when you have been almost shut up here for the past three weeks?"

But he merely inclined his head and left the room. Fool that he was, he had scarce been able to think of anything else all evening but this moment. He just hoped she had not changed mind. Five hundred pounds was a considerable inducement, of course, but he was of the opinion that if Jane

Ingleby had decided she did not want to sing, even five thousand pounds would not convince her.

He had been pacing the hall, leaning heavily on his cane, for two minutes after sending Hawkins up for her before she appeared on the staircase. She stopped on the third stair up and turned into a decent imitation of a statue—a pale, grim statue with its lips set in a thin, hard line, who nevertheless looked like an angel. The light, simply styled muslin dress did wonders for her form, accentuating her tall, slender grace. Her hair—well, he simply could not remove his eyes from it for a long moment. It was not elaborately styled. It was not a mass of curls and ringlets, as he had half expected. It was dressed up, but all the usual severity was gone. It looked soft and healthy and shiny and elegant. And pure gold.

"Well, well," he said, "the butterfly has fluttered free of its cocoon."

"It would be much better if we did not do this," she said.

But he moved to the bottom of the staircase and reached up a hand for hers, holding her eyes with his own.

"You will not turn craven on me now, Jane," he said. "My guests await my special guest."

"They will be disappointed," she warned him.

It was entirely unlike her to cower. Not that she was doing that exactly. She was standing straight with her chin lifted proudly. She also looked as if she might have sent roots down into the third stair.

"Come," he said, using his eyes shamelessly to compel her.

She came down to the second stair, and when he turned his hand palm down, she set her own hand on his and allowed him to lead her toward the drawing room. She had the bearing of a duchess, he thought with what might have been amusement under different circumstances. And in the same moment he felt as if scales had fallen from his eyes. An orphan? Raised in an orphanage? Turned out on the world to make her own way in life now that she had grown up? He did not think so. He was a fool ever to have been taken in by that story.

Which made Jane Ingleby a liar.

"'Barbara Allen' first," he said. "Something that is familiar to my fingers while they limber up."

"Yes. Very well," she agreed. "Are *all* your guests still here?"

"Hoping that forty-eight or forty-nine of them have retired to their homes for their beauty sleep, are you?" he asked her. "Not one has left, Jane."

He felt her draw deep, steadying breaths as a liveried footman leaped forward to open the drawing room doors. She lifted her chin a little higher.

She looked like a fresh garden flower amid hothouse plants, he thought as he led her inside and between two lines of chairs, on which his guests were seating themselves again and from which they looked with curiosity at his guest.

"Oh, I say." It was Conan Brougham's voice. "It is Miss Ingleby."

There was a buzz as those who knew who Miss Ingleby was explained to those who did not. They all, of course, knew about the milliner's assistant who had distracted the Duke of Tresham's attention during his duel with Lord Oliver and had then become his nurse.

Jocelyn led her into the open space occupied by the pianoforte at the center of the room. He released her hand.

"Ladies, gentlemen," he said, "I have persuaded Miss Ingleby to share with you what is surely the most glorious singing voice it has ever been my privilege to hear. Unfortunately she does not have an accompanist who can do her justice, only me. I dabble along, you see, with five thumbs on each hand. But I daresay no one will notice once she begins to sing."

He arranged the tails of his coat behind him as he seated himself on the bench, set his cane on the floor beside him, and curved his fingers over the keys. Jane was standing exactly where he had left her, but in truth he was not paying her much mind. He was terrified. He who had faced the wrong end of a pistol in four separate duels without flinching shied away from playing the pianoforte for an audience who would not even be listening to him, but to Jane. He felt exposed, almost naked.

He concentrated his mind on the task at hand and began playing the opening bars of "Barbara Allen."

Her voice was breathless and slightly shaking for the first two lines of the first verse. But then she settled down, as did he. Indeed, he soon forgot his own task and played more from instinct than deliberate intent. She sang the song better, more feelingly, than he had yet heard it, if that were possible. She was the sort of singer, he realized, who responded instinctively to an audience. And his guests were a very attentive audience indeed. He was sure no one moved in any way at all until the last syllable of the ballad had faded away. And even then there was a pause, a moment of absolute silence.

And then applause. Not the muted applause of a gathering of the *beau monde* being polite to one of its own, but the enthusiastic appreciation of an audience who had for a number of minutes been transported into another dimension by a truly talented artist.

Jane looked surprised and somewhat embarrassed. But quite composed. She inclined her head and waited for the applause to die away and be replaced by an expectant hush.

She sang Handel's "Art Thou Troubled?" It was surely one of the loveliest pieces of music ever composed for a contralto voice. Jocelyn had always thought so. But this evening it seemed that it must have been written especially for her. He forgot about the difficulty he had had in improvising an authentic-sounding accompaniment for the words. He simply played and listened to her rich, disciplined, but emotionally charged voice and found his throat aching, as if with tears.

" 'Art thou troubled?' " she sang. " 'Music will calm thee. Art thou weary? Rest shall be thine; rest shall be thine.' "

He must have been troubled and weary for a long, long time, Jocelyn found himself thinking. He had always known the seductive power of music to soothe. But it had always been a forbidden balm, a denied rest. Something that was soft, effeminate, not for him, a Dudley, a Duke of Tresham.

" 'Music.' " She drew breath, and her rich voice soared. " 'Music calleth, with voice divine.' "

Ah, yes, with voice divine. But a Dudley only ever spoke with a firm, manly, very human voice and rarely ever listened at all. Not at least to anything that was outside the realm of his active daily life, in which he had established dominance and power. Certainly not to music, or to the whole realm of the spirit that music could tap into, taking its listener beyond the mere self and the finite world of the senses to something that could only be felt, not expressed in words.

The pain in his throat had not eased by the time the song came to its conclusion. He closed his eyes briefly while applause broke the silence again. When he opened them, it was to see that his guests were rising one by one to their feet, still clapping, while Jane looked deeply embarrassed.

He got up from the bench, ignoring his cane, took her right hand in his, and raised it aloft between them. She smiled at last and curtsied.

She sang the light and pretty but intricate "Robin Adair" for an encore. He would doubtless inform her tomorrow that he had told her so, Jocelyn thought, but he knew that tonight he would be unable to tease her.

She would have fled from the room after that. She took a couple of hurried steps toward the opening between the lines of chairs that led to the doors. But his guests had broken ranks and had other ideas. The entertainment was over. It was suppertime. And Ferdinand had stepped into her path.

"I say, Miss Ingleby," he said with unaffected enthusiasm. "Jolly good show. You sing quite splendidly. Do come to the supper room for refreshments."

He was bowing and smiling and offering his arm and us- ing all the considerable charm of which he was capable when he turned his mind from horses and hunting and boxing mills and the latest bizarre bets at the clubs.

Jocelyn felt unaccountably murderous.

Jane tried to escape. She offered several excuses, but within seconds Ferdinand was not the only one she had to convince. She was surrounded by guests of both genders eager to speak with her. But though her position at Dudley House as his nurse and the circumstances of her hiring were doubtless in- triguing to people who throve on gossip and scandal, Jocelyn did not believe it was those facts alone that drew so much at- tention her way. It was her voice.

How could he have listened to it two nights ago, he won- dered now, without realizing that it was not just an extraordi- narily lovely voice? It was also a well-trained voice. And good voice training was surely not something anyone came by at an orphanage, even a superior one.

She was borne off toward the dining room on Ferdinand's arm, with Heyward walking at her other side, engaging her in an earnest discussion of Handel's *Messiah*. Jocelyn turned his attention to his other guests.

Her voice teacher, whom her father had brought to Cornwall at considerable expense, had given it as his opinion that she could sing professionally if she chose, that she could hold her own in Milan, in Vienna, at Covent Garden—anywhere she liked. That she could be an international star.

Her father had pointed out gently but firmly that a career, even such an illustrious one, was out of the question for the daughter of an earl. Jane had not minded. She had never felt the need to win public acclaim or fame. She sang because she loved to sing and because she liked to entertain friends and relatives.

But this evening's success at Dudley House was seductive, she had to admit. The house itself had been transformed into a splendid wonderland with every candle in every chandelier and candleholder lit and vases of lavish and expertly arranged flowers everywhere. Everyone was flatteringly kind. Almost all the guests approached her in the dining room, some just to smile and tell her how much they had enjoyed her performance, many to talk with her at greater length.

She had never been to London before. She had never moved in exalted circles. But there was a wonderful feeling of *rightness* about being with this company. These were her people. This was the world to which she belonged. If her mother had lived longer, if her father had retained his health, she would as a matter of course have come to London for a Season. She would have been brought to the great marriage mart for the serious business of selecting a suitable husband. She felt at home with the Duke of Tresham's guests.

She had to make a deliberate effort to remind herself that she was not really one of them. Not any longer. There was a huge obstacle between herself and them, put there when Sidney, drunk and offensive, had decided to try to seduce her as an inducement to persuade her to marry him. He had been going to ravish her—with the full connivance of his equally drunken friends. But she had never been one to endure bullying meekly. She had swung a book at his head.

And so had begun the string of events that had made a fugitive of her. But some fugitive! Here she was in the very midst of a select gathering of the *ton*, behaving as if she had not a care in the world.

"You must excuse me," she murmured, smiling and getting to her feet.

"Excuse you?" Lady Heyward regarded her with gracious surprise. "Absolutely not, Miss Ingleby. Can you not see that you have become the guest of honor? Heyward will persuade you to stay, will you not, my love?"

But Lord Heyward was deep in earnest conversation with a dowager in purple topped by a matching plumed turban.

"Allow me," Viscount Kimble said, taking Jane by the elbow and gesturing to the chair she had just vacated. "You are the mystery of the hour, Miss Ingleby. One moment hurrying to work across Hyde Park, the next nursing Tresh like a gray shadow, and now singing like a trained nightingale. Permit me to interrogate you." He smiled with practiced charm, softening the effect of his words.

Lady Heyward, still on her feet, was clapping her hands to draw all attention her way.

"I absolutely refuse to allow everyone to drift away after supper," she said, "when it is scarce past midnight. I refuse to allow Tresham to be the laughingstock tomorrow. We are going to have dancing in the drawing room. Mrs. Marsh will play for us, will you not, ma'am? Shall I give the order for the carpet to be rolled back, Tresham, or will you?"

"Dear me," his grace said, his fingers curling about the handle of his quizzing glass. "How extraordinarily kind of you to be so solicitous of my reputation, Angeline. I shall give the order." He left the room.

"You really must excuse me," Jane said firmly a few minutes later, after giving vague answers to the questions Lord Kimble had asked her. "Good night, my lord."

"I shall have a new reason for calling upon Tresham during the next few days," he told her, bowing over her hand, which he raised to his lips. His eyes looked appreciatively into her own.

Another dangerous gentleman, Jane thought as she hurried from the room, bidding several people good night as she went. And one who must surely know how devastatingly attractive pale blue and silver evening clothes looked with his blond hair.

But slipping off to the privacy of her room was not to be easy at all tonight, she saw as she approached the drawing room. The Duke of Tresham was coming out, leaning on his cane. Several of his guests were already back there, she could see through the open door. More were coming from the supper room.

"Going to bed, Jane?" he asked her. "When it is not even an hour past midnight?"

"Yes, your grace," she said. "Good night."

"Poppycock!" he told her. "You heard Angeline. In her estimation you have become the guest of honor. And despite her appalling taste in dress—shocking pink, you will have observed, does not become her, especially when accompanied by frills and flounces and those unfortunate blue plumes she has in her hair—despite all that, Jane, there is no higher stickler than my sister. You will come into the drawing room."

"No," she said.

He raised his eyebrows. "Insubordination? You will dance, Jane. With me."

She laughed. "And your cane too?"

"Now, that, Jane," he said, lifting it and pointing it at her, "is a low blow. I shall dance without my cane. A waltz, in fact. You will waltz with me."

He had moved to stand between her and the route to the staircase. She could tell from a glance at his face that he was in one of those moods that would not brook denial. Not that she would not put up a good fight on that account. He could not force her to dance, after all.

"You never waltz," she told him.

"Now who told you that?" he asked her.

"You did," she reminded him. "In my hearing. When someone mentioned Almack's one day."

"I will make an exception tonight," he said. "Do you waltz, Jane? Do you know the steps?"

It was her way out. All she needed to do was say no. And indeed she had never performed the steps at any public assembly, only with Charles and a few of their friends at private gatherings. But she was suddenly assailed by a deep longing to waltz here at Dudley House among her peers before she disappeared somewhere she would never be found. To waltz with the Duke of Tresham. Suddenly the temptation was overwhelming.

"She hesitates," the duke murmured. He leaned closer. "You must not deny it now, Jane. Your silence has betrayed you." He offered his arm. "Come."

She hesitated only a moment longer before laying her arm along his and turning into the drawing room.

To dance.

To waltz with the Duke of Tresham.

One thing was very clear to Jocelyn as he sat conversing with a few of his more elderly guests while the younger ones danced an energetic country dance. Jane Ingleby was going to have to go soon. Away from Dudley House. Away from him.

She had indeed become the focus of attention. She was not dancing, but she was surrounded by a veritable court of admirers, among them Kimble and Ferdinand, both of whom should have been dancing. She looked somewhat incongruous in her sprigged muslin dress and simple coiffure when every other lady present was decked out in silks and satins and jewels with elaborate plumes and turbans. But she made every one of them look fussy and overdressed.

She was simplicity itself. Like a single rose. No, a rose was too elaborate. Like a lily. Or a daisy.

There would indeed be questions if he kept her here any longer. Surely it must be apparent to all his guests, as it should have been to him for the past three weeks, that she was a lady from the top of her head down to her toenails. The impoverished orphan of an impoverished gentleman, at a guess. But a lady nonetheless. An extraordinarily lovely one.

He was going to have to find her employment elsewhere— a thoroughly depressing thought, which he would put out of his head for tonight. The country dance had ended. He got to his feet, leaving his cane propped against the chair. Putting his full weight on his right leg did not cause undue pain, he was relieved to find. He made his way toward Mrs. Marsh at the pianoforte.

"Take your partners, gentlemen," he announced after consulting her, "for a waltz." He moved in the direction of Jane and had the misfortune to meet the eyes of both Kimble and Brougham as he did so. Both were looking at him rather as if he had sprouted another head. He knew why. It was common knowledge that the Duke of Tresham never waltzed. He extended his right hand. "Miss Ingleby?"

"You will suffer for this," she warned him as they took their places on the polished floor, from which the carpet had been rolled back. "You will probably be forced to spend the next two weeks with your leg up on a cushion."

"Then you may have the satisfaction of saying you told me so," he said, setting his right hand behind her waist and taking her right hand in his left.

He never waltzed, for the simple reason that it was far too intimate a dance for a man who had become adept at avoiding matrimonial traps. But he had always thought that if the occasion and the woman were ever right, he would find the waltz truly enchanting.

The time was right and so was the woman.

Her spine arched pleasingly beneath his hand. The curve of her other arm and her hand resting on his shoulder brought her tantalizingly close to him though their bodies did not once touch as they twirled about the room, their eyes on each other, the other dancers and the spectators forgotten, as if they did not exist. He could feel her body heat and smell the faint aroma of roses that seemed to cling about her.

She danced divinely, as if her feet did not quite touch the floor, as if she were a part of himself, as if they were both a part of the music or it a part of them. He found himself smiling at her. Although her face remained in repose, it seemed to him that an answering warmth beamed through her blue eyes.

It was only as the music drew to an end that he realized two things—that he had inadvertently let go of his customary haughty aloofness, and that his leg was aching like a thousand devils.

"I am going to bed," she said breathlessly.

"Ah, Jane," he said softly, "I cannot come with you. I have a houseful of guests."

She withdrew herself from his arms as everyone changed partners or returned to the sidelines.

"But I will escort you to your room," he told her. "No, you may not look significantly down at my leg. I am not a cripple, Jane, and will not behave like one. Take my arm."

He did not care who saw them leave together. He would not be gone long. And she would not be here at Dudley House much longer to fuel any gossip. That was clearer than ever to him.

The hall and staircase seemed very quiet in contrast to the buzz of conversation they had left behind in the drawing room and could still hear. Jocelyn did not attempt conversation as they ascended slowly—he had not brought his cane with him. He did not speak at all until they were walking along the dimly lit corridor to Jane's room.

"You were as much of a success as I knew you would be," he said then. "More so, indeed."

"Thank you," she said.

He paused outside her room, standing between her and the door.

"Your parents," he said, "must have been very proud of you."

"Y——" She caught herself in time. She looked keenly at him, as if to see whether his words had been a mere slip of memory. "The people who knew me were," she said carefully.

"But a talent is not something to be unduly proud of, your grace. My voice is something for which I can take no credit. It was given me, just as was your ability to play the pianoforte as you do."

"Jane," he said softly before dipping his head and setting his lips to hers.

He did not touch her anywhere else. She did not touch him. But their lips clung softly, warmly, yearningly for many moments before one of them drew back—he was not sure who.

Her eyes were dreamy with latent passion, her cheeks flushed with desire. Her lips were parted and moist with invitation. And his own heartbeat was drumming in his ears and threatening to deafen him to reality. Ah, Jane, if only . . .

He searched her eyes with his own before turning and opening her door. "It is as well that I have guests below, Jane. This will just not do, will it? Not for much longer. Good night."

Jane fled into her room without a backward glance. She heard the door close behind her before spreading her hands over her hot cheeks.

She could still feel his hand at her waist as they waltzed. She could still feel his heat, still smell his cologne, still feel the sense of perfect rhythm with which they had moved to the music. She could still feel the waltz as an intimate, sensual thing, not the sheer fun it had been when danced with Charles.

Yes, it was as well there were guests downstairs.

She could still feel his kiss, not fierce, not lascivious. Much worse. A soft, longing kiss. No, it would not do. Not for *much* longer. Not for *any* longer, in fact. A great yawning emptiness opened up somewhere deep inside her.

11

The Brighton race was to begin at Hyde Park Corner at half-past eight the following morning. Fortunately it was shaping up to be a clear, windless day, Jocelyn discovered when he stepped outside, leaning on his cane.

He climbed up unaided to the high seat of his curricle, and waved away his groom, who would have jumped up behind. He was only going to the park and back, after all. He was going to give Ferdinand some last words of encouragement—not advice. Dudleys did not take well to advice, especially from one another.

He was very early, but he wanted to spend a few minutes with his brother before the crowds arrived to cheer the racers on their way to Brighton. There were a number of gentlemen who would ride their horses behind the curricles, of course, so that they could witness the end of the race and celebrate with the winner in Brighton. Ordinarily Jocelyn would have been one of them—no, ordinarily he would have been one of the *racers*—but not this time. His leg was considerably better than perhaps it should feel when he had waltzed on it last evening, but it would be foolish to subject it to a long, bruising ride.

Ferdinand was flushed and restless and eager as he checked his new team and chatted with Lord Heyward, who had arrived even before Jocelyn.

"I am to be sure to tell you from Angeline," Heyward was saying with an ironic lift of one eyebrow, "that you are to win at all costs, Ferdinand, that you are to take no risks that will break your neck, that the honor of the Dudley name is in your hands, that you are not to worry about anything but your own safety—and a great deal more in the same contradictory vein, with which I will not assail your ears."

Ferdinand grinned at him and turned to bid Jocelyn a good morning.

"They are as eager as I to be on the way," he said, nodding in the direction of his horses.

Jocelyn raised his quizzing glass to his eye and looked over the curricle, which his brother had bought impulsively a few months before entirely on the grounds that it looked both smart and sporty. He had complained about it ever since, and indeed there was something clumsy about it that one detected only in the handling of it. Jocelyn had driven it once himself and had never felt any burning desire to repeat the experience.

The odds were against Ferdinand in this race, though Jocelyn did not despair of his wager. Youth and eagerness were on his brother's side as well as a certain family determination never to come in second at any manly sport. And those chestnuts were certainly a pair that Jocelyn coveted himself. The curricle was the weakness.

Lord Berriwether, Ferdinand's opponent, was driving up amid a veritable cavalcade of horsemen come to cheer him on. All of them would have wagered on him, of course. A few of them called good-naturedly to Ferdinand.

"A prime pair, Dudley," Mr. Wagdean cried cheerfully. "A pity they have three lame legs apiece."

"Even more of a pity when they win," Ferdinand retorted, grinning, "and show up Berriwether's pair, which has no such excuse."

Berriwether was showing his unconcern with the opposition by flicking at an invisible speck of dust on his gleaming top boots with his whip. The man looked more suitably dressed for a stroll on Bond Street than a race to Brighton. But he would be all business, of course, once the race was under way.

"Ferdinand," Jocelyn said impulsively, "we had better switch curricles."

His brother looked at him with undisguised hope. "You mean it, Tresham?"

"I have a better regard for my wager than to send you off to Brighton in that bandbox," Jocelyn replied, nodding at the red and yellow curricle.

Ferdinand was not about to argue the point further. In a matter of minutes—and with only five minutes to spare before the scheduled start of the race—his groom had unhitched his curricle from the chestnuts and switched it with the duke's.

"Just remember," Jocelyn said, unable after all to resist the urge to give advice, "it is somewhat lighter than yours, Ferdinand, and more instantly responsive to your maneuvering. *Slow down* on the bends."

Ferdinand climbed up to the high seat and took the ribbons from his groom's hand. He was serious now, concentrating on the task ahead.

"And bring it back in one piece," Jocelyn added before stepping back with the rest of the spectators, "or I'll skin you alive."

One minute later the Marquess of Yarborough, Berriwether's brother-in-law, raised the starting pistol skyward, there was an expectant hush, the pistol cracked, and the race began amid a roar of cheers and a cloud of dust and a thundering of hooves.

It looked, Jocelyn thought, gazing rather wistfully after the curricles and the throng of riders, rather like a cavalry charge. He turned toward Ferdinand's curricle and exchanged a few pleasantries with some other spectators.

He wished then that he had brought his groom after all. He would have to go home in order to have his horses stabled and the curricle put away in the carriage house before proceeding to White's. But he need not go inside the house. He had no reason to do so and every reason *not* to.

He had kissed her again last evening. And had admitted that they could not go on as they were. The matter had to be dealt with. She had to go.

The trouble was, he did not want her to go.

He should have driven around to the mews, he remembered as he drove into Grosvenor Square and approached the front doors of Dudley House. He was not concentrating. He would drive around the square and back out of it.

But just as he gave his horses the signal to proceed, a series of incidents, which happened so fast that even afterward he was not sure of the sequence, changed all his plans. There was a loud snapping sound, a sudden lurching of the curricle to the left, a snorting and rearing of the horses, a shout in a male voice, a scream in a female's. And a painful collision of his body with something hard enough to knock the breath out of him.

He was lying facedown on the roadway outside his own doors when rational thought returned. With the sound of frightened horses being soothed behind him, with the feeling that every bone in his body must have been jarred into a new position, and with someone stroking his hair—what the devil had happened to his hat?—and assuring him in a marvelous exercise of utter female stupidity that he would be all right, that everything would be all right.

"Bloody hell!" he exclaimed ferociously, turning his head to one side and viewing from ground level the ruin of his brother's curricle, which was listing sharply to one side on its snapped axle.

Every house on the square, it seemed, was disgorging hordes of interested and concerned spectators—had they all been lined up at the windows to witness his humiliation?

"Just catch your breath," Jane Ingleby said, her hand still in his hair. "A couple of the servants will carry you inside in a moment. Don't try to move."

That was all he would need to cap the mortification of one of the most wretched months of his life.

"If you cannot talk sense," he said, shaking his head irritably to rid himself of her hand, "I suggest that you not talk at all."

He planted his hands on the ground—there was a ragged hole in the palm of one of his expensive leather gloves, he noticed, with raw flesh within—and hoisted himself upward, ignoring the silent screaming of muscles that had just been severely abused.

"Oh, how foolish you are!" Jane Ingleby scolded, and to his shame he was forced to set a heavy hand on her shoulder—again.

But he was gazing narrow-eyed at Ferdinand's curricle.

"It would have snapped when he was out in the country driving at breakneck speed," he said.

She frowned up at him.

"It is Ferdinand's curricle," he explained. "The axle has broken. He would have been killed. *Marsh!*" he bellowed at his head groom, who was still soothing the horses while someone from another house was unhitching them from the vehicle. "Examine that curricle with a fine-tooth comb as soon as you have a chance. I want a report within the half hour."

"Yes, your grace," his groom called.

"Help me inside," Jocelyn commanded Jane. "And stop

your fussing. I'll have bruises and scrapes for you to tend to your heart's content once we have reached the library, I do not doubt. I have not broken any bones, and I did not land on my right leg. At least, I do not think I did. Someone did this. Deliberately."

"To kill Lord Ferdinand?" she asked as they went inside. "So that he would lose the race? How absurd. No one could want to win a bet or a race that badly. It was an accident. They do happen, you know."

"I have enemies," he said curtly. "And Ferdinand is my brother."

He hoped fervently that the curricle was all that had been tampered with. This had the signature of the Forbes brothers all over it. Underhanded, sneaky bastards.

Jane had risen with a firm determination to take her leave of Dudley House that very day. Her usefulness here, what little there had been, was at an end. The three weeks were over. And what she had agreed to and done last evening for the entertainment of the duke's guests had been the ultimate madness. Fifty members of the *beau monde* had seen her—really *seen* her—when she was dressed, if not quite in the splendor of evening garments that would have set her on a level with them, at least in a manner that set her noticeably above the level of a maid.

It was surely only a matter of time before the search for her led to the circulation among the *ton* of a description of her appearance. Indeed she was puzzled that it had not already happened. But when it did, a number of last evening's guests were going to remember Jane Ingleby.

She had to leave Dudley House. She had to disappear. She would take the five hundred pounds—another madness, but she had every intention of holding the Duke of Tresham to his end of their bargain—and go into hiding. Not in London.

She would go somewhere else. She would walk clear of town before trying to board any public conveyance.

Jane was determined to leave. Even apart from every other reason, there was last night's lingering kiss, which had come alarmingly close to exploding into uncontrolled passion. It was no longer possible for her to remain at Dudley House. And she would not allow herself to indulge in any personal longing. For the moment at least she could not allow herself to have any personal feelings.

She fetched warm water and ointments and bandages as soon as she had settled him in the library. She was sitting on a stool before the fireside chair, rubbing ointment into his badly scraped palms, when his groom was admitted.

"Well?" his grace demanded. "What did you find, Marsh?"

"The axle had definitely been tampered with, your grace," his groom told him. "It was not natural wear and tear that made it go like that."

"I knew it," the duke said grimly. "Send someone reliable over to my brother's stable, Marsh. No, better yet, go yourself. I want to know exactly who has had access to that curricle during the past few days. Especially yesterday and last night. Deuce take it, but surely both he and his groom were careful enough to inspect the vehicle when it was to be used in a lengthy race."

"I know you and I both would if it had been you, your grace," the groom assured him.

He went on his way, and Jane found herself being scowled at.

"If you are planning to use those bandages," he said, "forget it. I am not walking around with two mittened paws for the next week or so."

"Those cuts will be painful, your grace," she warned him.

He smiled grimly at her, and Jane sat back on the stool. She knew that his mind was distracted with the morning's events and with anxiety for his brother's safety. But the time had come. She could wait no longer.

"I am going to leave," she said abruptly.

His smile became more crooked. "The room, Jane?" he said. "To put the bandages away again? I wish you would."

She did not answer but merely stared at him. He had not for a moment misunderstood her, she knew.

"You would leave me, then?" he said at last.

"I must," she said. "You know I must. You said so yourself last night."

"But not today." He frowned and flexed the fingers of his left hand, which was less badly scraped than the other. "I cannot cope with another crisis today, Jane."

"This is not a crisis," she told him. "I have had temporary employment here and now it is time for me to leave—after I have been paid."

"Perhaps," he said, "I cannot afford to pay you today, Jane. Did I not agree to give you the colossal sum of five hundred pounds for last evening's performance? I doubt Quincy keeps that much petty cash on hand."

Jane blinked her eyes, but she could not quite clear them of the despicable tears that rushed to them.

"Do not make a joke of it," she said. "Please. I must leave. Today."

"To go where?" he asked her.

But she merely shook her head.

"Don't leave me, Jane," he said. "I cannot let you go. Can you not see that I need a nurse?" He held up his hands, palms out. "For at least another month?"

She shook her head again and he sat back in his chair and regarded her, narrow-eyed.

"Why are you so eager to leave me? Have I been such a tyrant to you, Jane? Have I treated you so badly? Spoken to you so irritably?"

"That you have, your grace," she told him.

"It is because I have been pampered and fawned over since my youth," he said. "I did not mean anything by it, you know. And you have never let me browbeat you, Jane. *You* have been the one to browbeat *me*."

She smiled, but in truth she felt like bawling. Not just because of the frightening unknown into which she would be going but because of what she would be leaving behind, though she had tried determinedly not to think of it all morning.

"You must leave here," he said abruptly. "On that we are agreed, Jane. After last night it is even more imperative that you leave."

She nodded and looked down at her hands in her lap. If she had hoped he would try harder to persuade her to stay on the slim excuse of his scraped hands, she was to be disappointed.

"But you could live somewhere else," he said, "where we could see each other daily away from the prying eyes and gossiping tongues of the *beau monde*. Would you like that?"

She raised her eyes slowly to his. She could not possibly misunderstand his meaning. What she could not believe was her own reaction, or lack of it. Her lack of outrage. Her yearning. The temptation.

He was looking steadily back at her, his eyes very dark.

"I would look after you, Jane," he said. "You could live in style. A home and servants and a carriage of your own. Clothes and jewels. A decent salary. A certain freedom. Far more freedom than a married woman enjoys, anyway."

"In exchange for lying with you," she said quietly. It was not a question. The answer was too obvious.

"I have a certain expertise," he told her. "It would be my delight to use it for your pleasure, Jane. It would be a very fair exchange, you see. You cannot tell me in all honesty, can you, that you have never thought of sharing a bed with me? That you have never wanted it? That you are in any way repelled by me? Come, be honest. I will know if you lie."

"I do not have to lie," she said. "I do not have to answer at all. I will have five hundred pounds plus my three weeks' salary. I can go wherever I want and do whatever I want. That is a fortune for a frugal person, your grace. I am not compelled to accept *carte blanche* from you."

He laughed softly. "I do not believe, Jane," he said, "that I would ever be fool enough to try to compel you to do anything. I am not seducing you. I am not tempting you. I am offering you a proposition, a business one, if you wish. You need a home and a source of income beyond what you already have. You need some security and someone to take your mind off your lone state, I daresay. You are a woman with sexual needs, after all, and you are sexually drawn to me. And I need a mistress. I have been womanless for an alarmingly long time. I have even taken to cornering nurses outside their rooms when I escort them there and stealing kisses. I need someone I can visit at my leisure, someone who can satisfy my own sexual needs. You can, Jane. I desire you. And of course I have the means with which to enable you to live in style."

And in hiding.

Jane looked at her hands, but her mind was considering his offer. She could not quite believe that she was doing so, but she deliberately stopped herself from reacting with simple horror and outrage.

Even assuming she was never caught, she could never go back to being Lady Sara Illingsworth. She could never come into the inheritance due her on her twenty-fifth birthday. She had to think practically of her future. She had to live somewhere. She had to work. Five hundred pounds would not last forever no matter how frugally she lived. She was perfectly capable of taking employment fitted for a gentlewoman—as a teacher or governess or lady's companion. But to do so she would have to make application, she would have to have references, she would have to risk discovery.

The alternative was to grub out an existence at menial tasks. Or to become the Duke of Tresham's mistress.

"Well, Jane?" he asked into the lengthy silence that had followed his last words. "What do you say?"

She drew a deep breath and looked up at him.

She would not have to leave him.

She would lie with him. Outside wedlock. She would be a mistress, a paid woman.

"What sort of a house?" she asked. "And how many servants? How much salary? And how are my interests to be protected? How am I to know you will not dismiss me out of hand as soon as you have tired of me?"

He smiled slowly at her. "That's my girl," he said softly. "Feisty."

"There is to be a contract," she told him. "We will discuss and agree to its terms together. It is to be drawn up and duly checked and signed by both of us before I become your mistress. In the meanwhile I cannot stay here. Is there already a house? Are you one of those gentlemen who keeps a house especially for your mistresses? If so, then I will move to it. If we cannot come to an agreement on a contract, then I will, of course, move out again."

"Of course I have such a house," he said. "Empty of all but two servants at present, I hasten to add. I will take you there later, Jane, after Marsh has returned with news from my brother's stable. I have to do something to fill in the time before word comes from Brighton. We will discuss terms tomorrow."

"Very well." She got to her feet and picked up the bowl and the bandages. "I will have my bag packed and will be ready to leave whenever you summon me, your grace."

"I have the feeling," he said with deceptive meekness as she reached the door and turned the handle, "that you are going to drive a very hard bargain, Jane. I have never before had a mistress who insisted upon a contract."

"The more fool they," she said. "And I am not your mistress yet."

He was chuckling softly when she closed the door.

She leaned back against it, thankful that there were no servants in sight. All her bravado went from her, and with it all the strength in her legs.

What on earth had she just done?

What had she agreed to—or *almost* agreed to?

She tried to feel a suitable degree of horror. But all she could really feel was enormous relief that she would not be leaving him today, never to see him again.

12

It was a house he had owned for five years. It was on a decent street in a respectable neighborhood. He had had it decorated and furnished at great expense. He had hired decent, reliable servants, two of whom had been there for all five years, staying to maintain the house even when it had no occupant.

It was a house of which Jocelyn was fond, representing as it did a world of private and sensual delights. And yet as soon as he stepped across the threshold with Jane Ingleby, he felt uncomfortable.

It was not just the house. It was the whole idea of her becoming his mistress. He wanted her, yes. In bed. In all the usual ways. Yet somehow the idea of Jane Ingleby as his mistress did not seem quite to fit.

"Jacobs," he said to the butler, who bowed deferentially, "this is Miss Ingleby. She will be living here for a while. You and Mrs. Jacobs will take your orders from her."

If Jacobs was surprised to find his master choosing a mistress from among the working classes—she was, of course, wearing the cheap gray cloak and bonnet she had worn in Hyde Park—he was far too well trained to show it.

"We will do our best to see to your comfort, ma'am," he said, bowing to her.

"Thank you, Mr. Jacobs," she said, inclining her head regally before he withdrew discreetly to the nether regions of the house.

"They will hire more servants, of course," Jocelyn said, taking Jane's elbow and beginning a tour of the house with her. "Shall I give the orders, or would you prefer to be in charge of it yourself?"

"Neither yet," she said coolly, looking around the sitting room with its lavender carpet and furnishings, its pink draperies and frilled cushions. "I may not be staying longer than a few days. We have no agreement yet."

"But we will." He guided her toward the dining room. "I shall come in the morning for our discussion, Jane. But first I will take you to a modiste I know on Bond Street. She will measure you for the clothes you will need."

"I will wear my own clothes, thank you," he was not surprised to hear, "until I am your mistress. If we come to an agreement on that point, then you may summon a dressmaker here if you wish. I am not going to set foot on Bond Street."

"Because it will be known that you are my mistress?" he asked, watching her run her fingertips over the polished surface of the round dining table—it could be considerably enlarged to seat guests, but when dining alone with his mistress he preferred to be within touching distance. "You think that a matter for shame? I assure you it is not. Courtesans of the highest class, Jane, are almost on a par with ladies. Above them in some ways. They often have considerably more influence. You will be highly respected as my mistress."

"If I become your mistress, your grace," she said, "I will be neither ashamed nor proud. I will be taking the purely practical step of securing employment that will be both lucrative and congenial to me."

He laughed. "Congenial, Jane?" he said. "You bowl me over with your enthusiasm. Shall we go upstairs?"

He wondered if she felt as passionless as she looked. But he remembered the two embraces they had shared and drew his own conclusions, especially from the one in the music room. She had been anything but passionless on that occasion. And even outside her room, after she had sung for his guests, there had been a yearning that he might have kindled had he chosen.

He was still in the doorway of the bedchamber when she, a few steps ahead of him, turned toward him.

"One thing must be made perfectly clear even today," she said, her hands clasped at her waist, her chin lifted as if for battle, a martial gleam in her eyes. "If I decide to stay, everything in this house has to be changed."

"Indeed?" He raised his eyebrows and his quizzing glass and took his time looking about the room. The wide, canopied, mahogany bed with its intricately carved posts was covered in brocaded silk, with the same silk pleated in a rosebud design on the canopy. The bed curtains were of heavy, costly velvet, as were the window draperies. The carpet was soft and thick underfoot.

All were a rich scarlet.

"Indeed!" she replied firmly, pure scorn in her voice. "This house is disgusting. It is a caricature of a love nest. I will not sleep in this room even alone. I will certainly not lie here with you. I would feel like a whore."

Sometimes one had to take a stand with Jane Ingleby. The trouble was he was unaccustomed to taking stands since nobody had ever made it necessary before now.

"Jane," he said, planting his booted feet apart, clasping his hands at his back, schooling his features into their most forbidding aspect, "I believe it is necessary to remind you that I am not the one being offered employment. I have made you an offer, which you are free to accept or reject. There are plenty who would rush to take your place here given half a chance."

She stared at him.

"My mistake, your grace," she said after a few silent moments, during which he had to concentrate hard not to shift uncomfortably from foot to foot. "I thought we had agreed to discuss terms. But I see you have reverted to that ridiculous posturing as autocratic aristocrat, whose will no sane person would even dream of crossing. You had better go and give someone else half a chance. I am leaving."

She took one purposeful step toward him. Only one. He stood his ground in the doorway. She could try going through him if she wished.

"What is so objectionable about the house?" he was weak enough to ask her. "I have never before had a single complaint about it."

But she was quite right, damn it. He had felt it as soon as he had stepped inside the house with her. It was is if he had been entering a strange dwelling and seeing it for the first time. This house was just not Jane.

"I can think of two words to describe it," she said. "I could probably think of a whole dictionary full if I had more time. But those that leap to mind are *sleaze* and *fluff*. Neither of which is tolerable to me."

He pursed his lips. Those two words perfectly described the house. He had had the sitting room designed for a feminine taste, of course, not his own. Or what he had imagined was feminine taste. Effie had always appeared perfectly at home there. So had Lisa and Marie and Bridget. And this room? Well, in candlelight it could always heighten his sexual desire. The predominant reds did marvelous things to the color of naked female flesh.

"It is one of my first conditions," she said. "This room

and the sitting room. They are to be redone to my instructions. This point is not negotiable. Take it or leave it."

"One of?" He raised his eyebrows. "Tell me, Jane, am I to be allowed to write some conditions of my own into this contract of ours? Or am I to be your slave? I would like to know. Actually the prospect of being a slave has a certain appeal. Does it come with chains and whips?" He grinned at her.

She did not smile.

"A contract is a two-way agreement," she said. "Of course there will be certain things that you will insist upon. Like unlimited access to my—"

"Favors?" he suggested when she floundered.

"Yes." She nodded briskly.

"Unlimited access." He gazed steadily at her and was gratified to see that the rosiness in her cheeks owed nothing to the redness of her surroundings. "Even when you are unwilling, Jane? Even when you have a headache or some other malady? You would agree in writing to act the martyr even if my appetites prove insatiable?"

She thought for a moment. "I imagine it would be a reasonable demand for you to make, your grace," she said. "That is what mistresses are for, after all."

"Poppycock!" He narrowed his gaze on her. "If that is the attitude with which you approach the liaison, Jane, I want none of you. I do not want a body to plow whenever my sexual urges are out of control. There are innumerable brothels I might use for such a purpose. I want someone with whom to relax. Someone with whom to take the ultimate pleasure. Someone to pleasure in return."

The color deepened in her cheeks, but she kept her spine straight and her chin raised.

"What if you came here ten days in a row and I said no each time?" she asked him.

"Then I would consider myself a damnable failure," he said. "I would probably go home and blow my brains out."

She laughed suddenly and looked so vividly beautiful and golden amid the scarlet that he felt his breath catch in his throat.

"How absurd!" she said.

"If for ten straight days a man cannot entice his mistress into bed," he said meekly, "he might as well be dead, Jane. What is there for him to live for if his sexual appeal is gone?"

She tipped her head to one side and regarded him thoughtfully. "You are joking," she said. "But you are half serious too. Being a *man* is very important to you, is it not?"

"And being a *woman* is not important to you?"

She considered her answer. It was characteristic of her, he had noticed before, not always to rush into saying the first thing that came into her head.

"Being *me* is important to me," she said. "And since I am a woman, then I suppose being a woman is important too. But I do not have a mental image of what a perfect woman is, of what other people look for in me because I am a woman. I do not slavishly pattern my appearance or my behavior on any image. I need to be true to myself."

Jocelyn felt a sudden wave of amusement.

"I have never stood in this doorway before," he said, "halfway across the room from a woman, discussing the nature of gender and sexuality. We should by now, you know, have consummated our intent to contract a certain relationship. We should be lying exhausted and naked and mutually satisfied on that bed."

This time there was no other way to describe her face than to say she blushed.

"I suppose," she said, "you expected that once you had got me here I would succumb to your devastating charm and the allure of this room?"

It was exactly what he had expected—or hoped for anyway.

"And I suppose," he said with a sigh, "you will not allow me to lay one lascivious finger on you until this room looks like a monk's cell. Go ahead, then, Jane. Give your orders to Jacobs. Do whatever you wish with my house. I will do my part and pay the bills. Shall we go back downstairs? I daresay Mrs. Jacobs has a tea tray ready and is bursting with curiosity to catch a glimpse of you."

"She can bring it to the dining room," Jane said, sweeping past him when at last he stepped to one side of the doorway.

"Where will you sleep tonight?" he asked, following her down. "On the dining room table?"

"I will find somewhere," she assured him. "You need not concern yourself about it, your grace."

He walked away from the house an hour later, cane and painfully scraped palm and all, having dismissed his town carriage earlier. He was eager to hear Marsh's report from Ferdinand's stable. It might be impossible to prove that any of the Forbeses had had access to the curricle. But all he needed was the possibility that the broken axle had come courtesy of one of them.

Then they would have the Duke of Tresham to deal with.

He wondered if word had yet arrived about the result of the race. Unusually for him, all he was really concerned about was that Ferdinand had got to Brighton safely.

He should never have suggested that Jane Ingleby become his mistress, he thought. There was something all wrong about it.

And yet his loins ached for her.

Why had the damned woman not simply tiptoed on past that morning in Hyde Park when she had seen that there was a duel pending, as any decent woman would have done?

If he had never set eyes upon her, he would not now be walking around with the curious sensation that either he or his world was standing on its head.

She slept on the sitting room sofa. The color scheme and all the frills and knickknacks were in atrociously bad taste, but at least it was not as vulgar a room as the bedchamber.

While they had talked in that room during the afternoon, she had had lurid, uncomfortable images of lying tangled with him on the bed amid all that scarlet silk. She did not know what full sexual arousal felt like, but it must be something very like what she had felt then. What she had agreed to—or was about to agree to—had become appallingly real to her.

How could she be his mistress? she had asked herself, sitting upright on the sofa before lying down to sleep. She simply could not do it unless she felt something for him as a person. Did she? She did not *love* him, of course—that would be patently rash. But did she like him? Feel some affection for him? Some respect?

She thought of their endless verbal scraps—and smiled unexpectedly. He was a haughty, tyrannical, thoroughly irritating man. But she had the distinct impression that he enjoyed the way she stood up to him. And he *did* respect her opinions, even if he never admitted as much. The fact that she was alone tonight, their liaison unconsummated, was proof enough of that. And there was his strangely admirable sense of honor. He had faced Lord Oliver in a duel rather than call Lady Oliver a liar.

Jane sighed. Ah, yes, she liked him well enough. And, of course, there was the artistic, more sensitive side to his nature, which she had glimpsed that night in the music room. And his intelligence. And his sense of humor. All the many fascinating facets of his character that he kept carefully hidden away from the world.

And there was their mutual desire for each other. Jane felt no doubt that it *was* mutual. If she had been just any woman, any prospective mistress to him, he would have sent her on her way as soon as she raised the question of a contract. But she must remember—always, for as long as their liaison lasted—that it was only passion he felt. Sexual passion. She must never mistake the feelings of the Duke of Tresham for love.

It was not going to be easy to be his mistress.

Jane slept on the sofa and dreamed of Charles. Her closest friend. Her beau. Like someone from another lifetime. He was sitting in the rose arbor at Candleford with her, telling her about his sister's new baby and telling her too how they would set up their own nursery as soon as they were able after her twenty-fifth birthday freed her to marry whomever she chose.

She awoke with wet cheeks. She had deliberately not thought of Charles after her flight from home. She had succeeded all too well. Why had she not thought of going to him now that she had the money with which to travel? Was he still at his sister's in Somersetshire? Or had he returned to Cornwall? She could have found a way to reach him without being caught. He would surely know what to do, how to protect her, how to hide her if necessary. Most important of all, he would believe her story. He knew how desperately eager the new Earl of Durbury was that she marry his son. He knew how despicable Sidney could be, especially when he was in his cups.

She could still do it, of course. She had been paid yesterday before leaving Dudley House. She had not yet become the Duke of Tresham's mistress. She could leave before he came back and avoid the necessity of giving up her virtue.

The very idea of such a fate would surely have brought on a fit of the vapors just a few weeks ago. Now, with surprising belatedness, she had thought of a decent alternative.

But the trouble was that she did not love Charles. Not as a woman should love her husband. Not as Mama had loved Papa. She had always known it, of course. But she had always *wanted* to love Charles because she liked him and because he loved her.

If she went to him now, if he somehow extricated her from the tangle she was in, she would be bound to him for life. She would not have minded just a few weeks before. Friendship and affection would have been enough.

No longer.

Was being the duke's mistress preferable to honorable marriage with Charles, then?

It was a question Jane could not answer to her own satisfaction before his grace's arrival in the middle of the morning. It was a question whose answer she recognized with some reluctance after she had heard his knock and had opened the sitting room door to see him step into the hall and hand his hat and gloves and cane to Mr. Jacobs. He brought all his energy and restlessness and sheer maleness with him—and Jane realized she had missed him.

"Jane." He strode toward her, and they retreated into the sitting room together. "He won. By scarcely the length of his horses' noses. He was behind a full length coming into the final bend, but he accelerated into it and took Berriwether by surprise. They thundered into Brighton almost neck and neck. But Ferdinand won, and three-quarters of the members of White's have gone into mourning."

"He came to no harm, then?" she said. "I am glad." She might have commented again on how foolish such races were, but he looked so very pleased with himself. And she really was glad. Lord Ferdinand Dudley was a pleasant, charming young man.

"No. No harm." He frowned suddenly. "He does not choose his servants wisely, though. He has a valet who does not allow for the fact that a man sometimes turns his head without warning while being shaved. And he has a groom who allows half the world into his stable and carriage house the day before a race in order to admire the tools of his master's trade. There is no proving who arranged for Ferdinand's death during that race."

"But you suspect Sir Anthony Forbes or one of his brothers?" she asked him. She seated herself on the sofa, and he sat beside her.

"More than suspect." He looked about the room as he spoke. "It is the way they work. I did something to their sister; they do something to my brother. They will be sorry, of course. I will deal with them. What have you done to this room?"

She was relieved at the change of subject.

"I have just removed a few things," she told him. "All the cushions and a few of the ornaments. I have ideas for extensive changes to both this room and the bedchamber. I would not be needlessly extravagant, but even so the cost would be considerable."

"Quincy will take care of the bills," he said with a careless wave of one hand. "But how long is all this going to take, Jane? I have the feeling you are not going to allow me to bed you until everything is to your liking, are you?"

"No," she said with what she hoped was suitable firmness. "A week should be sufficient once the order is given. I have spoken to Mr. Jacobs, and he says the suppliers will fall all over themselves to be prompt as soon as he mentions your name."

The duke did not answer her. Obviously the truth of that statement was no surprise to him.

"Let us discuss this contract, then," he said. "Apart from *carte blanche* to tear down my house and rebuild it, what are your demands, Jane? I will pay you a monthly salary five times higher than what I paid you as a nurse. You will have your own carriage and as many servants as you deem necessary. You may clothe yourself in as much finery as you wish with all the accessories and direct the bills to me. I will be generous with jewels, though I would prefer to buy those myself. I will take on full responsibility for the support and future placement of any children of our liaison. Have I missed anything?"

Jane had turned suddenly cold. Her own naïveté quite mortified her.

"How many children do you presently have?" Foolishly she had not thought of becoming with child.

His eyebrows rose. "You can always be relied upon to ask

unaskable questions, Jane," he said. "I have none. Most women who make their living by such arrangements as this know how to prevent conception. I assume you do not. You *are* a virgin, are you not?"

It took a great deal of fortitude to keep her eyes from sliding away from his very direct gaze. She wished blushes were as much within her control.

"Yes." She kept her chin up. "There is one expense you do not need to burden yourself with. I do not need a carriage."

"Why not?" He rested one elbow on the back of the sofa and set his closed fist against his mouth. His dark eyes did not look away from hers. "You will need to shop, Jane, and get out to see the sights. It would be unwise to rely upon me to take you about. Shopping bores me. When I come here, I will be far more eager to take you to bed than out for a drive."

"The servants can shop for food," she said. "And if you object to the clothes I wear, you can send dressmakers here. I have no wish to go out."

"Is what you are about to do so shameful to you, then?" he asked her. "You really feel you cannot show your face to the world ever again?"

She had answered that the day before. But it would be as well, she thought, if he believed it. Strangely, it was not true. Life had become a practical business, which she must direct and control as best she was able.

He did not speak again for some time. The silence stretched between them while he stared broodingly at her and she gazed back, uncomfortable but unwilling to look away.

"There is an alternative," he said at last. "One that would bring you fame and fortune and great esteem, Jane. One that would save you from the degradation of bedding with a rake."

"I do not consider it degrading," she told him.

"No?" He lifted his free hand and cupped her chin. He ran his thumb lightly across her lips. "I am not intimate with the inner circles of high culture, Jane, but I daresay my word carries some weight almost everywhere. I could introduce you to Lord Heath or the Earl of Raymore, two of the more prominent patrons of the arts. I have every confidence that if either one of them heard your voice, he would set your feet on the road to fame. You are that good, you know. You would not need me."

She gazed at him in some surprise. He wanted her—she did not doubt that. But he was prepared to let her go? Even to help her be independent of him? Quite unconsciously she parted her lips and touched her tongue to the pad of his thumb.

His eyes met and held hers. And she felt raw desire knife down inside her. She had not intended to provoke such a moment. Neither had he, she suspected.

"I do not want a career as a singer," she said.

It was the truth even apart from the fact that she could not flirt with danger by going before the public gaze again. She did not want to use her voice to earn a living. She wanted to use it for the pleasure of people who were close to her. She had no yearning for fame.

He leaned forward and set his mouth where his thumb had been. He kissed her hard.

"But you do want one as my mistress?" he said. "On your terms? What are they, then? What do you want that I have not already offered?"

"Security," she said. "I want your agreement to pay my salary until my twenty-fifth birthday even if you should dismiss me before then. Provided I am not the one to break our agreement, of course. I am twenty now, by the way."

"For five years," he said. "And how will you support yourself after that, Jane?"

She did not know. She was supposed to come into her inheritance then—all of her father's fortune that had not been entailed on his heir. But of course she might never be able to claim it. She would not suddenly stop being a fugitive simply because she had reached the magic age of freedom.

She shook her head.

"Perhaps," he said, "I will never tire of you, Jane."

"Nonsense!" she told him. "Of course you will. And long before four and a half years have passed. That is why I must protect my future."

He smiled at her. He did not smile nearly often enough. And altogether too often for her peace of mind. She wondered if he knew what devastating charm his smile hinted at.

"Very well, then," he said. "It will be written into the contract. Salary until dismissal or your twenty-fifth birthday, whichever comes later. Anything else?"

She shook her head. "What about your conditions?" she asked him. "We have come to an agreement on what you will do for me. What must I do for you?"

He shrugged. "Be here for me," he said. "Have sexual relations with me whenever I can persuade you that you want them as much as I do. That is all, Jane. A relationship between a man and his mistress cannot be legislated, you know. I will not even try to insist upon obedience and subjection, you see. You would not be able to keep such a promise even if you could be persuaded to make it. And damn me for a fool for saying this aloud, but I believe it is your very impudence that attracts me. Shall I have Quincy draw up the contract and bring it here for your perusal? I imagine he will be vastly diverted by such a task. I will not bring it myself, Jane. I will not come again until you send for me. I will assume when I do hear from you that the bedchamber abovestairs is ready for use."

"Very well, your grace," she said as he got to his feet. She stood up too. A week was going to seem like an eternity.

He framed her face with his hands. "That will have to change too, Jane," he said. "I cannot have you *your gracing* me when we are in bed together. My name is Jocelyn."

She had not known his name. No one had ever used it in her hearing. "Jocelyn," she said softly.

His very dark eyes were normally hard and quite opaque. It was impossible to see more of the man than he was willing to reveal—and that was usually not very much, she suspected. But for a moment after she spoke his name, Jane had the distinct feeling that something opened up behind his eyes and that she was falling into them.

For only a moment.

He dropped his hands and turned toward the door.

"One week," he said. "If the renovations are not complete by then, Jane, a few heads are going to roll. You will warn all the workmen involved?"

"Yes, your grace," she said. "Jocelyn."

He looked over his shoulder at her and opened his mouth to speak. But he changed his mind and strode from the room without saying another word.

13

Many of Mick Boden's acquaintances envied him his job. There was a certain glamour about being one of the famed Bow Street Runners. The common fallacy was that he spent his working days literally running to earth all of London's and half of England's most desperate criminals and hauling them off to the nearest magistrate and the just reward for their dastardly deeds. They saw his life as one of endless adventure and danger and action—and success.

Most of the time his job was routine and rather dull. Sometimes he wondered why he was not a dockyard worker or a crossing sweeper. This was one of those times. Lady Sara Illingsworth, a lady of a mere twenty years who had grown up in the country and presumably had no town bronze, was proving to be unexpectedly elusive. In almost a month of searching he had discovered no trace of her beyond those first few days.

The Earl of Durbury still stubbornly insisted she was in

London. There was nowhere else she could have gone, he claimed, since she had no friends or relatives elsewhere apart from an old neighbor now living with her husband in Somersetshire. But she was not there.

Something told Mick that the earl was right. She was here somewhere. But she had not returned to Lady Webb's, even though the baroness was now back in town. She had not contacted either her late father's man of business or the present earl's. If she had been spending lavishly, she had not been doing it in any of the more fashionable shops. If she had been trying to sell or pawn any of the stolen jewels, she had not done it at any of the places Mick knew about—and he prided himself on knowing them all. If she had tried to secure respectable lodgings in a decent neighborhood, she had not done so at any of the houses on whose doors he and his assistants had tirelessly knocked. She had not sought employment in any of the houses at which he inquired—and he had asked at all the likely possibilities except the grandest mansions in Mayfair. She would not have been foolhardy enough to apply at one of those, he had concluded. None of the agencies had been applied to by anyone bearing any of the names Mick thought she might be using. None remembered a tall, slim, blond beauty.

And so he found himself yet again with nothing to report to the Earl of Durbury. It was lowering. It was enough to make a man think seriously about changing his line of work. It was also enough to arouse all a man's stubborn determination not to be thwarted by a mere slip of a girl.

"She has not gone into service, sir," he said with conviction to an exasperated, red-faced earl, who was doubtless thinking of the hefty bill he had run up at the Pulteney in a month. "She would not have sought employment as a governess or lady's companion—too public. For the same reason she would not have taken work as a shop clerk. She would have to work somewhere she would not be seen. Some workshop. A dressmaker's or a milliner's, perhaps."

If she was working at all. The earl had never told him exactly how much money the girl had stolen. Mick was beginning to suspect it could not have been much. Not enough to enable her to live in style, anyway. Surely such a young, inexperienced woman would have made mistakes by now if she had had a vast fortune to tempt her into the open.

"What are you waiting for, then?" his lordship asked coldly. "Why are you not out searching every workshop in London? Are the illustrious Bow Street Runners to be outsmarted by a mere girl?" His voice was heavy with sarcasm.

"Am I searching for a murderess?" Mick Boden asked. "How is your son, sir?"

"My son," the earl said irritably, "is at death's door. You are searching for a murderess. I suggest you find her before she repeats her crime."

And so Mick began his search anew. London, of course, had more than its fair share of workshops. He just wished he knew for sure what name the girl was using. And he wished that she had not somehow managed to hide her blond hair, apparently her most distinctive feature.

It was a long week. Jocelyn spent far too much of it drinking and gaming by night and trying to whip himself into shape during the day by spending long hours honing his fencing skills and building his stamina in the boxing ring at Gentleman Jackson's. His leg was responding well to exercise.

Ferdinand was incensed when he learned what had happened to his curricle and was determined to ferret out the Forbes brothers, who had dropped out of sight the day after the duel, and slap a glove in all their separate faces. At first he would not agree that it was his brother's quarrel. It was his life, after all, that had been threatened. But Jocelyn was insistent.

Angeline had had a fit of the vapors at the news of the

broken axle, had summoned Heyward from the House, and then, to divert her shaken nerves, had bought a new bonnet.

"I wonder that there is any fruit left on any of the stalls at Covent Garden, Angeline," Jocelyn observed, viewing it with a pained expression through his quizzing glass as he rode through Hyde Park at the fashionable hour one day and came across her sporting it as she drove in an open barouche with her mother-in-law. "I daresay it is all decorating that monstrosity on your head."

"It is all the crack," she replied, preening, "no matter what you say, Tresham. You simply must promise not to drive a curricle again. You or Ferdie. You will kill yourselves and I will never recover my nerves. But Heyward said it was no accident. I daresay it was one of the Forbeses. If you do not discover which one and call him to account, I shall be ashamed to call myself a Dudley."

"You do not now," he reminded her dryly before tipping his hat to the Dowager Lady Heyward and riding on. "You took your husband's name when you married him, Angeline."

He was not as impatient as his brother and sister to find the Forbeses and punish them. The time would come. They must know it as surely as he did. In the meantime, let them remain in their hiding place, imagining what would happen when they finally came face to face with him. Let them sweat it out.

Several people asked about Jane Ingleby. She had created even more of a stir with her singing than he had expected. He was asked who she was, if she was still employed at Dudley House, if she was to sing anywhere else, who her voice teacher had been. Viscount Kimble even asked him outright one evening at White's if she was his mistress—a question that won for himself a cool stare through the ducal quizzing glass.

Strange, that. Jocelyn had never before been secretive about his mistresses. Indeed, he had often used the house for dinners and parties when he wished them to be a little less formal than such occasions at Dudley House inevitably were. His mistresses had always also been his hostesses—a role that would fit Jane admirably.

But he did not want his friends to know she was in his keeping. It seemed somehow unfair to her, though he would not have been able to explain if he had tried. He told them she had had temporary employment with him and was now gone, he knew not where.

"A devilish shame, Tresham," Conan Brougham said. "That voice ought to be brought to the attention of Raymore. She could earn a more than decent living with it."

"I would have offered her employment myself, Tresh," Kimble said, "on her back, that is, not with her voice. But I feared I might be trespassing on your preserves. If you hear where she is, you might drop a word in my ear."

Jocelyn, feeling unaccustomedly hostile to one of his closest friends, changed the subject.

He walked home alone later that same night despite the danger of attack by footpads. He had never feared them. He carried a stout cane and he was handy with his fives. He would rather enjoy a scuffle with two or three ruffians, he had often thought. Perhaps any ruffians who had ever spotted him had been intelligent enough to estimate correctly their chances against him. He had never been attacked.

The mention of Jane Ingleby had made him unbearably restless. It had been five days, and it had seemed more like five weeks. Quincy had personally taken over that silly contract on the second day. To Jocelyn's surprise she had signed it. He had expected her to haggle over a few small details out of sheer perverseness.

She was officially his mistress.

His virgin, unbedded mistress. How everyone who knew him would jeer if they knew he had engaged a mistress who had banished him from his own house, insisted upon a written contract, and kept the relationship unconsummated a full week after he had made her the proposition.

He laughed aloud suddenly, stopping in the middle of an empty, silent street. Ornery Jane. Even during the consummation she would doubtless not play the part of timid, shrinking virgin being deflowered.

Innocent, naive Jane, who did not realize how clever she was being. He had desired her a week ago. He had yearned for her five days ago. By now he was on fire for her. He was finding it difficult to think of anything else. Jane with her golden hair, into whose web he could hardly wait to be ensnared.

He was forced to wait two more days before a note finally arrived. It was characteristically brief and to the point.

"The work on the house is complete," she wrote. "You may call at your convenience."

Cool, unloverlike words that set him ablaze.

Jane was pacing. She had sent the note to Dudley House immediately after breakfast, but she knew that often he left home early and did not return until late at night. He might not read the note until tomorrow. He might not come for another day or two.

But she was pacing. And trying in vain not to look through the front-facing windows more often than once every ten minutes.

She was wearing a new dress of delicate spring-green muslin. High-waisted, with a modest neckline and short, puffed sleeves, it was of simple design. But it was expertly styled to mold and flatter her figure above its high waistline and to fall in soft folds to her ankles. It had been very costly. Accustomed to the prices of a country dressmaker, Jane had been shocked. But she had not sent the Bond Street modiste and her two assistants away. The duke had selected them and sent them with specific instructions on the number and nature of garments she was to have.

She had selected the fabrics and designs herself, favoring light colors over vivid ones and simplicity of design over the ornate, but she had not argued over the number or the expense, except flatly to insist upon only one walking dress and only one carriage dress. She had no intention of walking or driving out any time soon.

He would not have given her *carte blanche* over the house renovations if he had not intended coming back, she thought as she leaned close to the window yet again early in the afternoon. He would not have sent the modiste or the contract. Indeed, he had sent the latter twice, first two copies for her to peruse and sign and return, and then just one copy to keep, with his own signature—*Tresham*—scrawled large and bold beneath her own. Mr. Jacobs had witnessed her signature, Mr. Quincy his.

But she could not shake the conviction that he would not come back. The week had been endless. Surely by now he must have forgotten her. Surely by now there was someone else.

She could not understand—and did not care to explore—her own anxiety.

But all anxiety fled suddenly to be replaced by a bursting of joy when she saw a familiar figure striding along the street in the direction of the house. He was walking without a limp, she noticed before turning and hurrying to open the sitting room door. She stopped herself from rushing to open the front door too. She stood where she was, waiting eagerly for his knock, waiting for Mr. Jacobs to answer it.

She had forgotten how broad-shouldered he was, how dark, how forbidding in aspect, how restless with pent-up energy, how—male. He was frowning as usual when he handed his hat and gloves to the butler. He did not look at her until he had done so. Then he strode toward the sitting room and fixed his eyes on her at last.

Eyes that looked not only at her dress and face and hair, she thought, but on everything that was her. Eyes that burned into her with a strange, intense light she had not seen there before.

The eyes of a man come to claim his mistress?

"Well, Jane," he said, "you have finished playing house at last?"

Had she expected a kiss on the hand? On the lips? Soft lover's words?

"There was much to do," she replied coolly, "to convert this house into a dwelling rather than a brothel."

"And you have done it?" He strode into the sitting room and looked around, his booted feet apart, his hands at his back. He seemed to fill the room.

"Hmm," he said. "You did not tear down the walls, then?"

"No," she said. "I kept a great deal. I have not been unnecessarily extravagant."

"One would hate to have seen Quincy's face if you had been," he retorted. "He has been somewhat green about the gills for the past few days as it is. I understand that bills have been flooding in."

"That is at least partly your fault," she told him. "I did not need so many clothes and accessories. But the dressmaker you sent said you were adamant and she dared not allow your orders to be contradicted."

"Some women, you see," he said, "know their place, Jane. They know how to be submissive and obedient."

"And how to make a great deal of money in the process," she added. "I kept the lavender color in here, as you can see, though I would not have chosen it had I been planning the room from scratch. Combined with gray and silver instead of pink, and without all the frills and silly knickknacks, it looks rather delicate and elegant. I like it. I can live here comfortably."

"Can you, Jane?" He turned his head and looked at her—again with those burning eyes. "And have you done as well with the bedchamber? Or am I going to find two hard, narrow cots in there and a hair shirt laid out on each?"

"If you find scarlet a necessary titillation," she said, trying to ignore the thumping of her heart and hoping it did not betray itself in her voice, "then I daresay you will not like what I have done to the room. But I like it, and that is what counts. I am the one who has to sleep there every night."

"I am being forbidden to do so, then?" He raised his eyebrows.

That foolish blush again. The one sign of emotion it was impossible to disguise. She could feel it hot on her cheeks.

"No," she said. "I have agreed—in writing—that you are to be free to come and go as you please. But I daresay you do not intend to *live* here as I do. Only to come when you . . . Well, when you . . ." She had lost her command of the English language.

"Want sex with you?" he suggested.

"Yes." She nodded. "Then."

"And I am not allowed to come when I do not?" He pursed his lips and regarded her in silence for a few uncomfortable moments. "Is that in the contract? That I can come here only for sex, Jane? Not for tea? Or conversation? Or perhaps just to sleep?"

It would be like a real relationship. It was too seductive a thought.

"Would you like to see the bedchamber?" she asked.

He regarded her for a few moments longer before the smile came—that slight smile that lit his eyes and lifted the corners of his mouth and turned Jane's knees weak.

"To see the new furnishings?" he asked her. "Or to have sex, Jane?"

She found his raw choice of words disconcerting. But any more euphemistic way of phrasing it would mean the same thing.

"I am your mistress," she said.

"Yes, so you are." He strolled closer to her, his hands still at his back. He dipped his head closer and gazed into her eyes.

"No sign of steely martyrdom. You are ready for the consummation, then?"

"Yes." She also thought she was ready to collapse in an ignominious heap at his feet, but that fact had nothing to do with a weak resolve, only with weak knees.

He straightened up and offered his arm.

"Let us go, then," he said.

The furnishings had not changed, only the color scheme. But he would scarcely have known he was in the same room if someone had blindfolded him, picked him up bodily, and deposited him here. It was all sage green and cream and gold. It was elegance itself.

If there was one thing Jane Ingleby had an abundance of, it was good taste, plus an eye for color and design. Another skill learned at the orphanage? Or at the rectory or country manor or wherever the devil it was she had grown up?

But he had not come to inspect the room's furnishings.

"Well?" Her eyes were bright, her cheeks flushed. "What do you think?"

"What I think, Jane," he said, narrowing his gaze on her, "is that I will see your hair down now at last. Take out the pins."

It was not dressed with its customary severity. It was waved and coiled in a manner that complemented the pretty, elegant dress she wore. But he wanted to see it flowing free.

She removed the pins deftly and shook her head.

Ah. It reached to below her waist, as she had said it did. A river of pure, shining, rippling gold. She had appeared beautiful before. Even in the hideous maid's dress and the atrocious cap she had been beautiful. But now . . .

There simply were not words. He clasped his hands behind him. He had waited too long to rush now.

"Jocelyn." She tipped her head to one side and looked

directly at him with her very blue eyes. "I am on unfamiliar ground here. You will have to lead the way."

He nodded, wondering at the great wave of—oh, not desire exactly that washed over him. Longing? That sort of gut-deep, soul-deep yearning that very occasionally caught him unawares and was shaken firmly off again. He associated it with music and painting. But now it was his name that had aroused it.

"Jocelyn is a name that has been in my family for generations," he said. "I acquired it when I was still in the womb. I cannot think of a single soul until now who has spoken it aloud to me."

Her eyes widened. "Your mother?" she said. "Your father? Your brother and sister? Surely—"

"No." He shrugged out of his tight-fitting coat and opened the buttons of his waistcoat. "I was born heir to my present title. I was born with an earl's title, Jane. My family all used it until I became Tresham at the age of seventeen. You really are the first to call me by my given name."

He had suggested it. He had never done so with his other mistresses. They had called him by his title, just like everyone else. He remembered now being shaken to hear his name on Jane's lips a week ago. He had not expected it to bring such a feeling of—of intimacy. He had not realized how he had longed for such intimacy. Just that. Someone calling him by name.

He tossed his waistcoat aside and untied the knot of his neckcloth. She was watching him, her hands clasped at her waist, cloaked in gold.

"Jocelyn," she said softly. "Everyone should know what it is like to be called by name. By the name of the unique person one is at heart. Do you want me to undress too?"

"Not yet." He pulled his shirt off over his head and pulled off his Hessian boots. He kept his pantaloons on for the time being.

"You are very beautiful," she surprised him by saying, her eyes on his naked torso. Trust Jane to make such a remark! "I suppose I have offended you by using that particular word. It is not masculine enough, I daresay. But you are not handsome. Not in any conventional sense. Your features are too harsh and angular, your coloring too dark. You are only beautiful."

An experienced courtesan could not have aroused him so deftly even with the most cunningly erotic words.

"Now what have you left me to say about you?" he asked, stepping forward and touching her at last. He framed her face with his hands, sliding his fingers into the warm silk of her hair. "You are not pretty, Jane. You must know that. Prettiness is ephemeral. It passes in a season. You will be beautiful when you are thirty, when you are fifty, when you are eighty. At twenty you are dazzling, breathtaking. And you are mine." He dipped his head and touched his parted lips to hers, tasting her with his tongue before withdrawing a couple of inches.

"Yes, Jocelyn." Her teeth bit into her soft, moist lower lip. "For now I am yours. According to our contract."

"That damned thing." He chuckled softly. "I want you to want me, Jane. Tell me it is not just the money or this house or the obligation that wretched piece of paper has put you under. Tell me you want me. *Me*—Jocelyn. Or tell me truthfully that you do not and I will leave you to the enjoyment of your home and salary for the next five years. I will not bed you unless you want me."

He had never particularly cared before. All conceit aside, he knew he was not the sort of man who repelled women who earned their living in bed. And it had always been a matter of pride with him to give pleasure where he took it. But he had never cared whether a woman wanted *him* or just the wealthy, rakish aristocrat with the dangerous reputation. In fact, if he had thought about it, he probably would have decided that he did not want any woman close enough to desire *him*.

He had never before been Jocelyn to anyone. Not to

anyone in his family. Not to any woman. Not even to his closest friends. He would rather turn and leave now and never return than let Jane lie on her back on that bed simply because she felt obliged to. It was a somewhat alarming realization.

"I want you, Jocelyn," she whispered.

There was no doubt she meant it. Her blue eyes were focused fully on his. She was speaking the simple truth.

And then she leaned forward, letting every part of her body rest lightly against him. She set her lips to the hollow at the base of his throat. It was a gesture of sweet surrender.

All the sweeter because it seemed uncharacteristic of Jane. He knew her well enough to realize it was something she would never do merely because surrender was expected of her.

He felt strangely gifted.

He felt curiously wanted. In a way he had never felt in his life before.

"Jane," he said, his face in the silk of her hair. "Jane, I need to be inside your body. Inside *you*. Let me in."

"Yes." She tipped back her head and gazed into his eyes. "Yes, I will, Jocelyn. But you must show me how. I am not sure I know."

Ah. Jane to the end. She spoke in her cool, practical voice—which he suddenly realized was a mask for nervousness.

"It will be my pleasure," he told her, his mouth against hers as his fingers tackled the buttons down the back of her dress.

14

She was not nervous.

Oh, yes, she was.

She was nervous in the sense that she did not know quite what to do and was afraid of being gauche.

But she was not afraid. Or in any way horrified at what she was doing. Or ashamed. And she had spoken no lie. She wanted him. She desperately desired him. And he *was* beautiful—all solid, hard muscle with broad shoulders and chest, narrow waist and hips, long legs. He was warm and smelled of some musky cologne.

He was Jocelyn, and only she had ever spoken the intimacy of his name. She knew all about the importance of names. Only her parents had ever called her by her middle name, her *real* name, the one that seemed somehow to encompass her true identity. Her parents and now Jocelyn. She had tried to stop him from calling her Jane, but he had done so regardless.

And so in some inexpressible way they knew each other

intimately even before the physical knowing, which was just beginning. He was unclothing her. Her nakedness did not embarrass her. She saw herself through the look in his dark eyes and knew that she was beautiful and desirable.

She gave him back the look.

"Jane." He set his hands lightly at her waist and drew her against him. She inhaled slowly at the feel of his bare chest brushing her nipples. "We are ready for bed. Come and lie down."

For a moment the coldness of the sheet against her back took her breath. She had changed the colors of the room but not the materials. Satin, she had guessed, was an erotic accompaniment to what would happen in this bed.

She watched him finish undressing. He did not turn his back and she did not look away. She was to become as familiar with the look and feel of his body as she was with her own. Why begin with shyness or coyness?

She knew pretty well what happened. She had lived all her life in the country, after all. But even so she was shocked. There surely could not be room.

He was smiling that half-inward smile of his when he climbed onto the bed beside her and propped himself on one elbow to look down at her.

"You will become accustomed to both the sight and feel of it, Jane," he said. "I have never had a virgin. I suppose there will be pain and blood this first time, but I promise you pleasure too. And I will not put this terror inside you until your body is ready for it. It is my task to see that it is made ready. Do you know anything of foreplay?"

She shook her head. "I have never even heard the word."

"It means what it says." His eyes still laughed gently at her. "We will play, Jane, for as long as we need before I mount your body and ride us both to satiety. I daresay you do not know much if anything about the ride either, do you? The pain will be over before it begins. You will enjoy it, believe me."

She did not doubt it. There was already an ache of something that was not quite pain along her inner thighs and up into her belly. Her breasts had tightened to a strange, tingling soreness.

"You are doing it already, are you not?" she said. "Playing? With words?"

"We could sit at opposite ends of a room and arouse each other to fever pitch with only words," he said, grinning suddenly. "And maybe we will do it one of these days. But not today. Today is for touch, Jane. For exploring each other with hands and mouths. For stripping away the otherness that holds us from merging into the oneness we crave. We *do* crave it, do we not? Both of us?"

"Yes." She lifted a hand and cupped one of his cheeks. "Yes, Jocelyn. I want to be a part of your name, a part of the person who bears that name, a part of the soul inside that person. I want to be one with you."

"You, me, we, us." He lowered his head and spoke against her mouth. "Let us invent a new pronoun, Jane. The unity of I and the plurality of we melded into a new numberless word for Jane and Jocelyn."

She opened her mouth beneath his, suddenly ravenous and shaken by the words they had spoken—and those they had not. This was not the way she had expected it to be. This was not man and mistress. This was lover and beloved.

It had not been a part of the bargain. Either for her or— surely—for him.

But it was what was happening.

She realized too late, as his tongue plundered her mouth and his hands gave her an intimation of the magic and sensual delights ahead, what this was all about. She understood, far too late, why she had taken this option rather than any of the other more proper and rational ones. She understood why she had accepted his proposition without either outrage or horror.

This was love. Oh, perhaps not *love* exactly. But this was being in love. This was wanting to give and give to the beloved until everything that was oneself had been gifted away. And wanting to receive and receive until the emptiness had been filled again with a mingling of what was herself and him.

He was right. There was no word. No pronoun. There never was a word for the deepest realities.

"Jane."

His hands, his skilled fingers, his mouth were everywhere. He knew unerringly where and how to touch her, where to brush with feather-light fingertips, where to tickle, where to pulse his fingers, where to massage, where to pinch and scratch. He knew where to kiss, where to lick, to suck, to nip with his teeth.

She had no idea how long it went on. And she had no idea how she knew where to touch him, how to caress him, when to change the nature of each caress. But she did know, as if she had always known, as if there were a deep well of femininity on which to draw for the beloved without the necessity of any lesson.

Perhaps it was that hers was not just any woman's body and his not just any man's. Some instinct told her that this was usually done in darkness and with eyes tightly shut, that usually all the pleasure was hugged tightly to oneself, the pleasure-giver shut out. Even in her inexperience she sensed that lovers did not always love with eyes open and focused on each other's whenever it was feasible to do so.

"Jane."

He spoke her name over and over, as she did his. She was his beloved, as he was hers.

The ache, the yearning, the need became more persistent and more localized. She needed him *there*.

Here.

Now.

His hand, between her thighs, worked light, deft magic in her most secret place and built a frenzy of desire.

"Jocelyn." She set her hand over his wrist. "Jocelyn." She did not know what she needed to say. But he understood.

"Slick and warm and ready," he said, his mouth coming to hers again. "I am going to mount, Jane. Lie still and stay relaxed. When I am deep, we will begin the final pleasure."

"Come," she said to him. "Oh, please come."

His whole weight bore her down into the mattress, holding her immobile while his thighs came between hers and pressed them wide and his hands slid beneath her. By sheer instinct she twined her legs about his. And then he raised his head and looked down into her face, his eyes heavy-lidded with passion. But not blind passion. He looked deep into her own eyes.

And then she felt him hard against the pulsing ache of her entrance. And pressing through it, pushing slowly but firmly, filling her, stretching her, alarming her. There was the sudden premonition of pain, the certainty that he could come no farther. He was too big.

"Jane." There was something like contrition in his eyes. "If I could only take the pain for you. But it always falls to the woman to do the suffering." He pushed hard, frowning as he gazed into her eyes.

There was an involuntary tensing, a fear of pain, and— and an awareness that the moment had passed, that he was deep. That he was inside her body. And inside her heart. Inside herself. She smiled at him.

"I am still alive."

He grinned and rubbed his nose across hers.

"That's my girl," he said. "I could not expect tears and vapors from Jane Ingleby, could I?"

She clenched her muscles about the unfamiliar thick hardness inside her and closed her eyes to revel in the wonder of it.

But he had promised more. And now that the dreaded moment of her lost virginity was over, all the longing, all the aching came flooding back.

"What is the ride?" she asked, opening her eyes again. "Show me, Jocelyn."

"Lie still if you wish," he told her. "Ride with me if you wish. There are no rules here in our bed, Jane, and nothing in that foolish contract either that applies to this. Just you and me and what is mutually pleasurable."

He lowered his head then to rest in her hair on the pillow. He withdrew slowly to the brink of her—and pressed inward again.

There was no pain this time. Only wetness and heat and soon the rhythmic thrust and withdrawal of a riding motion to which her own body soon adjusted and matched. A carnal, energetic, blissful mating of bodies that was focused *there*, where her woman's body had opened to him and his man's body had penetrated deep. And yet the sensation went beyond that localized physical point. This was the mating of man and woman, of Jocelyn and Jane. It was a ride to union, to that wordless moment at which the I and the you of the two of them would lose focus and meaning. The moment in which the plurality of we would become singular.

Desire, yearning, need—all became pain and reaching, reaching . . .

"Now, Jane." He lifted his head again. His lips touched hers. His eyes looked into her own. "*Now.* Come. Come with me. Now, Jane."

Yes, now. All the way. Now. All the way to nothingness, to everything. To oblivion, to the ultimate knowing. To oneness.

Yes, now.

"*Jocelyn!*"

Someone cried his name. Someone murmured hers.

She felt a final, blissful gush of heat and knew that the mating was complete.

There was murmuring after that, and lightness and coolness as he moved off her, and more murmuring, and the comfort of his damp chest against hers as he drew her onto her side against him, his arm about her, and the coziness of bedcovers over her shoulders.

"Jane." She heard her name once more. "I am not sure you are still capable of saying you are alive."

She smiled sleepily. "Mmm," she said with a sigh. "Is this heaven, then?"

She was too tired to hear his chuckle. She slid into a delicious slumber.

Jocelyn did not sleep. He was thoroughly sated but also uneasy. What the devil had he been babbling? He hoped she had not been listening.

Of course she had been listening.

What they had just done had been done together. They had not been separate entities giving and taking a purely physical pleasure. They had been—damnation, he could not stop thinking the way he had been speaking. He had become her, and she had become him. Not that that was it either. They had both, together, become a new entity that was both of them and neither of them.

He was going to end up in Bedlam if he was not careful.

It had been something quite beyond his experience. And certainly beyond his intentions. He had wanted a mistress again. Someone to bed at will. Something really quite basic and simple. He had desired Jane. She had needed a home and employment.

It had all made perfect sense.

Until she had let her hair down. No, that had only fueled his desire.

Until she had called him by name. And said something else. What the devil was it she had said? He rubbed his cheek over the warm silk of her hair and hugged her a little closer.

Everyone should know what it is like to be called by name. By the name of the unique person one is at heart.

Yes, that was what had done it. Those few foolish words.

From birth he had been an earl with the rank of a marquess, heir to a dukedom. All his education, formal and informal, had been designed to train him to take over his father's title and his father's character when the time came. He had learned his lessons well. He had taken over both at the age of seventeen.

. . . the unique person one is at heart.

He had no heart. Dudleys generally did not.

And he had no unique character. He was what his father and everyone else had always expected him to be. For years now he had hugged about himself like a cloak his reputation as a dark, ruthless, dangerous man.

Jane's hair was fragrant with the smell of roses that always clung about her. It made him think of country gardens in the early summer. And filled him with a strange yearning. Strange, because he hated the country. He had been to Acton Park, his own estate, only twice since leaving there after a bitter quarrel with his father when he was sixteen—once for his father's funeral less than a year later, and once for his mother's four years after that.

He had intended never to go back until he was carried there one day for his own burial. But he could close his eyes now as he held Jane tightly and remember the rolling, wooded hills to the east of the house, where he and Ferdinand and Angeline had played robbers and highwaymen and Robin Hood and explorers. And where sometimes, when alone, he had played poet and mystic, breathing in the smells of elemental nature, sensing the vastness and the mystery of this nebulous thing called life, trying to formulate his thoughts and feelings and intuitions into words, trying to write them down as poetry. And occasionally liking what he had written.

He had torn up every word in a passion of anger and disgust before he left home.

He had not thought of home in a long age. Not of *home* at least, even though he kept a careful eye on the running of the estate. He had even forgotten that Acton Park ever had been home. But it had. Once upon a time. There had been a nurse who had given them discipline and affection in generous measures. She had been with them until he was eight or nine. He could even remember why she had been dismissed. He had had a toothache and she had been holding him on her lap in the nursery, cradling his sore face with her large, plump hand and crooning to him. His father had come into the nursery unannounced—a rare event.

She had been dismissed on the spot.

He, Jocelyn, had been sent down to his father's study to await the thrashing that had preceded the pulling of his tooth.

The Duke of Tresham, his father had reminded him with every painful swish of the cane across his backside, did not raise his sons to be girls. Especially not his heir.

"Jocelyn." Jane was awake again. She tipped back her head to look at him. Her beautiful face was flushed and heavy-lidded, her lips rosy and swollen from his kisses. She seemed cloaked and hooded in fragrant, shining gold. "Was I dreadfully gauche?"

She was one of the rare women, he thought, for whom passion and sexuality were instinctive. She had given both unstintingly this afternoon as if she did not know what it was to be hurt. Or belittled. Or rejected.

But before he could answer, she set one fingertip lightly to the bridge of his nose to cover the frown line there.

"What is it?" she asked. "What is the matter? I *was* gauche, was I not? How foolish to have imagined that because it was earth-shattering for me, it must have been so for you too."

Foolish Jane so to expose herself to ridicule and pain. He took hold of her wrist and lowered her hand.

"You are a woman, Jane," he told her. "An extraordinarily lovely woman. With everything in the right place. I was well pleased."

Something happened to her eyes. Something closed up behind them. He recognized his sudden irritation for what it was. It was shame that his throat and chest were aching with unshed tears. And anger that she had brought him so low.

He should never have told her to call him by name.

"You are angry," she said.

"Because you talk of earth-shattering experiences and make me feel that I must have misled you," he said curtly. "You are employed as my mistress. I have just been putting you to work. I always take pains to make work congenial to my mistresses, but work is what it is. You have just been earning your living."

He wondered if she felt the lash of his words as stingingly as he. He hated himself, which was nothing new except that the passion of his self-hatred had long ago become muted to a disdain for the world in general.

"And giving good value for money," she said coolly. "I would remind you, your grace, that you employ me for the use of my body. You are not paying for my mind or my emotions. If I choose to find part of my employment earth-shattering, I am free to do so provided at the same time I open my body for your use."

For one moment he was in a towering rage. If she had dissolved into tears, as any normal woman would have done, he could have lashed himself harder by treating her with scorn. But typically of Jane, she was scolding him with cool dignity despite the fact that she was lying naked in bed with him.

He chuckled. "Our first quarrel, Jane," he said. "But not our last, I suspect. I must warn you, though, that I would not have your emotions engaged in this liaison. I would not have you hurt at its inevitable ending. What happens in this room is sex. Nothing else. And you were not gauche. It was as good a session of sexual intercourse as I have ever experienced. Better, in fact. There, are you reassured?"

"Yes," she said, her voice still cool. "Thank you."

He was aroused again——by his anger, by her cool refusal to be chastised, by her golden beauty, by the faint smell of roses. He did what he had to do to reassert his control over the afternoon's business. He turned her onto her back and mated with her again, but this time he concentrated all his powers on keeping the act carnal, even clinical. Man and mistress. Nothing more.

And then he slept, lulled by the sound of rain against the window.

"I thought perhaps you would wish to stay for dinner," she said.

"No."

They were dressed again and back downstairs in the sitting room. But he had not seated himself as she had. He had gone first to stand in front of the fireplace to stare down into the unlit coals. Then he had paced to the window to stare out at the rain.

He filled the sitting room with his presence and energy. Looking at his immaculate elegance, his proud, erect posture, his powerful shoulders and thighs, Jane found it hard to believe that just half an hour ago he had been lying naked with her in the bed upstairs. It was already hard to believe any of it had happened despite the physical evidence of soreness and tender breasts and unsteady legs.

"I have a dinner engagement," he said. "And there is an infernal ball to be attended tonight. No, I did not come to stay, Jane. Merely to consummate our liaison."

It was not going to be easy, being his mistress. She had never expected it to be. He was an arrogant man of uncertain temper. He was accustomed to having his own way, especially with women. But it was going to be especially hard to cope with his strange, sudden mood swings.

She would have felt hurt by his words, belittled by them, as she had when he had spoken in a similar manner in bed earlier. But she realized that the words were not spoken carelessly but quite deliberately. She was not sure why. To remind her that she was his mistress, not his lover?

Or to convince himself that she meant nothing to him beyond a female body to be used for his pleasure?

Despite all her ignorance and inexperience, she would swear that the first time he had entered her he had not been using her. She had not been a mere woman's body. It had not been just carnal pleasure.

He had made love to her. *With* her.

He was ashamed now of having shown such weakness.

"That is a relief, then," she said coolly. "There are several rearrangements to some of the other rooms that I hoped to start today, but I have already lost most of the afternoon."

He looked over his shoulder at her without turning and regarded her steadily.

"You will not be put in your place, Jane, will you?"

"If you mean," she replied, "that I will not allow you to make me feel like a whore, your grace, the answer is no, I will not. I will be here whenever you need me. It is our agreement. But my life will not revolve around your visits. I will not spend my days gazing wistfully from the window and my evenings listening expectantly for the door knocker."

She remembered guiltily how she had paced back and forth to the windows all morning. She would not do it again.

"Perhaps, Jane," he said softly, his eyes narrowing dangerously, "I should send a message in advance whenever I wish to bed you to ask if you can fit me into your busy schedule."

"You were not listening," she told him. "I signed a contract, and I mean to keep it and to see that you do too."

"What *do* you do with your time?" He turned from the window and looked about the empty room. "Do you go out?"

"Into the garden at the back," she said. "It is rather pretty, though it needs work. I have ideas and have started to implement them."

"Do you read?" He frowned. "Are there any books here?"

"No." He should know very well there were not.

"I will take you to Hookham's Library tomorrow morning," he said abruptly, "and buy you a subscription."

"No!" she said sharply. She relaxed again. "No, thank you, Jocelyn. I have plenty to do. It takes a great deal of time and energy to convert a brothel into a home, you know."

"That was unprovoked impudence, Jane, and unworthy of you." He looked very large and menacing, standing before her chair, his booted feet apart, his frown still in place. "I suppose if I told you I would come to take you walking in Hyde Park, you would be too busy for that too?"

"Yes." She nodded. "You do not need to put yourself out on my account."

He stared at her for a long time, his expression so unreadable that she could see nothing in him of the man who had loved her with unmistakable passion such a short time ago. He looked hard and humorless and untouchable.

Then he bowed to her abruptly, turned, and strode from the room.

She gazed in surprise at the door he had closed behind him and listened to the sounds of the front door being opened and then shut again. He was gone. Without a word of farewell or any hint of when he might come again.

This time she felt hurt.

Desolate.

15

*T*he room next to the sitting room had been furnished with a daybed, a plusher than plush carpet, an inordinately large number of mirrors, which multiplied one's reflection at least ten times, depending on where one stood, sat, or lay, and the inevitable cushions and knickknacks.

In Jane's estimation it had been used either as a private retreat by the duke's ex-mistresses who enjoyed their own company more than anyone else's, or as an alternative to the bedchamber. She suspected the latter.

It was a room she had ignored while the two main rooms were being refurbished. But now, at her leisure, she was making it into her own domain. The lavender sitting room was now elegant, but it was not *her*.

The mirrors and the daybed were banished—she did not care what happened to them. She sent Mr. Jacobs out on a special commission to purchase an escritoire and chair and paper, pens, and ink. Mrs. Jacobs in the meantime was sent to buy fine linen and an embroidery frame and an assortment of colored silken threads and accessories.

The den, as Jane thought of the room, would become her private writing and sewing room. She would indulge there her passion for embroidery.

She sat stitching in her den, a fire crackling cozily in the hearth, during the evening following the consummation of her liaison. She pictured Jocelyn at a grand dinner party and then moving on to a great squeeze of a ball, and tried not to feel envious. She had never had her come-out Season. There had been the year of mourning for her mother. Then her father had been too ill though he had urged her to accept Lady Webb's offer to sponsor her. But she had insisted on staying to nurse him. And then there had been his death and her year of mourning. And then the circumstances that had brought her under the new earl's guardianship.

Would Jocelyn dance tonight? she wondered. Would he waltz?

But she would not indulge in depressing thoughts.

For a moment her heart lifted when she heard a tap on the den door. Had he come back? But then she saw the butler peering around the door, his expression wary.

"I beg your pardon, ma'am," Mr. Jacobs said, "but there are two great boxes just now arrived. What would you like done with them?"

"Boxes?" Jane raised her eyebrows and set her embroidery aside.

"From his grace," the butler explained. "Almost too heavy to lift."

"I am not expecting anything." She got to her feet. "I had better come and see for myself. You are sure his grace sent them?"

"Oh, yes, ma'am," he assured her. "His own servants brought them and explained they were for you."

Jane was intrigued, especially when she saw two large crates in the middle of the kitchen floor.

"Please open one of them," she said, and Mrs. Jacobs fetched a knife and the butler cut the string that held one of the boxes closed.

Jane pushed back the lid, and all the servants—the butler, the housekeeper, the cook, the housemaid, and the footman—leaned forward with her to peer inside.

"Books!" The housemaid sounded vastly disappointed.

"Books!" Mrs. Jacobs sounded surprised. "Well. He never sent books here before. I wonder why he sent them now? Do you read, ma'am?"

"Of course she does," Mr. Jacobs said sharply. "Why else would she want a desk and paper and ink, I ask you?"

"Books!" Jane said almost in a reverential whisper, her hands clasped to her bosom.

She could see from the ones on top that they were from his own library. There were a Daniel Defoe, a Walter Scott, a Henry Fielding, and an Alexander Pope visible before she touched a single volume.

"It seems a funny sort of gift to me," the housemaid said, "begging your pardon, ma'am. P'raps there's something better in the other box."

Jane was biting hard on her upper lip. "It is a priceless gift," she said. "Mr. Jacobs, are the boxes too heavy for you and Phillip to carry into the den?"

"I can carry them on my own, ma'am," the young footman said eagerly. "Shall I unpack them for you too?"

"No." Jane smiled at him. "I shall do that myself, thank you. I want to see all the books one at a time. I want to see what he has chosen for me."

By happy chance there was a bookcase in the den though it had been covered with tasteless ornaments before Jane had cleared it off.

She spent two hours kneeling beside the boxes, drawing out one book at a time, arranging them pleasingly on the shelves, pondering over which she would read first.

And occasionally blinking her eyes fast and even swiping at them with her handkerchief when she thought of him going home this afternoon and handpicking all these books for her. She knew he had not simply directed Mr. Quincy to do the choosing for him. The books included ones she had mentioned as her particular favorites.

If he had sent her some costly piece of jewelry, she would not have been one fraction as well pleased. Such a gift would not even dent his purse. But his books! His own books, not ones he had purchased for her. He had taken them from his own shelves, and among them were his personal favorites too.

Some of the loneliness had gone from the evening. And some of the bewilderment at his leaving so abruptly during the afternoon, without a word of farewell. He must have gone straight home and spent time in his library. Just for her sake.

She must not, Jane told herself firmly, allow herself to fall any deeper in love with him. And she must not—she absolutely *must not*—let herself *love* him.

He was a man humoring a new mistress. Nothing more.

But she read happily until midnight.

The next morning the Duke of Tresham rode in Hyde Park at an hour when he often met some of his friends there on Rotten Row. The rain had stopped sometime during the night and the sun shone, making diamonds of the moisture on the grass. Fortunately for his need for distraction, he ran into Sir Conan Brougham and Viscount Kimble almost immediately.

"Tresh," the viscount said by way of greeting as Jocelyn joined the group, "we were expecting you at White's for dinner."

"I dined at home," Jocelyn told him. And he had. He had been unable to dine with Jane as his feelings had been rubbed raw and he had not wanted her to know it. And although he had dressed to go out, he had not done so. He was not quite sure why.

"Alone?" Brougham asked. "Without even the delectable Miss Ingleby for company?"

"She never did dine with me," Jocelyn said. "She was a servant, if you will remember."

"She could be my servant any time," Kimble said with a theatrical sigh.

"And you were not at Lady Halliday's," Brougham observed.

"I stayed home," Jocelyn said.

He was aware of his friends exchanging glances before they broke into merry laughter.

"Ho, Tresham," Brougham said, "who is she? Anyone we know?"

"A fellow cannot claim to have spent an evening at home alone without incurring suspicion?" Jocelyn spurred his horse into a canter. But his friends, who adjusted the speed of their mounts to match that of his, were not to be deterred. They rode one on either side of him.

"Someone new if she kept him from dinner at White's and the card room at Lady Halliday's, Cone," Kimble said.

"And someone who kept him awake all night if this morning's ill temper is anything to judge by, Kimble," Brougham observed.

They were talking across Jocelyn, both grinning, just as if he were not there.

"Go to the devil," he told them.

But they both greeted his uncharitable invitation with renewed mirth.

It was a relief to see Angeline approaching on foot beyond the fence with Mrs. Stebbins, one of her particular friends. They were out for a morning stroll.

"Provoking man!" Angeline exclaimed as soon as Jocelyn rode within earshot. "Why are you always out when I call,

Tresham? I made a particular point of going to Dudley House yesterday afternoon as Heyward informed me you had left White's before luncheon. I was quite sure you must have gone home."

Jocelyn fingered the ribbon of his quizzing glass. "Were you?" he said. "It would be redundant to inform you that you were wrong. To what, may I ask, did I owe the show of sisterly affection? Good morning, Mrs. Stebbins." He touched the brim of his hat with his whip and inclined his head.

"Everyone is talking about it," Angeline said while her friend made his grace a deep curtsy. "I have heard it three times in the past two days, not to mention Ferdie's speaking of it when I saw him yesterday. So I daresay you have heard it too. But I must have your assurance that you will do nothing foolish, Tresham, or my nerves will be shattered. And I must have your promise that you will defend the family honor at whatever cost to yourself."

"I trust," Jocelyn said, "you intend sooner or later to enlighten me on the topic of this fascinating conversation, Angeline. Might I suggest sooner as Cavalier is still frisky?"

"It *was* being said," she explained, "that the Forbes brothers fled town in fear of retaliation from you for what they tried to do to Ferdie."

"As well they might," he commented. "They have some modicum of wisdom among the three of them if that was indeed the reason for their disappearance."

"But now," she said, "it is known for absolute certain—is it not, Maria?" She turned to Mrs. Stebbins for confirmation. "Mr. Hammond mentioned it at Mrs. Bury-Haugh's two days ago and everyone knows that his wife is second cousin to Mrs. Wesley Forbes. So it must be true."

"Incontrovertibly, I would say," Jocelyn agreed dryly, using his quizzing glass to peruse the other walkers beyond the fence and the other riders within.

"They are not satisfied," Angeline announced. "Can you

imagine the gall of them, Tresham? When Ferdie might have been killed? They are not satisfied because you took the curricle and came to no worse harm than to ruin a pair of leather gloves. *They* are still vowing vengeance on *you!* When everyone knows that *you* are now the one with the grievance. They have gone for reinforcements and are expected back at any moment."

Jocelyn turned about with a flourish to look at the grassy expanse behind him. "But not quite yet, Angeline," he said. "The reinforcements to which you refer are presumably the Reverend Josiah Forbes and Captain Samuel Forbes?"

"It will be five against one," she declared dramatically. "Or five against two if one counts Ferdie as he insists one must. It would be five against three if Heyward would not insist in his odious manner that he will not involve himself in childish capers. I will wheedle a gun out of him and start practicing my marksmanship again. I am a Dudley, after all."

"I beg you to desist," Jocelyn said firmly. "None of us would know which side was in more danger from you if you were to prove as adept at shooting now as you were as a girl." He raised his glass again and looked her over from head to ankles. "That is a surprisingly elegant bonnet you are wearing," he said. "But the poppy red flowers are a lamentably poor match for the pink of your walking dress."

"Lord Pym met us ten minutes ago," she said with a toss of her head, "and observed, foolish man, that I look like a particularly delectable meadow in which he could only wish he were strolling alone. Did he not, Maria?"

"Indeed?" Jocelyn's manner became instantly frosty. "I trust, Angeline, you reminded Lord Pym that you are the sister of the Duke of Tresham?"

"I sighed soulfully and then laughed at him," she said. "It was harmless gallantry, Tresham. Do you believe I would allow any man to take liberties with me? I shall tell Heyward about it and he will toss his glance at the ceiling and then tell me . . .

well." She blushed and laughed again, nodded to Kimble and Brougham, took Maria Stebbins's arm, and resumed her promenade.

"London needs some new scandal," Jocelyn observed as he rode onward with his friends. "It seems that no one has anything else to talk about these days except those cowardly scoundrels who claim kinship with Lady Oliver."

"They are doubtless shaking in their boots, by Jove," Viscount Kimble said, "since Joseph Forbes was rash enough to claim responsibility on behalf of all of them for your scraped palms. But they are probably hatching more mischief too—nothing as direct as a challenge, of course."

"They may not have a choice—except loss of face and the last vestiges of their honor," Jocelyn said. "But enough on the subject. I am sick to death of it. Let us enjoy the fresh air and sunshine."

"To blow away the cobwebs?" Brougham asked. He looked beyond Jocelyn to address their other friend again. "Did you notice, Kimble, that according to Lady Heyward, Tresham was from home yesterday afternoon? Was he with you?"

"He was not with me, Cone," the viscount replied, all seriousness. "Was he with you?"

"I did not set eyes on him between yesterday morning and this," Brougham said. "She must be *very* new and *very* frisky."

"The devil!" Kimble drew his horse to such an abrupt halt and threw back his head to laugh with such loud merriment that he was almost unseated and had to exercise considerable skill to bring his mount under control again. "Right under our noses, Cone," he said when he was able. "The answer, I mean."

Conan Brougham's and Jocelyn's horses were prancing a little distance away.

"The delectable Miss Ingleby!" Kimble announced. "You rogue, Tresh. You lied. You do have her in your keeping. And she kept you from your friends and your obligations and your bed—your own bed, that is—most of yesterday and all night. She must have lived up to all the considerable promise she showed."

"It has been staring us in the face, has it not?" Brougham agreed with a grin. "You actually danced—*waltzed*—with her, Tresham. And could not take your eyes off her. But why the secrecy, old chap?"

"I do believe," Kimble said with an exaggerated sigh, "I am going to go into mourning. I have been considering hiring a Bow Street Runner to search for her."

"You two," Jocelyn said with his customary hauteur, "may go to the devil with my blessing. Now if you will excuse me, breakfast awaits at Dudley House."

At first silence and then their laughter followed him as he rode off unhastily in the direction of home.

It was not like that, he kept thinking foolishly. It was not *like* that.

But if it was not like that—a man with a new mistress enjoying the novelty of a new female body with which to pleasure himself—then what *was* it like?

He hated the thought of even his closest friends snickering over Jane.

She must have heard him coming. She was standing in the doorway of the sitting room again, wearing primrose yellow today—another new dress of classically simple design. She had perfect taste in clothing, it seemed, once she had been forced out of the cheap gray monstrosities.

He handed his hat and gloves to the butler and moved toward her. She smiled at him with dazzling warmth and held out both hands, completely throwing him off stride. He had been feeling out of charity with the world and even with her and had been irritated with himself for being unable *not* to come to her again this afternoon.

"Thank you," she said, and squeezed his hands when he gave them to her. "How can I ever thank you sufficiently?"

"For the books?" He frowned. He had forgotten about the books. He had intended to take her straight up to bed today, to have his brisk pleasure of her before leaving to get on with the rest of his day, undistracted by thoughts of her. He had intended to get this relationship properly on track. At the same time he had hated the thought of Kimble's or Brougham's ribald remarks, which he was sure to hear this evening, and his own knowledge that there was truth in them.

"A mere nothing," he said curtly. He freed his hands and motioned for her to precede him into the sitting room.

"To you, perhaps," she said. "But to me, everything. You cannot know how I have missed reading since I came here."

"Then why the devil," he asked her irritably, closing the door and looking about the room, "did you not let me take you to the library?"

And why the deuce was she so ashamed to be seen? His other mistresses had never been more happy than when he escorted them somewhere where they would be seen in his company.

She was probably the daughter of a damned clergyman. But he would be double damned before he would start feeling guilt at having had her virtue.

She would not answer his question, of course. She smiled again, tipping her head to one side.

"You are in a black mood this afternoon," she observed. "But I am not to be cowed by it. Has something happened that you would like to talk about?"

He almost laughed.

"The Forbes brothers have slunk off out of town to bring on reinforcements," he said. "They are afraid to confront me with the odds of three against one. They are planning to increase them to five against one. They will discover that the odds are still in my favor. I derive a certain relish out of dealing with bullies and cowards."

She sighed. "Men and their pride," she said. "I suppose you will still be brawling when you are eighty, if you should live so long. Will you sit down? Shall I order tea? Or do you wish to go straight upstairs?"

Suddenly, strangely, alarmingly, he did not want her. Not in bed. Not now. It just seemed too—too what? Sordid? He almost laughed again.

"Where are the books?" he asked. "In the bedchamber? The attic?"

"In the next room," she said. "I have converted it for my own use when you are not here. I think of it as my den."

He hated the sitting room. Even though it was now elegant and tasteful, it still reminded him of a waiting room, an impersonal space in which certain civilities were observed before the inevitable adjournment to the bedchamber. And there were no personal touches here that made it Jane's sitting room.

"Take me there," he commanded.

He might have guessed that Jane would not simply turn and meekly lead the way.

"It is my room," she said. "This is where I entertain you—and occasionally, perhaps, in the dining room. The bedchamber is where I grant you your contractual rights. The rest of the house I consider my personal domain."

Jocelyn pursed his lips, undecided whether to bark at her for the satisfaction of seeing her jump with alarm or to throw back his head and laugh.

Contractual rights, by thunder!

"Miss Ingleby." He made her his most elegant bow. "Would you grant me the privilege of seeing your den?"

She hesitated, bit her lower lip, and then inclined her head.

"Very well," she said, and turned to leave the room ahead of him.

The room was Jane. He felt that as soon as he stepped

through the door. He felt as if for the first time he was entering her world. A world that was elegant and genteel on one hand, industrious and cozy on the other.

The fawn-colored carpet and draperies had always made the room look dreary, and all the attempts of her predecessors to brighten the room with cushions and shawls and garish gewgaws had only emphasized the gloom. The mirrors, added by Effie, had merely multiplied the gloom. He had made it a habit never to set foot in here.

Now the fawn colors, which Jane had made no attempt to mask, made the room seem restful. The daybed was gone. So, not surprisingly, were all the mirrors. Some graceful chairs had been added as had a desk and chair, the former strewn sufficiently with papers to indicate that it was not for display purposes only. The bookcase was filled with his books though one lay open on the small table next to a fireside chair. In front of the chair at the other side of the hearth was an embroidery frame over which was stretched a piece of linen. About it were strewn silken threads and scissors and needles.

"May I sit down?" he asked.

She indicated the chair by the book.

"If you wish," she said, "you may deduct the cost of the desk and chair from my salary since they were purchased for my private use."

"I seem to recall," he said, "that I gave you *carte blanche* for the house renovations, Jane. Do stop saying ridiculous things and sit down. I am too much the gentleman, you see, to seat myself before you do."

She felt uncomfortable, he could see. She perched on the edge of a chair some distance away.

"Jane," he said impatiently, "sit at your embroidery frame. Let me see you work. I suppose it is another skill you learned at the orphanage?"

"Yes," she said, moving her place and picking up her needle.

He watched her in silence for a while. She was the picture of beauty and grace. A lady born and bred. Fallen indeed on hard times—forced to come to London to search for employment, forced to take work as a milliner's assistant, forced to become his nurse, forced to become a mistress. No, not forced. He would not take that guilt on himself. He had offered her a magnificent alternative. Raymore would have made her a star.

"This has always been my vision of domestic bliss," he said after a while, surprising himself with the words, which had been spoken without forethought.

She looked up briefly from her work.

"A woman beside the fire stitching," he said. "A man at the other side. Peace and calm about them and all well with the world."

She lowered her head to her work again. "It was something you never knew in your boyhood home?" she asked.

He laughed shortly. "I daresay my mother did not know one end of a needle from the other," he said, "and no one ever told either her or my father that it is possible occasionally to sit around the hearth with one's family."

No one had told him those things either. Where were these ideas coming from?

"Poor little boy," she said quietly.

He got abruptly to his feet and crossed to the bookcase.

"Have you read *Mansfield Park*?" he asked her a minute or so later.

"No." She looked up briefly again. "But I have read *Sense and Sensibility* by the same author and enjoyed it immensely."

He drew the volume from the shelf and resumed his seat.

"I shall read to you while you work," he said.

He could never remember reading aloud, except at his lessons as a boy. He could not remember being read to either until Jane had done it when he was incapacitated. He had found the experience unexpectedly soothing though he had never listened attentively. He opened the book and began reading.

"'About thirty years ago, Miss Maria Ward, of Huntingdon, with only seven thousand pounds, had the good luck to captivate Sir Thomas Bertram, of Mansfield Park. . . .'"

He read two chapters before stopping and lowering the book to his lap. They sat in silence for a while after that. In a silence that seemed to him thoroughly comfortable. He was sprawled in his chair, he realized. He could nod off to sleep with the greatest ease. He felt . . . How *did* he feel? Contented? Certainly. Happy? Happiness was something he had little or no acquaintance with and set no store by.

He felt shut off from the world. Shut off from his usual self. With Jane. Who was certainly shut off from her world and usual self, whatever they might be. Could this be perpetuated? he wondered. Indefinitely? Forever?

Or could it at least become an occasional retreat, this room that was so much Jane and in which he felt comfortable, restful, contented—all alien to his normal way of life?

He should put an end to these foolish, unrealistic, and uncharacteristic dreams without further ado, he thought. He should take his leave—or take her to bed.

"What is it you are working on?" he asked her instead.

She smiled without looking up. "A tablecloth," she said. "For the dining room table. I had to find *something* to make. Embroidery has always been a passion with me."

He watched her for a while longer from beneath lazy eyelids. The frame was tilted away from him so that he could not see the pattern. But the silks were autumnal colors, all tastefully complementary.

"Will your hackles rise," he asked, "if I come and look?"

"No indeed." She looked surprised. "But you are under no obligation to be polite, you know. You can have no interest in embroidery."

He did not deign to answer. He hauled himself out of the deep, comfortable chair, setting his closed book on top of her open one as he did so.

She was working a scene of autumn woods across one corner of the cloth.

"Where is the pattern from which you work?" he asked her. He wanted to be able to see the whole picture.

"In my head," she told him.

"Ah." He understood then why it was a passion with her. It was not just that she was skilled with her needle. "It is an art with you, then, Jane. You have a fine eye for color and design."

"Strangely," she said, "I have never been able to capture my visions on paper or canvas. But through my needle pictures flow easily from my mind to the fabric."

"I was never any good at portraying scenes," he said. "I always felt that nature did so much better than I could possibly do. Human faces are a different matter. There is so much life and character to capture."

He could have bitten his tongue as soon as the words were out. He straightened up in some embarrassment.

"You paint portraits?" She looked up at him, bright interest in her eyes. "I have always thought that must be the most difficult form of art."

"I dabble," he said stiffly, wandering to the window and gazing out at the small garden, which was looking remarkably well tended, he noticed. Had those roses always been there? "Past tense. I dabbled."

"I suppose," she said quietly, "it was not a manly pursuit."

His father's language had been far more graphically scathing.

"I would like to paint you," he heard himself saying. "There is a great deal in your face even apart from exquisite beauty. It would be an enormous challenge."

There was silence behind him.

"Upstairs we will satisfy our sexual passions," he said. "In here we could indulge all the others, Jane, if you wished it. Away from the prying eyes and sneering lips of the world. This is what you have created in this room, is it not? A den, as you call it, a haven, where you can be yourself, where all the other facts of your life, including being my mistress, can be set aside and you can be—simply Jane."

He turned his head. She was looking steadily at him, her needle suspended above her work.

"Yes," she said.

"And I am the last person with whom you would wish to share the room." He smiled ruefully at her. "I will not insist. In future you will entertain me in the sitting room whenever we are not in the bedchamber."

"No." She let a few moments pass before elaborating. "No, I will no longer think of this room as mine but as ours. A place in which our contract and our relative stations in life have no application. A place where you may paint and read, where I may embroider and write, a place where there can be a woman at one side of the hearth and a man at the other. A place of quiet and peace, where all is well with the world. You are invited to make yourself at home here whenever you wish, Jocelyn."

He gazed at her over his shoulder for a long time without saying anything. What the devil was happening? There could be only one reason, one passion to bring him to this house. He did not want any other reason. He might become dependent upon it—upon her. And yet his heart ached and yearned with hope.

For what?

"Would you like tea?" She was threading her needle into the linen and getting to her feet. "Shall I ring for the tray?"

"Yes." He clasped his hands at his back. "Yes, please."

He watched her do so.

"There is plenty of spare room in here," he said. "I am going to have a pianoforte brought here. May I?" He could scarcely believe he was actually asking permission.

"Of course." She looked gravely at him. "It is *our* room, Jocelyn. Yours as well as mine."

He thought for one moment that it might be happiness that rushed to engulf him. But he soon recognized it as an equally unfamiliar emotion.

Terror.

16

✤

*J*ane went to bed early, but she could not sleep. She stopped trying after half an hour. She got out of bed, lit a candle, pulled a warm dressing gown over her linen nightgown, slipped her feet into her slippers, and went back downstairs to her den. Their den. Their haven, he had called it.

Mr. Jacobs was still up. She asked him to build up the fire again. The young footman brought the coals and asked if there was anything else he could fetch for her.

"No, thank you, Phillip," she said. "That will be all. I can find my own way to bed when I am tired."

"Yes, ma'am," he said. "Don't forget to put the guard about the fire, then, when you leave, ma'am."

"I won't." She smiled. "Thank you for reminding me. Good night."

"Good night, ma'am," he replied.

She would read until she was too tired to keep her eyes open, she decided. She seated herself beside the fire, in the chair Jocelyn had occupied during the afternoon, and picked up a book. Not the one from which he had read. She left that where it was. Perhaps he would wish to continue with chapter three next time he came. She opened her book to the page at which she had left off reading the night before and set it on her lap.

She gazed into the fire.

She should not have allowed him in here. She knew that she would no longer think of this room as hers. It was theirs. She could *feel* his presence here. She could see him as he had been earlier, sprawled comfortably but not inelegantly in this chair. She could hear his voice reading from *Mansfield Park* as if he were as lost in the story as she had been. And she could see him standing at the window. . . .

It was unfair. She could have coped with her new life if their relationship had proceeded, as she had expected, along purely sexual lines. She knew enough to realize that sex was not love, especially sex between a rakish duke and his mistress. She did not know what *this* was.

He had spent longer than two hours in this room with her this afternoon—with his mistress—without once touching her. He had not taken her to bed. After tea, during which they had discussed the war and political reform—she was a pacifist, he was not; she was unreservedly in favor of reform, he was far more cautiously so—he had got to his feet quite abruptly, made her a bow, bade her a good afternoon, and gone on his way.

He had left her feeling empty inside. Though that could not be strictly true or she would not also have felt all churned up—her body, her mind, her emotions.

For almost the whole time they had been here together in the den, he had not been the Duke of Tresham. He had been Jocelyn. But Jocelyn with far fewer reservations than she was accustomed to. Jocelyn without any mask. A person in need of being himself as he had never been before. A man in need of friendship and acceptance and—ah, yes.

Jane sighed aloud.

A man in need of love.

But she doubted he would ever accept that ultimate gift even if he acknowledged the need to himself.

She doubted even more that he was capable of returning the gift.

And who was she to offer? A fugitive. A murderess—no, not that. She was even beginning to believe it herself. She did not think the blow she had given Sidney would have killed him in itself.

She shuddered at the memories.

And then she set her head back against the chair and listened to the sounds of Mr. Jacobs or Phillip at the front door, locking up for the night. A moment later there was a tap on her door.

"Come in," she called. It must be midnight or later. The servants should be in bed.

He looked powerful and satanic, covered from neck to ankles in a long black opera cloak. He stood in the doorway, one hand still on the knob, while her stomach performed a complete somersault and she knew that indeed the afternoon had been disastrous to her.

"Still up?" he asked. "I saw light beneath the door."

"Do you have your own key?" she asked him.

"Of course," he replied. "This is my house."

She got to her feet and moved toward him. She had simply not expected him.

And then a strange thing happened. He took his hand from the doorknob as she approached and spread his arms to the sides, revealing the white silk lining of the cloak and the elegant black and white evening clothes he wore beneath. But Jane did not really notice the splendor of his appearance. She kept walking and was soon enveloped in the folds of his cloak while she lifted her face and he lowered his own both at the same time.

It was a long and deep and fierce embrace. But the strange thing was that it was not sexual—not entirely so anyway. Jane had little experience with embraces, but she knew instinctively that he was not just a man kissing his mistress prior to taking her to bed. He was Jocelyn. And he was kissing her, Jane.

By the time the embrace ended he was the Duke of Tresham again.

"I will be putting you to work tonight, Jane," he said.

"Of course." She stood back and smiled.

And then gasped with alarm when he caught her hard by the wrist and gazed down at her with hard, cold eyes.

"No!" he said fiercely. "You will not smile at me in that way, Jane, like a jaded coquette hiding her weary cynicism behind a cool smile of invitation. There is no *of course* about it. If you do not want me, then tell me to go to hell and I will go."

She jerked her wrist out of his grasp. "What do you expect when you speak of putting me to work?" she asked angrily. "Does a woman go to *work* for a man in bed when she wants him? When you call it work you make a whore of me."

"You are the one," he reminded her, his eyes as cold as steel, "who speaks of contractual obligations and rights. What does that make of me? It makes me someone who has purchased access to your body. Someone who has bought the services of a whore. It makes of you a woman who is working when she lies on her back for me. Don't use righteous anger on me, Jane, and expect me meekly to bow my head. You may go to the devil for all I care."

"And you may . . ." But she forced herself to stop and to draw a steadying breath. Her heart was pounding like a hammer. "We are quarreling again. Was it my fault this time? I am sorry if it was."

"It is that infernal contract that is to blame," he grumbled.

"Which is my fault." She smiled briefly at him. "I really am pleased to see you, Jocelyn."

The anger and the coldness faded from his face. "Are you, Jane?"

She nodded. "And I really do want you."

"Do you?" He gazed broodingly at her, his eyes very black.

Could this be the Duke of Tresham? Unsure of himself? Uncertain of his welcome?

"I am saying it inside the room where we agreed our contract would bear no sway," she said, "so it has to be the truth. Come to bed with me."

"I have come from the theater," he explained. "I was invited back to Kimble's for supper with his party and said I would walk there rather than crowd a carriage. But I found my legs carrying me here instead. How do you interpret that, Jane?"

"I daresay," she said, "you were in need of a sharp quarrel with someone who would not back down from you."

"But you were the first to apologize," he reminded her.

"Because I was wrong," she told him. "I do not insist upon winning an argument at any cost, you see. Not like some I know."

He grinned wolfishly at her. "Which means, I suppose," he said, "that as usual you have had the last word, Jane. Come, then. Since it is what I came for and since you have invited me, let us go to bed."

Physical desire made her breathless again as she stepped past him and preceded him up the stairs. He did not come immediately after her, she noticed. He had paused to set the guard in front of the dying fire.

Which was probably, she guessed with an inward smile, one of the most domesticated things he had ever done.

Kimble would tease him mercilessly in the morning. Jocelyn did not care. When had he ever cared what anyone—even his closest friends—thought or said about him? And the teasing would at least be good-natured.

The truth was he had had to come back tonight. He had been more disturbed by the strange events of the afternoon than he cared to admit. He had had to come back just to get some normalcy back into his relationship with his mistress. To put her to work.

It had been a mistake to use those exact words to her, of course. But he was not accustomed to tiptoeing his way about other people's sensibilities.

He undressed, doused the candles, and climbed into bed with her. He had instructed her to keep on her prim and pretty nightgown. There was something surprisingly erotic about grasping its hem and lifting it up her legs and over her hips to her waist. He did not want foreplay tonight. He wanted to do what he had come to do before somehow the whole scene became unfamiliar again. He slid his hand between her thighs and felt her. She was ready enough. He turned onto her with his full weight, spread her legs wide with his knees, slid his hands beneath her, and entered.

She was soft, warm, relaxed heat. He began to work her with firm, vigorous strokes. He tried to think of her simply as a woman. He tried to think of his need as simply sexual.

He failed miserably on both counts.

He rarely kissed in bed. It was unnecessary, and it was too personal for his taste. He kissed her.

"Jane," he murmured into her mouth, "tell me you wanted me to come back, that you have thought of nothing but me since this afternoon."

"Why?" she whispered. "So that you can warn me again not to become dependent upon you? I am not sorry you came. I am glad. This feels good."

"Damn you," he said. "Damn you."

She was silent while he worked. But just as he felt the climax approach and was about to deepen and quicken his rhythm, he felt her arms close about his waist and her feet slide up the bed and her thighs hug his hips while she tilted her pelvis to allow him deeper access.

"Jocelyn," she whispered, "don't be afraid. Please don't be afraid."

He was driving toward release and did not hear the words consciously. But after he had finished, when he lay exhausted beside her, he heard their echo in his mind and thought he must have imagined them.

"Come here," he said, reaching out a hand to touch her.

She curled up against him, and he lowered her nightgown, drew up the bedclothes, wrapped his arms about her, pillowed his cheek against the top of her head, and fell asleep.

He had frequently spent nights at the house and staggered home at dawn to sleep. He had never *slept* a night at the house. When he had come this time, he had intended a few hours of vigorous sport just to remind both Jane and himself of the basic nature of their liaison.

He awoke when daylight was pouring into the room. Jane, tousled and flushed and delicious, was still asleep in his arms.

He drew free of her and swung himself out of bed, waking her in the process. She smiled sleepily at him.

"My apologies," he said stiffly as he pulled on his evening clothes. "I daresay according to that infernal contract I have no right intruding on your privacy when I am not actually asserting my rights. I will be gone in a moment."

"Jocelyn," she said with soft reproach, and then she had the unmitigated gall to laugh.

With glee.

At him.

"I amuse you?" He scowled at her.

"I do believe," she said, "you are *embarrassed* that you slept instead of spending the night demonstrating your renowned prowess as a lover. You seem always to have to prove your superior manhood."

The fact that she was perfectly right did not improve his mood.

"I am delighted to have amused you at least," he said, throwing his cloak about him with a vicious swing of his arm and buttoning it at his throat. "I shall do myself the honor of calling upon you some other time when I have need of you. Good morning."

"Jocelyn," she said softly again when he already had the door of the bedchamber open. He looked back at her with haughtily raised eyebrows. "It was a wonderful night. You are lovely to sleep with."

He did not wait to discover if she mocked him or not. He stepped through the door and closed it none too quietly behind him.

Devil take it, he thought, noticing the clock in the hallway as he descended the stairs and noticing too with a grimace that Jacobs was waiting there to let him out, it was seven o' clock. He had been here for seven hours. He had been in her bed for seven hours, and he had had intercourse with her once. *Once!*

He bade the butler a curt good morning and strode off down the street, noticing with some satisfaction that the twinge of stiffness in his right leg was becoming less pronounced each day.

You are lovely to sleep with.

Jocelyn chuckled despite himself. She was right, goddammit. It had been a lovely night, and he felt more refreshed by his sleep than he had in a long while.

He would go home to bathe and change, he decided, and then go shopping—for a small pianoforte and for sketching and painting supplies. Perhaps the best thing to do about this whole extraordinary situation was to go along with it, let it happen, let it proceed in its own way and at its own pace to its inevitable conclusion. Sooner or later he would grow weary of Jane Ingleby. He had of every woman he had ever known or bedded. He would of her too—perhaps in a month, perhaps in two, perhaps in a year.

In the meantime, why not just enjoy the novel feeling of being—ah, yes, the fateful words that hovered in the background of his thoughts and threatened to verbalize themselves.

Why not?

Why not enjoy the feeling of being in love?

Why not revel in the ultimate foolishness for once in his life?

Working in the garden later that same morning, enjoying the exercise, loving the brightness and heat of the sun on her back, Jane came to a decision.

She was in love with him, of course. Worse than that, she thought she was also growing to *love* him. There was no point in trying to deny her feelings and no use whatsoever in trying to fight them.

She loved him.

But it would not do, of course. She was not foolish enough to imagine that he would ever love her in return, though she knew that he was in the grip of a serious obsession with her. Besides, even if he ever did love her, there could be no happily-ever-after to expect. She was his mistress. And she was who she was.

But she could not live forever as a fugitive. She should never have given in to the cowardly impulse that had sent her scurrying into hiding in the first place. It had been so unlike her normal self. She was going to have to come out of hiding and do what she ought to have done as soon as she discovered that Lady Webb was not in London to help her.

She was going to find the Earl of Durbury if he was still in town. If he was not, she was going to find out where the Bow Street Runners had their headquarters and go there. She was going to write to Charles. She was going to tell her story to anyone who would listen. She was going to embrace her fate. Perhaps she would be arrested and tried and convicted of murder. Perhaps that would mean a hanging or at the very least transportation or lifelong imprisonment. But she would not give in meekly. She would fight like the very devil to the last moment—but not by running away and hiding.

She was going to come out into the open at last and *fight*.

But not just yet. That was the agreement she made with herself as she pulled weeds from about the rosebushes and turned the soil until it was a richer brown. A definite time limit must be set so that she would not continue to procrastinate week after week, month after month. She was going to give herself one month, one calendar month, starting today. One month to be Jocelyn's mistress, his love, though he would not be aware of the latter, of course. One month to spend with him as a person, as a friend in the den, if he ever returned there, as a lover in the bed upstairs.

One month.

And then she was going to give herself up. Without telling him. There might be scandal for him, of course, when it became known that he had harbored her at Dudley House for three weeks, or if anyone knew that she had been his mistress here. But she would not worry about that. His life had been one scandal after another. He appeared to thrive on them. She thought he would probably be rather amused by this particular one.

One month.

Jane leaned back on her heels to inspect her work, but Phillip was approaching from the direction of the house.

"Mr. Jacobs sent me, ma'am," he said, "to tell you that a new pianoforte just arrived and an easel and other parcels too. He wants to know where you want them put."

Jane got to her feet, her heart soaring, and followed him back to the house.

One glorious month, in which she would not even try to guard her feelings.

One month of love.

There followed a week during which Jocelyn almost totally ignored his family, the Olivers, the Forbeses, and all topics of gossip with which the *ton* continued to entertain itself. A week during which he rode in the park most mornings and spent an hour or two afterward breakfasting at White's and reading the papers and conversing with his friends, but during which he attended few social functions.

Kimble and Brougham were highly diverted, of course, and very inclined to ribaldry. Until, that was, the three of them were walking along a fortunately deserted street on the way from White's one morning and Kimble opened his mouth.

"All I can say, Tresh," he said, pretending to sound bored, "is that when the delectable Miss Ingleby has finally exhausted you, you may pass her on to me, if you please, and I will see if I can exhaust *her*. I daresay I know a trick or two she will not have learned from you. And if—"

His monologue was rudely interrupted when a fist collided with the left side of his jaw and with a look of blank astonishment he crashed to the pavement. Jocelyn looked with scarcely less astonishment at his own still-clenched fist.

"Oh, I say!" Conan Brougham protested.

Jocelyn spoke curtly to his friend, who was gingerly fingering his jaw. "Do you want satisfaction?"

"Oh, I say," Brougham said again. "I cannot be second to *both* of you."

"You should have told me, old chap," Kimble said ruefully, shaking his head to clear it before scrambling to his feet and brushing at his clothes, "and I would not have flapped my jaws. By Jove, you are in love with the wench. In which case the punch was understandable. But you might have been more sporting and warned me, Tresh. It is not the most comfortable of experiences to walk into one of your fists. No, of course I am not about to slap a glove in your face, so you need not look so damned grim. I meant no disrespect to the lady's honor."

"And I did not mean to endanger our friendship." Jocelyn extended his right hand, which his friend took rather warily. "It is all very well for you and Conan to tease, Kimble. I would do no less to you. But no one else is to be drawn into this. I will not have Jane publicly dishonored."

"I say!" Brougham sounded suddenly indignant. "You do not believe we have been spreading the word, Tresham? The very idea! I did not believe I would live to see the day when you would be in love, though." He laughed suddenly.

"Love be damned!" Jocelyn said gruffly.

But apart from that one incident, almost the whole of his attention for the week was taken up by the house where Jane lived and where he spent most of his time—in two separate but strangely complementary capacities. He spent his afternoons and several of his evenings in their den with her, almost never touching her. He spent his nights in the bedchamber with her, making love to her and sleeping with her.

It was a magical week.

A week to remember.

A week of such intense delight that it could not possibly last. It did not, of course.

But before it ended, there was that week. . . .

17

Once or twice they strolled in the garden, and Jane showed him what she had already done with it and explained what she still intended to do. But most of the time they spent indoors. It was a misty, wet week anyway.

Jane had simply abandoned herself to sheer pleasure. She spent hours stitching by the fire, necessary because of the damp chill, the autumn woods spreading in glorious profusion across one corner of the linen cloth, then another. Sometimes he read to her—they had reached almost the halfway point of *Mansfield Park*. More often in the evenings he played the pianoforte. The music was almost all his own composition. Sometimes it was halting, uncertain at the start, as if he did not know where the music came from or where it was going. But she came to recognize the point at which it went beyond an activity of the mind and hands and became one simply of the heart and soul. Then the music flowed.

Sometimes she stood behind him or sat beside him and

sang—mostly folk songs and ballads with which they were both acquainted. Even, surprisingly, a few hymns, which he sang with her in a good baritone voice.

"We were paraded to church every Sunday," he told her, "to cushion our superior backsides on the plush family pew— though never, at our peril, to squirm on it—while lesser mortals sat on hard wood and gawked in awe. And you, Jane? Were you orphans marched in a neat crocodile, two by two, to sit on backless benches and thank God for the many blessings He had showered on you?" His hands played a flourishing arpeggio.

"I always enjoyed church," she said quietly. "And there are always blessings for which to be thankful."

He laughed softly.

Most often during the afternoons he painted. He did not want after all, he decided, to paint just her face. He wanted to paint *her*, as she was. Jane had looked sharply at him when he said that, and he had raised his eyebrows.

"You think I am going to drape you in a lascivious pose on the floor, Jane, dressed only in your hair?" he asked. "I would put you to better use than to paint you if I did that, believe me. As I will show you tonight. Yes, definitely. Tonight we will have candles and nakedness and hair, and I will show you how to pose for me like the Siren you could be if you set your mind to it. I will paint you at your embroidery. That is when you are most yourself." He gazed narrow-eyed at her. "Quiet, industrious, elegant, engaged in creating a work of art."

And so he painted as she stitched, both of them silent. He always stripped off his coat and waistcoat before he began and donned a large, loose shirt over his good one. As the days passed it became smudged and streaked with paint.

He would not let her see the painting until it was finished.

"I let you see my embroidery," she reminded him.

"I asked and you said yes," he replied. "You asked and I said no."

To which logic there was no further argument.

She worked at her embroidery, but she watched him too. Covertly, of course. If she looked too directly or stopped work too long, he frowned and looked distracted and grumbled at her. It was hard sometimes to realize that this man who shared her most intimate space with such mutual ease was the same man who had once told her he would make her wonder if starvation would not be better than working for him. The infamous, heartless Duke of Tresham.

He had the soul of an artist. Music had been trapped within him most of his life. She had not yet seen any product of his brush, but she recognized the total absorption in his work of the true artist. Much of the harshness and cynicism disappeared from his face. He looked younger, more conventionally handsome.

And entirely lovable.

But it was not until the fourth evening that he really began to talk, to let out in words the person who had lurked behind the haughty, confident, restless, wicked facade he had shown the world all his adult life.

He was enjoying the novelty of being in love, though he kept reminding himself that it was *just* novelty, that soon it would be over and he would be on safe, familiar ground again. But it saddened him, at the same time as it reassured him, that Jane would ever look to him just like any other beautiful woman he had once enjoyed and tired of, that the time would come when the thought of her, of *being* with her, both in bed and out, would not fill him with such a welling of gladness that it seemed he must have taken all the sunshine inside himself.

His sexual passion for her grew lustier as the week advanced. He could not be satisfied with the almost chaste encounters of their first two times together, but set out to teach her—and himself—different, more carnal, more prolonged

delights. The previous week he might have exulted in the bed
sport with his new mistress and proceeded with the rest of his
life as usual. But it was not the previous week. It was *this* week.
And this week there was so much more than just bed sport.
Indeed, he suspected that bed was good between them just because there was so much else.

He dared do things he had craved as a boy—play the
pianoforte, paint, dream, let his mind drift into realms beyond
the merely practical. He was frustrated by his painting and ex-
hilarated by it. He could not capture the essence of her, perhaps because he looked too hard for it and thought too much
about it, he realized at last. And so he relearned what had
once been instinctive with him—to observe not so much with
his senses or even his mind but with the mindless, wordless aspect of himself that was itself part of the essence it sought.
He learned to stop forcing his art to his will. He learned that
to create, he somehow had to allow creation to proceed
through him.

He would not have understood the concept if he had ever
verbalized it. But he had learned that words were not always
adequate to what he yearned to express. He had learned to
move beyond words.

Gradually the woman who had become the grand obsession of his life took form on the canvas.

But it was words that finally took him into a new dimension of his relationship with his mistress on the fourth
evening. He had been playing the pianoforte; she had been
singing. Then she had sent for the tea tray and they had drunk
their tea in companionable silence. They were both sitting idle
and relaxed, one on each side of the hearth, she gazing into
the fire, he gazing at her.

"There were woods in Acton Park," he said suddenly, apro-
pos of nothing. "Wooded hills all down the eastern border of
the park. Wild, uncultivated, inhabited by woodland creatures
and birds. I used to escape there for long hours of solitude

until I learned better. It was when I came to realize that I could never paint a tree or a flower or even a blade of grass."

She smiled rather lazily. For once, he noticed, she was leaning back in her chair, her head against the headrest.

"Why?" she asked.

"I used to run my hands over the trunks of trees," he explained, "and even stand against them, my arms about them. I used to hold wildflowers in the palm of my hand and run grass blades between my fingers. There was too much there, Jane. Too many dimensions. I am talking nonsense, am I not?"

She shook her head, and he knew she understood.

"I could not even begin to grasp all there was to grasp," he said. "I used to feel—how does one describe the feeling? Breathless? No, totally inadequate. But there was a feeling, as if I were in the presence of some quite unfathomable mystery. And the strange thing was, I never wanted to fathom it. How is that for lack of human curiosity?"

But she would not let him mock himself. "You were a contemplative," she said.

"A what?"

"Some people—most people, in fact," she said, "are content with a relationship with God in which they have Him pinned down with words and in which they address Him in words. It is inevitable that all of us do it to a certain extent, of course. Words are what humans work with. But a few people discover that God is far vaster than all the words in every language and religion of the world combined. They discover tantalizing near glimpses of God only in silence—in total nothingness. They communicate with God only by giving up all effort to do so."

"Damn it, Jane," he said, "I do not even believe in God."

"Most contemplatives do not," she said. "Or not at least in any God who can be named or described in words or pictured in the imagination."

He chuckled. "I used to think it blasphemous," he said,

"to believe that I was more like to find God in the hills than at church. I used to delight in the blasphemy."

"Tell me about Acton," she said quietly.

And he did. He talked at length about the house and park, about his brother and sister, about the servants with whom he had had daily contact as a child, including his nurse, about his play, his mischief, his dreams, his fears. He resurrected a life he had long ago relegated to a dim recess of memory, where he had hoped it would fade away altogether.

There was silence at last.

"Jocelyn," she said after a few minutes, "let it all become part of you again. It *is* whether you wish it to be or not. And you love Acton far more than you realize."

"Skeletons, Jane," he told her. "Skeletons. I should not have allowed any of them out. You should not be such a restful companion."

"None of them seem very threatening," she commented.

"Ah," he said, "but you do not know what is crowding behind them, Jane." He got to his feet and held out a hand for hers. "Time to put you to work upstairs." But he grinned at her when her eyes sparked. "And time for you to put me to work. Will you, Jane? Hard, physical labor? I'll show you how to ride me, and you can use me for your pleasure as long as you choose. Come and ride me to exhaustion, Jane. Make me beg for mercy. Make me your slave."

"What nonsense!" She got to her feet and set her hand in his. "I have no wish to enslave you."

"But you already have, Jane," he said meekly, his eyes laughing at her. "And never tell me my words have not aroused you. There is a certain telltale flush in your cheeks and breathlessness in your voice that I am coming to recognize."

"I have never pretended," she told him primly, "that duty is not also pleasure."

"Come and let me show you, then," he said, "how very

pleasurable it will be to do the riding rather than always to be ridden, Jane. Let me show you how to master me."

"I have no wish——" But she laughed suddenly, a sound of delight he enjoyed coaxing from her. "You are not my master, Jocelyn. Why should I wish to be yours? But very well. Show me how to ride. Is it like a horse? I ride horses rather well. And of course *they* have to be taught who is in charge, wonderful creatures."

He laughed with her as he led her from the room.

He finished the portrait on the last day of the first week, late in the afternoon. He had a dinner engagement during the evening, which fact was a disappointment to Jane, but she expected that he would come back for the night. One week of her precious month was already over, though. There were only three left. She coveted every day, every hour.

She loved to watch him paint even more than she loved watching him play the pianoforte. With the latter, he very quickly entered a world of his own, where the music flowed effortlessly. At his easel he had to labor more. He frowned and muttered profanities as much as he was absorbed in his task.

But finally he finished. He cleaned his brush and spoke.

"Well," he said, "I suppose you have been sneaking peeks every time I leave the house."

"I have not!" she said indignantly. "The very idea, Jocelyn! Just because it is something *you* would undoubtedly do."

"Not if my word were given," he said. "Besides, I would never need to sneak peeks. I would boldly look. Come and see it, then. See if you like yourself."

"It is finished?" He had given no indication that he was nearing the end. She threaded her needle through the cloth and jumped to her feet.

"Come and discover the truth of my claim that I merely dabble," he said, shrugging as if he did not care what her verdict was, and busying himself with the task of cleaning his palette.

Jane was almost afraid to look then, afraid that indeed she would find an inferior product about which she would have to be tactful. Though he would tear her to pieces, she knew, if she were less than brutally honest.

Her first impression was that he had flattered her. She sat at her work, every line of her body elegantly arched. Her face was in profile. She looked industrious and absorbed by what she was doing. But she never saw herself thus, of course. In reality it was a good likeness, she supposed. She flushed with pleasure.

Her second impression was that the likeness or otherwise of the portrait was really not the point. She was not looking at a canvas produced merely so that the sitter might exclaim at the flattering likeness. She was gazing at something—something more.

The colors were brighter than she had expected, though when she looked critically she could see that they were accurate. But there was something else. She frowned. She did not know what it was. She had never been a connoisseur of art.

"Well?" There were impatience and a world of hauteur in his voice. And a thread of anxiety too? "Did I not make you beautiful enough, Jane? Are you not flattered?"

"Where . . . ?" She frowned again. She did not know quite what it was she wished to ask. "Where does the *light* come from?"

That was it. The painting was an excellent portrait. It was colorful and tasteful. But it was more than just a painting. It had *life*. And there was light in it, though she was not quite sure what she meant by that. Of course it had light. It was a vivid daytime scene.

"Ah," he said softly, "have I done it then, Jane? Have I really captured it? The essence of you? The light is coming from *you*. It is the effect you have on your surroundings."

But how had he *done* it?

"You are disappointed," he said.

She turned to him and shook her head. "I suppose," she said, "you never had an art master. It would not have been allowed for a future Duke of Tresham. Jocelyn, you are a man in every sense that you think important. You must dare to be more fully a man as you have been in this room this week. You have an amazing talent as a musician, an awesome talent as a painter. You must continue to use them even when I am gone. For your own sake as much as that of the world."

It was typical of him, of course, to choose to comment on a very small point.

"You are going to leave me, then, Jane?" he asked. "Go to greener pastures, perhaps? To someone who can teach you new tricks?"

She recognized the source of the insult. He was embarrassed by her earnest praise.

"Why should I leave you," she asked briskly, "when the terms of the contract are so favorable to me provided you are the one who does the leaving?"

"As I will inevitably do, of course," he said, regarding her through narrowed eyes. "There is usually a week or two of total infatuation, Jane, followed by a few more weeks of dwindling interest before a final severance of the relationship. How long have I been totally besotted with you now?"

"I would like to have time to practice skills other than just embroidery," she said, returning to her chair and folding her silk threads to put away in her workbag. "The garden needs more work. There are all those books to be read. And there is much writing I wish to do. I daresay that once your interest dwindles, I shall find my days richer and filled to overflowing with any number of congenial activities."

He chuckled softly. "I thought," he said, "we were not supposed to quarrel in this room, Jane."

"I thought," she replied tartly, "the Duke of Tresham was not to be brought into the room. I thought we had agreed not to allow him over the threshold, nasty, arrogant man. The very idea of telling me *when* I might expect to find your interest in me waning and how long I might expect to enjoy your wearying favors after that. Come here looking as if you believe you are doing me a favor, Jocelyn, and you will be leaving faster than you arrived, believe me. I have to consent, remember, before you so much as touch me."

"You like the portrait, then?" he asked meekly.

She set down her workbag and looked at him, exasperated.

"Must you always try to hurt me when you feel most vulnerable?" she asked. "I love it. I love it because you painted it and because it will remind me of this week. But I suspect that if I knew more about painting I would love it too because it is great art. I believe it is, Jocelyn. But you would have to ask an expert. Is the painting mine? To keep? Forever?"

"If you want it, Jane," he said. "Do you?"

"Of *course* I want it. You had better go now or you will be late for your dinner."

"Dinner?" He frowned, then appeared to remember. "Oh, *dinner*. To hell with it. I shall stay here and dine with you, Jane."

One more evening of her month to hug to herself.

They drank tea after dinner and he read to her from *Mansfield Park* while she sat relaxed in her chair. But after that they sat in companionable silence until he started talking about his boyhood again, as he had done for the past two evenings. Having started, it seemed he could not stop.

"I believe you should go back, Jocelyn," she said when he paused. "I believe you need to go back."

"To Acton?" he said. "Never! Only for my own funeral."

"But you speak of it with love," she said. "How old were you when you left?"

"Sixteen," he told her. "I swore I would never go back. I never have, except for two funerals."

"You must have still been at school," she said.

"Yes."

She did not ask the question. That was so like Jane. She would not pry. But the question might as well have been shouted out. She sat quietly and receptively. Jane, to whom he had opened so much of himself in the past week.

"You do not want to know, Jane," he told her.

"I think perhaps," she said, "you need to tell."

That was all she said. He gazed into the fire and remembered the initiation. The moment at which he had become his father. And his grandfather. A true Dudley. A man.

"I was sixteen and in love," he said. "With a neighbor's fourteen-year-old daughter. We swore undying love and fidelity. I even managed to get her alone once and kissed her—on the lips. For all of three seconds. It was very serious, Jane."

"It is not always wise to mock our younger selves," she said, responding to his tone of irony as if she were an octogenarian. "Love is as serious and painful a business to the young as it is to older people. More so. There is so much more innocence."

"My father got wind of it and became apprehensive," he said. "Though doubtless if he had waited I would have been sighing over some other maiden two or three months later. It is not in the nature of a Dudley to be constant in love, Jane—or even in lust, for that matter."

"He separated you?" she asked.

"There is a cottage." He set his head back and closed his eyes. "I mentioned it to you before, Jane. With its inhabitant, an indigent female relative ten years my senior."

"Yes," she said.

"There was a pool not far from her cottage," he said.

"Idyllic, Jane. At the foot of the hills, green with the reflections of trees, loud with birdsong, secluded. I used to go there often in the summer to bathe rather than frolic in the lake closer to the house. She was there one day before me, bathing, wearing only a thin shift."

Jane said nothing when he paused.

"She was suitably flustered," he said, "as she came out of the pool, looking as if she wore nothing at all. And then she laughed and joked and was charming. Can you picture it, Jane? The accomplished, well-endowed courtesan and the ignorant, virgin youth? That first time we did not even make it back to the cottage. We rutted on the grass beside the pool. I discovered what went where and what happened when it was in deep enough. I do believe all was accomplished inside thirty seconds. I thought myself one devil of a dashing fellow."

Jane's eyes were closed, he noticed when he opened his own.

"She was my first obsession." He chuckled. "The day after that I went to the cottage, and the day after that again. I labored mightily on that last occasion, having quickly learned that I could make the pleasure last considerably longer than thirty seconds. I was proud and exhausted when I was finally finished demonstrating my prowess. And then she started to talk, Jane, in a very normal, very amused voice.

"'He is an apt pupil and shows enormous promise,' she said. 'Soon *he* will be teaching *me* tricks.' And then before I could get my head up to discover what the devil she was talking about, another voice, Jane. My father's. Coming from the doorway of the bedchamber behind me.

"'You have done very nicely, Phoebe,' he said. 'He was bucking lustily enough between your thighs.' He laughed when I jumped off the bed on the opposite side from my clothes as if I had been scalded. He was standing with one shoulder propped against the doorway as if he had been there for some time. He had, of course, been watching and assessing my performance, probably exchanging winks and leers with his mistress. 'No need for embarrassment,' he told me. 'Every man ought to be deflowered by an expert. My father arranged it for me; I have arranged it for you. There is no one more expert than Phoebe, though today is your last with her, my boy. She is off-limits as of this moment. I cannot have my son sowing his oats in my woman, can I, now?'"

"Oh," Jane said softly, bringing Jocelyn's mind back to the present with a jolt.

"I gathered my clothes up and ran out of the cottage," he said, "without even stopping to dress first. I needed to vomit. Partly because my father had watched something so terribly private. Partly because it was his *mistress* with whom I had been dallying, and he had planned it all. I had not known until then that he even had mistresses. I had assumed he and my mother were faithful to each other. There was never anyone more naive than my boyhood self, Jane."

"Poor boy," she said quietly.

"I was not even allowed to vomit in peace." He laughed harshly. "My father had brought someone riding with him—his neighbor, father of the girl I fancied myself in love with. And out strode my father on my heels to share the joke in all its lurid details. He wanted to take us both to the village inn to toast my newly acquired manhood with a glass of ale. I told him he could go to hell, and I repeated the invitation at greater length when we were at home later. I left Acton the next day."

"And for this you have felt guilt ever since?" Jane asked. He discovered suddenly that she had got up from her place and crossed in front of the hearth to stand before his chair. Before he realized what she was about to do, she sat on his lap and burrowed there until her head was on his shoulder. His arms closed about her in sheer reflex action.

"It felt like incest," he said. "She was my father's *whore*, Jane."

"You were at the mercy of a ruthless man on one hand and a practiced courtesan on the other," she told him. "It was not your fault."

"I was in love with an innocent young girl," he said. "And yet I spared her not one thought as I rutted with a woman ten years my senior whom I thought to be a relative. I learned one valuable lesson from the experience, though, Jane. I was my father's son through and through. I *am* my father's son."

"Jocelyn," she said, "you were *sixteen*. No matter who you were, you would have had to be superhuman—or subhuman—to resist such a powerful temptation. You must not blame yourself. Not any longer. Those events did not prove that you have a depraved nature. Far from it."

"It took me a few years longer to prove that," he said.

"Jocelyn." He could feel her fingers playing with a button on his waistcoat. "Tell me something. Someday in the future when you have a son, will you ever do that to him? Initiate him with one of your own mistresses?"

He drew breath slowly and imagined it—the precious human who would be his son, product of his seed, and the woman with whom he would slake his appetites rather than remain true to his wife. Coming together, performing while he watched.

"I would sooner tear out my heart," he said. "My nonexistent heart."

"Then you are not your father," she said, "or your grandfather. You are yourself. You were a sensitive, artistic, romantic boy, who had been repressed and was finally cruelly seduced. That is all, Jocelyn. You have allowed your life to be stunted by those events. But there is much life left to you. Forgive yourself."

"I lost my father on that day," he said. "I lost my mother soon after, once I had arrived in London and learned the truth about her."

"Yes," she said sadly. "But forgive them too, Jocelyn. They were products of their own upbringing and experience. Who knows what demons they carried around inside them? Parents are not just parents. They are people too. Weak like all the rest of us."

His fingers were playing with her hair. "What made you so wise?"

She did not answer for a while. "It is always easier to look at someone else's life and see its pattern," she said, "especially when one cares."

"Do you care about me, then, Jane?" he asked, kissing the top of her head. "Even now you know those most sordid of all details about my past?"

"Yes, Jocelyn," she said. "I care."

They were the words that finally broke his reserve. He did not even realize he was weeping until he felt wet drops drip onto her hair and his chest heaved convulsively. He froze in horror. But she would not let him push her away. She wrapped her free arm about his neck and burrowed deeper. And so he sobbed and hiccuped ignominiously with her in his arms and then had to search for a handkerchief to blow his nose.

"Dammit, Jane," he said. "Dammit."

"Tell me," she said. "Do you have any kindly memories of your father? Anything at all?"

Hardly! But when he thought about it, he could remember his father teaching him to ride his first pony and playing cricket with him and Ferdinand.

"He used to play cricket with us," he said, "when we were young enough to saw at the air with our bats and hurl the ball all of six inches ahead when bowling. It must have been as exciting for him as watching grass grow."

"Remember those times," she said. "Find more memories like that. He was not a monster, Jocelyn. He was not a pleasant man either. I do not believe I would have liked him. But he was not a monster, for all that. He was simply a man. And even when he betrayed you, he thought somehow that he was doing something necessary for your education."

He kissed the top of her head again, and they lapsed into silence.

He could not quite believe that he had relived those memories at last. Aloud. In the hearing of a woman. His mistress, no less. But it felt strangely good to have spoken. Those ghastly, sordid events seemed less dreadful when put into words. *He* seemed less dreadful. Even his father did.

He felt peaceful.

"Skeletons are dreadful things to have in our past, Jane," he said at last. "I do not suppose you have any, do you?"

"No," she said after such a long silence that he thought she was not going to answer at all. "None."

"Come to bed?" he asked her with a sigh almost of total contentment. "Just to sleep, Jane? If I remember correctly, we were rather energetically busy most of last night. Shall we just sleep tonight?"

"Yes," she said.

He almost chuckled aloud. He was going to bed with his mistress.

To sleep.

His father would turn over in his grave.

18

*J*ocelyn went straight home the following morning, as he usually did, to bathe and shave and change before sallying forth to his clubs and engaging in his other morning activities. But Hawkins was waiting for him as he crossed the threshold, bursting with important information. Mr. Quincy wanted a word with his grace. At his earliest convenience.

"Send him to the library in half an hour," Jocelyn said as he made his way to the stairs. "And send Barnard up to me. Warn him that I feel no burning need of his personal company, Hawkins. Suggest to him that I will need hot water and my shaving gear."

Michael Quincy stepped into the library thirty minutes later. Jocelyn was already there.

"Well?" He looked at his secretary with raised eyebrows. "Some crisis at Acton, Michael?"

"There is a person, your grace," his secretary explained.

"He is in the kitchen and has been there for two hours. He refuses to go away."

Jocelyn raised his eyebrows and clasped his hands at his back. "Indeed?" he said. "Do I not employ enough footmen to pick up this—this *person* and toss him out? Am I expected to do it myself? Is this why the matter has been brought to my attention?"

"He is asking about Miss Ingleby, your grace," Quincy explained.

Jocelyn went very still. "About Miss Ingleby?"

"He is a Bow Street Runner," his secretary told him.

Jocelyn merely stared at him.

"Hawkins referred him to me with his questions," Quincy explained. "I told him I knew nothing about any Miss Ingleby. He said he would wait and speak with you, then. When I told him he might have to wait a week before you found a moment to spare for him, he said he would wait a week. He is in the kitchen, your grace, and shows no sign of going away."

"With questions about Miss Ingleby." Jocelyn's eyes narrowed. "You had better show him up, Michael."

Mick Boden was feeling uncomfortable. Only very rarely did his work bring him to any of the grand mansions of Mayfair. Truth to tell he was rather in awe of the aristocracy. And the owner of Dudley House was the Duke of Tresham, reputedly the sort of man even his peers feared to tangle with.

But he knew he was close. The servants were all lying their heads off, every last one of them. None of them knew any Miss Jane Ingleby, including his grace's secretary, whom, to his shame, Mick Boden had taken for the duke himself at first, so grand a nob was he.

Mick knew when people were lying. And he knew why these people were lying. It was not that they were protecting her or hiding her but that they were servants who valued their employment. And clearly one rule of that employment was that one did not open one's mouth to strangers about any inhabitant of the house, even fellow servants. He could respect that.

And then the butler, a man who had the habit of sniffing the air as if to catch the dirty odor of lesser mortals, appeared in the kitchen and fixed his disdainful eye upon Mick.

"Follow me," he said.

Mick followed him, out of the kitchen, up the steep stairs, and through the baize door that led into the back of the hall. The sudden splendor of the main part of the house fairly took his breath away, though he concentrated upon not showing that he was impressed. The secretary was waiting there.

"His grace will give you five minutes," he said. "I will show you into the library. I shall wait outside to show you off the premises when you have been dismissed."

"Thank you, sir," Mick Boden said.

He was a little nervous, but he strode purposefully enough into the library after the butler had opened the door. He came to a halt six steps inside the door and planted his feet wide on the carpet. He held his hat with both hands and bobbed his head civilly. He would not bow.

The duke—he supposed it must be the duke this time—was standing in front of an ornate marble fireplace, his hands clasped at his back. He was wearing riding clothes, but they were so well tailored and fit so perfectly that Mick immediately felt conscious of the cheapness of his own clothes, on whose nattiness he prided himself. He was being regarded steadily from eyes so dark Mick would swear they were black.

"You have a few questions for me," the duke informed Mick. "You are a Bow Street Runner?"

"Yes, sir. Mick Boden, sir." Mick resisted the urge to bob his head again. "I have been informed, sir, that you have a Miss Jane Ingleby in your service."

"Have you?" His grace raised his eyebrows and looked very forbidding indeed. "And who, may I ask, did the informing?"

"Madame de Laurent, sir," Mick Boden said. "A milliner. She employed Miss Ingleby until a month or so ago, when the young lady gave her notice and explained she was coming here to work for you."

"Indeed?" The duke's eyes narrowed. "And what is your interest in Miss Ingleby?"

Mick hesitated, but only for a moment. "She is wanted, sir," he said, "for dastardly crimes."

His grace's fingers found and curled about the handle of his quizzing glass, though he did not raise it to his eye.

"Dastardly crimes?" he repeated softly.

"Theft, sir," Mick explained. "And murder."

"Fascinating," the duke commented just as softly, and Mick, a good judge of character, knew without any doubt that this could be a very dangerous man indeed. "And a Banbury tale?"

"Oh, no, sir," Mick said briskly. "It is quite true. The name is an alias. In reality she is Lady Sara Illingsworth, who murdered Mr. Sidney Jardine, son and heir of the Earl of Durbury, and then ran off with the earl's money and jewels. You might have heard about the incident, sir. She is a desperate fugitive, sir, and it is my belief she is here in this house."

"Dear me," his grace said after a short silence. "I perceive that I am fortunate indeed not to have woken one morning during the past month to find my throat slit from ear to ear."

Mick felt intense satisfaction. At last! The Duke of Tresham had as good as admitted that she was at Dudley House.

"She is here, sir?" he asked.

The duke raised his quizzing glass halfway to his eye. "*Was* here," he said. "Miss Ingleby was employed for three weeks as my nurse after I was shot in the leg. She left a couple of weeks ago. You must pursue your search elsewhere. I believe Mr. Quincy is waiting in the hall to show you out."

But Mick Boden was not ready to be dismissed just yet.

"Can you tell me where she went, sir?" he asked. "It is very important. The Earl of Durbury is beside himself with grief and will not know a moment's peace until his son's murderess has been brought to justice."

"And his jewels returned to his safe at Candleford," the duke added. "Miss Ingleby was a servant here. Am I to know where *servants* go after they leave my employ?" His eyebrows rose haughtily again.

Mick knew he had just slammed into a brick wall. He had come so close.

"That will be all?" his grace asked. "The interrogation is ended? I confess an eagerness for my breakfast."

Mick would have liked to ask more questions. Sometimes, even when people were not deliberately hiding information, they knew more than they realized. Perhaps the girl had said something about her future plans, dropped some hint, confided in some fellow servant. But it was unlikely, he admitted. She knew she was a fugitive. Doubtless she had heard, during her weeks in this house, that the Runners were after her.

"Well?" There was a force of arrogant incredulity behind the one word.

Mick bobbed his head again, bade the Duke of Tresham a good morning, and took his leave. The duke's secretary showed him out through the front door, and the Bow Street Runner found himself on Grosvenor Square, feeling that he was back where he had started.

Though perhaps not quite.

He had heard about the duel even before Madame de Laurent had mentioned it. The Duke of Tresham had been shot in the leg and incapacitated for three weeks. The rest of London's nobs had probably beaten a path to his door to keep him company. The girl had been his nurse. She must surely have been seen by some of those visitors. Some of them might be more forthcoming than the duke himself.

No, he had not come up against a brick wall after all, Mick Boden decided. Not yet at least.

He would find her.

All the evidence had been staring him in the eyeballs, Jocelyn thought as he stood at the library window watching the Bow Street Runner make his slow way out of the square. Staring so closely, in fact, that it had thrown his mind out of focus and he had just not seen it.

She had clearly been brought up a lady. She had demonstrated all the attributes of a lady from the start except genteel dress. She spoke with a refined accent; she bore herself proudly and gracefully; she was literate; she could play the pianoforte with competence if not with flair; she could sing superbly—with a trained voice and a knowledge of composers like Handel; she could command and organize servants; she was not awed by a man with a title, like himself, even when he was overbearing by nature.

Had he for one moment believed her story that she had been brought up in an orphanage? For *one* moment, perhaps. But he had realized for some time that she had lied about her background. He had even idly wondered why. There was something about her past that she wanted to keep private, he had concluded. He had never been unduly curious about the secrets people chose to keep hidden.

Lady Sara Illingsworth.

Not Jane Ingleby, but Lady Sara Illingsworth.

His eyes narrowed as he gazed out onto the now empty square.

He had consistently misinterpreted the biggest clue of all—her reluctance to be seen. She had not wanted to venture outside Dudley House when she was here except into the garden; she did not want to venture outside the house where she was now. She had been very reluctant to sing for his guests.

She had chosen to become his mistress rather than pursue what could undoubtedly be a brilliant career as a singer.

He had thought she was ashamed, first of what people would think her relationship to him might be and then of what that relationship really was. But she had shown no other sign of shame. She had negotiated their foolish contract with practical good sense. She had redecorated her house because she would not be made to feel like a whore living in a brothel. There had been no shrinking from her fate the afternoon of the consummation of their liaison, no tears or other sign of remorse afterward.

His mind should have worked its way around to understanding that she was afraid to be seen in public lest she be recognized and apprehended. He had simply not seen the obvious—that she was in hiding.

That she was wanted for theft and murder.

Jocelyn stepped back from the window, paced to the other side of the room, and set his hands flat on top of the oak desk.

He did not care a fig for the fact that he was harboring a fugitive. The notion that she was dangerous was patently absurd. But he cared the devil of a bit over the fact that he had discovered her identity too late.

Offering employment as his mistress to a penniless orphan or even to a destitute gentlewoman was a perfectly unexceptionable thing to do. Offering the same employment to the daughter of an earl was a different matter altogether. Perhaps it should not be. If they lived in a perfect society, in which all people were seen as equals, it would make no difference.

But they did not.

And so it did make a difference.

He had had the virginity of Lady Sara Illingsworth, daughter of the late Earl of Durbury of Candleford in Cornwall.

He was not at this particular moment feeling kindly disposed toward Lady Sara Illingsworth.

Damn her. He thumped one fist down hard on the desk and clenched his teeth. She should have told him. She should have enlisted his aid. Did she not realize that he was exactly the sort of man to whom she could openly admit the worst without fear that he would have a fit of the vapors and send for the Runners? Did she not understand that he must hold men like Jardine in the utmost contempt? The devil! He pounded his fist hard onto wood again. What had the bastard done to her to provoke her into killing him—if he *was* dead? What had she suffered since in guilt and fear and loneliness?

Damn her all to hell! She had not trusted him enough to confide in him.

Instead she had locked and bolted a shackle about his leg and thrown away the key. Even if it had been done unwittingly—in fact, *undoubtedly* she had not intended it since she trusted him so little—it had been done effectively indeed.

For that he would find it hard to forgive her.

Damn the woman!

And something else. Oh, yes, there was something else. He had bared his soul to her last evening as he had never done to any other human being. He had trusted her that much.

But she did not return his trust. Ever since he had first set eyes upon her, she must have been suffering unbearable torment. Yet she had kept it all from him. Even last night.

Skeletons are dreadful things to have in our past, Jane, he had said to her. *I do not suppose you have any, do you?*

No, she had replied. *None.*

Damn her!

Jocelyn's fist banged onto the desk once more, causing the inkpot to jump in its silver holder.

Jocelyn spent the day at his clubs, at Jackson's boxing saloon, at a shooting range, at the races. He dined at White's and spent a couple of hours at an insipid soiree, at which his sister informed him that he had become quite the stranger and that she had talked Heyward into taking her to Brighton for a few weeks in the summer to mix with Prinny's set and sample the pleasures of the Pavilion. His brother, who also commented that he had become a stranger, was seething with indignation.

"The point is, Tresham," he said, "that the Forbeses are still hiding yet are still spreading the word that *you* are the one afraid to meet *them*. Not to mention what they must be saying about me hiding behind my big brother's coattails. What are you planning to do about them? That is what I want to know. I have never known you to drag your feet like this. If they do not show up within the week, I am going in search of them myself. And bedamned to that toplofty elder brother pronouncement that they are your concern. It was me they tried to kill."

Jocelyn sighed. Yes, he *had* procrastinated. All because of an infatuation for a woman.

"And me they hoped to humiliate," he said. "I will deal with them, Ferdinand. Soon." He refused to discuss the matter further.

But while he had been dallying with his *mistress* for the past week, talking and reading and dabbling with music and art, he had been allowing his reputation to tarnish. It would not do.

It was not until late evening that he finally contrived to get Brougham and Kimble alone. They were strolling together to White's from the soiree.

"You have not, either of you, mentioned the name of my mistress to anyone, have you?" he asked.

"The devil, Tresham." Brougham sounded irritated. "Do you need to ask when you requested us specifically not to?"

"If you do, Tresh," Kimble said with ominous calm, "perhaps I should plant you a facer. You have simply not been yourself lately. But maybe the question was rhetorical?"

"There is a person," Jocelyn explained, "a Runner with oiled hair and shudderingly awful taste in clothes but with shrewd eyes, who will very possibly be asking questions soon about Miss Jane Ingleby."

"A *Bow Street* Runner?" Brougham stopped walking.

"Asking about *Miss Ingleby*?" Even in the darkness of the street Kimble's frown was visible.

"Alias Lady Sara Illingsworth," Jocelyn explained.

His friends stared at him in silence.

"He will be questioning you among others," Jocelyn assured them.

"Miss Jane Ingleby?" Kimble's expression had become a blank mask. "Never even heard of her. Have you, Cone?"

"Who?" Brougham frowned.

"No, no," Jocelyn said gently, and began to walk again. His friends fell into step on either side of him. "It is known that she nursed me during my recuperation from my injury. I admitted as much this morning when the person was standing in my library doing his damnedest not to look servile. For three weeks. After which she left my employ. But who am I to have followed the progress beyond my doors of a mere servant?"

"*Was* there such a servant?" Brougham asked carelessly. "I confess I did not notice, Tresham. But I tend not to notice other people's servants."

"Was she the one who *sang* at your soiree, Tresh?" Kimble asked. "Pretty voice for those who like that sort of music. A pretty enough girl too for those who like simple country misses in muslin when all the ladies present are clad enticingly in satins and plumes and jewels. Whatever *did* happen to her?"

"Thank you," Jocelyn said briskly. "I knew I could trust you."

"I say, though, Tresham," Brougham asked, his voice returned to normal, "what *did* happen with Jardine? You are not about to ask us to believe, I hope, that Lady Sara murdered him in cold blood because he apprehended her stealing."

Kimble snorted derisively.

"I do not *know* what happened," Jocelyn said through his teeth. "She has not seen fit to confide in me. But let me say this. Jardine had better be dead as the proverbial doornail. If he is not, it will be my distinct pleasure to make him wish he were."

"If you need any help," Brougham offered, "look no further than yours truly, Tresham."

"What are you going to do about Lady Sara, Tresh?" Lord Kimble asked.

"Thrash her within an inch of her life," Jocelyn said viciously. "Get to the bottom of that ridiculous story. Get leg shackled to her and make her sorry for the rest of her life that she was ever born. In that order."

"Leg shackled." Conan Brougham winced. "Because she is your mistr—" He was overtaken suddenly by a fit of coughing, brought on perhaps by a sharp dig in the ribs from Viscount Kimble's elbow.

"Leg shackled," Jocelyn repeated. "But first I am going to get foxed. Inebriated. Drunk as a lord. Three sheets to the wind."

The trouble was, of course, that he never seemed able to get drunk when he wanted to, no matter how much he imbibed. He rather believed, by the time he left White's alone at something past midnight, that he had consumed a vast quantity of liquor. But unless he was drunker than he realized, he was walking a straight line in the direction of his mistress's house, and he still felt only coldly furious instead of passionately angry. How could he thrash her—not that he ever could literally beat her or any other woman. How could he deliver one of his famous tongue-lashings, then, if he could feel no heat with his anger?

By the time he had reached the house and let himself in with his key, he could think only of humiliating her, of reminding her of her very subordinate position in his life. He was going to have to marry the woman, of course, even if she did not realize it yet. She would be his wife in name. But she would soon understand that always, for the rest of her days, she would be less to him than a mistress.

19

He came after midnight, long after Jane had given up expecting him, though she was still up, pacing from the den to the dining room to the sitting room, knowing that something was terribly wrong. She was in the den, gazing at his portrait of her, her arms wrapped defensively about her waist, when she heard his key in the outer door. She hurried to meet him, picking up a candlestick as she went. But she mustered the self-respect to step quietly into the hall. She was glad of that restraint a moment later.

He was wearing his black opera cloak. He removed his silk hat and gloves with careful deliberation before turning to look at her. When he did so, Jane found herself gazing at the Duke of Tresham—that stranger from her past. The dark, cold, cynical, and surely inebriated Duke of Tresham. She smiled.

"Upstairs!" he commanded with cold hauteur and a slight jerk of his head in the direction of the stairs.

"Why?" She frowned.

He raised his eyebrows and looked at her as if she were a worm beneath his foot.

"Why?" he asked softly. "*Why*, Jane? Have I mistaken the address, by any chance? But my key fit the lock. Is this not the house at which I keep my mistress? I have come to avail myself of my mistress's services. I need a bed in order to do that comfortably and her person on that bed. The bed is upstairs, I believe."

"You are foxed!" she said, matching him in coldness.

"Am I?" He looked surprised. "But not too foxed to find my way to my mistress's house. Not too foxed to climb the stairs to her bed. Not too foxed to get it up, Jane."

She flushed at his coarseness and stared at him while her heart felt too like a leaden weight to be capable of breaking. But it would break, she knew, once this night was over. Fool! Oh, fool, not only to have fallen in love with him, but to have dreamed that he had fallen for her too.

"Upstairs!" He pointed again. And then he nodded. "Ah, I have realized the reason for your hesitation. I forgot to say please. *Please* go upstairs, Jane. Please remove all your clothes and hairpins when you get there. Please lie on your back on the bed so that I may avail myself of your services. Please keep your end of our contract."

His voice was colder than ice. His eyes were as black as the night.

She had no good reason to refuse him. It had never been part of their bargain that he must love her before she would grant him her favors. But she felt suddenly disoriented, as if a week—the most precious week of her life—had just been erased without a trace. As if she had dreamed it. As if he had never become her companion, her friend, her lover. Her soul mate.

When all was said and done, she was merely his mistress.

She turned and preceded him up the stairs, the candlestick held high, her heart turned to stone. No, not that. A stone felt no pain. She blinked back tears. He would not see such a sign of weakness in her.

Never!

"I have come here, Jane," he said a few moments later, standing inside the door of her bedchamber, his expression quite inscrutable—except that there was something about him that spoke of inebriation and threatened danger, "to be entertained by my mistress. How are you going to entertain me?"

It felt again as if the past week had not been. If it had not, of course, she would have found nothing particularly offensive in his words. There *was* nothing offensive in them. She must not respond as if she thought there were. She must simply forget the past week. But she hesitated too long.

"You do not have a headache, by any chance, Jane?" There was heavy irony in his voice. "Or your courses?"

Her courses were due within the next few days, and she had been feeling a justifiable anxiety about them. But she would not worry before she must. She had known the consequences of such a liaison from the start. There was even a clause in the contract that dealt with children of their affair.

"Or are you simply repulsed by me tonight?" he asked, looking more dangerous than ever with his eyes narrowed on her. "Are you going to exercise your prerogative, Jane, and send me off to hell, my lust unsatisfied?"

"No, of course not." She looked at him calmly. "I will be pleased to entertain you, your grace. What else do I have to think of and dream of and plan for during all the long hours when you are not here, after all?"

"It is reassuring to discover, at least," he said as he strode toward her and the bed, "that you have not lost your saucy tongue, Jane. I would certainly not enjoy you meek and submissive on your back. Now, what sensual delights can you dream up for me?"

She had learned a number of skills during the past week and a half. She had learned not to be shy of her own sexuality or his. It was clear that he really was going to wait for her to entertain him. He took up a stand beside the bed, his feet apart, his hands clasped at his back, and gazed at her with raised eyebrows. It was more than a little disconcerting and very definitely upsetting in light of what she had hoped their next encounter would be like.

She undressed slowly, teasing him with tantalizing glimpses of naked flesh, a little at a time. She folded each garment and turned to set it down on a chair. When she was naked, she lifted her arms and drew the pins from her hair one at a time until it cascaded about her. She smiled. Perhaps after all she could tease him out of his embarrassment over last evening—if that was what this abrupt change in him was all about.

He was still wearing his cloak, but he had thrown it back over his shoulders. He made no effort to hide the telltale bulge of his arousal pushing at the tight fabric of his evening knee breeches. Yet he did not move. His expression remained impassive.

She undid the buttons at his neck and let his cloak fall to the floor behind him. But in doing so she brushed against him and discovered something she had not known before—that there was something erotic about being naked with someone who was fully clothed.

"Sit down," she invited him, indicating the bed.

He raised his eyebrows, but he sat on the side of it, bracing his feet apart, setting his hands behind him on the bed, supporting himself on his arms.

"You are learning wicked lessons that I have not taught you, Jane," he said, watching as she unbuttoned his breeches and freed him of their silken confines. "What do you have in store for me? Mouth play?"

She knew instinctively what he meant. And though with her mind she thought it disgusting, she knew with her body that it would not be so. But she did not believe she could do it, even so. Not yet. Not unless the time should ever arrive when they could come together as lovers rather than as man and mistress.

She took him in her hands, caressed him, stroked him while he watched what she did with narrowed eyes. Then she knelt astride him on the bed, placed him at her entrance, and bore down on him. She stayed upright, her spine slightly arched backward, her fingertips on the satin of his evening coat at his shoulders. She looked into his eyes.

"Good, Jane," he said. "Entertaining." But he still did not move. He was long and rigid inside her, but he did not move. She could smell liquor on his breath.

He had taught her to ride. But she had done it before while he lay flat and she had leaned over him. And he had ridden with her, stride for stride. They had both labored toward the ultimate pleasure.

Tonight he sat still and watched her with his dark, dangerous eyes.

She was slick and wet and pulsing with desire. She would have liked nothing better than to feel him respond in more than just simple arousal, to have allowed him to lead the way to completion. But he would not do it. There was a darkness in him that she could not seem to lighten. He was still punishing both himself and her, she thought, for what he must see as the humiliation of his disclosures the evening before.

She kept her weight on her spread knees and calves. And she rode him. Not as she had done before, inner muscles clenching and unclenching to the rhythm of ascent and descent. There was a certain defense in such motions, a certain control over the rising and cresting of passion—at least until the final moments. This time she moved without defenses, her inner muscles relaxed, no barrier against the rigid hardness onto which she impaled herself time and time again as she rode the rhythm of sex. She arched her spine more, tipped back her head, closed her eyes, and braced her hands on his silken knees behind her.

She tried to show him with her body that she cared, that she would withhold nothing from him when he needed her. And despite his strange, bleak mood, she sensed that he *did* need her.

She did not know for how many minutes she continued while he remained hard and motionless. But desire became a raw ache, and ache became indistinguishable from pain before finally—ah, blessedly—his hands came to her hips and clamped there so unexpectedly hard that her rhythm and all her control shattered even as he thrust urgently and repeatedly up into her, pumping past the barrier she had deliberately not erected. She could hear herself sobbing as if she listened to someone else a great distance away. She heard the growl of his climax and felt the hot gush of his seed.

Union. Ah, the blessed union. He would be consoled now. They would lie together, warm and sated, and talk. She would reassure him and he would be Jocelyn again instead of the dark, dangerous Duke of Tresham.

Tomorrow she would be able to confide her own dark secrets to him.

She was panting and damp and chilly with perspiration. She still straddled him on the bed, her legs wide and stiff. He was still embedded in her. She lifted her head and smiled dreamily at him.

"Vastly entertaining, Jane," he said briskly. "You are becoming skilled indeed at your profession. You are beginning to be worth every penny of your salary." He lifted her off him, turned her so that she sprawled on the bed, and got to his feet. He began to button himself up again.

He might as well have hurled a pitcher of ice water over her.

"And you, of course," she said, "have always been a master of the veiled insult. I perfectly well understand that this is what I am paid to do. You do not need to remind me just because you let down your guard last evening and embarrassed yourself by telling me things you deeply regret telling." She pulled the bedcovers up to cover herself. Suddenly she felt very naked indeed.

"You are insulted, Jane," he asked her, "to be told that you are remarkably skilled in bed? I do not often pay that compliment, you know." He was throwing his cloak about his shoulders.

"I am *insulted*," she told him, sitting up and holding the covers to her breasts, "that you would think it necessary to degrade me, your grace, with this talk of skills and salary. I am insulted that you are ashamed of having confided in me merely because I am a woman and your mistress to boot. I thought we had become friends—and friends *do* talk to each other. They do confide in each other and share their deepest secrets and their deepest wounds. I was mistaken. I should not have forgotten that you pay my salary for *this*." She indicated the bed with one sweeping arm. "And now I am tired. I have been working hard earning my living. Kindly leave, your grace. Good night."

"Friends *confide* in each other, Jane?" He was glaring at her quite intently, his eyes very black. For a moment she felt frightened. She thought he was going to lean over and grab her. Instead he made her a sudden, ironically deferential bow and strode from the room.

Jane was left cold and trembling and lonelier and unhappier than she had ever been in her life before.

As he made his way home to Grosvenor Square, Jocelyn's mood was black indeed. He now thoroughly despised himself—a satisfyingly familiar feeling, at least. He felt as if he had raped her—though he had approached her in very much the way he had been accustomed to approaching his mistresses in the past. And he despised her. She ought not to have allowed him within touching distance of her tonight, but in fact she had serviced him like an experienced courtesan.

He hated her for lulling him all week into a belief that he had found a friend, a soul mate, as well as a damned good bed partner. For somehow inducing him to lower all his defenses, to share with her everything that was his most secret self. For somehow keeping him from noticing that she received but gave nothing except her body in return, that there was nothing reciprocal in their relationship.

She had taken his trust but had kept herself well hidden behind the position of mistress and the alias of Jane Ingleby. Yet she had dared just now to lecture him on the nature of true friendship.

She had taken *everything* from him, even the love of which he had thought himself no longer capable.

He hated her for fooling him into hoping that after all life was worth living. For stripping away all the comfort of the hard cocoon inside which he had lived for ten years.

He hated her.

He could not even *think* of her as Sara.

She was Jane.

But Jane Ingleby did not exist.

He could feel the satisfying beginnings of a headache as he neared home. If he was fortunate, he would have the distraction of a colossal hangover by morning.

From his position in the shadows of a darkened doorway across the street, Mick Boden watched, first as the Duke of Tresham strode off down the street and then as the light in what must be the bedchamber of the house was extinguished. The house was clearly a love nest—the duke had let himself in with his own key, stayed long enough for a prolonged mount or two in that room where the candlelight had appeared just after his arrival, and had then stridden off homeward, looking well satisfied with himself.

It had been a long day. There was no point in hanging

about any longer. It was scarcely likely that the mistress would emerge from the house to gaze after her lover, or even appear in the window since she had not done so in order to wave good night to him.

But she must come out sometime—probably tomorrow to go walking or shopping. All he needed was a glimpse of her. At least then he would know if the duke's fancy piece could possibly be Lady Sara Illingsworth, alias Miss Jane Ingleby. Mick Boden had a certain intuition about the female occupant of that house, and during his years as a Bow Street Runner he had learned to trust his intuition.

He would come back in the morning, Mick decided, and watch the house until she came out. He could set an assistant to such a mundane task, of course, since there were other courses of inquiry that he really should pursue, but his curiosity and even a certain respect for the woman had been aroused during his long, frustrating search for her. He wanted to be the first to see her and the one to apprehend her.

20

Jocelyn missed his usual morning ride in the park. He was too busy dealing with a fat head and a queasy stomach and a valet who opened back his curtains on bright sunshine and then appeared surprised to discover that his master was lying in his own bed, the sunlight full on his face.

But Jocelyn would not allow himself the luxury of nursing a hangover and terrorizing his staff for too long. There were things to do. Fortunately he had had a chance to talk with Kimble and Brougham the evening before. The same could not be said of the Earl of Durbury, who never appeared in public—just like his niece or his cousin or whatever Lady Sara Illingsworth was to him.

The man was still in town, though, and still at the Pulteney, Jocelyn discovered when he called there in the middle of the morning. And willing to receive the Duke of Tresham, though he might have been puzzled by the request. They had never had more than a nodding acquaintance, after all. He was standing in his private sitting room after Jocelyn had first sent up his card and then been escorted up by the earl's man.

"Tresham?" he said by way of greeting. "How do you do?"

"Very well, I thank you," Jocelyn replied, "when it is considered that I might at this moment be lying in my bed at home with my throat slit. Or in my grave, more like, since Lady Sara Illingsworth has been gone from my house for longer than two weeks."

"Ah, yes, have a seat. Let me pour you a drink." The Bow Street Runner had clearly reported to the earl recently, then. "Do you know where she is, Tresham? Have you heard something?"

"Nothing, thank you," Jocelyn said of the drink while his stomach churned unpleasantly. He availed himself of the offer of a chair. "You must understand that when she was in my employ she dressed the part of a servant and used an alias. She was a mere employee. It did not occur to me when she left to ask where she was going."

"No, of course not." The earl poured himself a drink and sat at the square table in the middle of the room. He looked disappointed. "Those damned Runners are not worth a quarter of what they charge, Tresham. Devilish incompetent, in fact. I have been kicking my heels here for well over a month while a dangerous criminal runs loose among an unsuspecting populace. And for three weeks of that time she was at Dudley House. If I had only known!"

"I was fortunate indeed," Jocelyn said, "to escape harm. Murdered your son, did she? My condolences, Durbury."

"Thank you."

The man looked distinctly uncomfortable. So much so, in fact, that Jocelyn, gazing keenly at him while giving an impression of almost bored indolence, drew his own conclusions.

"And robbed you to add insult to injury," he said. "Having spent three weeks at Dudley House, Lady Sara must be well aware that it is full of costly treasures. I have been apprehensive since learning her identity yesterday morning that she might attempt a burglary and murder me too if I am unfortunate enough to stumble upon her at the wrong moment."

The earl looked keenly back at him, but Jocelyn was long practiced in the art of giving nothing whatsoever away with his facial expression.

"Quite so," the earl agreed.

"I quite understand your, ah, *ire*," Jocelyn said, "in having had a mere female relative—and a dependent one too, I daresay—cause you such personal pain and expose your authority to such public ridicule. If I were in your shoes, I would be waiting as impatiently as you for her capture so that I could put my horsewhip to effective use about her hide before the law takes its turn. It is the only way with rebellious women, I have heard. I would mention two things to you, though—my reason for coming, in fact."

The Earl of Durbury looked unsure whether he had just been insulted or commiserated with.

"I have questioned some of my servants," Jocelyn explained—he had done no such thing, of course, "and they assure me that the nurse I knew as Miss Jane Ingleby had only one small bag of possessions with her at Dudley House. Which leaves a question in my mind. Where has she hidden the fortune in money and jewels that she took from you? Has the Bow Street Runner you employ thought of approaching the search from that angle? Find the treasure and there will surely be a clear trail to the woman."

He paused, eyebrows raised, for the earl to respond.

"It is an idea," his lordship conceded stiffly. Jocelyn was confirmed in his suspicion that there *was* no treasure, or at least not any significant amount of it.

"He would certainly be better employed looking for the money and jewels than following me," Jocelyn added amiably.

The Earl of Durbury looked sharply at him.

"I suppose," Jocelyn continued, "he concluded from his interview with me yesterday morning that I am the sort of man who would derive a certain titillation out of bedding a woman who might rob me of my last farthing while I sleep and split open my skull with the sharp end of an ax for good measure. One can understand his conclusion. I do have a certain reputation for reckless, dangerous living. However, although I found it rather amusing yesterday to be followed wherever I went, I do believe I would find it tedious to have the experience repeated today."

The earl clearly did not know what his Runner had been up to most of yesterday. He stared blankly.

"Not that it has been happening yet today," Jocelyn admitted. "I daresay he is camped out again before the house of a certain, ah, *lady* whom I visited last night. The lady is my mistress, but you must understand, Durbury, that any mistress I employ is under my full protection and that anyone who harasses her will have me to answer to. You will perhaps consider it pertinent to explain this to your Runner—I am afraid his name escapes my memory at the moment." He rose to his feet.

"I most certainly will." The Earl of Durbury looked thunderous. "I am paying the Runners an exorbitant amount *to watch your mistress's house,* Tresham? This is outrageous."

"I must confess," Jocelyn said as he picked up his hat and gloves from a table beside the door, "that it is somewhat distracting while one is engaged in, ah, *conversation* with a lady to know that the window is being watched from the outside. I will not expect such a distraction again tonight."

"No, indeed," the earl assured him. "I shall demand an explanation for this from Mick Boden, believe me."

"Ah, yes," Jocelyn said as he let himself out of the room, "that was the name. Wiry little man with well-oiled hair. Good day to you, Durbury."

He felt satisfied with the morning's visit as he sauntered down the stairs and out of the hotel, despite the headache that had settled in for a lengthy stay just behind his eyes. The morning was almost over. He just hoped that, untrue to form, she would not poke as much as her nose out through the door of her house before the watchdog was removed. But it was unlikely. She never went out except into the back garden. And now, of course, he understood why.

During a morning of ferociously hard work tackling a corner of garden wilderness she had not worked on before, Jane convinced herself that the end had come. He had spoken of it himself—the infatuation, the gradual loss of interest, the final severance of all ties.

The infatuation was over, killed by his own indiscretion— or what he apparently saw as an indiscretion anyway. The loss of interest, Jane suspected, would not be gradual but sudden. Perhaps she might expect a few more night visits like last night's. But one day soon Mr. Quincy would arrive to make arrangements for the ending of the liaison. Not that there would be much to discuss. The contract took care of most details.

Then she would never see Jocelyn again.

She tore recklessly at a clump of nettles, which stung painfully even through her gloves.

It was just as well, she told herself. She was going to turn herself in to the Bow Street Runners anyway. Soon she would be able to do it without any encumbrance. Soon her fate would not much matter to her, though she would, of course, from sheer principle fight to clear herself of the ridiculous charges against her. Ridiculous except for the fact that Sidney was dead.

She reached for another clump of nettles.

She had convinced herself so well that she was surprised when Jocelyn arrived early in the afternoon. She heard the rapping of the door knocker as she was changing into a clean dress upstairs. She waited tensely to hear his footsteps on the stairs. But it was Mr. Jacobs's hesitant knock that sounded on her door.

"His grace requests the honor of your company in the sitting room, ma'am," the butler informed her.

Jane's heart sank as she set down her brush. They had not used the sitting room for over a week.

He was standing before the empty fireplace, one arm propped on the high mantel, when she stepped into the room.

"Good afternoon, Jocelyn," she said.

He was looking his usual dark, cynical, arrogant self, his eyes quite inscrutable. His mood had not improved since last night, then. And suddenly she realized why he had come. He would not send Mr. Quincy, of course. He would tell her himself.

This was the end. After just a week and a half.

He inclined his head but did not return her greeting.

"It was a mistake," she said quietly. "When you asked if you could see the room next door, I should have held firm and said no. You want a mistress, Jocelyn. You want an uncomplicated physical relationship with a woman. You are afraid of friendship, of emotional closeness. You are afraid of your artistic side. You are afraid to confront your memories and admit to yourself that you have allowed them to blight your life. You are afraid to let go of your image of yourself as a pure man. I should not have encouraged you to indulge your inner self. I should not have been your friend. I should have kept our relationship to what it was meant to be. I should have entertained you in bed and encouraged you to live all the rest of your life beyond the confines of this house."

"Indeed?" There was pure ice in his voice. "Do you have any other pearls of wisdom for me, Jane?"

"I will not hold you to our contract," she said. "It would be criminal of me to insist that you support me for four and a half years when our liaison has lasted a mere week and a half.

You are free of me, your grace. As of this moment. By tomorrow I shall be gone. Even today if you wish."

It would be better today. To leave without having any time to think about it. To go to the Pulteney Hotel. Or to seek out the Bow Street Runners if the earl was not there.

"You are quite right," he said after staring at her in silence for an uncomfortably long time. "Our contract is void. It has a fatal flaw."

She lifted her chin a notch, realizing only as he spoke that she had been desperately hoping he would argue, try to persuade her to stay, be simply Jocelyn again.

"I believe," he said, "contracts are void if one of the parties uses an alias. I am no legal expert. Quincy would know. But I believe I am right, Sara."

Foolishly, she did not notice for a moment. There was only a strange chill at her heart. But it was only a moment. The name he had used seemed to hang in the air between them as if the sound of it had not died away with his voice.

She sat down abruptly on a chair close by.

"That is not my name," she whispered.

"I beg your pardon." He made her an ironic half bow. "I forget that you insist upon formality. I should have said *Lady* Sara. Is that better?"

She shook her head. "You misunderstand. It is not my *name*. I am Jane." But she spread her hands over her face suddenly and found they were shaking. She lowered them to her lap. "How did you find out?"

"I had a visitor," he said. "A Bow Street Runner. I understand that in his search for Lady Sara Illingsworth he called at the milliner's shop of a certain Madam Dee Lorrent. I suppose he meant Madame de Laurent. Coincidentally your former employer, Jane, as well as Lady Sara's. The Runner came to the intelligent conclusion that you were one and the same."

"I was going to tell you." She realized even as she spoke how lame her words sounded.

"Were you?" He raised his quizzing glass and regarded her through it with cold hauteur. "Were you indeed, Lady Sara? Pardon me for not believing you. You are as accomplished a liar as I have met. I am afraid of friendship and emotional closeness, am I? You ought not to have become my friend, ought you? To my shame I became your dupe. For a short while. No longer." He dropped his quizzing glass and it swung on its ribbon.

The temptation was to beg him to believe her, try to explain that after the emotional intensity of his own disclosures two evenings ago she had decided to wait to tell her own story. But he would not believe her. She would not believe him if the situation were reversed, would she?

"Does he know where I am?" she asked. "The Bow Street Runner?"

"He followed me here last night," he told her, "and stood outside while you were pleasuring me upstairs. Oh, do not be alarmed. I have called off the hunt, at least in this particular place, though I do not imagine he is deceived. He is more intelligent than his current employer, I believe."

"Is the Earl of Durbury still at the Pulteney?" she asked. "Do you know?"

"He was there this morning when I called upon him," he said.

Her face felt cold and clammy. There was a ringing in her ears. The air she breathed felt icy. But she would not faint. She *would* not.

"Oh, I have not betrayed you, Lady Sara," he told her, his eyes narrowing.

"Thank you," she said. "I would rather turn myself in than be dragged in. If you will give me a minute to fetch my bag from upstairs, you may see me off the premises and assure yourself that I am gone. Unless you have told anyone that I am your mistress, no one need know. I daresay Mr. Quincy and the servants here are discreet. It would be a condition of their employment, would it not? The scandal need not touch you too nearly." She got to her feet.

"Sit down," he told her.

The words were so quietly spoken but with such cold command that she obeyed without thinking.

"Are you guilty of any of the charges against you?" he asked her.

"Murder? Theft?" She looked down at the hands clasped in her lap. Her fingers, she noticed dispassionately, were white with tension. "I hit him. I took money. Therefore, I am guilty."

"And jewels?"

"A bracelet," she said. "It is in my bag upstairs."

She would offer no explanations, no excuses. She owed him none now. Yesterday it would have been different. He would have been her friend, her lover. Now he was nothing at all.

"You hit him," he said. "With an ax? With a pistol?"

"With a book," she said.

"With a *book*?"

"The corner of it caught him on the temple," she explained. "He was bleeding and dizzy. If he had sat down all might have been well. But he came after me, and when I stepped aside he lost his balance and cracked his head on the hearth. He was not dead. I had him carried upstairs and tended him myself until the doctor arrived. He was still not dead when I left, though he was unconscious."

There, she had given in to the urge to explain after all. She was still watching her hands.

"He kept coming after you," Jocelyn said quietly. "Why was he coming after you in the first place? Because he had caught you stealing?"

"Oh, that nonsense," she said contemptuously. "He was going to ravish me."

"At *Candleford*?" His voice was sharp. "At his father's home? His father's ward?"

"They were gone," she told him, "the earl and countess. They had left for a few days."

"Leaving you alone with Jardine?"

"And with an elderly relative as chaperone." She laughed. "She likes her port, does Cousin Emily. And she likes Sidney too—*liked* Sidney, that is." There was an uncomfortable churning in her stomach. "He got her drunk and sent her off early to bed. There were only a few of his friends there that evening and his own servants."

"The friends did not defend you?" he asked. "And were not to be depended upon to tell the truth in an investigation into the death of Jardine?"

"They were all inebriated," she said. "They were urging him on."

"Was he not afraid," Jocelyn asked, "of the consequences of ravishing you after his father had returned?"

"I suppose," she said, "he counted upon my being too ashamed to say anything. He counted upon my meekly agreeing to marry him. And it would have been the earl's solution even if I had told. It is what they both wanted and had urged upon me ceaselessly until I almost *was* ready to go at them both with an ax."

"A reluctant bride," he said. "Yes, that would appeal to Jardine. Especially when she is as lovely as a golden goddess. I am not well acquainted with Durbury, though I did not find myself warming to him this morning. Why did you steal and run away and go into hiding under an alias and make yourself look as guilty as sin? It seems uncharacteristic of Jane Ingleby. But then she does not exist, does she?"

"I took fifteen pounds," she said. "In the year and a half since my father's death, the earl had given me no allowance. There was nothing on which to spend money at Candleford, he told me. I believe he owed me far more than fifteen pounds. The bracelet was my father's wedding gift to my mother. Mama gave it to me on her deathbed, but I asked Papa to keep it in the safe with all the other family jewelry. The earl had always refused to give it to me or to acknowledge it as mine. I knew the combination of the safe."

"Foolish of him," Jocelyn said, "not to have thought of that."

"I was not running away," she said. "I had had enough of them all. I came to London to stay with Lady Webb, my mama's dearest friend and my godmother. Lord Webb was to have been my guardian jointly with my father's cousin, the new earl, but he died and I suppose Papa did not think of having someone else appointed. Lady Webb was not at home and not expected back soon. That was when I panicked. I started to realize that Sidney might have been badly hurt, that he might even have died. I realized how the taking of the money and the bracelet would be construed. I realized that none of the witnesses was likely to tell the truth. I realized I might be in deep trouble."

"All the deeper," he said, "for your decision to become a fugitive."

"Yes."

"Was there no one at Candleford or in its neighborhood to stand your friend?" he asked.

"My father's cousin is the earl," she explained. "Sidney is—was—his heir. There was no one powerful enough to shield me, and my dearest friend was from home in Somersetshire on an extended visit with his sister."

"He?" The question was asked with soft emphasis.

"Charles," she said. "Sir Charles Fortescue."

"Your friend?" he said. "And beau?"

She looked up at him for the first time in several minutes. Shock was beginning to recede. He had no business interrogating her. She was under no obligation to answer him. She was merely his ex-mistress. And she had no intention of accepting any pay for the past week and a half or of taking with her any of the clothes he had bought her.

"And beau," she replied steadily. "We were to marry, but not for a long time. I am not permitted to marry without the earl's consent until I am five and twenty. We would have married on my twenty-fifth birthday."

"But will not now do so?" He had his glass to his eye again, but Jane would not be cowed by it. She continued to look steadily at him. "He will not fancy marrying a murderess, Lady Sara? How unsporting of him. And he will not marry a fallen woman? How unchivalrous."

"*I* will not marry *him*," she said firmly.

"Quite right too," he said briskly. "The laws of our land prohibit bigamy, Lady Sara."

She *wished* he would not keep calling her that.

"Bigamy?" Had Charles met and married someone else? she thought foolishly without even stopping to wonder how she expected the Duke of Tresham to know that fact even if it were true.

"Sir Charles Fortescue," he said coldly, "would not be permitted by law to marry my wife. One hopes, I suppose, that his heart will not be broken, though I have not noticed him rushing about London, moving heaven and earth to find you and clasp you to his bosom. One hopes, perhaps, that *your* heart will not be broken, though frankly I cannot say that I much care."

Jane was on her feet.

"Your wife?" she said, her eyes wide with astonishment. "*Your wife?* How utterly preposterous. You think you owe me marriage just because you have suddenly discovered that I am Lady Sara Illingsworth of Candleford rather than Jane Ingleby from some orphanage?"

"I could not have phrased it better myself," he said.

"I do not know what you have planned for the rest of the

afternoon, your grace," she told him, looking into his cold, cynical face and feeling the full chill of his total indifference to her as a person, "but I have something of importance to do. I have a visit to the Pulteney Hotel to make. If you will excuse me." She turned resolutely to the door.

"Sit down," he said as quietly as before.

She swung to face him. "I am not one of your servants, your grace," she said. "I am not—"

"*Sit down!*" His voice, if anything, was even quieter.

Jane stood staring at him for a few moments before striding across the room until she stood almost toe to toe with him.

"I repeat," she said, "I am not one of your servants. If you have something more to say to me, say it without this ridiculous posturing. My ears function quite well enough when I am on my feet."

"You try my patience to the limit, ma'am," he said, his eyes narrowing dangerously.

"And mine is already tried *beyond* the limit, your grace," she retorted, turning toward the door again.

"Lady Sara." His icy voice stopped her in her tracks. "We will have one thing straight between us. Soon—within the next few days—you will be the Duchess of Tresham. Your personal wishes on this matter are not to be consulted. I am quite indifferent to them. You will be my wife. And you will spend the rest of your life ruing the day you were born."

If she had not been so white with fury, she might well have laughed. As it was she took her time about seating herself in the nearest chair, arranging her skirts neatly about her before looking up into his eyes, her own carefully cool.

"How utterly ridiculous you make yourself when you decide to play the part of toplofty aristocrat," she told him, folding her hands in her lap and pressing her lips tightly together. She girded herself for the inevitable battle.

21

He was surprised by the force of his hatred for her. He had never hated anyone—except perhaps his father. Not even his mother. It was unnecessary to hate when one did not feel strongly about anyone. He wished he could feel nothing but indifference for Lady Sara Illingsworth.

He could almost succeed when he thought of her by that name. But his eyes saw Jane Ingleby.

"You will not be forced to behold your ridiculous husband very often, you will be relieved to know," he told her. "You will live at Acton, and you know how fond I am of my main country seat. You will see me only once a year or so when it becomes necessary to breed you. If you are very efficient you will have two sons within the first two years of our marriage and I may consider them enough to secure the succession. If you are extraordinarily clever, of course, you may already be increasing." He lifted his quizzing glass and regarded her abdomen through it.

Her lips had already done their familiar disappearing act. He was glad she had pulled herself together. For a while she had looked pale and shaken and abject. He had found himself almost pitying her. She was glaring at him with her very blue eyes.

"You are forgetting one thing, your grace," she said. "Women are not quite slaves in our society, though they come dangerously close. I have to say 'I do' or 'I will' or whatever it is brides say to consent to a marriage. You may drag me to the altar—I will concede your superior physical strength—but you will be considerably embarrassed when I refuse my consent."

He knew he should be delighted by her obvious reluctance. But she had duped him, humiliated him, made a fool of him once. Her will would not prove stronger than his on this particular matter.

"Besides," she added, "I am not yet of age. And according to my father's will I cannot marry below the age of five and twenty without the consent of my guardian. If I do, I lose my inheritance."

"Inheritance?" He raised his eyebrows.

"Everything my father owned except Candleford itself was unentailed," she explained, "and his title, of course. His other estates, his fortune—everything, in fact—will be mine at the age of five and twenty, or my husband's if I marry with consent before then."

Which explained a great deal, of course. Durbury had the title and Candleford and control of everything else at the moment. He would have permanent control if he could persuade Lady Sara to marry into his family—or if he could make her life so uncomfortable that she would rashly elope with someone else before her twenty-fifth birthday.

"I suppose," he said, "if you break the rules Durbury himself inherits everything?"

"Yes."

"He may inherit everything, then," he said curtly. "I am enormously wealthy. I do not need my wife to bring me a fortune."

"I suppose," she said, "if I am convicted of murder I will be disinherited. Perhaps I will even d-die. But I will fight to whatever end is in store for me. And I will marry no one, whatever the outcome. Not Charles. Not you. At least not until I am five and twenty. Then I will marry or not marry as I choose. I will be free. I will be dead or imprisoned or transported, or I will be free. Those are the alternatives. I will be no man's slave in the guise of wife. Certainly not yours."

He gazed at her in silence. She did not look away, of course. She was one of the few people, man or woman, who could hold his scrutiny. She held her chin high. Her eyes were steely, her lips still in their thin, stubborn line.

"I should have seen it sooner," he said, as much to himself as to her. "The essentially cold emptiness at the core of you. You are sexually passionate, but then sex is an essentially carnal thing. It does not touch the heart. You have the strange ability of opening yourself to other people's confidences. You convey an image of sympathy and empathy. You can take in and take in, can you not, like some cold-hearted creature warming itself with its victim's blood. One does not notice that in effect you give nothing back. Jane Ingleby, bastard of some unknown gentleman, reared in a superior orphanage. That was all you gave me—lies. And your Siren's body. I am weary of arguing with you. I have other calls to make, but I will return. You will stay here until I do."

"I have hurt you," she said, getting to her feet. "You will be pleased to know that you have had your revenge. If my heart was not cold before, it is now. I have given and given of my very self because your need has been so great. I was not given a chance to reach out for myself, for the comfort of your understanding and sympathy and friendship. There was not enough time—just one week and it ended so abruptly yesterday. Go. I am weary too. I want to be alone. You feel betrayed, your grace? Well, I do too."

He did not stop her this time when she turned to leave the room. He watched her go. He stood where he was for a long time.

His heart ached.

The heart he had not known he possessed.

He could not trust her. He would not trust her. Not again.

Had he betrayed her? *Had* it been sympathy and friendship and love she had given after all? *Had* she intended sharing herself with him as he had shared himself with her?

Jane.

Lady Sara Illingsworth.

Ah, Jane.

He strode from the room and from the house. It was only when he was some distance away that he remembered ordering her to remain until he returned. But she was not one to take orders meekly. He should have made her promise. Devil take it, he should have thought of that.

But surely she would not leave the house now. Surely she would wait.

He did not go back.

If Lady Webb was surprised when her butler handed her a card on a tray and informed her even before she could look at it that the Duke of Tresham was standing in her hall below requesting the honor of a few minutes of her time, she did not show it by the time Jocelyn was announced. She rose from a small escritoire, where she was apparently engaged in writing letters.

"Tresham?" she said graciously.

"Ma'am." He made her a deep bow. "I thank you for granting me some of your time."

Lady Webb was an elegant widow of about forty with

whom he was acquainted, though not well. She moved in a more civilized set than any with which he usually consorted. He held her in considerable respect.

"Do have a seat," she offered, indicating a chair while she seated herself on a sofa close by, "and tell me what brings you here."

"I believe," he said, taking the offered chair, "you have an acquaintance with Lady Sara Illingsworth, ma'am."

She raised her eyebrows and regarded him more keenly. "She is my goddaughter," she said. "Do you have any news of her?"

"She was employed at Dudley House as my nurse for three weeks," he said, "after I had been shot in the leg in a, ah, duel. She came upon me in Hyde Park while it was happening. She was on her way to work at a milliner's at the time. She was using an alias, of course."

Lady Webb was sitting very still. "Is she still at Dudley House?" she asked.

"No, ma'am." Jocelyn sat back in his chair. He was experiencing extreme discomfort, a feeling relatively unknown to him. "I did not know her real identity until a Bow Street Runner came to speak with me yesterday. I knew her as Miss Jane Ingleby."

"Ah, Jane," Lady Webb said. "It is the name by which her parents called her. Her middle name."

Foolishly it felt good to hear that. She really *was* Jane, as she had told him earlier.

"She was a servant, you must understand," he said. "She had temporary employment with me."

Lady Webb shook her head and sighed aloud. "And you do not know where she went," she said. "Neither do I. Is that why you have come here? Because you are outraged to know that you were duped into giving sanctuary to a fugitive? If I knew where she was, Tresham, I would not tell you. Or the Earl of Durbury." She spoke the name with disdain.

"You do not believe, then," he asked, "that she is guilty of any of the charges against her?"

Her nostrils flared, the only sign of emotion. She sat straight but gracefully on her seat, her back not touching it. Her posture was rather reminiscent of Jane's—a lady's posture.

"Sara is no murderer," she said firmly, "and no thief either. I would stake my fortune and my reputation on it. The Earl of Durbury wanted her to marry his son, whom she held in the utmost contempt, sensible girl. I have my own theory on how Sidney Jardine met his end. If you are lending your support to Durbury by coming here in the hope that you will learn more from me than he did a few days ago, then you are wasting your time and mine. I would ask you to leave."

"Do you believe he is dead?" Jocelyn asked with narrowed eyes.

She stared at him. "Jardine?" she said. "Why would his father say he was dead if he were not?"

"*Has* he said it?" Jocelyn asked. "Or has he merely not contradicted the rumor that has been making the circuit of London drawing rooms and clubs?"

She was looking steadily at him. "Why are you here?" she asked.

All day he had wondered what exactly he would say. He had come to no satisfactory conclusion. "I know where she is," he said. "I found her other employment when she left Dudley House."

Lady Webb was on her feet instantly. "In town?" she asked. "Take me to her. I will bring her here and give her sanctuary while I have my solicitor look into the ridiculous charges against her. If your suspicions are correct and Sidney Jardine is still alive . . . Well. Where is she?"

Jocelyn had risen too. "She is in town, ma'am," he assured her. "I will bring her to you. I would have brought her now, but I had to be sure that she would find a safe haven here."

Her gaze became shrewd suddenly.

"Tresham," she asked, as he had feared she would, "what other employment did you find Sara?"

"You must understand, ma'am," he said stiffly, "that she gave me a false name. She told me she had been brought up in an orphanage. It was clear that she had had a genteel upbringing, but I thought her destitute and friendless."

She closed her eyes briefly, but she did not relax her very erect posture. "Bring her to me," she said. "You will have a maid or some respectable female companion with her when she arrives."

"Yes, ma'am," he agreed. "I do, of course, consider myself affianced to Lady Sara Illingsworth."

"Of course." There was a certain coldness in the eyes that regarded him so keenly. "It just seems a rather sad irony that she has escaped from one blackguard merely to land in the clutches of another. Bring her to me."

Jocelyn made her a bow, resisting the urge to don his usual expression of cynical hauteur. At least the woman had enough integrity not to be rubbing her hands with glee at the thought of netting the Duke of Tresham for her goddaughter.

"Enlist the help of your solicitor by all means, ma'am," he said. "In the meantime I will be doing my own part to clear the name of my betrothed and to release her from the bonds of an inappropriate guardianship. Good day."

He left her standing straight and proud and hostile in the middle of her drawing room. Someone to whom he could quite safely bring Jane. A friend at last.

Jane remained in her bedchamber for a whole hour after Jocelyn had left, doing nothing but sit on the dressing table stool, her slippered feet side by side on the floor, her hands clasped in her lap, her eyes glazed as they gazed unseeing at the carpet.

Then she got up and removed all her clothes, everything that had been bought for her. She took from her wardrobe the plain muslin dress, the serviceable shift, and the stockings she had worn to London and dressed again. She brushed out her hair and braided it tightly so that it would fit beneath her gray bonnet. She pulled on the bonnet and matching cloak, slipped her feet into her old shoes, drew on her black gloves, and was ready to go. She picked up her bag of meager possessions—and the priceless bracelet—and let herself quietly out of her room.

Unfortunately Phillip was in the hallway below. He looked at her in surprise—she had never been out before, of course, and she was very plainly dressed.

"You are going out, ma'am?" he asked redundantly.

"Yes." She smiled. "Just for a walk and some fresh air, Phillip."

"Yes, ma'am." He hurried to open the door for her and looked uncertainly at her bag. "Where shall I tell his grace you have gone, ma'am, if he should return?"

"That I have gone for a walk." She retained her smile as she stepped out onto the doorsill. She immediately felt the panic of one who fears falling off the edge of the world. She stepped resolutely forward. "I am not a prisoner here, you know."

"No, of course, ma'am," Phillip was hasty to agree. "Enjoy your walk, ma'am."

She wanted to turn back to say a proper good-bye to him. He was a pleasant young man who had always been eager to please. But she merely walked on and listened to the sound of the door closing behind her.

Like a prison door.

Shutting her out.

It might have been just oversensitive nerves, of course. She realized that as soon as she sensed less than five minutes later that she was being followed. But she would not turn around to look. Neither would she quicken her pace—nor slacken it. She strode along the pavement at a steady pace, her back straight, her chin up.

"Lady Sara Illingsworth? Good afternoon, my lady."

The voice, reasonably pleasant, not raised, came from close behind her. She felt as if a reptile were crawling up her spine. Terror attacked her knees, nausea her stomach. She stopped and turned slowly.

"A member of the Bow Street Runners, I presume?" she said just as pleasantly. He certainly did not look the part. Neither tall nor large in girth, he appeared like nothing more than a poor man's imitation of a dandy.

"Yes, my lady. At your service, my lady," the Runner said, looking steadily at her, not making any obeisance.

Jocelyn had been wrong, then. He had not succeeded in lifting the watch on her house. He had described the Runner as shrewd, but he had not guessed that the man was too shrewd to allow himself to be ordered away from his prey when he knew she was close.

"I will make your task easy," she said, surprised by the steadiness of her own voice. Indeed, it was amazing how terror receded once one had faced it head-on. "I am on the way to the Pulteney Hotel to call upon the Earl of Durbury. You may escort me there and claim all the glory of having apprehended me, if you wish. But you will not come closer or touch me. If you do, I shall squawk very loudly—there are any number of carriages and pedestrians in sight. I shall make up every story I can think of to convince my audience that you are stalking and harassing me. Do we have an agreement?"

"It is like this, my lady." The Runner's voice sounded pleasantly regretful. "Mick Boden does not let criminals escape him once he has them in his sights. I don't foolishly let them off the leash just because they are ladies and know how to talk sweet. And I don't make bargains with them. You come quiet after I have tied your hands behind you under your cloak, and you will not embarrass yourself. I do know that ladies don't like to be embarrassed in public."

The man might be shrewd, but he certainly was not wise. He took a purposeful step toward Jane, one hand disappearing inside a deep pocket. She opened her mouth and screamed— and screamed. She startled even herself. She had never been a screamer, even as a child. The Runner looked both startled and aghast. His hand jerked out of his pocket, clutching a length of rope.

"Now, there is no need to take on so," he said sharply. "I'm not going to—"

But Jane never did discover what it was he was not going to do. Two gentlemen rode up at a smart trot and proceeded to dismount from their horses. A hackney coach stopped abruptly on the other side of the street, and its burly driver jumped down from the box while shouting directions to a young sweeper to hold the horses' heads. An elderly couple of respectable middle-class demeanor, who had passed Jane a few moments before, turned and hurried back. And a giant of an individual, who looked as if he might well be a pugilist, had materialized seemingly from nowhere and hugged Mick Boden from behind, pinioning his arms to his sides. It was this action that cut the Runner's sentence in half.

"He accosted me," Jane informed her gathering rescuers. "He was going to tie me up with *that*"—she pointed one genuinely shaking finger at the rope—"and abduct me."

Everyone spoke up at once. The pugilist offered to squeeze harder until the villain's stomach came spurting out his mouth. The coachman suggested taking him in the hackney to the nearest magistrate, where he would surely be sentenced to hang. One of the gentlemen riders gave it as his opinion that it would be a shame for such a slimy toad to swing before his facial features had been rearranged. The elderly gentleman did not know why such a villainous-looking thug should be allowed to roam the streets of a civilized city, terrorizing its womenfolk. His wife set a motherly arm about Jane's shoulders and clucked and tutted with mingled concern and outrage.

Mick Boden had recovered his composure even though he could not free himself. "I am a Bow Street Runner," he announced in a voice of authority. "I am engaged in apprehending a notorious thief and murderess and would advise you all not to interfere in the workings of justice."

Jane lifted her chin. "I am Lady Sara Illingsworth," she said indignantly, hoping that none of the gathered spectators had heard of her. "I am on my way to visit my cousin and guardian, the Earl of Durbury, at the Pulteney Hotel. He will be very vexed with me when I confess that I came out without my maid. The poor girl is nursing a chill. I should have brought a footman instead, of course, but I did not understand that desperate men will accost ladies even in broad daylight." She drew a handkerchief from the pocket of her cloak and held it to her mouth.

Mick Boden looked reproachfully at her. "Now, there was no need of all this," he said.

"Come, my dear," the elderly lady said, linking her arm through Jane's. "We will see you safely to the Pulteney Hotel, will we not, Vernon? It is not far out of our way."

"You go on, my lady," one of the riders told her. "We know where to find you if you are needed as a witness. But I've a mind to do the law's work for it without bothering any magistrate. You go on."

"Now see here," Mick Boden was saying as Jane took the offered arm of the elderly gentleman and proceeded along the street, protectively flanked by him and his wife. Under other circumstances she might have been amused. As it was, she felt a mingling of boldness—now at last she was *doing* something—and apprehension. He had been going to *tie* her hands.

She thanked her escort most profusely when they arrived before the doors of the Pulteney, and promised that never again would she be foolish enough to step out alone onto the streets of London. They had been so kind to her that she felt guilt at the way she had deceived them. Although she was, of course, no thief and no murderer. She stepped inside the hotel.

A few minutes later, she was knocking on the door of the Earl of Durbury's suite, having declined the offer to have his lordship informed of her arrival while she waited in a lounge downstairs. She recognized her cousin's valet, Parkins, who answered her knock, and he recognized her. His jaw dropped inelegantly. Jane stepped forward without a word for him, and he jumped smartly to one side.

She found herself in a spacious and elegant private sitting room. The earl was seated at a desk, his back to the door. Despite herself, her heart was thumping in her chest, in her throat, in her ears.

"Who was it, Parkins?" he asked without turning.

"Hello, Cousin Harold," Jane said.

Jocelyn intended to waste no time in taking Jane to Lady Webb's. It really would not do for her to remain where she was for a moment longer than necessary. He would have Mrs. Jacobs accompany her in his carriage.

But getting his carriage necessitated riding through Hyde Park. And in riding through the park he came quite coincidentally upon an interesting scene. There was a largish group of gentlemen on horseback some distance from the path along which he rode, several of them talking and gesticulating excitedly.

Some quarrel was brewing, he thought. Normally he would not have hesitated to ride closer and discover what was going on, but today he had more important matters to attend to and would have continued onward if he had not suddenly recognized one of the loudly gesturing gentlemen as his brother.

Ferdinand quarreling? Perhaps getting himself into deep waters from which his Dudley nature would not permit him to withdraw until he was in over his head? Well, the least he himself could do, Jocelyn decided with a resigned sigh, was go and lend some moral support.

His approach was noted, first by those who were not themselves involved in the loud altercation that was proceeding, but then even by its participants. The crowd turned as one man to watch him come and a curious hush descended on them.

The reason for it all was almost instantly apparent to Jocelyn. There they were at last, all five of them in a body together—the Forbes brothers. Terrified, no doubt, to show their individual faces anywhere in London, they were presenting a collective front to the world today.

"Tresham!" Ferdinand exclaimed. He looked about at the brothers in some triumph. "*Now* we will see who is a cowardly bastard!"

"Dear me." Jocelyn raised his eyebrows. "Has anyone here been using such shockingly vulgar language, Ferdinand? I am vastly relieved I was not present to hear it. And who, pray, was the recipient of such an uncharitable description?"

Although he was a prosy bore in a pulpit, the Reverend Josiah Forbes, to give him his due, was no sniveling, sneaky knave. He rode forward without any hesitation until he was almost knee to knee with Jocelyn, made a grand production of taking off his right glove, and then spoke.

"You were, Tresham," he said. "Cowardly bastard *and* debaucher of wedded virtue. You will meet me, sir, if you wish to dispute either of these accusations."

He leaned forward and slapped his glove across Jocelyn's cheek.

"Gladly," Jocelyn said with languid hauteur. "Your second may meet with Sir Conan Brougham at his earliest convenience."

The Reverend Forbes's place was taken by Captain Samuel Forbes, resplendent in his scarlet regimentals, and amid the buzz of heightened excitement among the spectators, Jocelyn was aware that the remaining Forbeses were forming a wavering queue behind. He yawned delicately behind one hand.

"And you will meet me over the matter of my sister's honor, Tresham," Captain Forbes said, and slapped *his* glove across the same ducal cheek.

"If fate permits me," Jocelyn told him gently. "But you will understand that if your brother has spattered my brains across a field of honor before I am able to keep our appointment, I will be forced to decline your invitation—or at least Brougham will on my posthumous behalf."

Captain Forbes wheeled his horse away, and it was apparently Sir Anthony Forbes's turn. But Jocelyn held up a staying hand and looked from one to the other of the three remaining brothers with careful disdain.

"You must forgive me," he said softly, "if I beg to decline the opportunity of meeting any of the three of you on a field of honor. There is no honor in attempting to punish a man without first challenging him face to face. And I make it a personal rule to duel only with gentlemen. There is nothing gentlemanly about attempting to wound a man by killing his brother."

"And nothing safe about it either," Ferdinand added hotly, "when that brother can stand up to answer the cowardly trick for himself."

There was a smattering of applause from the ever-growing circle of spectators.

"You three," Jocelyn said, raising his whip and pointing it at each of the brothers in turn, "will take your punishment at the end of my fists here and now, though I suggest we move to a more secluded area. I will take on all of you at once. You may defend yourselves since I *am* a gentleman and would not take unfair advantage even of rogues and scoundrels by having you tied down. But there will be no rules and we will have no seconds. This is *not* a field of honor."

"Oh, I say, Tresham," Ferdinand said with cheerful enthusiasm, "well done. But it will be two against three. This is my quarrel too and I will not be left out of the satisfaction of sharing in the punishing." He dismounted as he spoke and led his horse in the direction of the grove of trees toward which Jocelyn had pointed. Beyond it there was more grass but no paths, and so it was rarely used by those riders and pedestrians who frequented the park daily.

The three Forbes brothers, as Jocelyn had guessed, could not avoid the meeting without losing face. The other gentlemen crowded after them, delighted by the unexpected opportunity of watching a mill in Hyde Park of all places.

Jocelyn stripped off his coat and waistcoat while his brother did the same thing beside him. Then they both strode out into the grassy ring, formed by the crowd of acquaintances who had gathered to watch.

It really was a vastly uneven contest, Jocelyn realized with some disappointment and contempt before even two minutes had passed. Wesley Forbes liked to use his booted feet and clearly hoped to disarm his opponents with one well-placed kick to each. Unfortunately for him, Ferdinand, who had quick reflexes, caught his boot in midair with both hands just as if it were a ball and held him off balance while he used one of his considerably longer legs to poke the man sharply in the chin.

After that, and to enthusiastic cheering from the vast majority of the spectators, it was two against two.

Sir Anthony Forbes, who landed one lucky punch to Jocelyn's stomach, tried for some time to match his opponent strike for strike, but soon he began blubbering about its being unfair to fight him when it was Wes who had tampered with the curricle.

The crowd jeered.

"Perhaps it is poetic justice, then," Jocelyn told him as he jabbed at Sir Anthony's defenses and waited longer than was really necessary before delivering the *coup de grâce*, "that I should be punishing the wrong brother."

At last he let fly with a left hook and a right uppercut, which felled his opponent like a wicket going down before a cricket ball.

Ferdinand meanwhile was using Joseph Forbes's stomach as a punching ball. But hearing the general cheer as Sir Anthony went down, he ended his own bout with one pop to the man's face. Joseph's knees buckled under him and he rolled on the ground, clutching his bloody nose. He did not attempt to get up.

Jocelyn strode over to the other two brothers, who had watched in silence. He nodded courteously enough. "I shall await further word from Sir Conan Brougham," he said.

Ferdinand, without a visible mark on his body, was pulling his coat back on and laughing gaily. "One could have wished for all five," he said, "but one must not be greedy. Well done, Tresham. That was inspired. No duels for those three but simple punishment. And audience enough to tell the tale for weeks to come. We have reminded everyone of the consequences of annoying a Dudley. Come to White's?"

But Jocelyn had just grown aware of how much time had been used up in this encounter.

"Perhaps later," he said. "For now I have something of extreme importance to attend to." He looked assessingly at his brother, waving off the gentlemen who would have come to congratulate them and mounting his horse. "Ferdinand, there is something you can do for me."

"Anything." His brother looked both surprised and gratified. It was not often that Jocelyn asked something of him.

"You might spread the word," Jocelyn said, "subtly, of course, that it has turned out that Miss Jane Ingleby, my former nurse and the main musical attraction at my soiree, is in reality Lady Sara Illingsworth. That I have found her by happy chance and taken her to Lady Webb's. That all the rumors surrounding her name are about to be proved as exaggerated and groundless as most rumors are."

"Oh, I say." Ferdinand looked vastly interested. "How did you find out, Tresham? How did you find *her*? How——"

But Jocelyn held up a staying hand. "You will do it?" he asked. "Is there any grand *ton* entertainment tonight?" He was dreadfully out of touch.

"A ball," Ferdinand said. "Lady Wardle's. It is bound to be a horrid squeeze."

"Drop word there, then," Jocelyn said. "All you need do is mention the bare facts once. Twice perhaps for good measure. No more than that."

"What——" Ferdinand began, but Jocelyn had his hand up again.

"Later," he said. "I have to go take her to Lady Webb's. This is going to be a near-run thing, Ferdie. But we will pull it off."

It felt rather good, he thought as he rode onward, to have made the discovery that his brother could also be a friend, as he had been when they were boys.

So there were two more duels to face—after he had dealt with this whole damned mess with Jane. Would she out of sheer principle, he wondered, be as prickly about being escorted to Lady Webb's as she had been about everything else earlier on?

Dratted, exasperating woman!

22

*T*he Earl of Durbury whipped around, his eyes widening in astonishment.

"So," he said, getting to his feet, "you have been ferreted out at last, have you, Sara? By the Bow Street Runner? Where is he?"

"I am not perfectly sure," Jane said, strolling farther into the room in order to set her gloves and bonnet down on a small table. "The group of men who prevented him from abducting me had not decided what to do with him when I continued on my way here. I have come quite voluntarily to see you. To commiserate with you on your loss. And to demand what you mean by setting up a Bow Street Runner outside my house as if I were a common criminal."

"Aha," the earl said sharply. "He was right, then, was he? I might have guessed it. You are a strumpet, Tresham's doxy."

Jane ignored him. "Your hired Runner," she said, "who would have engaged in melodrama by dragging me here with my hands tied behind my back, called me a thief. What have I stolen, pray, that is yours and not mine? And he called me a murderess. In what sense am I criminally responsible for Sidney's death when he fell and banged his head while trying to grab hold of me so that he might ravish me and force me into marrying him? He was alive when I left Candleford. I had him carried upstairs to his bed. I tended him myself until the doctor *I sent for* arrived. I am sorry despite everything that he died. I would not wish for the death even of a despicable creature like Sidney. But I can hardly be held responsible. If you wish to try to have me convicted of his murder, I cannot stop you. But I warn you that you will merely make yourself look ridiculous in the public eye."

"You always did have a wicked, impudent tongue, Sara," her cousin said, clasping his hands at his back and glowering at her. "We will see whether the word of the Earl of Durbury carries more weight with a jury than that of a common whore."

"You bore me, Cousin Harold," Jane said, seating herself on the nearest chair and hoping that the shaking of her knees was not evident. "I should like some tea. Will you ring for service, or shall I?"

But he was given no chance to make a choice. There was a knock on the door, and the silent valet turned to answer it. The Bow Street Runner stepped into the room, breathing rather heavily and looking somewhat disheveled. His nose was as red as a beacon and surely swollen. In one hand he clutched a handkerchief on which Jane could see bloodstains. A thin red line trickled from one nostril. He glared accusingly at Jane.

"I apprehended her, my lord," he said. "But to my shame I confess she is more sly and dangerous than I had anticipated. I will tie her up here and now if it is your wish and drag her to a magistrate before she can play any more of her tricks."

Jane felt almost sorry for him. He had been made to look

foolish. She guessed that such a thing did not happen often to upset his dignity.

"I shall be taking her back to Cornwall," the earl said. "She will meet her fate there. We will be leaving tonight, as soon as I have dined."

"Then if I were you," the Runner advised, "I would not trust her to sit meekly beside you in your carriage, my lord, or to enter inns along the way without kicking up a fuss and having you set upon by a parcel of ignorant fools who would not see the truth if it peered into their eyes. I would not trust her not to bash you over the head as she did to your son as soon as you nod off to sleep."

"I really have hurt your feelings," Jane said pleasantly. "But you cannot say I did not warn you that I would scream."

He looked at her with dislike. "I would have her trussed up hand and foot if I were you, my lord," he said. "And gagged too. And hire a guard to travel with you. I know a woman who would be willing to take on the task. My lady here would not play any of her tricks on Bertha Meeker, believe me."

"How ridiculous!" Jane said.

But the earl was looking uneasy. "She always was headstrong," he said. "She was never biddable despite all the kindnesses we showed her after her father's passing. She was an only child, you know, and spoiled atrociously. I want her back at Candleford, where she can be properly dealt with. Yes, do it, Boden. Employ this woman. But she must be here within two hours or it will be dark even before I leave London."

Jane had been feeling an enormous sense of relief. It had all been a great deal easier than she had anticipated. Indeed, she had been finding it hard to imagine that she had been so unexpectedly craven for so long. She should never even have been tempted to go into hiding, to give in to the terrors of what might happen if none of the witnesses was willing to speak the truth of what had happened at Candleford that night.

Now once again terror assailed her. They were going to tie her up and send her back to Cornwall as a prisoner with a female guard. And then she was going to be tried for murder. The air felt suddenly cold in her nostrils.

"In the meantime," Mick Boden said, his gaze fastening hastily on Jane again, "we will confine my lady to that chair so that you may have your dinner in peace. Your man will help me."

Anger came to Jane's rescue. She shot to her feet. "Stay where you are," she commanded the Runner with such hauteur that for a moment he halted in his tracks. "What an utterly gothic suggestion! Is this your idea of revenge? I have just lost the final vestiges of respect I felt for you and your intelligence. I will accompany you to Candleford of my own free will, Cousin Harold. I will *not* be hauled there like a common felon."

But the Runner had that length of rope out of his pocket again, and the valet, after one uneasy glance at the earl, who nodded curtly, took a few steps toward her.

"Tie her down," the earl said before turning away to shuffle the papers on his desk.

"Very well." Jane gritted her teeth. "If it is a fight you want, a fight you will get."

But this time she could not scream. It would be too easy for the earl to convince would-be rescuers that she was a murderess resisting arrest. And of course she would lose the fight—she was pitted against two men with her cousin to add his strength to theirs if it became necessary. Within a few minutes she was going to find herself back on her chair, tied hand and foot and probably gagged too. Well, she would not go down without leaving a few bruises and scratches on each of her assailants. All fear had vanished, to be replaced by a strange sort of exhilaration.

They attacked her together, coming around both sides of the chair and grabbing for her. She hit out with both fists and then with both feet. She twisted and turned, jabbed with her elbows, and even bit a hand that came incautiously close to her mouth. And without even thinking she used language with which she had become familiar in the past few weeks.

"Take your *damned* hands off me and go to the *devil*," she was saying when a quiet voice somehow penetrated the noise of the scuffle.

"Dear me," it said, "am I interrupting fun and games?"

By that time Parkins was hanging on to one of her arms while the Runner had the other twisted up painfully behind her back. Jane, panting for breath, her vision impaired by the hair that had fallen across her face, glared at her savior, who was lounging against the frame of the open door, his quizzing glass to his eye and grossly magnifying it.

"Go away," she said. "I have had *enough* of men to last me at least two lifetimes. I do not need you. I can do very well on my own."

"As I can see." The Duke of Tresham lowered his glass. "But such atrocious language, Jane. Wherever have you acquired it? Might I be permitted to ask, Durbury, why there is a male person—neither one a gentleman, I fear—hanging from each of Lady Sara Illingsworth's arms? It appears to be a strange, unsporting sort of game."

Jane caught sight of Mrs. Jacobs hovering outside the door, looking as if she were bristling with indignation. And Jane herself was feeling no less so. Why was it that two grown men, who had been quite ferocious enough to overpower her just a minute before, were now standing meek and motionless, looking as if for direction to one languid gentleman?

"Good day, Tresham," the earl said briskly. "Cousin Sara and I will be leaving for Candleford before dark. Your presence here is quite unnecessary."

"I came of my own free will," Jane said. "You are no longer responsible for me in any way at all, your grace."

He ignored her, of course. He addressed the Bow Street

Runner. "Unhand the lady," he said gently. "You already have a nose that is painful to behold. Are you responsible, Jane? My compliments. I would regret to have to give you eyes to match, my fine fellow."

"Now see here——" Mick Boden began.

But the ducal glass was to the duke's eye again and his eyebrows had been raised. Much as it was a relief to have her arm suddenly released, Jane could feel only indignation against a man who could rule merely through the power of his eyebrows and his quizzing glass.

"Dismiss this man," the duke instructed the Earl of Durbury. "And your servant. Should this contretemps draw the attention of other hotel guests and employees, you might find yourself having to explain why a supposedly murdered man is alive and well and living at Candleford."

Jane's eyes flew to the earl's. He was looking thunderous and rather purple in the face. But for the moment he said nothing. He did not protest. He did not contradict what had just been said.

"Exactly so," the Duke of Tresham said softly.

"One would equally hate it to become public knowledge," the earl said, "that you have been harboring a common felon in the guise of mis——"

"I would not complete that sentence if I were you," Jocelyn advised. "You will dismiss the Runner, Durbury? Or shall I?"

Mick Boden drew audible breath. "I would have you know——" he began.

"Would you indeed?" his grace asked with faint indifference. "But, my good man, I have no wish to hear whatever it is you would have me know. You may wish to leave now before I decide after all to call you to account for the arm-twisting I witnessed a short while ago."

For a moment it seemed as if the Runner would accept the challenge, but then he replaced his length of rope in his pocket and stalked from the room with a great show of bruised dignity. The earl's valet followed him out willingly enough and closed the door quietly behind him.

Jane turned on the earl, her eyes blazing. "Sidney is *alive*?" she cried. "And *well*? Yet all this time you have been hunting me as a *murderess*? You have allowed me to believe since I arrived here in this room that he is *dead*? How *could* you be so cruel? And now I know why we were to return to Candleford instead of facing a magistrate here. You still believe you can persuade me to marry Sidney. You must have windmills in your head—or believe that I do."

"There is still the matter of a vicious assault, which kept my son hovering between life and death for many weeks," the earl retorted. "And there is still the matter of a certain sum of money and a certain costly bracelet."

"Ah," Jocelyn said, tossing his hat and cane onto a chair just inside the door, "it is gratifying to know that my guess was correct. Jardine *is* still an active member of this vale of tears, then? My congratulations, Durbury."

Jane turned her indignation on him. "It was a *guess*?" she said. "A *bluff*? And why are you still here? I told you I did not need you. I will never need you again. Go away."

"I have come to escort you to Lady Webb's," he told her.

Her eyes widened. "Aunt Harriet's? She is here? She is back in town?"

He inclined his head before turning away to address her cousin. "It will be an altogether more convenient place than Candleford at which to call upon my betrothed," he explained.

Jane drew breath to speak. How dare he! But Sidney was alive and well. Aunt Harriet was back in London. She was to go there. It was all over, this nightmare with which she had lived seemingly forever. She closed her mouth again.

"Yes, my love," Jocelyn said gently, observing her.

"Your betrothed?" The earl was pulling himself together. "Now see here, Tresham, Lady Sara is twenty years old. Until she is five and twenty she may not marry or betroth herself to any man who does not meet with my approval. You do not. Besides, this betrothal nonsense is humbug if ever I heard any. A man of your ilk does not marry his whore."

Jane watched wide-eyed as Jocelyn took a few leisurely strides forward. A moment later the earl's toes were scraping the floor for something against which to brace his weight while his cravat in Jocelyn's hand converted itself into a convenient noose. His face turned a deeper shade of purple.

"I sometimes believe," Jocelyn said softly, "that my hearing is defective. I suppose I should have it checked by a physician before punishing a man for what I merely suspect he said. But lest I find that I am unable to restrain myself despite good resolutions, I would suggest, Durbury, that in future you speak very clearly and very distinctly."

The earl's heels met the floor again and his cravat resumed its former function, though somewhat more crumpled and askew than before.

Jane would not have been human if she had been able to resist a purely feminine rush of satisfaction.

"Your permission must be granted before I may arrange my nuptials with Lady Sara Illingsworth?" Jocelyn asked. "I will have it then, in writing, before you leave for Cornwall, which I believe you will do no later than tomorrow morning?" He raised his glass to his eye.

"*That* I will not be bullied into doing," the earl said. "Sara is my responsibility. I owe it to her dead father to find her a husband more suited to providing her lasting happiness than you, Tresham. Remember too that she assaulted and almost killed my son. Remember that she robbed me of both money and jewels. She must answer for those actions in Cornwall, even if only to me. I am her guardian."

"Perhaps," Jocelyn said, "these charges should be made in London, Durbury. Lady Sara will doubtless prove a difficult prisoner on the long journey to Cornwall. I will help you haul her off to a magistrate now. And then the *ton*, desperate for

novelty at this stage of the Season, will be able to enjoy the
entertainment of witnessing a gently nurtured lady being
prosecuted for whacking and felling a man twice her size with
a book. And for taking fifteen pounds from her guardian, who
had deprived her for longer than a year of the allowance to
which she was entitled. And for removing from a safe a
bracelet that was her own while leaving behind what is doubtless a costly hoard of jewelry that will be hers at her marriage
or on her twenty-fifth birthday. The *beau monde*, I assure you,
sir, will be vastly amused."

The Earl of Durbury's nostrils flared. "Are you by chance
attempting to blackmail me, Tresham?" he asked.

Jocelyn raised his eyebrows. "I do assure you, Durbury,
that if I were attempting blackmail, I would choose to hold
over your head the threat that my betrothed will charge you
with neglect of your duty to protect her in your own home
and your son with attempted ravishment. I am sure at least
one of the witnesses could be persuaded to tell the truth. And
I would add for good measure that if by some misfortune
Sidney Jardine's path should ever cross mine during the re-
mainder of both our lives, he will, within five minutes of such
a meeting, be picking his teeth out of his throat. You may
wish to convey that observation to him."

Jane felt another rush of unwilling satisfaction. It ought
not to have been so easy for him. It was not fair. Why could
no one stand up to the Duke of Tresham? All the bluster
drained out of Cousin Harold when he understood that his
plan to catch her, to lure her back to Cornwall, and to blackmail her into marrying Sidney was not going to work. And
that even withholding his consent to her marriage would have
consequences far worse than the loss of much of her father's
property and most of his fortune.

While Jane sat in indignant silence, totally ignored as if
her very existence were irrelevant, permission for the Duke of
Tresham to marry Lady Sara Illingsworth was duly given in

writing after Mrs. Jacobs and the valet had been summoned as witnesses.

After that, there was nothing left for Jane to do but smooth the creases from her cloak, put on her bonnet and gloves with slow deliberation while Mrs. Jacobs picked up her bag, and then march out of the room and down the stairs and out to the waiting carriage, with its ducal crest and cluster of servile sycophants waiting to bend and scrape and pay him homage. Jane climbed inside and seated herself, Mrs. Jacobs beside her. If it were really possible for a human being to burst with fury, Jane thought, she would surely do it. And serve him right too to have blood and brains and tissue raining down on the plush interior of his expensive town carriage.

He vaulted in and took the seat opposite.

Jane sat with straight back and lifted chin. She directed her gaze beyond the carriage windows. "I will avail myself of your escort to Lady Webb's," she said, "but we will be perfectly clear about one thing, your grace—and Mrs. Jacobs may be my witness. If you were the last man on earth and you were to pester me daily for a million years, I would not marry you. I *will* not do so."

"My dear Lady Sara." His voice was haughty and bored. "I do beg you to have some regard for my pride. A million years? I assure you I would stop asking after the first thousand."

She pressed her lips together and resisted the urge to answer him with some sufficiently cutting remark. She would not give him the satisfaction of a quarrel.

He had come to her rescue—of course he had. It was the sort of thing the Duke of Tresham would do. She had left the house without his permission. She had been his mistress. He had determined that he would do the honorable thing and marry her. She was his possession.

But he did not believe she had been his friend.

He did not believe she would have made him hers by telling him the full truth about herself.

He did not trust her. He did not love her. *Of course he did not love her.*

Fortunately the journey to Lady Webb's was short. But it was only as the carriage drew to a halt that Jane really thought about her. She must know that Jane was on the way. Did she know everything else? Would she welcome her?

But she had her answer even as a footman was opening the carriage door and putting down the steps. The door of the house opened and Lady Webb came outside, not just onto the doorsill, but all the way down the steps.

"Aunt Harriet!"

Jane scarcely noticed Jocelyn descending from the carriage and handing her down. It seemed that within a single moment she was enfolded in the safe arms of her mother's dearest friend.

"Sara!" she exclaimed. "My dear girl. I thought you would never come. I have quite worn a path in the drawing room carpet, I declare. Oh, my dear, dear girl."

"Aunt Harriet."

Jane was sobbing and hiccuping suddenly and being led up the steps into a brightly lit hall. She had been taken up the staircase to the drawing room and seated in an elegant chair beside the cheerful fire there and handed a lace-edged handkerchief to dry her eyes before she realized that they were alone, she and Lady Webb.

He had gone.

Perhaps forever.

She could not have been more emphatic in her rejection of him.

And good riddance too.

There had perhaps not been any bleaker moment in her whole life.

It was a busy morning. Jocelyn rode in the park, where he met Baron Pottier and Sir Conan Brougham. The latter had already spoken with the seconds of the two Forbes brothers and made arrangements for the duels to be fought on successive mornings one week hence in Hyde Park. He would single-handedly be bringing the park back into fashion as a venue for meetings of honor if he did not soon change the family of his dueling partners, Jocelyn thought wryly.

It was not a pleasant prospect. Two more men would be given their chance to snuff out his life. And he did not believe that the Reverend Josiah Forbes, at least, was one to be given the trembles by the famous black Tresham stare.

But Viscount Kimble joined them and then Ferdinand, and Jocelyn put the thought of the duels firmly behind him.

"Word spread last night like fire in a woodshed," Ferdinand said with a grin. "Miss Jane Ingleby turning out to be Lady Sara Illingsworth! It is the sensation of the hour, Tresham. Those people who were at your soiree and heard her sing were preening themselves at Lady Wardle's, I can tell you. Old Hardinge was trying to convince all who would listen that he had guessed it all along. She was far too genteel, he said, to be anyone but Lady Sara."

"Where did you find her, Tresham?" Baron Pottier asked. "And how did you discover the truth? When I think that every time we called on you at Dudley House, there she was. And we never so much as suspected."

"Is it true," Sir Conan asked, "that her name has been cleared, Tresham?"

"It was all a mistake." Jocelyn waved one careless hand and then tipped his hat to a couple of ladies who were riding in the opposite direction. "I spoke to Durbury last evening just before he set out for Cornwall. Jardine is not dead. Indeed, he has fully recovered from his little accident. Durbury came to town and hired a Runner to find Lady Sara simply to tell her there was nothing to worry about. The rumors spread, as rumors will, quite independently of him."

"But the theft, Tresham?" Baron Pottier asked.

"There was no theft," Jocelyn said. "How susceptible we all are to gossip. It makes one wonder if we need to find something better to do."

His friends laughed as if he had made the joke of the morning.

"But rumors have a nasty habit of lingering," Jocelyn continued, "unless there is something to take their place. I for one will be calling upon Lady Sara at Lady Webb's and even pursuing her acquaintance."

Baron Pottier roared with laughter. "Ho, Tresham," he said, "that will do it. That will create new gossip. It will be said that you are hankering after a leg shackle."

"Quite so," Jocelyn said agreeably. "One would certainly not wish the lady to be looked upon as someone who is somehow tainted, would one?"

"I will call upon her too, Tresham," Ferdinand said. "I want to take another look at Lady Sara now that I know she *is* Lady Sara. I say, this is famous!"

"It will be my pleasure to call upon her too, Tresh," the viscount said.

"I daresay my mother and my sister would be pleased to make her acquaintance," Sir Conan added. "I'll take them to call, Tresham. My mother has an acquaintance with Lady Webb."

His friends understood, Jocelyn was relieved to find. Kimble and Brougham had the advantage of knowing the full truth, of course, but even the other two seemed to realize there was a certain embarrassment in his having employed the lady as a nurse for three weeks. All were willing to do their part in drawing Jane into society, making her respectable, helping squash any vestiges of doubt about the charges that had been made against her.

The new sensation that would finally replace the old, of course, would be news that the Duke of Tresham was paying court to the woman who had once been his nurse.

All would be well. None of the few people who knew that Lady Sara Illingsworth had been his mistress would ever breathe a word of the fact. She would be safe, her reputation restored.

The conversation turned at length to a reliving of yesterday's fight.

He was at breakfast later, having decided to remain at home to read the papers before proceeding to White's, when Angeline arrived. She swept into the dining room unannounced.

"Tresham," she said, "whatever could you have been thinking of, you and Ferdie, to have taken on *three* of the Forbes brothers in the park yesterday? I was all aflutter when I heard. But how perfectly splendid that all three of them had to be carried to the nearest carriage, two of them quite insensible and the other with a broken nose. What a shame it was not all five. That would have been a glorious victory for the Dudleys, and I daresay you could have done it too. I suppose it is true that you have been drawn into dueling with the other two. Heyward says such information is not for a lady's ears, but he would not deny it so I daresay it is true. I shall not have a wink of sleep between now and then. You will be killed for sure, and what will I do then? And if you kill them, you will be forced to flee to Paris and Heyward *still* says he will not take me there, odious man, even though I would willingly forgo the pleasures of Brighton. And, Tresham, *what* is this I hear of the Ingleby woman's turning out to be Lady Sara Illingsworth?"

"Do have a seat, Angeline," Jocelyn said, waving one languid hand at the chair opposite, "and a coffee." He raised one finger in the direction of the butler at the sideboard. "And do remove that more than usually ghastly pea-green bonnet, I beg you. I fear it will interfere with my digestion."

"*Is* it true?" she asked. "Do tell me it is. It is just the sort of story we Dudleys revel in, is it not? You harboring an ax murderer as your nurse and presenting her to a select gathering of the *ton* as a nightingale. It is quite priceless." She went off into peals of merry laughter as Hawkins bent over her to fill her cup with coffee.

She had made no move to take off her bonnet. Jocelyn regarded it with distaste. "Lady Sara Illingsworth is now at Lady Webb's," he said. "I would be obliged if you would call upon her there, Angeline. The Lord knows why, but you are the only respectable Dudley—probably because a dry stick like Heyward married you and keeps you on some sort of rein, though heaven knows it is not a tight one."

She laughed merrily. "Heyward a dry stick?" she said. "Yes, he is, is he not? In public, at least."

Jocelyn's expression became more pained as her blush clashed horribly with the pink plumes of her bonnet.

"I shall certainly call at Lady Webb's," she said. "Heyward will escort me there this afternoon. I cannot resist having one more look at her, Tresham. Is she likely to be wielding an ax? How enormously exciting that would be. Heyward would be forced to risk his life in defending me."

"She hit Jardine over the head with a book," he said dryly, "when he was, ah, disrespectful. That is all, Angeline. The gentleman is alive and well, and it turns out that the stolen property was not stolen at all. A very dull story, in fact. But Lady Sara is not to be allowed to hover on the brink of society. She will need respectable people of good *ton* to draw her in."

"All of which Lady Webb will arrange for her," she said. "Why should you be interested, Tresham?" But she stopped after an uncharacteristically brief monologue, stared at him for a moment, her cup halfway to her mouth, set it down in its saucer again, and resumed her hilarity. "Oh, Tresham, you are *interested*! How absolutely famous! Oh, I cannot wait to tell Heyward. But he has gone to the House, provoking man, and I daresay he will not return until it is time to take me visiting. Tresham, you are *smitten*."

Jocelyn used his quizzing glass despite the fact that it enlarged the garish bonnet. "I am delighted to have caused you such amusement," he said, "but *smitten* and the Tresham name are mutually exclusive terms, as you ought to be aware. I will, however, be marrying Lady Sara. You will be pleased to learn that you are the first to know, Angeline, apart from the lady herself, of course. She has said no, by the way."

She stared at him, and for one fascinated moment he thought she had been robbed of speech.

"Lady Sara has said no." She had found her voice. "To you? To the Duke of Tresham? How absolutely splendid of her. I confess I scarcely noticed her when she was your nurse. She looked so very drab in gray. Whoever would wear gray when there are so many other colors to choose among? I was quite struck with her when she sang at your soiree. And she knew how to waltz. That should have been a clue, but I confess I did not pick up on it. But now she has refused you. I am going to like her. She must be a woman of spirit. Just what you need. Oh, I am going to love her as a sister."

"She has said no, Angeline," he said dryly.

She looked at him in incomprehension. "You are a Dudley, Tresham," she said. "Dudleys do not take no for an answer. I did not. Heyward was quite averse to marrying me for all of one month after I was first presented to him, I do assure you. He thought me empty-headed and frivolous and too talkative. The fact that I had you and Ferdie for brothers did not endear me to him either. But he did marry me. Indeed, he was horridly dejected the first time he asked and I said no. I feared he would go home and shoot himself. How could he not have fallen for my charms when I was determined that he should?"

"How indeed?" he agreed.

He was subjected to almost half an hour more of her incessant chatter before she took her leave. But he felt that the morning had been well spent. Jane's respectability was assured. And by dropping a word in a fertile ear, he had lined up on his side powerful forces with which to storm the citadel of her mulish determination not to have him.

He did wonder briefly why he would want to storm her defenses. He could not admit, after all, to any personal need of her. It was just her very stubbornness, of course. Jane Ingleby had always had the last word with him.

Well, Lady Sara Illingsworth would not. It was as simple as that.

He found himself wondering what he would wear when he paid her an afternoon call. Just as if he were some moonstruck schoolboy.

23

ou are looking peaked, Sara," Lady Webb said. "It is quite to be expected, of course, after all you have gone through. We will soon put the roses back in your cheeks. I just wish we could go outside this afternoon for a walk or a drive. The weather is so lovely. However, this is one of the afternoons on which it is known that I am at home to visitors. Vexing as it may be, my dear, we must be ready to receive them."

Jane was wearing a fashionable, high-waisted dress of sprigged muslin. It had been in the trunk of her belongings that had been delivered during the morning by Phillip and the Duke of Tresham's coachman. Her hair had been dressed by the maid who had been assigned to her care. But ready as she appeared to be to face an afternoon of socializing, she broached the subject that was troubling her.

"Perhaps it would be best," she said, "if I remained out of sight of your guests, Aunt Harriet."

Lady Webb, who had been looking out through the window, came to sit down on a chair opposite Jane's. "That is precisely what you must not do," she said. "Although neither of us has put it into words, Sara, I am fully aware of how you have been living for the last little while. Appalling as it is that you felt driven to such a life, it is over. No one need know. You can be very sure that Tresham will silence anyone of his acquaintance who suspects the truth. And of course he means to marry you. He is a gentleman and knows he has compromised you. He is not only prepared to do the honorable thing but will doubtless try to insist upon it."

"He is very good at that," Jane said bitterly. "But he knows better than to believe it will work with me."

"The Duke of Tresham has possibly the most unsavory reputation of any gentleman in town," Lady Webb said with a sigh. "Though perhaps I exaggerate. He is not known for any particular vice but only for wildness and the tendency to be at the center of every brawl. He is exactly like his father before him and his grandfather before that."

"No!" Jane said more hotly than she had intended. "He is not."

Lady Webb raised her eyebrows. But before she could say anything more, there was a tap on the drawing room door and the butler opened it and announced the first visitors—Sir Conan Brougham with Lady Brougham, his mother, and Miss Chloe Brougham, his sister. They were followed not many minutes after by Lord and Lady Heyward, the latter of whom made it very clear that she had come for the specific purpose of talking with Jane and scolding her for hiding her true identity while she was at Dudley House.

"I was never more surprised in my life as when Tresham told me about it," she said. "And never more gratified than to know he had discovered you and brought you here, Lady Sara. The very idea that you were an ax murderer! I go off into peals of laughter whenever I think about it, as Heyward will testify. I daresay Mr. Jardine was unpardonably rude to you. I met him once and received the distinct impression that he was a slimy villain. It was most forbearing of you to slap him merely with a book, and very poor spirited of him to make a fuss about it and run sniveling to his papa. In your place I would have reached for an ax."

"Lady Webb has been offering you this chair for the last two minutes, my love," Lord Heyward said, leading his wife away.

A large number of guests arrived after that. A few were Lady Webb's friends. Many were people Jane had met at Dudley House on various occasions—Viscount Kimble, Lord Ferdinand Dudley, and Baron Pottier among them. It did not take Jane long to understand who had sent them all or why they had come. The campaign was on to make her respectable again. Far from gratifying her, the knowledge infuriated her. Did he really believe that she could not manage her own life without his helping hand? She only wished he would come in person so that she could give him a piece of her mind.

And then he did.

He arrived alone, looking immaculate in a blue coat and biscuit-colored pantaloons so well fitting that he must surely have been poured into them and Hessian boots that one might have used as twin mirrors. And he was looking insufferably handsome, of course, although when she had started to think of him as handsome Jane did not know. And suffocatingly male. And armed with all his detestable ducal hauteur.

She hated him with a powerful hatred, but of course good manners prevented her from either glaring at him or demanding that he leave. This was not her drawing room, after all. She was as much a guest here as he.

He bowed to Lady Webb and exchanged civilities with her. He bowed distantly to Jane—just as if she were a speck of dust that had floated into his line of vision, she thought indignantly. He acknowledged with the lift of an eyebrow those

of his relatives and friends who were clustered about her—
Lady Heyward, Lord Ferdinand, Viscount Kimble among oth-
ers. And then he proceeded to converse with Mrs. Minter and
Mr. Brockledean for all of fifteen minutes.

She was *determined* not to speak to him, Jane had thought as
soon as he was announced. How *dare* he give her no opportunity to ignore him? Of course, she also wanted a chance to tell
him that he need not have bothered to send people here to
visit her or to try to restore respectability to her life. How *dare*
he not approach her to be upbraided and told to mind his
own business?

"It is really a very splendid new curricle, Ferdie," Lady
Heyward was saying. "It is far more dashing than the last one.
But you are bound to accept a wager from someone to prove
its superiority to any other. You must absolutely not accept.
Only consider my nerves if there were another race like the
last. Though I never tire of hearing about that final bend in
the road, around which you accelerated despite all Tresham's
and Heyward's warnings that you must drive with caution. I *do*
wish I had been there to witness it. Is it not tiresome sometimes, Lady Sara, to be a woman?"

He had got up from his place, Jane saw with her peripheral
vision. The Duke of Tresham, that was. He was about to take
his leave. He had turned toward her group. He was going to
approach and speak to her. She turned her head and smiled
dazzlingly at his brother.

"I understand you are a famous whip, Lord Ferdinand," she
said.

An eager, good-natured young man, whom she liked extremely well, he rose immediately to the bait.

"I say," he said, "would you care to drive in the park with
me tomorrow afternoon, Lady Sara?"

"I would love to, thank you," she replied warmly, looking
up into the dark eyes of the Duke of Tresham, who had
stopped at the outer perimeter of her group.

But if she had expected to see annoyance in his face, she was to be disappointed. He had the gall to look faintly amused.

"I came to take my leave of you, ma'am," he told her, slightly inclining his head.

"Oh," she said, still smiling, "is it you, your grace? I had quite forgotten you were here." It was about the most ill-mannered thing she had said in public in her whole life. She was enormously pleased with herself.

"Ah," he said, holding her gaze and speaking only loudly enough to be heard by her and her group. "Not surprising, I suppose, when I am renowned for avoiding the tedium of paying afternoon calls. But for you I made an exception as I so rarely have the opportunity to take tea with a former employee."

He turned and strolled away, having enjoyed the satisfaction of having the last word, Jane had no doubt. She glared hotly at his receding back, good manners forgotten, while the members of her group either stared at one another in astonishment or pretended to a sudden deafness and a need to clear their throats. Lady Heyward tapped Jane's arm.

"Well done," she said. "That was a magnificent setdown and took Tresham so much by surprise that he descended to sheer spite. Oh, how *well* I like you."

The conversation resumed until a short time later the guests began to take their leave.

"Never has one of my at-home afternoons been such a success," Lady Webb said with a laugh when everyone had left. "For which I believe we have the Duke of Tresham to thank, Sara."

"Well," Jane said more tartly than she had intended, "I am grateful to him, I am sure. If he should ever come back and ask specifically for me, Aunt Harriet, I am not at home."

Lady Webb sat down and regarded her houseguest closely. "Did he treat you so badly, then, Sara?" she asked.

"No," Jane said firmly. "I was forced into nothing, Aunt Harriet. He offered and I accepted. I insisted upon a written contract, and he kept its terms. He did not treat me badly."

Except that he made me love him. And worse, he made me like him. And then he discovered the truth and turned as cold as ice and would not trust me even enough to believe that I would have made myself as vulnerable to him as he had made himself to me. Except that he stood all my emotions on their heads and left me empty and bewildered and as wretchedly unhappy as it is possible to be.

She did not speak her thoughts aloud, but she did not need to.

"Except to make you fall in love with him," Lady Webb said quietly.

Jane looked sharply at her, but she could not stop the despicable tears from springing to her eyes. "I hate him," she said with conviction.

"I can see that," Lady Webb agreed with a faint smile. "Why? Can you tell me?"

"He is an unfeeling, arrogant monster," Jane replied.

Lady Webb sighed. "Oh, dear," she said, "you really *are* in love with him. I do not know whether to be glad or sorry. But enough of that. All day I have been considering what is to be done to help you put the past quite behind you. I will present you at the next Queen's Drawing Room, Sara, and the following day I will give you a come-out ball here. I am as excited as a girl. It will almost certainly be the grandest squeeze of the Season. You are understandably famous, my dear. Let us start making plans."

It would be the come-out Jane had dreamed of just a few years ago. But all she could think of now was that Jocelyn had come this afternoon, looking cold and haughty, and that he had almost entirely ignored her until he had a chance to insult her. How many afternoons ago was it since he had finished her portrait and then poured out his heart to her and wept while holding her on his lap?

It felt like a lifetime ago.

It felt as if it must have happened to two other people.

She hated him.

She believed the heavy ache in her heart would never go away.

And then she felt sudden panic. *Her portrait.* Her precious painting. She had left home without it!

Home?

Home?

All the fashionable world rode or drove or promenaded in Hyde Park late in the afternoon during the spring Season. Everyone came to see and be seen, to gossip and be gossiped about, to display and observe all the latest fashions, to flirt and be flirted with.

Jane was wearing a blue dress and pelisse and a plain straw bonnet tied beneath her chin with a wide blue ribbon. She carried a straw-colored parasol, which Lady Webb had lent her. She was perched on the high seat of Lord Ferdinand Dudley's new curricle while he wielded the ribbons, conversed amiably with her, and introduced her to a number of people who approached for the specific purpose of meeting the notorious Lady Sara Illingsworth, whose story had drawing rooms and club lounges abuzz again.

She smiled and chattered. The sun was shining, after all, and she was in the company of a handsome young gentleman who was going out of his way to be charming to her. He bore a remarkable resemblance to his brother, which fact she would not hold against him.

It was the thought of his brother that kept her from truly enjoying herself. Despite all that had happened during the past forty-eight hours—the release from fear, the return to being herself, living in her own world—she almost wished she could will herself back one week. This time last week they had

been together, he painting, she working at her embroidery.
Growing comfortable together. Becoming friends. Falling in
love.

All illusion.

This was reality.

And reality came riding up to Lord Ferdinand's curricle in
company with Viscount Kimble. The Duke of Tresham, that
was—it was even difficult now to think of him as Jocelyn—
looking dark and morose and unapproachable, quite his usual
self, in fact. He touched his whip to the brim of his hat, inclined his head to her, and bade her a good afternoon, while
the viscount smiled and reached for her hand to carry to his
lips and proceeded to make conversation for a few minutes.
The duke's black, expressionless eyes rested on her the whole
time.

Jane smiled and talked and twirled her parasol and agreed
to come driving in the park again the very next day with Lord
Kimble. Then they were gone and Jane, smiling gaily, fought
the lump that had formed in her throat and the ache it sent up
behind her nostrils and down into her bosom.

But there was no time to brood. There was Lord Ferdinand
to listen to and other people with whom to converse. Only
minutes after Jocelyn rode away, Lady Heyward drove up in an
open barouche, introduced Jane to the Dowager Lady
Heyward, and proceeded to talk.

"I am looking forward excessively to your come-out ball at
Lady Webb's," she said. "Our invitation was delivered late this
morning. I daresay Heyward will escort me, which is rare
enough for him as he finds balls tedious. Can you imagine being bored by *dancing*, Lady Sara? And you may not roll your
eyes in that odious way, Ferdie. I was not speaking to you.
Besides, everyone knows that you prefer fighting to dancing.
You will never know what palpitations I suffered on hearing
that you and Tresham had fought three of the Forbes brothers
the other day. Though as I told Tresham, the victory would

have been sweeter had you fought all five. I do not know why the other two stood by to watch their brothers being slaughtered."

"Angie," Lord Ferdinand advised, "take a damper."

But Jane had turned sharply to look at him. "You and his grace fought a few days ago?" she asked. "With *pistols*? And you *killed* three opponents?"

"Fists actually, ma'am." He looked decidedly embarrassed. "We rendered two of them unconscious, one apiece. The third was rolling on the ground nursing a broken nose. It would have been unsporting to hit him when he was down. You have no business speaking of such things in front of other ladies, Angie."

Lady Heyward rolled her eyes skyward. "I suppose it is ungenteel too, Ferdie," she said, "to be lying awake nights, my nerves positively shattered, because Tresham is to meet the other two Forbeses. I daresay it will be pistols. He will be killed for sure. Though I do think it rather grand of him to take on the *two* of them on two successive mornings. I have never heard the like before. One can only hope he lives to face the second meeting."

Jane felt as if every drop of blood in her body had drained downward to reside in her toes and set them tingling while the rest of her felt cold and clammy and faint.

"Angie," Lord Ferdinand said sharply, "that is gentlemen's business. If you have nothing better to talk about, I suggest you take that bird home that is perched on the brim of your bonnet and feed it birdseed before it expires. And water all those flowers while you are about it. How your neck can hold up all that clutter is beyond me. Good day, ma'am." He touched his hat to the dowager and gave his horses the signal to move on.

Jane was still not quite sure she would not pitch forward into insensibility. There was an annoying buzz in her ears. The pins and needles had found their way up to her hands.

"His grace is to fight another duel?" she asked. "*Two* more?"

"Nothing to bother your head over, Lady Sara," Lord Ferdinand said cheerfully. "I wish he would let me fight one of them, though, since it was me they tried to kill. But he won't, and when Tresham has his mind set on something, or against something as the case may be, there is no arguing with him."

"Oh, the foolish, foolish man!" Jane cried, anger saving her and sending the blood surging through her body again. "All for the sake of honor."

"Yes, precisely, ma'am," Lord Ferdinand agreed before very charmingly but very determinedly changing the subject.

Not one but two duels, Jane thought. On two successive mornings. He was almost certain to be killed. The odds against his surviving were double what they would normally be.

And it would serve him right too, she thought furiously.

But how would she be able to live on?

How could she live in a world that did not contain Jocelyn?

He missed Jane more than he would have thought possible. Oh, he called at Lady Webb's that first afternoon, of course, and was goaded into being unpardonably rude to Jane before a sizable audience merely because she had been pert to him and had smiled so dazzlingly at Ferdinand while accepting his offer to drive her in the park that Jocelyn had been sorely tempted to plant his own brother a facer. And he had ridden in the park when he knew she would be there, first with Ferdinand and then with Kimble, and had greeted her and exchanged civilities with her. No more than that. He had sensed from her mulish look and set lips that had he tried to say more, he would merely have precipitated another sharp quarrel—which he would have been perfectly happy to do if only they could have been private together.

He was determined to have her, of course. Not least, perhaps, because she was determined not to have him. But he knew it would be useless to follow his usual practice and try to force his will on her. She must be allowed time in which to adjust her mind to the change in her fortune.

He must allow her time in which to miss *him*. Surely she would do so. Although when he had first learned her real identity he had concluded that her sympathy for him must have been a shallow thing, he was no longer so sure. He remembered the comfortable accord they had established in that room she called their den. And there had been no mistaking her sexual passion for him. He bitterly regretted those last two visits he had paid her—one by night, the other by day. He had not handled the situation well.

He would give her time, he had decided at first. And he would give himself time. He had two duels to face, both with pistols. He found he could not face them with the casual ennui with which he had approached the other four. He was startlingly aware this time that he could die.

Perhaps on those other occasions that fact had been of less significance to him. Perhaps now he had something to live for.

There was Jane.

But how could he pursue her now when he might die? And how could he pursue her when she was still so bitterly angry with him, and his own sense of betrayal was still like a raw wound?

And so in the days before the first of the duels, against the Reverend Josiah Forbes, Jocelyn deliberately avoided any close encounter with Jane. He went to the house once and found himself prowling around their private room. He looked at her unfinished embroidered cloth, still stretched over the frame, and pictured her sitting straight-backed and graceful before it as she worked. He picked up *Mansfield Park* from the table

beside the chair where he had usually sat. He had never finished reading it. He played a melody on the pianoforte with
his right hand without sitting down. And he gazed at the portrait he had painted of her.

Jane, with the light of life and love glowing from inside her
and brightening the canvas. How could he ever have doubted
her? How could he have treated her with cold fury instead of
gathering her into his arms and inviting her to confide all her
secrets, all her fears in him? She had not let him down. It was
the other way around.

He summoned his lawyer to Dudley House and changed
his will.

And was haunted by that mental image of what he ought
to have done and had not done. He had not gathered her into
his arms.

He might never have another chance to do so.

If he could do it just once more, he began to think with
uncharacteristic sentimentality, he could die a contented man.

What utter, driveling balderdash, he thought in his saner
moments.

But then he discovered from Angeline that she was to attend a sizable but private party at Lady Sangster's. Jane, that
was. She was attending no public balls yet because she had neither been presented at court nor made her official come-out.
But she had accepted her invitation to the soiree.

To which Jocelyn had also been invited.

The night before the first of his duels.

24

It was quite unexceptionable for Jane to attend Lady Sangster's soiree, Lady Webb had assured her goddaughter. Indeed, it was desirable that she appear in public as much as possible before her official come-out. It must not seem that she had something to hide.

But it was the night before Jocelyn was to fight the first of his duels. Jane had not told Aunt Harriet. She had said nothing to anyone about it since quizzing Lord Ferdinand. She had scarcely slept or eaten. She could think of nothing else. She had considered going to Dudley House and begging him to stop the foolishness, but she knew it would be useless to do so. He was a man, with a man's sense of honor.

She went to the soiree, partly for Aunt Harriet's sake and partly for her own. Perhaps somehow it would distract her mind for the evening, even if not for the night ahead or the next morning until she had news. But even if he survived the morning, he had it all to do again the next day. She dressed with care in an elegant gown of dull gold satin and had her maid style her hair elaborately again. She even consented to having a little color rubbed artfully into her cheeks when her godmother commented that she looked beautiful but pale.

The Sangster soiree had been described as a private, select party. In fact, it seemed to Jane, it was a large gathering indeed. The double doors between the drawing room and a music room beyond had been thrown back, as had those leading to a smaller salon beyond. All three rooms were thronged with guests.

Lord and Lady Heyward and Lord Ferdinand were there, all three of them deep in animated conversation with other guests. How could they when they knew their brother was facing death in the morning, and on the morning following that? Viscount Kimble was there, smiling charmingly at a young lady with whom he was talking. How could he when one of his closest friends might die in the morning? He spotted Jane, made his excuses to the young lady, and came toward her to make his bow.

"I avoid insipid entertainments as I would the plague, Lady Sara," he said, smiling his attractive, dangerous smile at her. "But I was told that you were to be here."

"Is all the burden of lifting the evening above insipidity to be on my shoulders, then?" she asked, tapping him on the arm with her fan. Lady Webb had moved away to greet some friends.

"All of it." He offered his arm. "Let us find you a drink and an unoccupied corner where we may enjoy a tête-à-tête until someone discovers that I am monopolizing your company."

He was a charming and an amusing companion. Jane found herself over the next little while engaged in light flirtation and laughing a great deal—and all the while wondering how *he* could keep his mind on anything other than his friend's danger and how *she* could possibly force a laugh from her throat.

There was a loud buzz of conversation all around them. There was music coming from the middle room. She was firmly back in her own world, Jane thought, looking about. It was true that her appearance had caused considerable interest, perfectly well bred, of course, but nonetheless unmistakable. But no one had looked askance at her or been shocked at her temerity in appearing at a superior gathering of the *ton*.

It felt like an empty victory.

"I am utterly crushed," Lord Kimble said. "My best joke, and it has been received without even a smile."

"Oh," Jane said, instantly contrite, "I am so very sorry. *What* did you say?"

His smile was gentler than usual. "Let us see if music will distract you more effectively," he said, offering his arm again. "All will turn out well, you know."

So he *did* care. And he did know that she knew. And that she cared.

Lord Ferdinand was in the middle room, among the people grouped about the pianoforte. He smiled at Jane, took her hand in his, and raised it to his lips.

"I must protest, Kimble," he said. "You have had the lady to yourself for too long. It is my turn." He tucked her hand through his arm and led her closer to the pianoforte.

He was so very like his brother, Jane thought. Except that he was somewhat more slender and long-legged. And where there was darkness in Jocelyn, there was light in Lord Ferdinand. He was an easygoing, happy, uncomplicated young man, she guessed. Or perhaps not. Perhaps it was just that she had had more of a chance to learn the secret depths of Jocelyn's character during the time she had been his mistress— and friend.

"There are more people here than I expected," she said.

"Yes." He smiled down at her. "I have almost as little experience with such select gatherings as you, Lady Sara. I usually avoid them."

"Why did you not on this occasion?" she asked.

"Because Angie said you were to be here." He grinned at her.

It was very much what Viscount Kimble had said earlier. Were these two gentlemen so smitten with her, then? Or did they both know exactly what she had been to Jocelyn?

"Will you sing?" Lord Ferdinand asked. "If I can persuade someone to accompany you, will you? For me, if for no one else? You have the loveliest voice I have ever heard."

She sang "The Lass with the Delicate Air" to the accompaniment provided by Miss Meighan. The crowd about the pianoforte listened with greater attention than they had given the other performers. And more people came crowding in from the other rooms.

Among them the Duke of Tresham.

He was standing in the drawing room doorway when Jane smiled about her in acknowledgment of the applause that followed her song. Looking elegant and immaculate and not at all as one would expect a man to look who was to face death within hours.

Jane's eyes locked with his for an endless moment while a curious sort of hush descended on the music room. Then she looked away and smiled again, and conversations resumed as if there had been no break in them.

"The devil!" Lord Ferdinand muttered from beside her as she made to move away from the pianoforte so that another young lady could take her place. "What in thunder is *she* doing here?"

Lady Oliver was standing beside Jocelyn, Jane saw when she looked again. She was smiling up at him and saying something. He was looking down at her and replying. She was setting one hand on his arm.

Lord Ferdinand had recovered himself. "There are refreshments in the room across the hall," he said. "Shall we go there? Will you allow me to fill a plate for you? Are you hungry?"

"Ravenous," she said, smiling dazzlingly up at him and taking his arm.

Five minutes later she was seated at a small table with a heaped plate in front of her and four fellow guests in addition to Lord Ferdinand with whom to converse. She never afterward knew what was said to her or what she said in reply. Or what she ate, if anything.

He had come. Just as if a duel were nothing at all. Just as if his life meant nothing to him. And he had allowed *that woman* to touch him and talk to him without loudly and publicly spurning her. Making himself look not only guilty but also lacking the good taste to keep his distance from his supposed mistress, a married lady. Did a man's honor stretch so far?

Finally Lord Ferdinand led her out of the refreshment room and back across the hall to the salon and the two adjoining rooms. Was it too early, Jane wondered, to find Aunt Harriet and suggest that they return home? But how was she to live through even one more hour here without fainting or giving in to a fit of hysteria?

Someone stepped into the doorway of the salon as they were about to enter it. Jocelyn. He grasped her right wrist and looked at his brother but said not a word to him. Lord Ferdinand said nothing either, but merely slid his arm away from Jane's and stepped into the room without her. And even she said nothing. It was a strange moment.

He led her back into the hallway and turned left, drawing her away from the lighted area of the party until they reached the darkened recess of a doorway. He turned her back against the door and stood in front of her, still holding her wrist. His face was all darkness and shadows. Except that she could see his eyes, which gazed back into her own with such an intensity of passion, sorrow, longing, and desperation that she could only gaze back, mute and heartsick.

Neither of them spoke. But the silence was pregnant with unspoken words.

I might die tomorrow or the morning after.
You might leave me. You might die.
This may be good-bye.
Forever. How will I face forever without you?
My love.
My love.

And then he gathered her into his arms and held her tightly, tightly, as if he would fold her right into himself. She clung to him as if she would merge with him, become eternally one with him. She could feel him and smell him and hear his heartbeat.

For perhaps the last time.

He found her mouth with his in the darkness, and they kissed with openmouthed passion, heedless of the proximity of so many of their peers in the nearby rooms. Jane felt his heat, his taste, his maleness, his essence. But all that mattered was that he was Jocelyn, that he was the air she breathed, the heart that beat within her, the soul that gave her life meaning. And that he was here, warm and alive and in her arms.

She would never let him go. Never.

But he lifted his head, gazed down at her for a long moment, then released her and was gone. She listened to the sound of his footsteps receding down the hall in the direction of the salon and was alone.

More alone than she had ever been in her life before. She stared blankly into the almost dark hall beyond the doorway.

Neither of them had spoken a word.

"There you are," a voice said gently perhaps a minute later. "Allow me to escort you to Lady Webb, ma'am. Shall I ask her to take you home?"

She could not even answer him for a few moments. But then she swallowed and stepped resolutely out of the doorway. "No, thank you, Lord Ferdinand," she said. "Is Lady Oliver still here? Do you know? Will you take me to her, please?"

He hesitated. "I don't believe you need worry about her," he said. "Tresham is not—"

"I know that," she said. "Oh, I know that very well. But I wish to talk to her. It is time *someone* did."

He hesitated, but he offered his arm and led her back to the soiree.

Lady Oliver appeared to be having some difficulty working her way into any group. She was standing alone in the middle of the drawing room, fanning herself and smiling rather contemptuously as if to say that it was beneath her dignity to join any of the groups there.

"I'll wager she did not even receive an invitation," Lord Ferdinand muttered. "Lady Sangster would not have invited both her and Tresham. But she would be too polite, I suppose, to turn the woman away. Are you sure you wish to talk to her?"

"Yes, I am," Jane assured him. "You need not stay, Lord Ferdinand. Thank you. You are a kind gentleman."

He bowed stiffly to Lady Oliver, who turned and raised her eyebrows in surprise when she saw Jane.

"Well," she said as Lord Ferdinand walked away, "the notorious Lady Sara Illingsworth herself. And what may I do for you?"

Jane had intended to try to draw her away to the refreshment room, but it seemed they were in a small island of privacy, enclosed by the noise of group conversations and the sound of music coming from the next room.

"You may tell the truth," she said, looking very directly into the other woman's eyes.

Lady Oliver opened her fan and plied it slowly before her face. "The truth?" she asked. "And to which truth do you refer, pray?"

"You risked your husband's life and the Duke of Tresham's because you would not tell the truth," Jane said. "Now you would risk the lives of two of your brothers and that of his grace again. All because you have not told the truth."

Lady Oliver visibly blanched and her hand stilled. There was no mistaking the fact that she had just been dealt a severe shock, that she had not known about the duels until this moment. But she was evidently made of stern stuff. She pulled herself together even as Jane watched, and began fanning her face again.

"I count myself fortunate that I have brothers to defend my honor, Lady Sara," she said coldly. "What do you want? That I should call them off and save your lover? You might be better served if he died in a duel. It would save you the ignominy of being shed like a soiled garment when he is done with you. That is what Tresham inevitably does with his doxies."

Jane regarded her coldly and steadily. "You will not divert me from what I have sought you out to say, Lady Oliver," she said. "The Duke of Tresham was never your lover. But he has always been a gentleman. He will die rather than contradict a lady and cause her public humiliation. The question is, ma'am, are you a lady? Will you allow gentlemen to suffer and perhaps die because a lie serves your vanity more than the truth?"

Lady Oliver laughed. "Is that what he has told you?" she asked. "That he was never my lover? And you believed him? Poor Lady Sara. You are an innocent after all. I could tell you things. . . . But no matter. You have nothing more to say? I will bid you good evening, then. I have friends awaiting me."

"You will have an unenviable life ahead of you," Jane told her, "if someone is killed on account of your lie. A life in which your conscience will plague you every single day and every night too. Even in sleep you will not be able to escape it. I pay you the compliment, you see, of believing that you do have a conscience, that you are vain rather than depraved. I will not bid you a good evening. I hope it is not good. I hope you will be tormented by the mental images of what may happen during one or both of those duels. And I hope that before it is too late you will do the only thing that is likely to win back the respect of your peers."

She watched as Lady Oliver snapped her fan shut and swept away into the music room. And then she turned her head to find Lady Angeline on her brother's arm, Lady Webb on Viscount Kimble's, all waiting to gather her up into their company.

"Come, Sara," Aunt Harriet said, "it is time to go home. I am thoroughly fatigued from so much pleasurable conversation."

"I will take upon myself the pleasure of escorting the two of you out to your carriage, ma'am," Lord Kimble announced.

Lady Angeline stepped forward and hugged Sara hard. Uncharacteristically, she said nothing.

Lord Ferdinand did. "I will wait upon you early tomorrow morning, Lady Sara," he said.

To tell her if Jocelyn were alive or dead.

Jocelyn thought the night would never come to an end. But it did, of course, after endless hours of fitful sleep, vivid, bizarre dreams, and long spells of wakefulness. It was strange how different this duel felt from any of the four that had preceded it. Apart from an extra burst of nervous excitement on those other occasions, he could not remember having disturbed nights.

He rose earlier than necessary and wrote a long letter, to be delivered in the event that he did not return. After sealing it and pressing his signet ring into the soft wax, he raised it to his lips and closed his eyes briefly. He had held her once more in his arms. But he had been unable to utter a single word. He had been afraid of coming all to pieces if he had tried. He was not good at such words as had been needed. He had no previous experience.

Strange irony to have found love just when he had this morning to face. And tomorrow morning if he survived today.

Strange to have found love at all when he had not believed in its existence. When he had thought of marriage, even to her, as a trap.

He pulled on the bell rope to summon his valet.

Jane had not slept. She had tried, but she had lain awake, staring at the shadowed canopy above her head, feeling dizzy and sick to her stomach. In the end it had been easier to get up, dress, and curl up on the windowseat of her bedchamber, alternately cooling a burning cheek against the windowpane and huddling for warmth inside a cashmere shawl.

She should have *said* something. Why had she remained silent when there was so much to say? But she knew the answer. There were no words with which to express the deepest emotions of the heart.

What if he should die?

Jane shivered inside the shawl and clamped her teeth hard together to prevent them from chattering.

He had come through four duels with no mortal injury. Surely he could survive two more. But the odds were against him. And Lord Ferdinand, who had been no match for Jane's determined quizzing during their drive in the park, had revealed not only the place and time of the meeting but also the fact that the Reverend Josiah Forbes, despite his calling, was a cold fish and a deadly shot.

Jane's thoughts were interrupted by a scratching on her door. She looked at it, startled. It was very early in the morning. The door opened quietly, and her maid looked cautiously around it in the direction of the bed.

"I am here," Jane said.

"Oh, my lady," the girl said, peering into the semidarkness, "begging your pardon but there is a lady downstairs insisting on speaking with you. She got Mr. Ivy up out of his bed, she did, and he got me out of mine. She will not take no for an answer."

Jane was on her feet, her stomach churning, her head spinning.

"Who is she?" she asked. She *knew* who it must be, but she dared not hope. Besides, it was too late. Surely it was too late.

"Lady Oliver, my lady," her maid replied.

Jane did not pause to check her appearance. She dashed from the room and down the stairs with unladylike haste.

Lady Oliver was pacing the hallway. She looked upward when Jane came into sight and hurried toward the foot of the staircase. In the early dawn light, which was augmented by one branch of candles, Jane could see her agitation.

"Where are they?" she demanded. "Where are they to meet? Do you know? And when?"

"Hyde Park," Jane said. "At six."

"*Where* in Hyde Park?"

Jane could only guess that it would be the same place as before. But how could she explain exactly where that was? Hyde Park was a very large place. She shook her head.

"Why?" she demanded. "Are you going there?"

"Yes," Lady Oliver answered. "Oh, quick, quick. Tell me where."

"I cannot," Jane said. "But I can show you. Do you have a carriage?"

"Outside the door." Lady Oliver pointed. "Show me, then. Oh, quick. Run for a cloak and bonnet."

"There is not time," Jane said, hurrying past her visitor, grabbing her sleeve as she did so. "It must be well after five already. Come!"

Lady Oliver needed no urging. Within a minute they were seated in her carriage and on their way to Hyde Park.

"If he should die . . ." Lady Oliver dabbed at her nose with a handkerchief.

He could not die. He could not. There was too much living to be done. Oh, he could not die.

"He has always been the best of brothers," Lady Oliver continued, "and kinder to me than the others. He was the only one who would play with me as a girl and allow me to follow him around. He must not die. Oh, can that wretched coachman not go faster?"

They were in the park at last, but the carriage could not drive all the way to that private stretch of grass beyond the trees. The coachman, loudly berated by his mistress, set down the steps in haste, and Lady Oliver, looking reasonably respectable in cloak and bonnet and gloves, fairly tumbled out, followed by a bareheaded Jane in morning dress, shawl, and slippers.

"This way!" Jane cried, and broke into a run. She was not sure, of course. It might not be the right place. And even if it were, they might be too late. She listened tensely for the sound of shots above that of her own labored breathing and Lady Oliver's sobs.

It was the right place. As soon as they had stumbled through the trees, they could see the gathered spectators, all of whom were silent.

There could be only one reason for their silence!

The Reverend Josiah Forbes and the Duke of Tresham, both clad only in shirt, pantaloons, and Hessian boots, were back to back, pacing away from each other, their pistols pointing at the sky. They were stopping. They were about to turn to take aim.

"Stop!" Jane cried. "STOP!" She obeyed her own command and came to a full halt, pressing both fists to her mouth as she did so.

Lady Oliver screamed and stumbled onward.

Both gentlemen stopped. Jocelyn, without turning or lowering his pistol, found Jane out with a single glance. His eyes locked with hers across the distance. The Reverend Forbes both turned and lowered his pistol, frowning ferociously.

"Gertrude!" he bellowed. "Go away from here. This is no place for a woman. I will deal with you later."

Lord Oliver, looking both flustered and embarrassed, stepped forward from among the spectators and would have taken his wife's arm and propelled her firmly away. But she jerked her arm free.

"No!" she declared. "I have something to say."

Jane, returning Jocelyn's stare unwaveringly, nevertheless listened. It took her only a moment to realize that Lady Oliver had chosen to play the part of brave martyr, sacrificing her own reputation for the life of her dear brother. But it did not matter. At least she was doing what she should have done long ago, before the meeting of her husband with the Duke of Tresham.

Strange, Jane thought dispassionately. If Lady Oliver had done the right thing at the start, she herself would never have met Jocelyn. How fragile were the moments of chance on which the whole course of one's life hinged.

"You must not shoot Tresham, Josiah," Lady Oliver implored. "Neither must Samuel. He has done no wrong. There was never anything between him and me. I wanted there to be, but he would have none of me. I wanted to be the subject of a duel—it seemed grand and romantic to me. But I was wrong, and I will admit it now. You must not shoot an innocent man. You would have it on your conscience for the rest of your life. So would I."

"Even now you would defend your lover, Gertrude?" the Reverend Forbes asked, using the voice he must use from the pulpit, Jane guessed.

"You know me better," she told him. "If it were true, I would not so abase myself before an audience. I have simply decided to do what is right. If you still do not believe me, you may speak to Lady Sara Illingsworth, who came with me this morning. She was a witness to the snub I received from Tresham when I called upon him after the last duel. He was never my lover. But he was too much the gentleman to call me a liar."

Jocelyn, who still had not moved, did not look away from Jane. But even across the distance she could see one eyebrow lift in mockery.

Her fists, she realized, were still pressed to her mouth.

The Reverend Josiah Forbes was striding across the grass toward his dueling partner. At last Jocelyn turned and lowered his pistol.

"It seems I was mistaken, Tresham." The Reverend Forbes was still using his pulpit voice. "I owe you an apology and I withdraw my challenge. If you feel that you have a grudge against me, of course, then we will continue this meeting. My family is responsible, after all, for a dishonorable plot to harm yours." Jane guessed that he had taken three of his brothers severely to task for the incident with Lord Ferdinand's curricle.

"I believe," Jocelyn said with a languid sigh, "that small matter has already been avenged, Forbes. And as for this, you were merely doing what I would do for my own sister." He transferred the pistol to his left hand and extended his right.

There was a collective sigh from the spectators as the two shook hands and Captain Samuel Forbes stepped forward to offer his own apologies and withdraw his own challenge. Jane slowly lowered her hands and realized that she had left the imprint of eight fingernails on her two palms.

Lady Oliver swooned elegantly into her husband's arms.

An honorable reconciliation had just taken place. Soon enough Jocelyn was alone again and looking toward the trees once more. He held up his left hand, palm out, to discourage his friends from approaching while at the same time beckoning Jane imperiously with the fingers of his right hand.

Everything fled from Jane's mind except a mind-numbing

relief and an overpowering fury—fanned to breaking point by those beckoning fingers. As if she were a dog! As if he were incapable of coming to her. She hurried toward him until she stood almost nose to nose with him.

"You horrid man," she said, her voice low and trembling. "You *horrid*, arrogant, bull-headed man. I loathe you! You faced death here this morning, but you would have died without a word to me. Even last night—even then you spoke not a *word*. If I needed more evidence that you do not care *that* much for me"—she snapped her fingers in his face with a satisfyingly loud click—"I now have it in abundance. I never want to see you again. Do you understand me? Never. Stay away from me."

He looked back at her with lazy hauteur and no glimmering of remorse. "You came all this way at this hour of the morning and in this state of dishabille to command *me* to stay away from *you*, Lady Sara?" he asked with detestably cool logic. "You have flaunted propriety in order to tell me that I am *horrid*? Now, you will take my arm without further delay, and I will escort you to Oliver's carriage—I assume that is where the lady is being carried. I daresay that in the drama of the moment they will forget you if we do not hurry, and then you will be left with a score or two of gentlemen for your sole chaperons and escorts. It is not the sort of situation Lady Sara Illingsworth should find herself in when her reputation is still in a precarious state."

He offered his arm, but she turned away and began to stride in the direction of the carriage. He fell into step beside her.

"I suppose," he said, "all this was your idea? It made for wonderful drama. Saved in the nick of time."

"Not the nick of time part of it," she said coldly. "I merely suggested to Lady Oliver last evening that perhaps it was time to tell the truth."

"I owe my life to you, then." But his words were spoken haughtily and held no note of gratitude.

"You may return to your friends," she said as the carriage came into sight and it was clear that she would reach it in plenty of time to accompany the still-insensible Lady Oliver home again.

He stopped and bowed to her and turned away without another word. But she thought of something as he began to stride away.

"Jocelyn!" she called.

He stopped and looked at her over his shoulder, a strange light in his eyes.

"I left my embroidery behind," she said foolishly, unable even now to say what she wanted to say.

"I will bring it to you," he said. "No. Pardon me. You never wish to see me again. I will have it sent to you." He turned away.

"*Jocelyn!*"

Again the look over his shoulder.

"I left the *painting* behind."

It seemed to her that their eyes remained locked for long moments before he replied.

"I will have it sent," he said.

He turned and strode away from her.

Just as if last evening had never happened. And what *had* that been all about anyway? Just a stolen kiss between a man and his ex-mistress?

Jane turned and hurried toward the carriage.

25

Her embroidery, the painting, and *Mansfield Park* were delivered the same day. Phillip brought them, though Jane did not see him. All she knew for certain was that *he* did not bring them himself. She was glad he did not. His behavior during the morning had been imperious and cold and offensive. She had simply imagined that there was tender yearning in his kiss last evening, she decided. His not coming in person with her belongings saved her from having to refuse to see him. She never wanted even to hear his name again.

Which argument was seen for the nonsense it was the following morning when Lady Webb was still in her dressing room and the butler brought the morning post into the breakfast parlor.

"There is a letter for you, my lady," he said to Jane.

She snatched it from his hand and looked with eager anxiety at the name and direction written on the outside. But her heart immediately plummeted. It was not in the bold, careless hand of the Duke of Tresham. In her disappointment she did not immediately realize that she did nevertheless recognize the handwriting.

"Thank you," she said, and broke the seal.

It was from Charles. A rather long letter. It had come from Cornwall.

The Earl of Durbury had returned to Candleford, Charles wrote, bringing with him the news that Sara had been found and was now staying with Lady Webb. She would be reassured to know that the announcement had been made from Candleford that Sidney Jardine, who had for a long time been reputed to be at death's door, was finally recovering his health.

"I have been more distressed than I can say," Charles wrote, "that I was away from home when all this happened so that you did not have me to turn to with your troubles. I would have followed you to London, but where would I have looked? It was said that Durbury had hired a Bow Street Runner but that even he could not find you. What chance would I have had, then?"

But he might have tried anyway, Jane thought. Surely if he really loved her, he would have come.

"Durbury is also spreading another piece of news," the letter continued, "though surely it cannot be true. My belief is that it is for my benefit, Sara, to hurt and alarm me. You know how much he has always despised our partiality for each other. He says that he has given his consent to the Duke of Tresham to pay his addresses to you. I daresay you will be laughing merrily when you read this, but really, Sara—Tresham! I have never met the man, but he has a reputation as surely the most notorious rake in all England. I sincerely hope he is not pestering you with unwanted attentions."

Jocelyn, she thought. Ah, Jocelyn.

"I am going to come up to London," Charles wrote, "as soon as I have dealt with a few important matters of business. I will come to protect you from the advances of any man who believes that this unfortunate incident has made you deserving of all manner of insult. I shall come to fetch you home, Sara. If Durbury will not consent to our marriage, then we will marry without his consent. I am not a wealthy man and so hate to see you deprived of your own fortune, but I am well able to support a wife and family in comfort and even some luxury."

Jane closed her eyes and bowed her head over the letter. She was dearly fond of Charles. She always had been. For several years she had tried to convince herself that she was fond enough of him to marry him. But she knew now why she had never been able to love him. There was no fire in his own love. There was only bland amiability. He obviously had no clear understanding of all she had suffered in the past weeks. Even now he was not rushing to her side. There were a few matters of business to be dealt with first.

Jane felt bleak almost to the point of despair as she folded the letter and set it beside her plate. She had not thought specifically of Charles since coming to Aunt Harriet's. She had known, of course, that a match between them was now impossible, but only now, this morning, had she been forced to face that reality before she was quite ready to deal with it.

She felt as if somehow a comfortable lifeline had been finally severed. As if she were now thoroughly and eternally alone.

And yet he was coming to London.

She would write immediately and tell him not to, she decided, getting to her feet even though she had eaten no breakfast. It would be a waste of time and expense for him to come all this way. And breaking the news to him that she could not marry him would be more easily done on paper than in a face-to-face encounter.

It took Jocelyn a few days to realize fully that there was no more imminent threat of death, that the Forbeses and apparently Lord Oliver too were satisfied that Lady Oliver had told the truth during her dramatic interruption of the duel.

When Jocelyn *did* realize it, in the library one morning while he was reading over the latest report from Acton Park, he discovered that he was somewhat short of breath. And when he rested his elbows on the desk and held up his hands, he found with some fascination that they were shaking.

He was very thankful that Michael Quincy was not present to witness the phenomenon.

It was strange really since none of his previous duels had succeeded in bringing him eyeball to eyeball with his own mortality. Perhaps it was because he had never before come face to face with life and the desire to live it to the full. For the first time reading the dry, factual report of his steward brought on a powerful feeling of aching nostalgia. He wanted to *go* there, to see the house again with adult eyes, to roam the park and the wooded hills, remembering the boy he had been, discovering the man he had become.

He wanted to go there with Jane.

He ached for her. He would leave her alone until after her presentation, he had decided. He would dance with her at her come-out ball and then pay her determined court until she capitulated, which she would surely do. No one could defy his will forever.

But there was still a whole week left before the ball. He could not wait that long. He was too afraid that she would be the one to defy him, if anyone could. And while he waited, the likes of Kimble and even his own brother were squiring her all over town, oozing charm from every pore, and drawing from her the sort of dazzling smiles she had been very sparing of in her dealings with him. And then he was furious at himself for admitting to jealousy of all things. If she wanted another man, let her have him. She could go to the devil for all he cared. He amused himself with mental images of fighting Kimble and Ferdinand simultaneously—with swords. One in each hand.

And a cutlass between his teeth, he thought in self-derision. And a black patch over one eye.

"Deuce take it!" he told his empty library, bringing the side of his fist down onto the desktop for good measure. "I'll wring her neck for her."

He presented himself at Lady Webb's that same afternoon but declined her butler's invitation to follow him to the drawing room, where other visitors were being entertained. He asked to speak to Lady Webb privately and was shown into a salon on the ground floor.

Lady Webb, he knew, did not approve of him. Not that she was ill bred enough to voice her dislike, of course. And it was perfectly understandable. He had not spent his adult years cultivating the good opinion of respectable ladies like her. Quite the contrary. She did not like him, but she clearly recognized the necessity of his making her goddaughter an offer.

"Though if she refuses you," she told him before sending Jane down, "I will support her fully. I will not allow you to come here bullying her."

He bowed stiffly.

Two more minutes passed before Jane appeared.

"Oh," she said, closing the door behind her back and keeping her hands on the knob, "it is you, is it?"

"It was the last time I glanced into a looking glass," he said, making her an elegant bow. "Whom did you expect?"

"I thought perhaps it was Charles," she said.

He frowned and glared. *"Charles?"* All his good intentions fled. "The milksop from Cornwall, do you mean? The bumpkin who imagines he is going to marry you? He is in town?"

Her lips did their familiar disappearing act. "Sir Charles Fortescue," she said, "is neither a milksop nor a bumpkin. He has always been my dearest friend. And he is coming as soon as he is able."

"As soon as he is able," he repeated. "Where has he been during the past month or so? I have not noticed him dashing about London searching for you, rescuing you from the clutches of your uncle or your cousin or whatever the devil Durbury is to you."

"Where would he have looked?" she asked. "If the Bow Street Runners could not find me, what chance would Charles have had, your grace?"

"I would have found you." He narrowed his gaze on her. "The world would not have been large enough to hide you, *Lady Sara*, if I had been searching."

"Don't call me that," she told him. "It is not my name. I am Jane."

His mood softened and for the moment he forgot the irritation of Sir Charles Fortescue, milksop and bumpkin.

"Yes," he agreed. "Yes, it is. And I am not 'your grace,' Jane. I am Jocelyn."

"Yes." She licked her lips.

"Why are you cowering there, grasping the doorknob?" he asked her. "Are you afraid I will make a grab for you and have my wicked way with you?"

She shook her head and advanced farther into the room. "I am not afraid of you."

"Then you should be." He allowed his eyes to roam over her. She was clad in pale-lemon muslin. Her hair glowed. "I have missed you." But after all, he could not allow himself such vulnerability. "In bed, of course."

"Of course," she said tartly. "Where else could you possibly mean? Why have you come, Jocelyn? Do you still feel honor bound to offer for me because I am Lady Sara Illingsworth rather than Jane Ingleby? You insult me. Is the name so much more significant than the person? You would not have dreamed of marrying Jane Ingleby."

"You have always presumed to know my thoughts, Jane," he said. "Do you know my dreams now too?"

"You would not have married Jane Ingleby," she insisted. "Why do you wish to marry me now? Because it is the gentlemanly thing to do, like facing death in a duel rather than call a lady a liar? I do not want a perfect gentleman, Jocelyn. I would prefer the rake."

It was one of the rare occasions when his own temper was not rising with hers. The fact gave him a definite advantage.

"Would you, Jane?" He made his voice a caress. "Why?"

"Because the rake has some spontaneity, some vulnerability, some humanity, some—oh, what is the word I am looking for?" One of her hands was making circles in the air.

"Passion?" he suggested.

"Yes, precisely." Her blue eyes gazed angrily back into his. "I prefer you to be arguing and quarreling with me and insulting me and trying to order me about and reading to me and p-painting me and forgetting all about me and the rest of the world while you lose yourself in music. I prefer *that* man, odious as he can be. That man has *passion*. I will not have you acting the gentleman with me, Jocelyn. I *will* not."

He held his smile inside. And his hope. He wondered if she realized just how suggestive her final words had been. Probably not. She was still in a towering temper.

"Will you not?" He strolled toward her. "I had better kiss you, then, to prove how much I am not the gentleman."

"Come one step closer," she told him, "and I will slap you."

But she would not, of course, take one step back to put more distance between them. He took two steps closer until they were almost toe to toe.

"Please, Jane." He made his voice a caress again. "Let me kiss you?"

"Why should I?" Her eyes were bright with tears, but she would not look away. And he was not sure whether they were tears of anger or sentiment. "Why should I let you kiss me? The last time you made me believe you cared even though you said nothing. And then the morning after you *beckoned* with your fingers and looked cold and arrogant, just as if I were your dog being called to heel. Why should I let you kiss me when you do not care a fig for me?"

"A fig?" he said. "I do not even like figs, Jane. I like you."

"Go away," she told him. "You toy with me. I suppose I have much for which to thank you. Without you I would be in Cornwall now battling it out with Sidney and the Earl of Durbury. But I am not convinced you did not help merely for your pride's sake. You were not there for me when I really needed you to confide in. You—"

He reached out and set one finger across her lips. She stopped abruptly.

"Let me tell it," he said. "We grew close during that week, Jane. Closer than I have ever been to anyone else. We shared interests and conversation. We shared comfort and emotions. We became friends as well as lovers. More than friends. More than lovers. You convinced me without ever preaching at me that to be a whole person I had to forgive myself and my father too for what happened in the past. You convinced me that being a man does not consist of cutting off all one's finer feelings and more tender emotions. You taught me to feel again, to face the past again, to remember that there was joy as well as pain in my boyhood. And all this you did by just being there. By just being Jane."

She drew her head free of his finger, but he would not allow her to speak. Not yet. He cupped her chin in his hand.

"You told me," he said, "that you would have confided in me as I had in you if I had not discovered the truth about you just when I did. I should have believed you, Jane. And even when I first learned the truth, I should have reacted far differently than I did. I should have come to you. I should have taken you in my arms, as you had taken me the night before, told you what I had discovered, and invited you to tell me all, to trust me, to lean on me. I knew how difficult it was to relive some memories. I had got past that difficulty just the night before and should have been far more sensitive. I failed myself, Jane. And dammit, I failed you."

"Don't," she said. "You are despicable. I cannot fight you when you talk like this."

"Don't fight me," he told her. "Forgive me, Jane? Please?"

She searched his eyes as if to judge his sincerity. He had never seen her so defenseless. She was not even trying to hide her yearning to believe him.

"Jane," he said softly, "you have taught me that there really is love."

Two tears spilled over and ran down her cheeks. He blotted them with his thumbs, cupping her face with both hands, and then he leaned forward to kiss the dried spot on each cheek.

"I thought you were going to d-die!" she blurted suddenly. "I thought we would be too late. I thought I would hear a shot and find you dead. I had a feeling about it here." She patted her heart. "A premonition. I was desperate to reach you, to say all the things I had never said, to—to . . . oh, *why* can I never find a handkerchief when I most need one?" She was fumbling around at the pocketless seams of her dress, sniffing inelegantly.

He handed her a large white one.

"But you did reach me in time," he said, "and you did say all those things. Let me see if I can remember accurately. Horrid man? Arrogant? Bull-headed—that was a nasty one, Jane. You loathed me? I was never ever to come near you again? Have I missed anything?"

She blew her nose and then appeared not to know what to do with the handkerchief. He took it from her and put it away in his pocket.

"I would have died if you had died," she said, and he had the satisfaction of seeing that she was growing cross again. "Horrid, loathsome man. If you ever again get yourself into a

situation that invites a challenge from another man, I will kill
you myself."

"Will you, my love?" he asked her.

She compressed her lips. "You are determined to have me,
are you not?" she asked him. "Is this all a ruse?"

"If you knew what I am suffering, Jane," he said. "I am terrified that you are going to say no. And I know that if you do,
there will be no shifting you. Have pity on me. I have never
been in this position before. I have always been able to have
my own way with ease."

But she would only look back at him with the same expression on her face.

"What is it?" he asked her, but she shook her head slightly.
"Jane, I long to go home. To go back to Acton—with you. To
start creating our own memories and our own traditions there.
You thought you knew my dreams. But this is my dream. Will
you not share it with me?"

She pressed her lips even harder together.

"Why have you stopped talking to me?" He clasped his
hands at his back and leaned his head slightly closer to her.
"Jane?"

"This is all about *you*, is it not?" she blurted. "About what
you want? About your dreams? What about me? Do you even
care about me?"

"Tell me," he said. "What about you, Jane? What do you
want? Do you want me to go away? Seriously? Tell me if
you do—but quietly and seriously, not in a passion, so that I
will know that you mean what you say. Tell me to go and I
will."

Even facing Forbes's pistol a few days before had not filled
him with such terror.

"I am with *child*," she cried. "I have no choices left."

He recoiled rather as if she had punched him on the chin
with the full force of her fist. Good God! How long had she
known? Would she have told him if he had not come today?

Would she *ever* have told him? Ever have confided in him, trusted him, forgiven him?

She glared at him in the silence that followed her words. He clasped his hands so tightly behind his back that he felt pain.

"Ah, so," he said softly at last. "Well, this changes everything, Jane."

26

ady Webb opened Jane's dressing room door and
stepped inside. Dressed in midnight blue with matching
plumed turban, she formed a marked contrast to Jane,
who looked almost ethereal in a fashionable low-cut gown of
white lace over white satin, silver thread gleaming on the scal-
loped hem, the sash beneath her bosom, and the short scal-
loped sleeves. She wore long white gloves and silver slippers
and had a narrow white, silver-shot ribbon threaded through
her golden hair.

"Oh, Sara, my dear," Lady Webb said, "you are indeed the
daughter I never had. How fortunate I am. But how I wish
your poor mother could be here to see you on surely the most
important day of your life. You look positively beautiful."

Jane had been critically examining her appearance in the
long pier glass in her dressing room. She turned to her godmother.

"You said exactly the same thing yesterday when I was

forced to wear those horrid, heavy, old-fashioned clothes that the queen insists upon when one is being presented at one of her Drawing Rooms," she said. "I certainly feel better tonight."

"Your presentation at court was obligatory," Lady Webb said. "Your come-out ball is your personal, triumphant entry into society."

"Will it be a triumph, do you suppose?"

Jane picked up her fan from the dressing table. She was feeling a fluttering of anxiety about the evening ahead. All day there had been a great hustle and bustle in preparation for the ball. Since returning from a morning outing with her maid, she had watched in wonder as the ballroom was transformed before her eyes. It was decked out all in white and silver ribbons and bows and flowers, the only color provided by the lush green of leaves and ferns. The great chandeliers had been lowered and cleaned and filled with hundreds of new candles. The orchestra had arrived late in the afternoon and set up their instruments on the dais. The dining room had been set with all the best porcelain and crystal and silverware for a sumptuous supper banquet at midnight.

"Of *course* it will be a triumph," Lady Webb said, approaching Jane and hugging her, though not closely enough to rumple either of them. "How could it not? You are Lady Sara Illingsworth, daughter of the late Earl of Durbury and a great heiress. You are as lovely as the princesses of fairy tales. And you already have a considerable court of admirers."

Jane smiled ruefully.

"You could make any of a number of brilliant matches," her godmother told her. "Viscount Kimble, for example, has been markedly attentive and could be brought up to scratch, I believe. You need not feel obliged to allow Tresham to continue paying court to you—if he intends to do so, that is. He came and made you a decent offer—at least, I trust it was decent. But the choice is yours, Sara."

342   *Mary Balogh*

"Aunt Harriet," Jane said half reproachfully.

"But I will say no more on that subject," Lady Webb said briskly. "I have already said enough—perhaps too much. Come, we must go down to the ballroom. Our guests will be arriving soon. Cyril and Dorothy will be waiting for us."

Lord Lansdowne was Lady Webb's brother. She had invited him and his wife to help her host the ball. Lord Lansdowne was to lead Jane into the opening set of dances.

The ballroom had looked magnificent in the light of late afternoon. Now it looked nothing short of breathtaking. The candles had all been lit. They sparkled gold above all the white and silver, their light multiplied by the long mirrors along the walls.

It all looked, Jane thought, almost like a room prepared for a bridal ball. But it was her come-out they were celebrating tonight. And all must go well. Nothing must be allowed to spoil it. Aunt Harriet had given so much time and energy—as well as a great deal of money—to make sure that yesterday and today would be perfect for her goddaughter.

"Are you nervous, Sara?" Lady Lansdowne asked.

Jane turned to her with eyes that were tear-filled, despite herself. "Only insofar as I want everything to go well for Aunt Harriet's sake," she said.

"You look as fine as fivepence, I must say, my dear," Lord Lansdowne told her. "Now, if only I can disguise the fact that I have two left feet . . ." He laughed heartily.

Jane turned to Lady Webb, who was regarding her with a maternal eye. "Thank you so very much for all this, Aunt Harriet," she said. "My own mama could not have done better for me."

"Well, my dear. What can I say?" Lady Webb looked suspiciously dewy-eyed.

Fortunately, perhaps, there were some early guests arriving.

The four of them hurried to form a receiving line outside the ballroom doors.

The next hour sped by in a blur for Jane as she was formally presented at long last—at the advanced age of twenty—to her peers in the *ton*. There were familiar faces among those of strangers. Some people she felt she already knew quite well. There was the very handsome and charming Viscount Kimble, who Aunt Harriet seemed to believe was a prospective suitor for her hand. There was the amiable Sir Conan Brougham, and a few more of Jocelyn's friends, who had visited him at Dudley House while Jane was there. There was Lord Ferdinand Dudley, who bowed over her hand, raised it to his lips, and grinned at her with his attractive boyish charm. And there were Lord and Lady Heyward. The former bowed courteously, said all that was correct, and would have moved on into the ballroom if his wife had not had other ideas.

"Oh, Sara," she said, hugging Jane tightly at risk of grave damage to both their appearances, "you *do* look lovely. I am *so* envious of your ability to wear white. I look like a ghost in it myself and simply must wear brighter colors. Though Tresham and Ferdie are forever criticizing my taste, odious creatures. Is Tresham coming tonight? He would not give me a direct answer when I met him in the park this afternoon. Have the two of you had words? How splendid of you actually to quarrel with him. No one has ever been able to stand up to him before. I do hope you will not forgive him too readily but will make him suffer. But tomorrow, you know—"

But Lord Heyward had grasped her firmly by the elbow. "Come, my love," he said. "The line will be stretched down the stairs and across the hall and out to the pavement if we stand here talking any longer."

"*Have* you quarreled with the duke, Sara?" Lady Webb asked as they turned away. "You had so little to say for yourself after he called on you last week. Do you know if he intends to come tonight?"

But there really was a line of people waiting to be presented. There was no chance for further private talk.

He did come. Of course he came. He was late, but not *too* late. Jane and Lady Webb were still standing outside the ballroom doors with Lord and Lady Lansdowne while all was abuzz inside and the members of the orchestra were tuning their instruments. He was dressed in a tailed black, form-fitting evening coat with gray silk knee breeches, silver-embroidered waistcoat, sparkling white linen, lace, and stockings, and black dancing shoes. He was looking formal and correct and haughty as he bowed in turn to everyone in the receiving line.

"Lady Sara," he murmured when he came to Jane. He grasped the handle of his jeweled quizzing glass but did not raise it quite to his eye as he looked her over slowly from head to toe. "Dear me. Looking almost like a bride."

Oh, odious, odious man! He knew very well that white was almost obligatory for any lady making her come-out.

"Your grace," she murmured, emphasizing the words slightly in retaliation for his calling her Lady Sara. She dipped him a curtsy.

He did not linger but proceeded on into the ballroom. Jane turned her thoughts away from him. It was not easy to do but must be done. Tonight was for Aunt Harriet more than for herself.

Five minutes later Lord Lansdowne led her into the opening set of country dances. Jane relished the moment to the full. She was dancing at a grand London ball for the first time, and it was her own ball. It was a vigorous and intricate dance, one that had her flushed and laughing before it was over. Other couples had joined them on the dance floor, enough in fact to make it quite clear that tomorrow Aunt Harriet would be able to boast that the event had been a squeeze.

Jocelyn did not dance. Jane did not once look directly at him, but every moment she was aware of him, standing alone on the sidelines, dark and handsome, watching the dancing. At the end of the set, after Lord Lansdowne had returned her to Lady Webb's side and a few prospective partners had approached her, including Lord Ferdinand, she saw him turn and leave the ballroom.

Jocelyn prowled. There was no other word to describe his movements. Even he was aware of it as he moved from the ballroom to the card room to the refreshment room to the landing that connected all three rooms and back to the ballroom again. He could not settle anywhere, even though Pottier invited him to join a table of card players and Lady Webb offered to present him with a dancing partner. There was Ferdinand to deal with, of course. And Angeline.

"I do not know why you bothered to come, Tresh," the former said disapprovingly when they ran against each another on the landing while Ferdinand was on his way to the refreshment room and Jocelyn was about to enter the card room for the third time. "All you have done since you arrived is look damned morose and toplofty. If you have come to spoil the evening for her, I am here to tell you that I will not have it."

Jocelyn looked at his brother with pleased approval. Then he raised his quizzing glass to his eye. "You still have the same valet, Ferdinand?" he asked. "Despite the fact that he is still attempting to slice your throat? You are braver than I, my dear fellow."

Ferdinand frowned and fingered the small nick beneath his jaw on the right side while Jocelyn prowled off in the direction of the card room.

Angeline was a little more garrulous—but then, when was she not? It seemed that she applauded Jane for looking so radiantly happy when it was clear that Tresham must have quarreled with her. She hoped Jane would lead him a merry dance and never forgive him for whatever he had said to offend her. And he was no brother of hers if he did not immediately sweep Jane off her feet and make her an offer and positively refuse to take no for an answer.

"That is what I goaded Heyward into doing," she told him. She fanned her face while her brother looked at her with distaste.

"I wonder," he said, "if you are color blind, Angeline. It is the kindest explanation I can think of to account for your appalling choice of red and pink plumes to be worn side by side in your hair."

She ignored him. "You are going to marry Lady Sara in St. George's, Hanover Square, before the Season is over," she told him. "With all the *ton* in attendance. I absolutely insist upon it, Tresham. I shall plan it all myself."

"Heaven defend us," he murmured before bowing politely to her and continuing on his way into the ballroom.

It was almost time. A cotillion was coming to an end. A waltz was next. He stood close to the doors, his prowling forgotten, and watched Brougham lead a flushed and smiling Jane off the dance floor and return her to Lady Webb's side. The inevitable court of hopefuls gathered around. It looked as if Kimble had won the race. He was smiling and saying something to Jane. Jocelyn strolled forward.

"This," he said firmly when he was close enough, "is my dance, I believe, ma'am."

"Too late, too late," Kimble said flippantly. "I spoke first, Tresham."

Jocelyn regarded his friend with haughtily raised eyebrows as the fingers of one hand grasped the handle of his quizzing glass.

"Congratulations, my dear fellow," he said. "But the lady's

hand is mine nonetheless. Of course, if you care to argue the point—"

"Your grace," Jane began, sounding more embarrassed than angry. Jocelyn lifted his glass all the way to his eye and swung it in her direction. All the other bucks in attendance on her had frozen in place, he noticed, as if they were expecting fisticuffs to break out at any moment and were terrified that they might be involved.

"You have fought enough duels to last for the next decade or so, Tresh," Kimble said. "And I have no wish whatsoever to peer down the wrong end of your pistol, even if I know very well that you will shoot into the air when it comes to the point."

He bowed, had the temerity to wink at Jane, and strolled away.

"I cannot waltz, your grace," Jane reminded Jocelyn. "This is my come-out ball, and I have not yet had the nod of approval from any of the patronesses of Almack's to waltz at a public ball."

"Poppycock!" he said. "This is *your* ball, and you will waltz if you wish to. *Do* you?"

Lady Webb, who might have spoken up in protest, did not do so. The decision was Jane's. Did she have the courage? He looked directly into her eyes.

"Yes," she said, setting her hand on his sleeve. "Of course I do."

And so they took the floor together for the waltz, a move that drew considerable attention from most if not all of the gathered guests, Jocelyn noticed. He and Jane were an *ondit*, he realized, despite his efforts to see to it that they were not. And now he had goaded her into waltzing in defiance of the prevailing custom.

He did not care a tinker's damn what anyone thought. But she did, of course. This was her come-out ball, which Lady

Webb had prepared for her with such selfless enthusiasm. He gazed intently at her as he took her in his arms. How could he possibly behave himself as a gentleman ought and act as if she meant nothing at all to him? How could he possibly disguise what he felt for this woman? Even just touching her, like this . . . But he held her the regulation distance from his body and concentrated on keeping the heat he was feeling out of his gaze.

"It was quite odious of you," she said, "to say what you did when you arrived."

"Lady Sara?" he said. "But you are. And I was on my best behavior. Besides, you retaliated without a blink, Jane."

"Not that," she said. "The other thing."

"About your looking like a bride?" he said. "You do. All white lace and satin and blushes."

"Flushes," she said. "I have been dancing."

"With all your most loyal and persistent beaux," he agreed. "Jealous?"

He raised his eyebrows and did not deign to answer. Instead, he drew her closer. Scandalously close, in fact. He could sense the gossips murmuring and muttering behind fans and lorgnettes and gloved hands. Jane made no protest at all.

They did not talk after that. It was a spirited waltz tune that the orchestra played, and the dance floor was larger than the drawing room at Dudley House, where they had last waltzed together. He moved her about the perimeter of the floor, twirling her to the rhythm, his eyes locked on hers the whole while, their bodies almost touching.

There was no need of words. They had spoken plenty during the weeks of their acquaintance. Enough that they could sometimes converse quite eloquently without a single sound issuing from their lips. Despite good intentions, he made love to her with his eyes, heedless of any audience they might still have. She pressed her lips together, but she did not once look away. He was not going to spoil the evening, her eyes told him. For Lady Webb's sake he was not. She might have been goaded into possible scandal by waltzing with him, but she would not be persuaded into looking back at him as he was looking at her. Or into quarreling with him. And yet her eyes said other things too. They were far more expressive than she realized.

"Well, Jane," he asked her when he knew the waltz was drawing to an end, "what is your assessment? Is this the happiest day of your life?"

"Of course." She smiled slowly at him. "How could it not be? Are *you* happy?" she asked him.

"Bedamned," he told her.

There was a stranger with Lady Webb, he saw as he took Jane's arm to lead her back to her godmother. A young man who was dressed with perfect decency and propriety but with not the slightest flair of elegance or fashion. Someone who lived almost exclusively in the country, it would appear. The milksop and country bumpkin, if his guess was not quite wide of the mark.

It was a suspicion that was confirmed almost immediately, as soon as Jane's attention was drawn away from someone who said something to her in passing. She looked ahead to Lady Webb, her hand stiffened on his arm, and she hurried forward.

"Charles!" she exclaimed, holding out both her hands to the bumpkin, who was glaring at him, Jocelyn, as if he would dearly like to take him apart limb from limb.

"Yes, Sara," the young idiot said, finally looking at the woman who was reputed to be the love of his heart and taking her hands in his own. "I have come. You are quite safe now."

*   *   *

"I have come," Charles said again. "And in the very nick of time, it would appear, Sara. I found that fellow offensive."

Jane had her arm linked through his and was leading him in the direction of the refreshment room. Yes, Jocelyn really had behaved rather annoyingly. He had become the Duke of Tresham even before she had introduced the two men, all haughty ennui, his quizzing glass to his eye. And when she *had* introduced them, he had spoken with faint hauteur.

"Indeed?" he had said, looking Charles over. "Lady Sara's champion, I gather? Her trusty knight, who rode at a gallop to her rescue when she was within the very jaws of the dragon?"

Charles had swelled up almost visibly with indignation, but he had found nothing better to say than that he had been away from home at the time and that when he had arrived back it was to learn that even a Bow Street Runner had been unable to find her.

"Yes, quite so," Jocelyn had agreed with an audible sigh before inclining his head to Jane and Lady Webb and strolling away.

To her shame Jane had wanted to laugh. She had felt nothing but dismay and chagrin at seeing Charles in Aunt Harriet's ballroom. Surely he must have received her letter before leaving Cornwall. But he had come anyway.

"Yes, you have come," she said. "But why, Charles, when I wrote and told you not to?"

"How could I stay away?" he asked her.

"And yet," she said quietly, accepting the glass of lemonade he had taken off a tray for her, "you did not come when I most needed you, Charles. Oh, yes, I know." She held up a staying hand when he would have spoken. "You did not see the point in coming when you did not know where to look. It was sensible to remain at home."

"Yes, exactly," he agreed. "I have come now when I can do some good. I am happy that Lady Webb has arranged this ball for you. It is only fitting that Lady Sara Illingsworth be presented to the *ton*. But it is unfortunate that an event such as this exposes you to every rake and fortune hunter who cares to ask a dance of you."

"The guest list was prepared by Aunt Harriet," Jane explained. "And every partner I have had tonight has been approved by her. You insult her by saying such a thing, Charles."

"Well," he said, "you were waltzing with the Duke of Tresham, Sara, and he was taking inappropriate liberties with his eyes. Besides which, he had no business leading you into a waltz of all things. He will be causing you to be called fast. I know that he had a hand in finding you and bringing you here, so I suppose Lady Webb had no choice but to invite him. But he must not be encouraged. A man such as he has no honorable intentions toward any decent woman, believe me."

Jane sighed and sipped her drink. "Charles," she said, "I will not quarrel with you. We have always been friends, and I am grateful that you have cared enough to come all this way. But you really must not pass judgment on people you have not even met before, you know."

"His reputation is enough for me," he said. "Pardon me, Sara, but you have been gently nurtured and have lived a sheltered life far from places like London. I can understand that an experience like this tonight is exciting for you. But you must not abandon your roots. You belong in the country. You would not be happy here forever."

"No," she agreed, smiling softly into her glass. "You are right."

"Come home with me, then," he urged her. "Tomorrow or the next day or next week. Just come."

"Oh, Charles," she said, "I do wish you had read the letter I sent. I cannot go back to Cornwall. That phase of my life is over. I hope we can remain friends, but there—"

"He is not the one for you, Sara," he said urgently, interrupting her. "Believe me, he is not. He could bring you nothing but unhappiness."

"Which is exactly what I would bring you, Charles," she told him gently. "I feel a deep affection for you. But I do not love you."

"Love is something that grows between two married people," he said. "Affection is enough on which to start."

She set a hand on his arm. "This is neither the time nor the place, Charles," she said. "I have already missed one set of dances. If I do not return to the ballroom soon, I will miss another, and I would hate that."

"We will speak tomorrow, then," he said.

How she wished he had not come to London, she thought as he escorted her back to the ballroom. But she said no more.

Later in the evening, she was seated for supper at one of the long tables in the dining room, in company with friends and acquaintances, when Charles came to take the empty place opposite her. Jane smiled at him and introduced him to the people around them. He was quiet for a time while the rest of them chattered and laughed on a variety of topics.

Baron Pottier announced his intention of removing to Brighton for the summer, after the Season was over. It was where the Prince Regent went, and where half the *ton* followed him.

"Will you be going there, Lady Sara?" Lord Pottier asked.

"Oh, no, I think not," Jane said. "I would rather spend the summer in the country."

Viscount Kimble, seated at her side, caught her hand in his and raised it to his lips. "But Brighton would be empty of all attraction without you," he told her, his eyes twinkling. "I shall simply kidnap you and take you there myself."

"Oh, no, you will not," Lady Heyward said, laughing. "If there is any kidnapping to be done, it is I who will be doing it—with Heyward's help. Not that he would agree to do anything so dashing or dangerous, of course. With Ferdie's aid, then. We will kidnap Lady Sara and Tresham and bear them off to St. George's for a grand wedding. Will we not, Ferdie?"

Lord Ferdinand, seated across the table, next to Charles, grinned. "I would need the assistance of half a regiment of burly military types, Angie, if I were to try trussing up Tresham," he said.

Viscount Kimble sighed soulfully. "Alas," he said, "do not forget all about me or my heart will be broken, ma'am."

Jane laughed at him, and the conversation would doubtless have moved on to another subject. But Charles, perhaps not recognizing the light, teasing tone of the conversation, chose to speak up.

"As Lady Sara has said," he told the group, "she will be returning to the country for the summer. Perhaps sooner."

"Oh, yes," Lady Heyward agreed, laughing. "After the wedding. Now really, Ferdie—"

"Lady Sara will be returning to Cornwall. With me," Charles said with enough emphasis to attract the attention of everyone seated at their table. "We have long had an understanding."

"Charles!" Jane said sharply before explaining to the group at large. "We have been friends and neighbors all our lives."

"Tresham might have a thing or two to say about your *understanding*," Baron Pottier said. "Are you really going back to Cornwall, Lady Sara? Jardine notwithstanding?"

"I believe I will be able to protect my own betrothed from any further impertinences from that direction," Charles said.

"Charles, *please* . . ."

"Oh, you are mistaken, sir," Lady Heyward said merrily. "Lady Sara is going to marry my brother even though they have quarreled and have danced together only once this evening—"

"Stow it, Angie," Lord Ferdinand said. "The lady is looking embarrassed. Let's change the subject. Let's talk about the weather."

But Charles was not to be deterred. He actually stood up,

scraping back his chair with his knees. And somehow the action attracted general notice in the crowded dining room and the noise level dropped noticeably.

"Lady Sara Illingsworth will not be the object of any London buck's gallantries for much longer," he said, indignation vibrating in his voice. "I will be taking her home where she belongs. Not to Candleford, but *home.*"

Jane would have closed her eyes in mortification, but she glanced first at a dark-clad figure standing in the dining room doorway. He must have been on his way out, but he was standing still now, his quizzing glass in one hand, his attention on Charles.

"Mr. Fortescue," Lady Lansdowne asked from the end of their table, "are we to understand that you are announcing your betrothal to Sara?"

Jane's eyes locked with Jocelyn's in the doorway.

"Charles—" she said aloud.

"Yes, ma'am," Charles said, raising his voice and speaking now to an audience of every single guest at the ball. "I have the honor of announcing my betrothal to Lady Sara Illingsworth. I trust everyone will wish us happy."

A swell of sound in the dining room replaced the silence. But then Jocelyn took one step forward and a hush descended once more.

"No, no, no," he said, every inch the Duke of Tresham again. "I would wager that Lady Sara has not consented, and it is not good *ton*, you know, Fortescue, to make such an announcement unless the prospective bride has done so."

"Of course she has consented," Charles said testily. "We have had an underst—"

"*Have* you, Jane?" The ducal quizzing glass swung her way. "How naughty of you, my love."

Jane heard a feminine gasp at the duke's use of the endearment. While Jocelyn was actually *enjoying* himself, Jane was wishing for a black hole to swallow her up.

"She is *not* your love," Charles retorted, "and I would thank you for not—"

"Ah, but she is," Jocelyn said, taking a few more steps forward and lowering his glass. "And I must protest most forcefully against your imagined betrothal to her, my dear fellow. You see, much as I commend you for the concern you have shown for her well-being, I really cannot permit you to marry my wife."

There was another swell of sound, but it died away quickly to a chorus of hushing noises. No one wanted to miss a word of this drama, which would be repeated endlessly and with blissful relish in dozens of drawing rooms and gentlemen's clubs for days, even weeks to come.

"What?" Charles had turned pale, Jane saw in a quick glance at him. He was looking at her across the table. "Is this true? Sara?"

She nodded almost imperceptibly.

He stared at her for a few moments while there was another small swell of sound and more hushing noises, and then he turned without another word and stalked from the room, brushing past the duke as he went.

"Come, Jane." Jocelyn held out a hand toward her and she went to him on legs that were not quite steady. He was smiling as she had never seen him smile before—openly, warmly, radiantly.

"Ladies and gentlemen," he said as his hand closed about hers, "allow me, please, to present my wife, the Duchess of Tresham. Ma'am?" He bowed to Lady Webb. "I do beg your pardon that my hand has been forced. Jane insisted that nothing be allowed to spoil yesterday and today for you since you have worked so tirelessly to plan her presentation and her come-out. Both, of course, would have had to change for a married lady. And so I agreed that we would delay our announcement until tomorrow."

He settled Jane's hand on his arm and covered it with his free hand before looking around at all the gathered guests, though his eyes rested on his brother and sister as he spoke again. "We were married by special license this morning. We had a quiet wedding, as we both wished, with only my secretary and her grace's maid in attendance as witnesses."

He smiled down at Jane—that warm, wonderful, defenseless smile again—and raised her hand to his lips. There was already noise and movement in response to his announcement.

"My love," he murmured while he still could, "I was already quite determined to have my bride in my own home and my own bed for what will remain of our wedding night when your ball is over. I am no saint, you see."

"I have never wanted a saint," she told him. "I have only ever wanted you, Jocelyn."

He leaned toward her, his eyes on fire, and whispered with passionate intensity in her ear. "My love and my life. My Jane. And at last and forever *my wife*."

There was only a moment—a timeless moment—in which to smile radiantly at him and to realize with a shock of reality that it was really true. She was married to Jocelyn, her love, her heart's desire, her soul's mate. She was happier than anyone had any right to be. He was *her husband*.

And there was no further need to hide the fact.

Then Aunt Harriet was hugging her and shedding tears over her and scolding her and laughing. And Lady Heyward was catching her in her arms and talking a mile a minute. Lord Ferdinand was grinning at her and kissing her cheek and calling her sister. Viscount Kimble was pretending to clutch his broken heart and was also kissing her cheek. Jocelyn's friends were all pumping his hand and slapping his shoulder. His sister was crying all over his waistcoat despite his protests and declaring that her nerves would not stand the shock and she had never been more happy in her life and she would organize a grand wedding ball for next week and just let Heyward try to stop her, provoking man.

Everything became a blur after that as everyone moved back to the ballroom, congratulating the newly married couple, bowing, curtsying, shaking hands, hugging and kissing as they went. The resumption of the dancing was considerably delayed.

Finally they were alone in the dining room with Lady Webb, Lord and Lady Lansdowne, Lord and Lady Heyward, and Lord Ferdinand. Jocelyn drew Jane's shining new wedding ring from a pocket of his waistcoat, lifted her left hand, and slid it onto her ring finger, where it had resided so briefly during the morning.

"With this ring, my love," he said, and dipped his head to kiss her lips in full view of their small audience. He looked up at Lady Webb. "Now, ma'am, do you suppose the orchestra can be coerced into playing another waltz?"

"Absolutely," Aunt Harriet said.

And so they waltzed again—alone for the first five minutes, while everyone watched.

"I repeat," Jocelyn said as the music began—a slow, dreamy waltz tune this time, "you look almost like a bride, Jane. In fact, you look exactly like a bride. Mine."

"And the ballroom looks as if it had been decked out for a wedding ball," she said, giving him back look for look. "Ours."

And then he did something truly outrageous. He dipped his head and kissed her hard. He lifted his head, smiled wickedly at her, and kissed her softly. And then again with all the yearning and all the hope and all the love Jane knew was in his heart—and her own.

"She will never reform the dangerous Duke of Tresham," some unidentified voice said with startling clarity as Jocelyn twirled Jane into the dance.

"But whyever would she want to?" a female voice called back.

If *More than a Mistress* stole your
heart, get ready to be entranced
by the final book
in Mary Balogh's series featuring the
extraordinary Huxtable family.

A Secret Affair

CONSTANTINE'S STORY

Available from Delacorte in hardcover

Turn the page for a sneak peek inside.

A Secret Affair

"Good evening, Duchess," Mr. Huxtable said, strolling closer to her as her court opened up a path for him. "It is rather crowded in here, is it not? I see it is less so in the music room. Shall we stroll in there for a while?"

"That sounds pleasant," she said, handing her empty glass to a gentleman on her right and slipping her hand through Mr. Huxtable's arm.

It was a very solid arm she had taken, Hannah realized. And it was all clad in black, except for the crisp white cuff that showed at his wrist. His hand was dark-skinned and long-fingered and well manicured, though there was nothing soft about it. Quite the contrary. It looked as if it had done its fair share of work in its time. It was lightly dusted with dark hair. His shoulder was a few inches above the level of her own. He wore a cologne that wrapped itself very enticingly about her senses. She could not identify it.

The music room was indeed still half empty. Entertainments of this nature never did begin on time, of course. They began to stroll slowly about the perimeter of the room.

"And so," he said, looking down at her, "I am to be

consoled for my disappointments, am I, Duchess, by being granted the seat next to yours this evening?"

"Were you disappointed?" she asked.

"Amused," he said.

She turned her head and looked into his very dark eyes. They were quite impossible to read.

"Amused, Mr. Huxtable?" She raised her eyebrows.

"It is amusing," he said, "to watch a puppeteer manipulate the strings in order to make the puppet dance only to discover that the strings are not attached."

Ah. Someone who knew the game and refused to play by its rules—her rules, that was. She liked him the better for it.

"But is it not *intriguing*," she said, "when the puppet dances anyway? And proves that he is not a puppet after all, but that he does love to dance?"

"But you see, Duchess," he said, "he does not like dancing with the chorus. It makes him feel quite . . . ordinary. Indeed, he quite refuses to be an insignificant part of any such group."

Ah. He was setting out his terms, was he?

"But it can be arranged," she said, "that he dance a solo part, Mr. Huxtable. Or perhaps a pas de deux. Very definitely a pas de deux, in fact. And if he proves to be a superior partner, as I am confident he will, then he may be offered the security of exclusive rights to the part for the whole of a Season. There will be no need for any chorus at all. It may be dispensed with."

They turned to walk along the front of the room, between the shallow dais where the orchestra's instruments lay and the front row of gilt, velvet-seated chairs.

"He is to be on trial, then, at the start?" he said. "At a sort of audition?"

"I am not sure that will be necessary," she said. "I have

not seen him dance, but I am convinced he performs superlatively well."

"You are too kind and too trusting, Duchess," he said. "He is perhaps more cautious. If he is to dance a pas de deux, after all, he must be given an equal chance to try out *his* prospective partner, to discover if she is as skilled a dancer as he, to discover whether she will suit his style for a whole Season and not very quickly become tedious."

Hannah opened her fan with her free hand and fluttered it before her face. The music room was still not crowded, but it already felt stuffy and overhot.

"*Tedious,* Mr. Huxtable," she said, "is a word not in her vocabulary."

"Ah," he said, "but it is in *his*."

Hannah might have been offended or outraged or both. Instead, she was feeling very pleased indeed. The word *tedious* figured largely in her vocabulary—which meant she had just told yet another lie. Barbara would be upset with her if she could hear. Though it was very fortunate indeed that she could hear no part of this conversation. She would expire from shock. Most gentlemen of Hannah's acquaintance were tedious. They really ought not to set her on a pedestal and worship her. Pedestals could be lonely, barren places, and worship was just plain ridiculous when one was very mortal indeed.

They had turned to walk up the far side of the room.

"Ah," she said, looking ahead, "there are the Duke and Duchess of Moreland. Shall we go and speak with them?"

The duke was Mr. Huxtable's cousin, the one who looked like him. They might easily have passed for brothers, in fact.

"It seems," he murmured as she drew him in their direction, "that we shall."

The duke and duchess were very polite to her, very chilly to him. Hannah seemed to recall hearing that there was some sort of estrangement between the cousins. But she caught herself in time before censuring them mentally for quarreling when they were family. That would be rather like the pot calling the kettle black, would it not?

She had been right in her earlier assessment. The duke was the more handsome of the two men. His features were more classically perfect, and there was the surprise of his blue eyes when one expected dark. But Mr. Huxtable was, nevertheless, the more attractive of the two—to her, anyway, which was just as well given the fact that the duke was a married man.

"Mr. Huxtable and I are going to be seated now," Hannah said before the encounter could become too strained. "I am tired after having been on my feet for so long."

And they all nodded and smiled at one another, and Mr. Huxtable took her to sit in the middle of the fourth row back from the dais.

"It is not a promising sign," he said, "when a dancer's feet ache after she has been on them for a mere hour or so."

"But who," she said, closing her fan and resting it on his sleeve for a moment, "is talking about dancing? Why have you quarreled with the Duke of Moreland?"

"At the risk of sounding quite ill-mannered, Duchess," he said, "I am compelled to inform you that it is none of your business."

She sighed.

"Oh, but it is," she said. "Or will be. I will absolutely insist upon knowing everything there is to know about you."

He turned his very dark eyes upon her.

"Assuming," he said, "that after the audition you will be offered the part?"

She tapped the fan on his sleeve.

"After the audition, Mr. Huxtable," she said, "you will be *begging* me to take the part."

CONSTANTINE'S spring mistresses—Monty had once dubbed them that—were selected almost exclusively from the ranks of society's widows. It was a personal rule of his never to visit a brothel and never to employ either a courtesan or an actress. Or, of course, to choose a married lady, though there was a surprising number of them who indicated their availability. Or an unmarried lady—he was after a mistress, not a wife.

Many widows, he had always found, were in no great hurry to marry again. Though most of them did remarry eventually, they were eager enough to spend a few years enjoying their freedom and the sensual pleasure of a casual amour.

He almost always took a lover for the Season. Rarely more than one, and never more than one at a time. His lovers were usually lovely women and younger than he, though he never thought of beauty or age as a necessary qualification. He favored women who were discreet and poised and elegant and intelligent enough to converse on a wide variety of interesting topics. He looked for a certain degree of companionship as well as sexual satisfaction in a lover.

And this year?

He was standing on the wide cobbled terrace behind the Fonteyn mansion in Richmond—though *behind* and *before* were relative terms in this case. The front of the house faced toward the road and any approaching carriages and was really quite unremarkable. The back of the house, on the other hand, overlooked the River Thames, and between it and the river there were the terrace, the wide, flower-bedecked steps, the sloping lawn below them, bordered on one side by a rose arbor and a small orchard and on the other by a row of greenhouses, and another terrace, this one paved, alongside the river. A small jetty stretched into the water for the convenience of anyone desirous of taking out one of the boats that bobbed on either side of it.

And at the moment the back of the house, which might easily claim to be the real front, was bathed in sunshine and a heat that was tempered by an underlying coolness, as one might expect this early in the year. It was all very picturesque and very pleasant indeed.

It had been a bold move on the part of the Fonteyns to host a garden party this early in the Season, long before anyone else was prepared to take such a chance with the weather. Of course, there was a spacious ballroom inside the house as well as a large drawing room and doubtless other rooms large enough to accommodate all the guests in the event of chill weather or rain.

This year there was a new widow in town, and she was quite blatantly and aggressively offering herself to him as this Season's mistress. If one discounted her very obvious ruse of appearing hard to get, that was. He really had been amused by her behavior on Bond Street and at the Merriwether ball.

At the moment she was doing it again. She was standing on the lawn not far from the orchard, her hand on the arm of Lord Hardingraye, one of her old lovers with whom she had arrived half an hour ago. They were surrounded by other guests, both male and female, and she was giving the group her full attention as she twirled a confection of a parasol above her head. Inevitably it was white, as was everything else she wore. She almost always wore white, though she never looked the same on any two occasions. Amazing, that.

She had not once looked Constantine's way. Which might mean one of two things—she had not seen him yet, or she was no longer interested in pursuing any sort of connection with him.

He knew very well that neither possible explanation was the real one.

She was determined to have him. And she had certainly seen him. She would not have so studiously *not* looked at him if she had not.

He was amused again.

He sipped his drink and carried on a conversation with a group of his friends. He was in no hurry to approach her. Indeed, he had no intention of making the first move. If she wished to ignore him all afternoon, he would not leave brokenhearted.

But as he talked and laughed and looked about at all the new arrivals, smiling at some of them, raising a hand in greeting to others, he mulled over the question that had been bothering him for the past three days.

Did he really *want* the Duchess of Dunbarton as a lover?

He had said a very firm no to that question in Hyde Park, and he had meant it.

Most men would have thought the question a ludicrous one, of course. She was, after all, one of the most perfectly beautiful women anyone had ever set eyes upon, and, if it was possible, she had improved with age. She was still relatively young, and she was as sexually desirable as she was lovely. She was much sought after—an understatement. She could have almost any man she chose to take as a lover, and that did not exclude many of the married ones.

But . . .

Something made him hesitate, and he was not quite sure what it was.

Was it that *she* had chosen *him*? But there was no reason why a woman might not go after what she wanted just as boldly as a man could. When he decided upon a woman, after all, he always pursued her with determined persistence until she capitulated—or did not. Besides, was it not flattering to be singled out by a beautiful, desirable woman who could have almost anyone?

Was it that she was *too* available, then? Had her lovers not been legion while the old duke lived? Were they not likely to continue to be numerous now that she was finally free, not only of the duke but also of her obligatory year of mourning? But he had never balked at the prospect of competition. Besides, if it turned out that she expected to keep other lovers as well as him, he could simply walk away. He was not looking for love, after all, or anything like a marital commitment. Only for a lover. His heart was not going to be involved.

And she had said in so many words at the Heaton concert that while he was her lover no one else would be.

Was it, then, that she was too much of an open book, as he had told her at the concert? Everyone knew all about her. Despite the bedroom eyes and the half-smile she kept almost always on her lips, there was no real mystery about the woman, nothing to be uncovered a layer at a time, like the petals of a rose.

Except her clothing.

One never knew exactly what a woman was going to look like unclothed, no matter how many times one's eyes roamed over her clad body. One never knew exactly what she would *feel* like, how she would move, what sounds she would make . . .

"Constantine." His aunt, Lady Lyngate, his mother's sister, had come up behind him and laid a hand on his arm. "Do tell me you have not been down by the river yet. Or, if you have, do lie about it and tell me you will be delighted to escort me there."

He covered her hand with his own and grinned at her.

"I would not be lying, Aunt Maria," he said, "even if I had been down there a dozen times already, which I have not. It is always my pleasure to escort you anywhere you wish to go. I did not know you were in town. How are you? You grow lovelier with every passing year and every newly acquired gray hair. More distinguished."

He was not lying about that either. She was probably close to sixty years old and a head-turner.

"Well," she said, laughing, "that is the first time, I believe, I have been complimented on my gray hair."

She was still very dark. But she was graying attractively at the temples. She was Elliott's—the Duke of Moreland's—mother but had never cut their acquaintance just because her son rarely talked to him. Neither had Elliott's sisters.

"How is Cece?" he asked of Cecily, Viscountess Burden, the youngest of them and his favorite, as he led his aunt off the terrace and down the broad steps to the lawn. "Is her confinement to be soon?"

"Soon enough that she and Burden have remained in the country this year," she said, "much to the delight of the other two children, I am sure. What a good idea it was to set up tables on the terrace down there. One may sit and enjoy refreshments and be right by the water."

They proceeded to do just that and sat for ten minutes or so before being joined by three of his aunt's friends—a lady and two gentlemen.

"You will take pity on me, if you will, Lady Lyngate, and if your nephew can spare you," the single gentleman said after they had all chatted for a while. "We came down here to take out a boat, but I have always had an aversion to being a wallflower. Do say you will make up a fourth."

"Oh, indeed I will," she said. "How delightful! Constantine, will you excuse me?"

"Only with the greatest reluctance," he said, winking at her, and he watched as the four of them climbed into a recently vacated boat and one of the men took the oars and pushed out into the river.

"All alone, Mr. Huxtable?" a familiar voice asked from behind his shoulder. "What a waste of a perfectly available gentleman."

"I have been sitting here waiting for you to take notice and have pity on me," he said, getting to his feet. "Do join me, Duchess."

"I am neither hungry nor thirsty nor in need of rest," she said. "Take me into the greenhouses. I wish to see the orchids."

Did anyone ever say no to her, he wondered as he offered his arm. When she had announced at the Heaton concert that she would sit with *him* in the music room, had she even considered how embarrassed she might have been if he had refused to sit with *her*? But why should she fear rejection when even the crusty, crabby old Duke of Dunbarton had been unable to resist her after resisting every other woman for more than seventy years?

"I have been feeling dreadfully slighted," she said as she took his arm. "You did not come to greet me when you arrived."

"I believe," he said, "I arrived before *you* did, Duchess. And you did not come to greet *me*."

"Is it the woman's part," she said, "to go out of her way to greet the man?"

"As you have done now?"

He looked down at her. She was not wearing a bonnet today. Instead she was wearing an absurd little hat, which sat at a jaunty angle over her right eyebrow and looked—of course—quite perfect. Her blond curls rioted about it in an artless style that had probably taken her maid an hour or more to create. The white muslin of her dress, he could see now that he was close, was dotted with tiny rosebuds of a very pale pink.

"That is unkind repartee, Mr. Huxtable," she said. "What choice did you leave me? It would have been too, too tedious to have gone home without speaking with you."

He led her diagonally up the lawn in the direction of the greenhouses. And he gave in to a feeling of inevitability. She was clearly determined to have him. And for all his misgivings, he could not deny the fact that he was not at all averse to being had. Being in bed with her was going to be something of a wild adventure, he did not doubt. A struggle for mastery, perhaps? And mutual and enormous pleasure while they fought it out?

Sometimes, he thought, the prospect of extraordinary sensual pleasure was enough to ask of a liaison. The mysteries of a character that had some depths worth exploring could wait until another year and another mistress.

He really was capitulating with very little struggle, he thought. Which meant that she was very good at seduction. No surprise there. And he would not begrudge her that since it was beginning to feel rather pleasant to be seduced.

"Where is Miss Leavensworth this afternoon?" he asked.

"Mr. and Mrs. Park invited her to accompany them on a visit to some museum or other," she said, "and she preferred to go there than to come here with me. Can you *imagine* such a thing, Mr. Huxtable? And they are to take her to dinner afterward and then to the *opera*."

She shuddered delicately.

"You have never been to the opera, Duchess?" he asked. "Or to a museum?"

"But of course I have," she said. "One must not appear an utter rustic in the eyes of one's peers, you know. One must show some interest in matters of superior culture."

"But you have never enjoyed either?" he asked.

"I really *did* enjoy looking at Napoleon Bonaparte's carriage at . . . Oh, in *some* museum," she said, waving the hand that held her parasol in a dismissive gesture. "The one in which he rode to the Battle of Waterloo, I mean. He could not ride his horse because he was suffering with piles. Did you know that? The duke told me and explained what piles *are*. They sound like dreadfully painful things. Perhaps the Duke of Wellington won the battle on the strength of Napoleon Bonaparte's piles. I wonder if the history books will reflect that fact."

"Probably not," he said, feeling vastly amused. "History will doubtless prefer to perpetuate the modern eagerness to see Wellington as a grand, invincible hero, who won the battle on the strength of his grandness and invincibility."

"I suppose so," she agreed. "That is what the duke said too. *My* duke, that is. And he took me once to see the Elgin marbles and I was not at all *shocked* to see all those naked figures. I was not even vastly impressed by them. They were pale marble. I would far rather see the real flesh-and-blood man. Greek, that is. With sun-bronzed skin instead of cold stone. Not that a real-life man could ever be quite so perfectly beautiful, of course."

She sighed, and her parasol twirled again.

The minx, Constantine thought.

"And the opera?" he said.

"I never understand the Italian," she said. "It would all be very tedious if it were not for all the *passion* and the tragedy of everyone dying all over the stage. Have you noticed how all those dying characters sing the most glorious music just before they expire? What a waste. I would far prefer to see such passion expended upon *life*."

"But since opera is written for a living singer and an audience of living persons rather than for a dying character," he said, "then surely that is exactly what is happening. Passion being expended upon life, that is."

"I shall never see opera the same way again," she said, giving her parasol one more twirl before lowering it as they came to the first greenhouse. "Or hear it the same way. Thank you, Mr. Huxtable, for your insight. You must take me one evening so that I may hear it correctly in your presence. I will make up a party."

It was humid and very warm inside the greenhouse. It was filled with large banks of ferns down the center and orange trees around the glass walls. It was also deserted.

"How very lovely," she said, standing still behind the central bank and tipping back her head to breathe in the scent of the foliage. "Do you think it would be eternally lovely to live in a tropical land, Mr. Huxtable?"

"Unrelenting heat," he said. "Bugs. Diseases."

"Ah." She lowered her head to look at him. "The ugliness at the heart of beauty. Is there always ugliness, do you suppose? Even when the object is very, very beautiful?"

Her eyes were suddenly huge and fathomless. And sad.

"Not always," he said. "I prefer to believe the opposite— that there is always an indestructible beauty at the heart of darkness."

"Indestructible," she said softly. "You are an optimist, then."

"There is nothing else to be," he said, "if one's human existence is to be bearable."

"It is," she said, "very easy to despair. We always live on the cliff edge of tragedy, do we not?"

"Yes," he said. "The secret is never to give in to the urge to jump off voluntarily."

She continued to gaze into his eyes. Her eyelids did not droop, he noticed. Her lips did not smile. But they were slightly parted.

She looked . . . different.

The purely objective part of his mind informed him that there was no one else in this particular greenhouse, and that they were hidden from view where they stood.

He lowered his head and touched his lips lightly to hers. They were soft and warm, slightly moist, and yielding. He touched his tongue to the opening between them, traced the outline of the upper lip and then the lower, and then slid his tongue into her mouth. Her teeth did not bar the way. He curled his tongue and drew the tip slowly over the roof of her mouth before withdrawing it and lifting his head away from hers.

She tasted of wine and of warm, enticing woman.

He looked deeply into her eyes, and she gazed back for a few moments until there was a very subtle change in her expression. Her eyelids drooped again, her lips turned upward at the corners, and she was herself once more. It had seemed as if she were replacing a mask.

Which was an interesting possibility.

"I hope, Mr. Huxtable," she said, "you can live up to the promise of that kiss. I shall be vastly disappointed if you cannot."

"We will put it to the test tonight," he said.

"Tonight?" She raised her eyebrows.

"You must not be alone," he said, "while Miss Leavensworth is off somewhere dining and attending the opera. You might be lonely and bored. You will dine with me instead."

"And then?" Her eyebrows remained elevated.

"And then," he said, "we will indulge in a decadent dessert in my bedchamber."

"Oh." She seemed to be considering. "But I have another engagement this evening, Mr. Huxtable. How very inconvenient. Perhaps some other time."

"No," he said, "no other time. I play no games, Duchess. If you want me, it will be tonight. Not at some future date, when you deem you have tortured me enough."

"You feel tortured?" she asked.

"You will come tonight," he said, "or not at all."

She regarded him in silence for a few moments.

"Well, goodness me," she said, "I believe you mean it."

"I do," he said.